Virginia Macgregor is the author of *What Milo Saw*, *The Return of Norah Wells*, *Before I was Yours* and, most recently, the young adult novel *Wishbones*. Her work has been translated into over a dozen languages. After graduating from Oxford University, she worked as a teacher of English and Housemistress in three major British boarding schools. She holds an MA in Creative Writing, and was, for several years, Head of Creative Writing at Wellington College.

Virginia now writes full time. She is married to Hugh, who is Director of Theatre at St. Paul's School in Concord, New Hampshire. They moved to New Hampshire from the UK in July 2016 and live in St. Paul's with their two daughters, Tennessee Skye and Somerset Wilder.

Also by Virginia Macgregor

What Milo Saw
The Return of Norah Wells
Before I was Yours

For Young Adult Readers
Wishbones

VIRGINIA
MACGREGOR

you
found
me

SPHERE

First published in Great Britain in 2018 by Sphere

1 3 5 7 9 10 8 6 4 2

A CIP catalogue record for this book
is available from the British Library.

Hardback ISBN 978-0-7515-6525-6
Trade Paperback ISBN 978-0-7515-6524-9

Typeset in Granjon by M Rules
Printed and bound in Great Britain by
Clays Ltd, Elcograf S.p.A.

Papers used by Sphere are from well-managed forests
and other responsible sources.

Sphere
An imprint of
Little, Brown Book Group
Carmelite House
50 Victoria Embankment
London EC4Y 0DZ

An Hachette UK Company
www.hachette.co.uk

www.littlebrown.co.uk

For my two daughters: Somerset Wilder,
who kept me company while I wrote this, and
Tennessee Skye, whose love of elephants inspired
me to include them in my story.

The things one does not remember are as important; perhaps they are more important.

VIRGINIA WOOLF, *Moments of Being*

Under the tall, thick oaks, which have lived here for hundreds of years, in one of the oldest forests of Europe, stands an empty cottage. It's been empty for a while now.

Dim light streams in through the windows. Dust thickens the air. A vase of dried wildflowers sits on the kitchen table.

Outside, a child's swing shifts in the morning breeze.

Her father put it up on the day they moved here. Before they'd unpacked their boxes or screwed the lightbulbs into their sockets, he'd hung thick spools of rope from the branches, then fastened a plank of wood as a seat.

He was out there until midnight. Until there was no chance of having light in the house until morning.

On a summer day, like today, the leaves are so dense that the sun strains to get through. A shaft, every now and then, like the light which falls through the window of a church. But mostly shadows. And darkness.

On that day, when they moved in, the daughter had waited until midnight for him to finish. She was too old for it, she knew, but when she'd been the right age, they'd lived in a flat in the city, no garden or trees. And he'd always promised her a swing.

So there she was, under the moon, the backs of her thighs pressed into the rough wood.

She'd untied her plait, arched her body, tilted back her head and let her long, brown hair sweep the forest floor.

Then she'd closed her eyes and breathed in the scent of resin from the bleeding trees, the pine needles that carpeted the floor, the fleshy leaves.

And she'd listened to the birds, to the orchestra of what was now her home.

And she'd called out to him:

Higher, push me higher!

Her voice, clear as a bell, had echoed through the trees.

Higher!

He'd pushed her for hours, until they were too dizzy and tired to go on. And then, hand in hand, they'd stumbled back inside and gone to sleep.

Now, in the forest, on this hot summer's day, the swing, like the cottage, sits empty, spinning in the breeze.

Isabel

In London, in a bedsit perched above an Italian restaurant, Isabel stands at the window and shoos away a pigeon.

It's raining; the pigeon is trying to find shelter and she knows she should feel sorry for him, but she doesn't have the energy to look after yet another living creature.

He pecks at the concrete windowsill.

Silly bird, she thinks – no matter how hard she tries to get rid of him, he always comes back.

He inches closer to the window, as if daring her. A few steps more and he'll be inside, flying around the flat, and then she'll never be able to get him out.

Shoo!

She slams the window shut.

Behind her, her little girl stirs in her sleep.

Isabel goes and sits on the edge of the sofa bed and brushes River's hair out of her eyes. A tangle of thick brown curls, which she refuses to cut or tie up or brush, so different from Isabel's own thin blonde hair.

When River was a baby, people would look into her pram and then frown as they saw a child who had not one feature in common with her mother. It seems unfair that River should have inherited so much from him and nothing from her.

Sometimes, Isabel wonders whether River is hers at all. Whether maybe this has all been a strange dream.

She will have to wake her soon; today is the little girl's last day at primary school. She's growing up, moving away from her.

Being a mother is one long lesson in letting go, she'd read somewhere.

Only she's not ready for that, not yet.

David

Deep in the belly of the city, as the Tube train snakes its way to Euston Square, David pushes his fingers under his glasses and rubs his eyes. Sometimes he's so tired that he forgets which way he's going: whether he's heading home for a rest or whether he's going back to the hospital for another shift.

Someone shoves an elbow into the soft flesh of his stomach. He knows that his body is too big for such a small space. He senses how others resent it, as though he is taking up more than his allocated share.

He pushes his glasses back up his nose, takes a deep breath and tries to suck in the bulk of his stomach.

The train lurches to a stop. The doors open. The smell of metal and rain-damp clothes sweeps in. More commuters push each other into the already full train.

He is shoved deeper into the carriage.

A young woman catches his eye. Her short, jagged hair stands at angles, streaked with blondes and blacks, browns and ambers. She wears a man's shirt, sleeves rolled up. The tattoo of a crow sits on her arm. A buggy with three sleeping babies stands in front of her and she balances a toddler on her hip.

The young woman is eating sweets, those gummy bears that come in gold packets.

She doesn't look like a mother, thinks David. And then he feels guilty. He's thirty-nine and single with no prospect of getting married or having children – what does he know?

For a second, the young woman looks up and, noticing that she's being observed, folds her face into a scowl.

His gaze offends her, he thinks, just as those standing around him are offended by his size.

He looks down at his scuffed black shoes, at the frayed hem of his grey suit, and wonders what it would be like to be invisible.

Another lurch. Another stop. More pushing and shoving.

When he looks up again, she's gone.

Outside the entrance to London Zoo, a man sits on a bench. He stopped minding the rain a long time ago; it is part of him now, of his hair and beard and clothes. Soon, it will seep through his skin and start running through his veins, like a river. Like the sea.

How long have I been sitting here? he wonders.

He puts a hand in his pocket and feels for the small, silver charm. The upward curve of the trunk, the thick body and the sturdy legs. Sapphires for eyes.

He closes his eyes. If he listens carefully, especially early in the morning or late in the afternoon, before the visitors come to the zoo, he hears the animals.

He wonders where the elephants are. Where they sleep and eat and live.

Someone told him once that elephants use their trunks to soothe each other for comfort, like a human touch.

How long has it been since he's touched another person's skin? And whose skin was it?

He reaches into the lining of his jacket and pulls out an envelope, damp with rain – on it, a hand-drawn map of London. The paper sits limply in his hands. Each drop of rain makes the pictures dissolve further: the streets, the bridges, the zoo – the river that snakes through the city.

Someone drew it for him. Someone who wanted him to see these places.

He has to wait for her. He promised her that he'd wait.

River

River's eyes fly open. Right from the moment she wakes up, her body feels jittery, like she's channelling all the electricity whizzing around London.

She looks to the window and sees the pigeon balancing on the windowsill. Raindrops on his feathers. He looks up for a second, puffs out his chest, tilts his head and opens his beak just a fraction. She knows what's coming next – a low, mournful coo, so loud that it will fill the whole flat.

He's hungry, poor thing.

She puts her finger to her lips. *Shush*, she mouths and then points in the direction of Mum, who's standing in the kitchen, her back turned.

The pigeon is one of the many things she and Mum fight about. River believes he belongs here just as much as they do; Mum wishes he would leave them alone.

The bird flaps its wings.

Mum spins round, frowns and looks at the window, but he's gone – so fast, he may as well have been a ghost.

Good boy, River whispers to the grey sky.

Mum comes over and places a pill in River's palm: the one that keeps her calm and helps her focus. Sometimes. Then Mum sits down on River's rainbow quilt.

Along with pigeons, rainbows are one of River's very favourite things. It's impossible to see a rainbow without feeling happy. She thinks about them when she needs to stop her mind shooting off in a million different directions.

Today's a special day: it's River's last day at primary school. No more sitting still and trying to concentrate or being told to tie up her hair. No more uniform and silly rules about the colour her tights should be. Her whole body sighs with relief: just a long summer of running around doing as she pleases.

And after that? When the summer is over?

Well, she's told Mum that she's not going to secondary school. That no one can make her, not even the politicians Mum talks about, the ones who made that law about children having to go to school.

Mum gets up and walks to the window, mumbling something about needing umbrellas.

River wonders where her pigeon is now, whether he's found shelter somewhere else, at least until the sun comes out.

For a second, she pictures her pigeon, his wings spread wide, feathers glistening with rain, flying across the arc of a rainbow.

Today would be the perfect day for a rainbow, she thinks. A sign that anything could happen.

JULY

River

It takes River and Mum exactly thirty-three minutes to walk from their bedsit on Acacia Road, through Regent's Park, out of Chester Gate and to River's school. And then it takes another fifteen minutes for Mum to walk to the hospital where she works as a cleaner. They walk every day. Even if it rains or snows or blows so hard that River imagines them being swept up and off the ground and swirled around in the sky and dumped in the lion enclosure at London Zoo.

Mum says River needs the fresh air, but River knows it's for other reasons too.

Like that they don't have a car.

And that the bus is too expensive.

And, most of all, Mum knows that if River can burn off some of the energy rattling around in her body *before* she gets to school, there's a better chance that she'll sit still for five minutes and actually learn something.

Today it's raining. Really hard. Big sheets of water shoot off the side of River's umbrella. Her school shoes are soaked already.

River finishes her cereal bar and puts the wrapper in a park bin.

'Come on, Mum!' River yells through the rain.

Mum's dragging her feet today, which means she didn't sleep well. And her umbrella is so small it barely covers her head. But then Mum's small, both ways: vertically and horizontally. It won't be long before River is taller than her – maybe then Mum will listen to her.

Anyway, for once, River wants to get to school early. It's the last day of the summer term and her last day *ever* at Caius Primary, which means there won't be any lessons, just lots of assemblies and goodbye parties and – if the rain stops for a second – playing outside, which is the best bit about school. Whenever River spends too much time inside, her whole body starts to feel itchy, like her insides are going to burst out of her. She wishes she could go to a school where all the lessons happened outside. Even when it rained.

'Mum?'

River runs back down the path and finds Mum staring at a row of terracotta pots spilling over with red geraniums in the Italian Gardens. The flowers are covered in millions of raindrops: they sit there on the petals like big, shiny tears.

Red geraniums are Mum's favourites. Once she told River that, in Venice, they hang out of people's window boxes all summer long and that it makes the houses look like they're wearing bright red lipstick.

Mum loves Venice. She went there when she was really young.

Every day they stop here so that Mum can look at how the flowers are doing.

River takes Mum's hand. 'You okay, Mum?'

Mum bites her lip and nods. 'I just can't believe it's your last day at school. You're growing up so fast, River.'

River had always looked forward to growing up, but whenever Mum talks about it, she makes it sound like it's a bad thing.

They stand there for a while, listening to the drip, drip, dripping of the rain on their umbrellas.

'Come on, Mum,' River says.

They keep walking until they get to the second place they stop every day: the entrance to London Zoo. River likes animals as much as Mum likes flowers. She likes to see the latest posters and displays. And sometimes, she thinks she can hear a chimpanzee swinging through the trees; a hyena laughing; the penguins flapping their tuxedo wings before diving into the water. Sometimes, River wonders what would happen if the zookeepers forgot to lock the enclosures and all the animals ran out of the main gates and hung out in Regent's Park. She'd like that.

Mum walks ahead, checking her phone while River goes over to a noticeboard to see what events they're putting on this summer. Except something stops her before she gets there. Someone crying. And it's not like when Mum cries: small and hiccupy and sniffly. Whoever's crying is crying properly: big, noisy gulps.

River looks round to see where it's coming from.

There's a man sitting on a bench, just by the entrance to the zoo. He's all by himself and his head is in his hands. Everything about him is wet. His tangled brown hair is smushed down on his face and his jacket's dripping from the seams. His tie's soggy, his white shirt's so wet it's gone see-through, his suit trousers are sticking to his legs – and his feet are sitting in a puddle.

It's like he's gone for a swim with all his clothes on.

At first, River can't work out whether the drops plopping from the man's eyes are rain or tears, but from the gulping sound he was making a moment ago, he's obviously been crying. He's like one of those clowns whose face is painted to look happy and colourful yet still looks like the saddest person in the whole world.

River can't remember the last time she saw a man cry – a proper, grown-up one.

She goes over, sits beside him and tilts her umbrella to shield him a bit.

'Are you okay?' she asks.

He looks up at River and blinks; more tears drop out of his

eyes. Behind his tears his eyes are big and brown: they match the colour of his hair exactly. Although he looks kind of beaten down by the rain, he's not old. He must be about Mum's age. Which makes it weird that he's sitting here. People Mum's age usually have jobs they're rushing to at this time of the morning.

'What's your name?' River asks him.

'River – come back here!' Mum's voice carries over to them from further up the road.

The man looks up, startled.

'Don't worry – it's just Mum.' River rolls her eyes. She's been practising her eye-rolling for when people annoy her, like the teachers at school or the girls with neat hair who sit still in their chairs.

Jules, Mum's best friend, taught her: she's the best eye-roller in the world. Jules is basically like River's second mum; she lives with them and River spends more time with her than anyone else, mainly because Mum works so much.

River studies the man.

'What's your name, then?' she asks again.

He looks down into his hands, like he's trying to find his name written on his palms. River spots an inky smudge on his left forefinger. Maybe he's left-handed, like her. Maybe he holds his pen too low as well. Maybe, when he was little, teachers told him off for not holding his pen properly, like River's teachers do.

'Whatever's making you sad is probably not as bad as you think it is,' River says to him, gently.

That's what Jules tells her when she complains about school.

'Are you waiting for the zoo to open?' she asks.

He looks over to the entrance but doesn't answer.

The man smells damp and musty like River's clothes do when Mum forgets to take them out of the washing machine. He could be a homeless person, River thinks. But homeless people don't wear suits, do they?

Then River notices a stick propped up beside him against the bench. She wonders whether there's something wrong with his legs and whether that's why he's sitting in the rain getting soaked: because he can't move.

'River! You're going to be late for school!'

A moment later, Mum's standing in front of them. She stares at the man and River can tell that she's taking it all in: his blotchy, tear-stained face and his soggy clothes and his squelchy feet.

River stands up and pulls Mum to one side.

'I think he's sad,' she whispers.

Mum looks back at the man for a second and River can see that Mum's as nosy about him as she is. But then Mum takes River's hand and says, 'He probably just needs some time to himself. Come on, River, let's not bother him any longer.'

Mum gives River's hand a yank.

River pulls her hand away.

'That's not what Jules says to me when I'm sad, she says that it's best to share your worries. And you're always saying that Jules is wise and that I should listen to her.' River likes to use her Jules card: Mum listens to Jules more than anyone. 'Anyway, he's soaking. We can't just leave him.'

Mum goes over to the man. 'I'm sorry we disturbed you,' she tells him. 'River likes to talk to people.'

Mum doesn't mean people – she means strangers. She's told River off for doing it before. It's another thing that keeps Mum up at night: River talking to strangers and her fear that she'll be stolen away from her. Only most of the strangers River's met seem really nice – nicer, sometimes, than the non-strangers in her life.

'My name's River.' River holds out her hand. 'Mum called me

17

that because she loves Venice.' River pauses, realising that this probably doesn't make sense to someone who doesn't have the full story. 'And in Venice there are lots of canals, which are like rivers, but you can't really call your daughter Canal so she called me River.'

A bit of light comes back into the man's eyes.

Mum's obsessed with Italy. And not just the flower thing. She, Jules and River live over an Italian restaurant called Gabino's; they get the rent cheap because Mum cleans for the owner, who they call Grumpy Gabs because he doesn't ever seem happy about anything. Mum's promised that, one day, when they've saved up lots and lots of money, she'll take River to Venice on holiday and that they'll buy masks and lounge around on gondolas all day.

River waits for him to tell her his name back but he doesn't say anything. So she leans towards him and tries not to let the damp smell into her nose and says:

'I hope you feel better soon.'

The sky goes from dark grey to a lighter grey and suddenly, the rain stops.

River looks up. 'Phew!' She puts down her umbrella and gives it a shake. Then she grins at him. 'There might be a rainbow.'

Very slowly, the corners of the man's mouth turn up and, for a second, he doesn't look quite so sad any more.

'Do you like rainbows?' she asks.

He nods.

'So do I. They're probably my favourite thing in the whole world.'

The man's smile goes a little wider.

'I think we've bothered this gentleman long enough,' Mum says. 'Let's get going, River.'

But River doesn't want to go until she knows who he is.

'Don't you *have* a name?' she asks.

River likes to find out about people's names, especially unusual ones. Ones that come from faraway countries that she's never been to, names that roll around in her mouth and take a while to learn how to say properly. One of Mum's cleaning friends is called Ashur, which means great warrior, which is kind of cool. Though everyone calls him Ash because he's always sneaking out to smoke on the fire escape. And River likes the stories behind how people got their names, like how she got the name River and how Mum's friend is called Jules even though her real name is Juliet, which she hates because she thinks it sounds too girly. Jules likes Jules because she says it doesn't let people know whether you're a boy or a girl and that that's a good thing because there are enough people in the world trying to put you in boxes. River's a name like that too – for boys *and* girls.

River wonders what Jules would think about this man. She has strong opinions about most people.

'If we know your name, then we can be friends,' River says.

Then River wonders whether it would be possible to be someone's friend *without* ever knowing their name.

Mum tugs at River's arm and pulls her away.

River tries to think of a reason to persuade Mum to stay a little longer and then she hears a quiet voice behind her.

'I don't remember.'

River spins round. His voice sounds different from the way English people speak. It kind of rolls.

'You don't remember what?' River asks.

The man's looks right into River's eyes. 'I don't remember . . .' He coughs and takes a while to get his breath back. Then he looks back up at River with his big, sad, brown eyes and says: 'I don't remember my name.'

Isabel

Isabel sits in the waiting room of the neuropsychiatry ward next to the strange, quiet man River found sitting outside London Zoo.

Unable to find any clothes in lost property long enough for his beanpole limbs, she'd put him in a hospital gown and wrapped him in a towel. It will have to do for now.

His wet clothes are sitting in a carrier bag at his feet. They've soaked through the plastic and have left a puddle on the floor, which, as soon as she gets back to doing what she's meant to be doing right now – cleaning – Isabel will have to mop up.

She wonders what he'd look like in that suit if it were dry and clean and if he weren't sick. He's got smooth skin – the only wrinkles on his face are tiny smile lines by his eyes. His hair is a rich brown and although his eyes are sad, they're bright.

Isabel imagines that, before he got all wet and sick, he must have looked quite smart in his suit. He could easily have been just another commuter travelling through the city on his way to work. Someone with a nice office and a wife and children to go home to at night.

The man coughs. A huge, wracking cough that comes from deep inside his lungs. It doesn't sound good. Neither does the fact that he doesn't seem to have a clue about who he is or where he is or how he came to be sitting outside London Zoo.

When he keeps coughing, Isabel goes to get him a cup of water.

Only when she comes back, he's not there any more.

She spins round and sees him walking down the corridor. She breaks into a jog and catches his arm.

'Where are you going?'

He looks at her, his brown eyes wide.

Sometimes, when you meet someone, the feeling isn't of unfamiliarity or strangeness, but of remembering. Even if you know that you've never seen them before.

It's not the first time that Isabel's felt drawn to this otherness. There's a relief, somehow, in encountering a stranger, especially one from far away – from a place that doesn't know that she or this life of hers exists. It's how she'd felt when she went to Venice with Jules all those years ago – as if, in that brief window of time, everything that had gone before was forgotten and she could be someone new.

He keeps staring at her blankly. *God, he's lost,* Isabel thinks. *Really lost.*

'It's okay.' She presses his arm. 'Just come back and take a seat.'

The man looks away from her, down the corridor, in the direction he'd been heading.

'Come on, I got you some water,' Isabel says.

She steers him back to the seats and then hands him the cup of water.

He takes a sip.

'Thank you,' he says, pushing out the words through another cough.

Isabel's phone vibrates. It's a text from Ash:

Can't cover you for much longer.

If Isabel's supervisor, Stingy Simon, finds out that she's missed an hour of her shift, he'll dock her pay.

Be there in a minute, Isabel texts back.

Then she stands up and says to the man: 'Wait here.'

He nods and his eyes turn sad like when River asked for his name at the park. She hopes he doesn't start crying again. She feels she should say something to make him feel better, or maybe put her arm around his shoulders.

Isabel's heart contracts. Perhaps it wasn't just River who wanted to make sure he was okay.

'I'll be back in a moment,' she says gently.

Isabel walks down the corridor to the room where all the consultants hang out and have coffee. She knows she's meant to go through official procedures but official procedures take too long.

She knocks.

A doctor she hasn't seen before opens the door. A woman with white-blonde hair. Young. Much younger than Isabel. Isabel notices the woman's name badge: *Dr Reed.*

The doctor looks Isabel up and down, clocking her cleaner's uniform.

'Can I help you?' she asks.

'Could I speak to David, please?'

Dr Reed raises her thin eyebrows. *She has time for that*, thinks Isabel. *To take care of how she looks.*

'David?' the woman asks.

'Dr Deardorff. I need to ask him about a patient.'

He's the best psychiatrist on the ward. Probably in the whole of London. Patients get sent to him from all over the country, hard cases that other doctors haven't been able to work out.

Dr Reed frowns, tilts her head and makes a point of scanning the ID card hanging from Isabel's lanyard. 'A patient?'

Isabel wishes she'd never knocked on the door.

'I think he's busy . . .' the woman starts.

But then David pushes past her. 'Isabel! I thought I heard your voice.'

David is short and round, with thick-lensed glasses and dimples – the dimples make him look more like a child than a fully-grown man. But they also make him look warm and kind, less intimidating than the other doctors.

David never seems to go home and Isabel works long shifts, so their lives at the hospital have always overlapped.

David shoves the remains of a Jammie Dodger in his mouth, gulps hard and wipes some crumbs off his top lip. Then he takes a packet of Rennies out of his pocket. It's a routine Isabel's familiar with: Jammie Dodgers followed by Rennies.

'What can I do for you, Isabel?' he asks, chewing on a Rennie.

'I need your help.'

He swallows the rest of the tablet and then smiles at her, as if asking him for a favour is just about the nicest thing she could have done for him on this grey, rainy day.

'I'm sorry to disturb you ...' she stutters. 'I know you're busy—'

'Nonsense. What is it?'

'Would you mind looking at a patient?'

The young doctor is still hanging around. 'I've got this,' he says to her.

Dr Reed gives David a strained smile and slips back into the staff room.

'Lead the way,' David says.

He doesn't comment on the soggy plastic bag at the man's feet or why he's wrapped in a towel or what he has to do with Isabel. Instead, he shakes the man's hand and smiles.

It's not the first time Isabel has noticed the parallels between David and River: their frightening openness to the world.

'Hello, I'm Dr Deardorff.' He pushes his glasses up his nose.

The man nods.

David takes the man's elbow and helps him out of the chair.

The man reaches out for his stick, winces and rubs his knee.

'That giving you trouble?' David says, looking at the man's leg.

The man nods again.

David nods. 'We'll find you a bed and take a good look at everything.'

The man starts coughing, and keeps coughing for a good few minutes. David rubs his back in slow, gentle circles, like you would with a distressed child.

'We'll need to take a look at that too. You have been through the wars, haven't you?'

For a moment, the man looks at him, startled. 'The wars?'

David smiles warmly. 'It's just a turn of phrase.' He turns to Isabel. 'Coming, Nurse Rushworth?'

It's what he calls her when she helps with one of the patients. He's the only one at the hospital who knows that, long ago, that's what she was meant to be: a nurse.

'I've got to get back to work,' Isabel says. 'I'm sorry.'

David gives her a bow as she goes to leave. 'Of course.'

She turns back to David. 'Thank you for agreeing to help.'

As she watches the short, chubby doctor taking the weight of the tall, long-limbed man as they walk down the corridor, she thinks how there couldn't be a more unlikely pairing.

The sea, it's rising; waves lap at his body, as though he were the shore.

Soon, he thinks, *I will be washed away altogether. Maybe things will be easier then.*

He tries to lift his hands to his ears to block out the sound, but the clamp's in the way, holding his head in place.

It's nothing sinister, the doctor had said. *We just have to keep your head stable, to get a sharp picture.*

He thrashes his arms against the bed.

Why did he let them bring him here?

Clanging sounds, muffled through the foam in his ears. But still loud. Behind his closed eyes he sees a metal ladder bashing the side of a ship.

Clang. Clang. Clang.

It won't take long, the doctor had said. *Just a quick look to check that there's nothing obvious we're missing.*

But it feels like he's been in here for a lifetime.

Clang. Clang. Clang. Ricocheting between the bones of his skull.

It won't hurt, he'd said, pressing his arm.

But everything hurts.

He tries to move his head from side to side but it's held down by the clamp.

He wants to leave. He wants to be back outside under the sky, by the entrance to the zoo. To wait there.

Maybe if he found the strength to stand right at the place

where people went into the zoo, that would be better. Maybe he should never have sat down on the bench. People walk past benches. They don't see.

He opens his eyes. It's dark in here.

Where is the doctor?

Then he feels the button in his hand. He presses it over and over.

'Are you okay in there?' A voice comes to him.

It's not the doctor's voice.

Where is he?

And where is the nurse who brought him in? The mother of the little girl. The girl who found him.

Where are they now?

He opens his eyes. It's dark. Somewhere, far off, lights flash across the dark sea.

He has to get out.

He tries to stand up but he can't move.

I'm not meant to be here.

He shuffles his legs. His knee burns and tears.

We'll snap a picture of that too, the doctor had said. *Make sure there are no broken bones.*

He raises his hands to his head and bangs his fists against the walls.

Clang. Clang. Clang.

Everything's too loud in here.

And the sea, it's rising.

It can be a bit strange, but it's nothing to worry about, the doctor had said.

'Nearly done now,' the voice comes again, from outside.

I have to get out of here. I have to get back to the bench outside the zoo. I was never meant to leave.

He thrashes out again. Then he presses the button over and over. He's screaming now, his voice raw. He coughs. The words won't come out.

And the sea, it keeps rising.

'Let me go!' He screams it over and over, arching his back, contracting his muscles. 'Let me go!'

Isabel

'So, you found him in Regent's Park?' Ash asks, mopping the area around the nurses' station.

Besides Jules, Ash is Isabel's closest friend. Although they never really see each other outside the hospital, they started at the same time: they've been working alongside each other for over ten years.

'Yep.'

'And he doesn't remember his name?'

'Nope.'

'Are you going to check on him?'

'I don't know.'

'What do you mean, you don't know?'

'There's not much more I can do now. He's being looked after.'

'You're not curious?'

Curiosity gets you in trouble; having a daughter like River has taught her that.

'It was good of Dr Deardorff – I mean, he didn't have to help out. You know, he really is nice.'

'Yes, he is.' She pauses.

Ash props himself up on his mop, leans into Isabel and grins at her.

'He'd never say no to you.'

Isabel tugs at the collar of her cleaner's uniform. She hates the polyester against her skin.

'You could do worse,' Ash goes on.

'He's a consultant, Ash, and I'm a cleaner. And I'm done with men – present company excluded.'

The truth is that Isabel isn't done with men: she just isn't over the man she fell in love with eleven years ago. No, that's not true either. They were only together for a few hours; you have to be with someone longer than that to truly love them, don't you?

You're in love with the idea of him, Jules says. *And the idea's getting old.*

And she's right.

For years, Isabel has been in love with how he made her feel that night, and with how she felt about herself when her life was still full of possibilities. And now she's scared that she'll never find anyone who'll make her feel the same way. And she's scared that if she does, it'll happen again: she'll wake up one day and he'll be gone and she'll find herself alone.

And even if there weren't all that clutter in the way, when's she meant to find the time to fall in love again? She works extra shifts at the hospital, just to make ends meet, and when she's not here she's worrying about River.

Ash shakes his head. 'Well, we'll see.'

'We'll see about what?' David is standing behind them. He pushes his glasses up his nose and looks at her intently.

Ash winks at her. Isabel shoots him a look.

'I thought you were going to come up and check on our patient?' David says. 'He's been waiting for you.'

'Waiting for me?'

'You're the one who brought him in – he trusts you, Isabel.'

He's known me for five minutes, thinks Isabel, *he's probably just confused.*

And then she thinks of his big brown eyes and how he looks at her as though he's trying to find an answer in her face.

'Sorry,' she says. 'I have too much to do down here.'

29

David tilts his head to one side. 'He's had a bit of a rough morning,' he says.

Isabel looks up at him. 'He has?'

'He didn't take too well to the MRI. Keeps saying he wants to leave.'

'Poor guy,' Ash says.

'Yeah, he's been through a lot.' David fixes his eyes on Isabel in a way that she's all too familiar with: he wants her to help and he knows that she's going to say yes. 'He'd like to see you, Isabel.'

'He said that?'

David nods. 'You and River.'

David's known River nearly as long as he's known Isabel, and he's always letting her sneak onto the ward when Jules can't watch her.

Ash says the hospital is David's family, which always makes Isabel feel sad. Though she supposes she's not so different. She spends more time scrubbing this ward than she does doing anything else.

'He's quite taken with you both,' David adds. The tips of his ears glow red.

An awkward silence hangs between them, which, thank goodness, Ash cuts right through. 'Did you find out what's wrong with him?'

'His knee's in poor shape, but some physio will help ease the pain.'

'An accident?'

David rubs his temples. 'I've been staring at the X-ray for hours and I can't make head nor tail of it. It's not a break or sprain or fracture. It looks like maybe the ligaments were torn at some point, but not from physical activity, as you'd expect. It's like his whole leg has been stretched, somehow. Anyway, I'll organise some physio, and some anti-inflammatories will help with the pain, at least.'

'And the cough?' Isabel asks.

'His lungs are in bad shape too, but it makes more sense. He's got pneumonia.'

'From sleeping rough?' Ash asks.

'I imagine so. Under the right conditions, pneumonia can set in fast, especially in a depleted immune system.'

Isabel thinks back to this morning, when she first saw him: his beard; his long, knotty hair; the way the rain seemed to have gone right through to his bones, as though he'd been sitting on that bench for a lifetime.

She wonders whether it's possible that she and River have walked past him before and not noticed him. But really, she knows that's not possible.

'Anyway, the knee and the pneumonia are treatable,' David says. 'It's the amnesia that's proving to be more complicated.'

'You can't identify a cause for the memory loss?' Isabel asks.

Sometimes Isabel thinks about going to university and getting a nursing degree: there's so much she wants to understand about what makes people sick. But then she remembers that she's broke and getting old and that there's no time and brushes it off as a stupid idea.

'We're still running tests,' David says. 'He's probably experienced some kind of shock. I imagine he'll start remembering things again soon. This kind of amnesia doesn't usually last long.'

'This kind?' Isabel asks.

'When there's no sign of physical trauma to the brain.'

'Isabel said that he doesn't even remember his name – isn't that a bit weird?' Ash asks.

'It is strange,' David says. 'But we've got to give it time.' He turns to Isabel. 'When you first spoke to him, did he give you any information at all? Did you find any papers amongst his things? Did he have a bag or something?'

Isabel shakes her head. When she stuffed his wet clothes into a plastic bag, she didn't check the pockets. They were too wet. And he was watching; she didn't want to upset him by rifling through his things.

'That's what I feared.' David rubs his brow.

Isabel knows what David's thinking: if the man doesn't have any papers, he doesn't have an NHS number. Which means that they'll have to get the police involved – in case he's a missing person, or in case he's pretending that he's forgotten everything – including his name – because he's covering up something. They get people like that sometimes, being in London. Lost souls who gravitate to the capital because they think that, somehow, things will make sense here.

She thinks about going home to River and having to explain that, far from helping the man, they've just landed him in a whole lot more trouble. Or worse, that she's just escorted a wanted criminal to hospital.

But then criminals don't look that sad – do they?

'Could you delay things for a bit?' Isabel says. 'Perhaps we could pretend . . . ' Her voice trails off.

'That he's an English citizen?'

Isabel nods.

David pauses. He's a compassionate man and he's happy to bend the rules, but Isabel doubts whether even he would risk his career over a homeless man who's forgotten his name.

'I'm doing what I can,' David says.

'Has Mr Long seen him?'

Mr Long is the hospital manager who knows nothing about

medicine but is paid to make all the important decisions at the hospital. It drives Isabel crazy.

'Yes, he's seen him.'

'And?'

'He asked whether I'd contacted the authorities.'

'You mean the police?'

David nods.

Isabel feels her heart sink. The last thing this poor man needs is the police involved.

'And what did you answer?'

'I said that I was processing his paperwork.'

Isabel smiles. They both know that 'processing paperwork' is Mr Long's favourite phrase.

'And are you? Processing it?'

He smiles at her. 'In a manner of speaking.'

'So, you've bought us a bit of time?'

'A bit.'

'Thanks,' Isabel says.

David gives Isabel a nod. And then, before he turns away, he says:

'If you can, do bring River up to see him, I really think it will help.'

Through sleepy eyes, the man sees someone leaning towards him. He pushes himself back into the mattress, his heart hammering. And then he realises that it's okay, it's the woman who brought him here, her maroon uniform loose over her slight frame.

Maybe she's one of the senior nurses, he thinks.

He closes his eyes, not wanting to interrupt her. She adjusts his sheet, and tucks it around his body.

She pauses for a moment and then leans in closer, her breath warm against his neck. He feels her fingers brushing his hair from his forehead.

When he senses her move away, the man opens his eyes again. She's not like the other nurses who rush in and out and whisper about his dirty hair and his unshaven chin and his strange voice.

'Sorry, did I wake you?' she asks.

He shakes his head.

'Good. Dr Deardorff said you had to rest.' She pats a stack of newspapers on his bedside table. 'I found these in the recycling.'

He glances at the newspapers and the headlines swim in front of his eyes.

The sea pulls at his body.

He can't breathe.

He clamps his hands over his ears, closes his eyes and shakes his head.

'Are you okay?'

He opens his eyes, stares at her, looks over to the newspapers and pushes them off the table.

'Oh!' Her fingers flutter to her throat. She crouches down and gathers them up. Then she stands there, hugging the newspapers to her chest. 'I'm sorry. I thought they could help, maybe trigger a memory.' Her cheeks are flushed.

He shakes his head and looks down at his hands, his skin dark against the white bedsheets. He doesn't want to see these stories or these words.

Why is he here? He needs to get back to the entrance to the zoo.

'You must be tired,' she says. 'I understand.'

She means to be kind, he knows that. He wants to apologise, but his tongue and lips are too dry to form words. Every few hours, the other nurses come and bring him white paper cups with pills which have made everything feel far away, like there's a fog sitting between him and the rest of the world.

His body is heavy against the sheets. He wants to leave this place, but he doesn't know how to move.

He looks back up at her and forces a word into his throat.

'Isabel?' The name comes to him suddenly. The jolt of a memory. The fog clears for a second.

Her eyes light up. 'You remember me?'

He nods. 'Isabel,' he says again. And then he repeats it over and over in his head, scared that it too will slip away.

'You're not ready to get up yet,' she says, pushing down on his arm. 'And you've got to rest before River gets here.'

River, that name comes back to him too. *Not a canal*, she'd said.

'She'll wear you out in a second,' Isabel says. Then she looks at her watch.

'I'd better go and pick her up – last day of school.'

He wants to thank her again. For coming to see him. For not turning away from him when he threw the newspapers on the

35

floor. As she turns to leave he tries to catch her hand but he's too slow. He watches her walk away from him, so delicate it seems as though the light from the window is shining right through her.

Shifting his head towards the window, he tries to work out what time of day it is and how long he's been here. Every time he's opened his eyes, the light has been different: fluorescent light from above that hurts his eyes, sunlight filtering through the blinds, then darkness again. Each stage slips away from him before he can work it out.

Sounds drift into his room.

The voices of nurses and doctors walking past, their quick steps in the corridor.

The windows opening and shutting.

Machines bleeping.

Rain falling from the sky onto hot tarmac.

A phone ringing out from the nurses' station.

A man snoring behind a curtain.

And then a woman's voice, too loud:

'Who've we got here then?'

He feels sweat gathering at the base of his spine. He should have left when he had the chance. He should have persuaded the nurse to let him go.

A doctor stands over him: tall, her face full of angles.

A nurse hovers beside her and says: 'One of Dr Deardorff's patients. We're not sure who he is.' The nurse pauses. 'He can't remember his name.'

The doctor laughs. 'Can't or *won't*?'

'I don't know,' the nurse says, his voice hesitant like he's afraid to get the answer wrong.

They talk over him, as though forgetting has somehow made him deaf and dumb.

'No ID on him, I suppose?' the doctor asks.

The nurse shakes his head. 'Nothing.'

'And let me guess, Dr Deardorff hasn't filed a report on him?'

His knee starts hurting, a burning and tearing. He has to get away from here. A report? No, he shouldn't be here.

The nurse shakes his head again. 'Dr Deardorff said this was a special case, that we needed to give him some time.'

'He did, did he?' She screws up her eyes into narrow slits, juts out her sharp chin and leans in towards the man. 'You're not from around here, are you?'

The man's heart speeds up. Sweat runs down his temples.

The doctor smiles. 'Thought not.'

Then she walks away down the ward.

The man's heart beats faster. He starts coughing. The machine beside him bleeps.

'Please . . .' he stutters at the nurse. 'Please let me . . .' But he can't stop the coughing.

A moment later, Dr Deardorff's round, pink face appears in front of him, large, concerned eyes behind his glasses.

'I thought I said I needed you to rest?' He turns to the nurse, the one who was talking to the young doctor a moment ago. 'What happened here, Nurse Green?'

He looks down at his feet. 'He was fine a moment ago.'

The man keeps coughing. Dr Deardorff sits him up and rubs his back. When the coughing eases, he goes to fiddle with the drip until the machine stops bleeping.

'We're just trying to help you get better. And that means you need to rest.' He writes notes on the man's chart and then sits down on the side of the bed and looks the man in the eye. 'Can you do that for me?'

'I'd like to go, please,' the man says. His heart pounds in his ears. *I don't belong here*, he thinks.

'It's okay, it's okay.' Dr Deardorff places his hand on the man's arm.

The man feels the warmth and pressure of the doctor's hand on his arm, how it's been good to rest here for a while. But then he thinks about what that other doctor said. He shakes his head. 'No, I need to—' His breath catches in his throat. 'I need to go . . .'

'Go where?' Dr Deardorff asks gently.

The man knows that it must make him sound crazy: that he needs to be waiting by the entrance of the zoo. But what else can he say?

Dr Deardorff leans in and says quietly: 'Why don't you tell me where home is – why don't we start there?'

The man closes his eyes. He sees trees, tall as giants, and birds and grass and flowers, and high up above the trees, through their thick leaves, a big open sky. A swing.

And then he sees the entrance to the zoo again, where the little girl and her mother found him this morning.

'Do you know where home is?' Dr Deardorff asks again.

The man opens his eyes and, very slowly, shakes his head.

Isabel

Right now, Isabel should be polishing Mr Long's oversized desk upstairs, in the management suite. But instead, she's here, watching him sleep – the man who, a few hours ago, she didn't even know existed.

She glances at her watch. Stingy Simon has a thing about being on time, and he's always reminding her that *cleaning the hospital manager's office is a privilege*. Except he knows as well as she does that privilege doesn't come into it: Isabel is the only cleaner who'll do a good enough job to keep the manager happy.

So who cares if she's a few minutes late for once, she'll still do a better job than all of the other cleaners put together.

Isabel looks over at the bed. His lips move in his sleep. Maybe he's speaking to someone, she thinks, and maybe if she waits and listens long enough, she'll pick something up that will help him remember. That's more important than cleaning a stupid desk.

His thick, dark eyelashes brush his skin. She remembers how, when River was a baby, she would watch her dark eyelashes grow – how amazed she was by how different they were from her own, which are so pale they might as well not be there at all.

There are deep circles under the man's eyes, grey and purple, like bruises. Isabel brushes her fingertips across the paper-thin skin, wishing she could ease the tiredness. She's always thought that eyes were too fragile to carry the weight of all the things they had to see.

She notices that he hasn't touched his tray of food. She lifts it off the bedside table, takes it to a trolley in the corridor and then comes back, wipes the table down and passes her cloth over the rails of the bed. When she starts cleaning things, it's like a series of dominoes – one thing leads to another and, if there wasn't anyone to stop her, she could keep scrubbing at the world for ever.

Wasn't there a time when nurses did the cleaning in hospitals? When cleaning was seen as a form of care?

Her foot nudges into a soggy plastic bag on the floor: it's the one she put his clothes in this morning. His suit and tie and shirt and socks are all scrunched up. She shakes her head. She'd asked Nurse Green to make sure he hung the clothes up to dry, but of course, the nurses don't take orders from cleaners.

Isabel picks up the bag and puts it by her cleaning trolley to remind her to take it home. There's a laundrette a few shops down from the flat.

And then she hesitates.

She'd promised herself to stop getting so involved in the lives of patients. To stop talking to them too much, worrying about whether they're getting better, stepping in when the nurses don't have time to do the basics.

One of these days you'll get yourself in a whole heap of trouble, Jules told her recently. *Taking all those psychos under your wing.*

But Jules doesn't understand. They aren't psychos, they're ill, and showing an interest in the patients is the only thing that makes Isabel's job bearable.

And anyway, this man's different. He doesn't have anyone else.

Isabel puts her hand into the plastic bag and looks through the man's clothes. In the pocket of his trousers, she feels a tiny piece of metal. She pulls out an elephant charm and sits it in the palm of her hand. It's the kind that would go on a bracelet or maybe a necklace. She holds it to her throat for a second and closes her eyes. Her chest tightens. She takes a breath and places it on the man's bedside table and keeps looking through the pockets.

I'm doing this to help him remember, she tells herself.

As she folds up his clothes, ready to take home with her, she feels a piece of paper in the inside pocket of his blazer. It's an old, torn envelope, sodden from the rain. There's a picture on the back, and although the ink has run, she can just about make out that it's a hand-drawn map. She unfolds it gently. It's London, drawn like a cartoon: Big Ben, Westminster Bridge, the Thames, Trafalgar Square. And then she sees it, drawn disproportionately large: Regent's Park with a big red dot by the entrance to the zoo – the place where they found him this morning.

She grabs a tissue and dabs at the map.

The only two things in the world that this man owns: a tiny silver elephant and a rain-smudged map of London. No passport. No driving licence. No bank card. Not even a name.

She looks towards the bed. The man's eyes are open. He's been watching her.

'I was just ...' She holds up the plastic bag. 'I thought you might like to have your clothes washed.' She points to his bedside table. 'I put your things there ...' Her cheeks burn. 'They were in your pockets.'

He looks over at them briefly then closes his eyes a second. *Those long eyelashes*, she thinks. *One blink could cause a storm.* 'Thank you.'

She wants to ask him what they are and whether they mean anything, but she's already invaded his privacy by rifling through his clothes – he can do without being questioned by her too.

His face softens. 'Thank you for coming to see me.' He hesitates. 'Isabel.'

She can't place his accent. There's a clipped precision to his

English but it's definitely foreign. She wonders whether it's possible to forget your mother tongue.

She steps closer to the bed. 'You remember my name?'

He smiles. 'Yes.'

'I just wasn't sure ... what you can and can't remember, I mean.'

'I do not understand either. But I remember today. I remember you and your daughter. Her name is River – that is right, is it not?'

'Yes, yes, that's right.'

He smiles. 'Because of the Venice canals?'

Isabel feels a pinch. 'Yes.'

She notices that his hair is still matted, and that his skin smells of earth and rain, of the park that Isabel and River walk through every day.

'Hasn't Nurse Green taken you for a bath yet?' she asks.

He shakes his head.

Isabel looks at her watch. She's fifteen minutes late now. And Stingy Simon likes to check on her when she's working on the management rooms.

'Just a minute,' she says and runs over to the nurses' station.

'Nurse Green – you're looking after the ... ' Isabel stalls. 'After the gentleman in the cubicle over there, right?'

Nurse Green looks up at her, still young and new enough to be worried that he's been caught doing something wrong – though not young enough to be put out by a cleaner holding him to account.

'Does he need something?' Nurse Green asks.

'Why hasn't he had a bath yet?'

His cheeks flush pink. 'I was told not to.'

'By whom?'

'Dr Reed.'

Isabel's eyebrows shoot up. 'The new doctor?'

The woman who more or less told Isabel to get lost this morning?

Nurse Green nods and glances down the corridor at the young blonde doctor chatting to one of the senior consultants.

'He's Dr Deardorff's patient,' Isabel clarifies.

'Dr Reed said he wouldn't be here for long, so not to bother.'

'The length of his stay hasn't been established yet,' Isabel snaps back.

The nurses might dismiss Isabel as a cleaner, but she's certainly not going to give them the satisfaction of thinking they understand more about how this place works than she does: she's been here for ten years.

Nurse Green straightens his spine and raises his chin.

'I'll wait for Dr Deardorff to instruct me directly.'

'Helping the patients wash is your *job*,' Isabel snaps. 'You don't need to be instructed.'

He stares at Isabel for a moment, his fingers hover over the keyboard of the computer, and then he looks back down as though he hasn't heard her.

Isabel wonders why someone fresh out of nursing school wouldn't have the instinct – or the basic compassion – to help a patient have a warm bath when he's been sitting in the rain for God knows how long.

'Fine,' Isabel says and turns on her heel.

When she gets to the man she places her arm under his elbow and says, 'I'm taking you for a bath.'

She can show him where it is, make sure he gets in okay, wait for him to have a quick wash, bring him back and there'll still be time to give the manager's office a good clean.

Only, there's nothing quick about taking a frail man with pneumonia and a damaged leg for a wash.

He leans a little too heavily on her and she stumbles.

'Sorry,' she says, and then grips his arm tighter.

Isabel realises why he was sitting on that bench and why he got drenched: he didn't have the strength to move. The walk to the hospital this morning must have taken everything out of him.

Isabel shifts her arm from holding his elbow to fully supporting him round the waist. At first she can sense him holding his weight back so as not to be a burden on her but he can't keep that up for long – he's too weak. Eventually she's all but carrying him.

And when they get to the bathroom, Isabel realises that unless she goes into the cubicle with him, he's not going to have the strength to get into the bath on his own, let alone wash himself.

Her heart starts hammering. He's basically her age and she guesses that the last time he washed with someone else there it was his wife or his girlfriend or maybe his kid.

She takes a breath. She's being silly. Nurses and doctors do this all the time. This is no different from when she makes a bed or empties a bin or helps a patient at mealtimes when a nurse is busy.

She checks her watch again. Half an hour of her shift is gone. She considers texting Ash to cover for her again, but he already did her a favour this morning. And if Simon catches him in the managers' area, they'll both have to pay for it.

She sends up a silent prayer that Simon's got caught up micromanaging someone else.

'Let me help you with the bath,' Isabel says.

She's got this far, she's not going to give up now. What's more,

Isabel believes in the healing properties of water. When River cried as a baby, Isabel would put her in the bath and play with her until her little fingers and toes were as wrinkled as prunes.

A city floating on water: it's what had made her want to go to Venice all those years ago.

Perhaps the water will soothe him too, and maybe that will help him remember.

The man looks back down the corridor in the direction of his bed. 'Maybe we should go back.'

She notices a pink flush in his cheeks. He's embarrassed too, about her helping him take a bath. Maybe she should have waited for a nurse to get round to it.

But then she feels like he needs her, someone who makes him feel safe. He's been through so much.

She puts her hand on his arm. 'It'll be over before you know it.'

But when she's filled up the bath and they're both standing there, staring at the water, she feels her breath speeding up again.

Maybe she should give him some space to get changed.

But then he looks at her like he's waiting for her to help. So she steps forward and unties his gown; there's a tremor in her fingers but she keeps going. She folds it up and places it on the side of the sink and then comes back to him.

She puts her arms around his waist and helps him to sit on the edge of the bathtub. Then she kneels in front of him and pulls off his socks.

For a moment, she looks up and he looks back at her, his brown eyes wide and confused.

'Thank you,' he says. 'For helping me.'

She nods. 'Of course.'

He looks over his shoulder at the water. And then his brow

folds on itself and he closes his eyes and lifts his hands to his ears. He starts swaying.

'What is it?' she asks.

He shakes his head over and over. She notices a tremor in his legs.

'Are you okay?'

He keeps swaying, his hands clamped over his ears.

Gently, she pulls them away.

He opens his eyes and stares at her; she's never seen anyone look so scared.

'It won't take long,' Isabel says. 'It will make you feel better.'

He looks back at the water. All the blood has drained from his face.

Perhaps this wasn't a good idea, she thinks. She acts like she knows what she's doing, like she's just as competent as any nurse, but she's just a cleaner. How's she meant to help someone like this?

'Maybe you were right.' She pauses. 'Maybe we should go back.'

He turns back to her and looks right into her eyes:

'You are kind,' he says. 'You want to help me.'

'Yes – yes, of course.'

'I should have the bath.'

'I think it will help you feel better,' she says. 'The water. Being clean.'

Isabel knows it was a stupid thing to say. Whatever this man has been through, it's going to take a lot more than a bath to make him feel better. But it's all she has to give him right now.

'If you prefer, I could ask one of the nurses to come in—'

'No,' he says. 'I want you to stay. If you would still like to help me?'

Isabel touches his arm. 'Of course I do.'

She places her hands gently on his hips, manoeuvres him round and then takes one of his legs at a time and places them into the tub. Finally, she guides his body down into the warm water.

She senses his body relax into itself. Maybe a bath can't take away his worries but it can help his body in this moment and, for now, that's enough.

He sits in the water, his eyes closed.

'Would you like me to help you wash?' she asks.

He nods, his eyes still closed.

She kneels back down, takes the flannel, pulls his shoulders forward and then washes the planes of his back, his neck and his chest.

Part of this feels familiar, like she's bathing a child. Only he's not a child. He's a grown man, and she hasn't seen a man's body, not like this, for a long time.

She looks at the vertebrae scaling up his long back: it takes all the self-restraint she can muster not to trace them with her fingers. She loves human anatomy. It's the one part of nursing school she would have sailed through.

Isabel begins to wash his stomach but he puts his hand over hers, takes the flannel from her and then makes a weak attempt at cleaning the lower parts of his body.

She looks away for a moment, folds his socks, and puts them on top of his hospital gown.

After that, she comes back to the bath mat. He hands her the flannel; she squeezes it out, puts it on the side of the tub then sits back on her heels.

He's staring down at his hands now, rubbing at an ink stain on his left forefinger. She wonders how he got it – when the last time was that he held a pen and wrote a word.

'Shall I wash your hair?' she asks.

He shakes his head.

'I'll be gentle. I've had practice with River – she hates it when I get soap in her eyes.'

'It is not the soap.'

'Oh.'

'Maybe we could wash my hair next time.' His voice is shaky. 'Next time I have a bath.'

He makes it sound like she'll be here every time, kneeling beside the bathtub, helping him.

She leans over and brushes her fingers over the coarse hair of his beard.

'How about a shave?' she asks him.

He looks up at her. 'If it's no trouble.'

'No trouble.'

Perhaps, without the beard, he'll recognise himself better, she thinks.

She finds an old plastic razor and some shaving foam in the bathroom cabinet over the sink and lifts his chin.

He tilts his head to one side. 'Your husband is a lucky man.'

She laughs. 'My husband?'

He looks up at her, startled.

'You think I wash my husband?' She tries a joke to still her nerves. *You think I've ever done this before?* She gulps. *You think I have a husband?*

Wasn't it written all over her: that she was alone. That she hadn't loved another man in over ten years?

She smooths the razor over the angles of his face. *He looks younger already,* she thinks.

'I'm sorry,' he says. 'I just thought . . .'

'It's okay.' She rinses the shaver in the bathwater and starts on the other side of his face. 'I don't have a husband.'

His eyes widen. He sits up. She catches the skin by his ear. A small trail of blood drips down his face.

'I'm so sorry!' She stands back from the bathtub and grabs a tissue and dabs at the cut.

He takes the tissue from her. 'It's nothing.' He smiles again. 'It's better than I would have done.' He picks up the razor from the side of the bathtub. 'Will you finish?'

Her fingers are trembling but she nods and picks up the razor. Just one plane of skin to go now.

'What about River's father?' he asks.

Her fingers shake harder. She's beginning to wish that she'd never stopped by his bed.

'It's just the two of us.' She stands up, turns her back to him and throws the razor in the bin.

'I'm sorry,' she hears him say.

'It's okay, we're fine just the two of us.'

She's said that phrase so often that it feels like a pebble in her mouth: a round, polished, perfect lie.

'I'm a little tired,' he says. 'Would it be possible to get out now?'

She turns round. 'Of course.' The poor man must be exhausted.

He fixes his eyes on her. 'I'm sorry for my questions. It's just that learning about other people ... it helps.'

She touches his arm. 'It's okay, really.'

As he sits up, he splashes water over the edge. It sprays against her uniform.

'Hey!' Without thinking she reaches into the water and flicks it at him.

He closes his eyes and laughs. And then, when she's not watching, he scoops up a palm full of water and launches it at her.

In a few seconds, Isabel is soaked and they're both laughing and it's the first time she feels her body relax since before she offered to take him for a bath.

She likes his laugh, the depth of it, like it's a place rather than a sound.

She hears the bathroom door swing open. She must have forgotten to lock it.

'Isabel?'

A moment later, David is standing over them, staring. He's out of breath. Sweat runs down the sides of his face.

Isabel is soaking, the bathroom floor flooded with water; the man stands in the bathtub, barely covered by his towel.

David mops his brow. *Did he run here?*

'This isn't your job, Isabel.'

She's never heard him sound so stern.

She shakes some water out of her hair and straightens her uniform. 'I'm sorry.'

'You should have asked Nurse Green.'

'I did.'

'It's my fault.' The man sways; his legs look like they're going to buckle.

At the same moment, Isabel and David reach out and catch him just before he falls.

'He needed a wash,' Isabel hisses. 'And Nurse Green wasn't going to do it. So I did.'

David looks at her for a while. *He looks confused*, she thinks. This man coming into their lives so suddenly and so completely has confused all of them. They've never had a patient like this before.

Eventually, he says, 'I understand, Isabel. I understand.'

She lets out a breath and feels sorry for snapping at him. Of course he understands. It's what they both do: go beyond the remits of their jobs – go against protocol, even – to help the patients.

But somehow, this feels different.

David helps the man out of the bathtub. He struggles with the man's long, thin limbs, by the unsteadiness of his body.

Isabel steps forward to help but David holds out a palm. 'I can take it from here, Isabel. You'd better get back to work.'

And she knows he's right. She should have got back to work an hour ago. God knows what will happen if Simon finds out. But she still finds it hard to make her feet move.

'I'll bring River over later,' Isabel says to the man.

He puts a hand to his chest and gives her a small bow and mouths: *thank you*.

Out in the corridor, Isabel catches a glimpse of herself in one of the glass doors. And that's when she sees Simon coming up behind her. Her body sinks into itself.

'What are you doing here, Isabel?' he asks.

She doesn't answer.

'This isn't your cleaning area,' Simon says.

Simon's portioned out the hospital like they're his colonies. He has a colour-coded chart in his office in the basement. Isabel's a fan of organisation but there's something nasty about the way Simon manages things. Thank God he's only in charge of cleaners.

He pulls out his phone and calls up a replica of the chart. 'You're meant to be upstairs – Mr Long's office.'

'I got delayed.'

'Like you got delayed this morning?'

She should have known he'd find out.

He looks over her shoulder. 'And where's your trolley?'

'It's already upstairs,' she lies.

Please, please may he not have seen it standing next to the man's bed.

'I'll make up the time,' she adds.

'Of course you will. Tonight – before you go home.'

'I can't . . . ' She hesitates. 'I have to look after my daughter.'

Simon knows that Isabel never uses her single-mum card to get special treatment. River spends more time with Isabel's best friend than she does with her mum – that's how seriously Isabel takes her job.

'I'm sure you'll find a way.' He gives her a thin smile.

Isabel wants to reel off all the unpaid overtime she's done over the years and to remind him how she's twice as efficient as any other cleaner in the hospital. But she bites her tongue. She needs this job.

'Yes, I'll find a way,' she says.

'Good, good.' Simon clicks his heels together, turns, and disappears down the corridor, his head jutting forward, ready to catch the next person out.

'*Weasel*,' Isabel mutters under her breath.

River

River sits next to the man's bed and studies his face. Knots line his brow and his eyelids slope down. His beard's gone, which makes him look kind of younger and he smells clean so he must have had a wash.

She's itching for him to wake up so she can talk to him some more, but Mum said he needs to rest and not to disturb him.

But then Mum's busy cleaning so it's not like she'd know.

River touches the man's arm but he doesn't wake.

All day at school she hasn't been able to stop thinking about who he is and where he's from and why he was sitting in the rain on that bench outside the zoo.

Most of all, she hasn't stopped wondering what made him forget his name. Because that's something she just can't get her head around. Isn't your name the one thing that's meant to stick? The thing that's been with you from the second you were born?

Anyway, he's the most interesting thing that's happened to River in ages and she's going to make sure Mum lets her get to know him.

Her leg starts jiggling; she stands up and walks around the room to calm it down, like Jules taught her.

She notices a pile of napkins on the man's bedside table. Someone's drawn pictures of animals and people's faces in smudgy black biro; they're distorted with big noses and big ears and funny eyes, like cartoons, only they look more grown-up than cartoons.

River looks over to the bed again. His hands are resting on

top of the sheets; smudges of biro run along the forefinger of his left hand.

He drew all of these, she thinks.

One of the pictures makes her look closer. It's a woman and she doesn't look as distorted as the others. In fact, the bits that are bigger are the bits that make her look pretty: her almond shaped eyes shine out from her face and she's got delicate lips that tilt upwards like she's keeping a secret.

And she has a little mole just to the left of her top lip.

River lets out a small gasp, picks up the piece of paper and holds it to her eyes. Her breath catches in her throat. The woman in the picture looks like Mum. Only younger – much younger. And she's got a long thick plait hanging over her shoulder; Mum's hair is light and wispy as feathers.

And then River gets it. The man didn't draw Mum. Or not just Mum. He drew River too. The person in the picture is a mix of the two of them: Mum's face and River's dark hair.

River's heart skips. If he drew them like this, it must mean that he likes them. She knew it was right to bring him to the hospital.

The biro sits next to the pile of drawings. River picks it up and notices that the plastic is cracked and that there's no ink left inside.

She reaches into her schoolbag, pulls out her pencil case and her English exercise book, and places them on the bedside table. School's finished so it's not like she's going to need them.

She tears out the pages she's written on, the ones full of red corrections and comments with exclamation marks from her teacher, and shoves them in the bin by the door.

School's over. She doesn't need to be reminded about how rubbish she was at everything.

Then she comes back to sit next to the man.

His breath has gone rattly and his chest is heaving and even though he's asleep, it's like he's gasping for air. She wonders whether she should get someone, but then his breath stills again.

Mum said he was really sick and that because his immune system was low, his lungs got hurt from being out in the cold night after night; she said that it would take him a long time to get better. River knows she shouldn't be glad that the man is ill but it means he'll be here for longer, which means she can see him more. She wants him to stay long enough, at least for him to remember his name and where he's from, because he's bound to be someone exciting, she can feel it.

River looks at the man again. His eyes are still firmly shut. He might not wake up for ages.

She leans in and whispers in his ear. 'I'm going to get you some treats.'

Yesterday, River earned a bit of pocket money for helping Mum clean the loos in Gabino's, the Italian restaurant under their flat, so she should have enough for a bunch of flowers and some grapes. Mum's always getting patients those things to cheer them up. And the man definitely looks like he could do with cheering up. Plus, it'll help pass the time until he wakes up.

On the way to the lifts, River spots a woman doctor she's never seen before talking to the hospital manager, Mr Long. She's twisting her blonde hair between her fingers and nodding at everything he says and Mr Long's smiling back.

River wonders whether her mum and dad looked at each other like that when they were young and whether Dad was handsome, and whether Mum twisted her hair at him.

But when it comes to Dad, River basically knows nothing. Every time River brings him up, Mum changes the subject. And Jules won't say anything either.

It's one of the two things River isn't allowed to ask questions about: the other thing is her grandparents. She reckons that not asking about Dad and not asking about Mum's parents must be connected in some way, but she's not sure how.

In the eleven years of her life, these are the only things Mum's ever told River about Dad:

He's Italian.

Mum met him in Venice.

Mum was really young.

He only ever gets referred to as *The Italian*. Even by Jules. It's like they're scared to even say his name out loud.

River's not even sure she believes this stuff. She bets Mum made it up to keep River from asking more questions.

The truth is, Dad's probably a loser or a psychopath or just a guy who doesn't want to have a kid.

The doctor looks up, notices River staring at her and raises her eyes like River shouldn't have been looking. That's grown-ups all over: blaming you for stuff that's not your fault. If she didn't want her to look, she shouldn't be standing in the middle of the corridor like that.

River decides to give up on the lift and pushes through the doors that lead to the stairwell.

When she gets to the newsagent on the ground floor of the hospital she realises she only has enough money for the grapes. She really wanted to get the man some flowers too. Things should be cheaper in hospitals, River thinks. It's not like anyone wants to be sick just so they can get the grapes. Then she has an idea. She looks up and down the corridor to make sure Mum isn't around.

Mum doesn't let River walk around London on her own, even though she knows London better than Mum and even though, as Mum keeps reminding her, she's about to start secondary school, which means that, after the summer, she'll be walking around all over the place by herself.

Mum's logic is completely off.

River takes a breath and runs out of the hospital onto the busy street.

When River comes back to the man's cubicle, the bed's empty. It takes her a moment to notice that he's standing by the IV drip, easing it out of his arm and wincing.

His other arm is pressing down on the stick that he uses as a cane.

'Hey!' she calls over.

The man doesn't respond.

She dumps the red geraniums she picked from the Italian Gardens at Regent's Park next to the grapes.

'What are you doing?'

He looks at her, his eyes wild.

'Why are you up? You shouldn't be up. You're meant to be resting, Mum said. And so did Dr Deardorff. You're sick, really sick.' She nods at the IV drip. 'And I don't think you're meant to take that out, not by yourself, anyway.'

Maybe he's got ADHD, like I do, thinks River. Maybe he finds it hard to stay in bed all day long.

The man stares at her, but his eyes are a million miles away, like he's stepped back into himself.

'You don't look well,' she says. 'You should get back into bed. I can get Dr Deardorff.'

He shakes his head wildly. His knotty brown hair falls into his eyes.

'I have to go.' The man's words come out in jagged breaths. His skin looks grey and clammy. He definitely shouldn't be up.

'Go where?'

'To London Zoo.' He flutters his hand in the direction of the door. 'I have to go back there.'

His eyes stop looking far away and the storm comes back. He jerks his head around, like he's looking for a way to run off without anyone noticing.

'I really think you should stay here.'

He shakes his head again. 'I promised I'd wait for her there.'

'Wait for who?'

The knots on his brow bulge out. He rubs his forehead like he's trying to press them back in. He grabs at his hair, like he wants to tear it out. Then he puts his hands over his ears and closes his eyes and starts swaying.

River touches his arm, gently. 'It's okay . . . '

But he keeps shaking his head. He takes his hands away from his ears, pushes his body harder against his stick and takes some steps. River can tell that he's trying to go really fast but that his legs aren't listening – he's wobbling all over the place.

River holds his arm. 'Stop – you're going to fall.'

He yanks his arm out of hers and stumbles forward.

River grabs him again, holding both his arms this time. She uses all her strength to root him to the spot, which isn't easy because he's like double her height. But she's not going to give up: she found him and she persuaded Mum to bring him to hospital. She's not going to lose him now.

She keeps holding him tight and looks into his eyes.

'Who did you promise you'd wait for?' she asks again. 'Tell me, maybe I can help?'

'You can't help.'

'Well, how do you know that? You haven't even given me a chance. And I'm good at helping – *really* good.'

The storm in his eyes goes still again for a second. Then she feels the muscles in his arms relaxing. He drops his shoulders. And, very slowly, he sits back down on the bed. It's like all the air's gone out of him.

River's not sure which is worse – the man trying to tear out of the room or the man just sitting there, limp and sad.

River sits down beside him and asks him again: 'Who were you waiting for – outside the zoo?'

His shoulders slump even more.

'I don't remember ...' he says.

'But you know you're meant to meet someone?'

He nods.

'Well, that's a start. Maybe, if you take some time to get better, you'll remember who it was.'

River notices the man looking past her to the nurses' station. She follows his gaze. The doctor from before is still there but this time she's talking to a nurse.

'She does not want me here,' the man says, his eyes going stormy again.

'Who?'

'Dr Reed.' The man nods at the doctor.

'Don't be silly. You're sick and she's a doctor, of course she wants you here, we all do.'

The man bows his head so low it seems to disappear between his shoulders. 'I am not from here.'

'I thought you didn't know where you came from?'

'I don't ...'

'So how can you know you're not from here?'

River feels proud of her logic. Jules is always telling her that she's got a good analytical brain. Not that it's got her anywhere at school.

'I know that I'm not from here because people from here are allowed to be in the hospital,' the man says. 'And I am not allowed to be here.'

'Is that what Dr Reed said?'

'She did not need to.'

'Isn't Dr Deardorff your doctor?' River says.

Mum and Dr Deardorff have worked on the same ward for ten years.

'And Dr Deardorff is really nice. And Mum says he's the best doctor in the hospital.'

The man nods.

'Dr Deardorff says it's okay for you to be here, doesn't he?' River says.

The man nods again.

'Well, that's settled then.' She smiles. 'And anyway, I'd be sad if you left now.'

The man looks up at River. His eyes are a bit calmer now.

'You are kind,' he says.

'I am?'

'Yes. Like your mother.'

River scrunches up her nose. 'Like Mum?'

Mum didn't seem to want to take him to the hospital. Not at first, anyway.

He nods. 'You and your mother, you do not know me—'

'Of course we know you. We met this morning, at the zoo, remember?'

River wonders how this whole memory thing works. Whether having forgotten stuff in the past means that he'll keep forgetting things that are happening now too.

'I mean, you do not *really* know me.' He pauses. 'And still, you are kind.'

'Well, I've got all summer to get to know you – that is, unless you remember things before then and go home or something.' She pauses. 'I could help you ... if you like.'

The man's eyes brighten. The storminess has definitely settled for a bit.

'So, will you get back into bed?'

The man looks over to the nurses' station again. Dr Reed has disappeared.

'We can tell the nurse that the IV dropped out in your sleep.' River leans in and whispers. 'I promise I won't tell: it can be our secret.'

Keeping secrets is something else Jules says that River is good at. It's an important life skill, Jules says. And Jules is right: River would never give away anyone's secrets.

For the first time since she found him trying to leave, the man gives her a proper smile. He's got crooked teeth and his gums look red rather than pink but he's got a nice smile.

River helps him back to his bed and then takes his stick from him and turns it over in her hands. It's like a proper stick with knobbly bits, and the end's been polished where his palm has rubbed it over and over.

The man follows River's gaze. 'A dog brought it to me.'

'The stick?'

He nods. 'I threw it back for him, but he didn't want it.'

'Maybe he knew,' River says.

'Knew?'

'That you needed it – because you have a sore knee. Animals know things, much more than human beings do. It's only because they can't talk that people don't notice how clever they are.'

The man's smile goes even wider. Then he eases his legs back into bed. The effort makes his breath go wheezy. Even if he had tried to run away, he wouldn't have had the strength to get very far, thinks River.

When he's safely back in bed, she goes and finds a jam jar for the geraniums and places them on his bedside table. Mum says that geraniums don't last long out of the ground, but River hopes that they'll keep going long enough to cheer him up a bit.

As she adjusts the jam jar, she notices a small elephant charm on the table – and a piece of paper, wavy and stained with raindrops.

She picks them up and puts them on his lap.

'Did you find these too?' she asks. 'Like the stick?'

He stares down at the objects. Knots push up into his brow. River worries that he's going to flip out again and try to leave.

'Maybe someone left them here by mistake. I can give them to the nurse—'

'No,' the man says. 'No, they are mine.'

He picks up the elephant charm and turns it around between his fingers. His breathing goes wheezy again.

'I like elephants,' River says. 'And pigeons. All animals, really.' She looks up at him. 'Do you like animals as well? Is that why you were waiting outside London Zoo?'

'I can't remember.' He keeps staring at the charm in his fingers.

'Well, I think you'd like to see the elephants. They're not at London Zoo any more though.'

The man's face folds into a frown.

'It's okay. They didn't die or anything, they just moved them to Whipsnade. We could go there – I mean, when you're well enough. It's a bit further out, but it's definitely worth a visit.'

The man's eyes suddenly fill with tears.

'What made you sad?' River asks.

The man blinks. A few tears plop down his cheeks.

'I don't know,' the man says.

He puts the elephant charm down on his lap and then clutches at his hair again.

River takes his hands from his hair and puts them back down on the bedsheet.

'It's okay,' she says.

She thinks about how sometimes she feels sad – and even gets tearful – without knowing why. Like her body is feeling something that her brain can't make sense of.

River squeezes his hand. 'I promise we'll take you – and I always keep my promises.'

He nods and tries to smile but he still looks sad.

River's decided: as soon as he's better, they'll take him to see the elephants at Whipsnade. It can be a celebration of him getting out of hospital.

She picks up the piece of paper that was lying beside the elephant charm. It has pictures of roads and buildings on it. 'What's this?'

'I don't . . . ' He looks down at his hands and rubs at the ink stain on his left forefinger. 'I don't remember.'

'Can I borrow it?' River asks.

She thinks that maybe it will give her a clue about where he's from.

'I could trace over the lines that have gone all blurry. It could give us some clues, jog your memory.'

He nods again and closes his eyes. Mum's right, she has to be careful not to wear him out.

She folds up the piece of paper and puts it in her pocket.

'Before I go,' River says. 'I wanted to tell you that I've got something for you.'

He keeps his eyes closed but his lips smile slightly.

'A name.'

The man's eyes open. 'A name?'

River nods. 'Just until you remember your old one.'

The man waits for her to continue and River gets worried all of a sudden, in case he doesn't like it. It had seemed like a good idea when it had come to her.

'Reg,' she announces as proudly as she can. 'I think we should all call you Reg.'

River thinks everything and everyone should have a name. It's why she gave the pigeon who visits their flat the name Pablo, after Pablo Picasso. Because even though you can't see it, pigeons have millions of colours in their feathers and Pablo Picasso loved colours.

'Reg?' the man asks. It sounds funny in his accent.

River nods. 'For Regent's Park, where we found you.' She hesitates. 'I thought you'd like it.'

'Reg . . . ' the man says again, like he's trying it out.

'I think it's short for Reginald – which I looked up; it means being a wise, powerful ruler.'

The man laughs. 'I'm not sure it's the right name for me, then.'

'Well, I think it suits you. And we can't very well go around calling you nothing, can we? I mean, everyone needs a name.'

'I suppose so,' the man says.

'So, Reg it is?'

'Reg is what?' Mum walks in. Her top lip is sweaty and her hair's frizzy. Stingy Simon has made her work extra hard for the time she missed this morning.

'His for-now-name,' River says. 'For Regent's Park, where we found him.'

Mum shakes her head and sighs but not in a cross way. Then she notices the plaster hanging off Reg's arm from where his IV drip was.

She darts forward. 'What happened?'

'He had a bad dream and it popped out,' River says quickly.

Mum's eyebrows shoot up. 'Popped out?'

'Yep.' River's cheeks go pink.

It's something River and Mum have in common – they both blush at the drop of a hat. It's just River's luck to have inherited a skin condition rather than one of Mum's pretty features like her eyes or her lips or her tiny feet. At least, because River's skin is darker, her blushing doesn't show up as much as Mum's.

'IV drips don't just "pop out",' Mum says.

Officially, Mum might be a cleaner, but River reckons she knows more about medical stuff than all the doctors and nurses put together. A few years ago, she saved someone's life. He was choking on an olive at Gabino's and Mum did the Heimlich manoeuvre on him. The olive flew out of the man's throat and catapulted right across the restaurant. After a bit of coughing, the man was fine again. So obviously Mum knows that Reg's IV drip wouldn't just drop out.

But for the first time ever, Mum doesn't question River any further.

'We'll ask one of the nurses to sort it out later.'

Reg looks up at Mum with one of his sad smiles.

'Thank you.'

'My pleasure.' Mum's cheeks go a bit red, like River's.

'We'd better go home, River,' Mum says.

'Can I come back tomorrow?'

Tomorrow, River's meant to be with Jules. Which, usually, she'd love. Being with Jules is cool – definitely cooler than being at school. They hang out with the kids she nannies and spend all their time outside, mainly at Regent's Park or at the zoo.

But right now, Reg is more interesting than anyone and the

only place River wants to be is right here, helping him work out who he is and where he's from.

And it's not like she's going to get Jules to come here – she hates hospitals.

'I won't be any trouble,' River says. 'And maybe I can help Reg remember a few things.'

River is good at puzzles and treasure hunts and at linking up clues. Sometimes Jules organises a treasure hunt for River and the kids she's looking after in the park and if River works it out faster than anyone else, she gets this bolt of electricity that runs right up her spine and it's the best feeling ever.

'I'm sure Jules wouldn't mind,' River suggests. 'Not if we explain.'

Mum kisses the top of River's head. 'I'll have a think about it. Let's get you home, River.'

'See you tomorrow, Reg,' River says. And then, even though she doesn't know him very well, she goes and gives him a kiss on the cheek.

Reg looks up at her and smiles, a proper big one this time. Even the sad shimmer in his eyes seems to go away for a second.

'I would like that very much, Miss River,' he says.

David

Every day, after his shift, David stops by the newsagent in the hospital to buy a packet of Jammie Dodgers.

Before David's even got through the door, Milek, the young Polish man who owns the shop, rings up the biscuits.

'Good day at work?' Milek asks.

David thinks about how much has happened today: how he's keeping a man on the ward who doesn't have any papers and doesn't even remember his own name. And how, if someone were to ask him why he was going to so much trouble for a stranger, he'd have to say that of course it was for the patient. For a man who was lost and in distress. But he knew it was because he couldn't say no to Isabel.

'An interesting day,' David says.

'You going to see your mother?'

David nods.

'Well, give her my best,' Milek says.

'I will, thank you.'

Milek was the one who recommended The Birches when David mentioned that his mother needed to move to a nursing home. Milek's mother is there too. She likes the bingo, he said, and the food isn't bad. Most of all, it's close to the hospital, so David can visit her on his way home from work. David had tried to keep his mother at home as long as possible, but when her mind began to go and with his long shifts at the hospital, he knew that she needed round-the-clock care.

David realises that Milek, the shop-owner who sources

old-fashioned Jammie Dodgers for him, a man with whom he only ever exchanges a few words, probably knows more about David than anyone else in the world. He'd never spoken to anyone about his mother before. Not even to Isabel.

'See you soon,' Milek says.

As soon as he's standing on the pavement, David unravels the top of the packet of Jammie Dodgers, levers a biscuit out of the packet, eases apart the two sides and licks off the jam. He closes his eyes and, as the sweet jam melts between his tongue and the roof of his mouth, his body relaxes for the first time all day.

'Mum . . . it's me.' David sits next to his mother's armchair.

She stirs and opens her eyes. Her brow furrows.

'It's David, your son.'

Her brow relaxes. 'David,' she says, breathing the word out with relief. 'Have you been working hard at school?'

'At work, Mum, I've been at work. At the hospital.'

'Of course you have,' his mother says, patting his knee.

David looks at the black and white photograph of his father on the table next to his mother's armchair. He's in his Met uniform: a series of badges on his chest recognising a lifetime of service. It was taken a few days before he was stabbed by four teenagers. David was fifteen.

'Your tea's in the kitchen,' his mother says. 'Your father's going to be late home, so you don't need to wait for him.'

After the stabbing, his mother had gone into shock and after that, her mind retreated to David's childhood. She's been waiting for David's father to come home from work for the last twenty-five years.

David stays with her for an hour, breaking up bits of biscuit and popping them into her mouth, as he tells her about his day at the hospital.

'Sleep well, Mum,' he says, kissing the top of her soft grey hair. She's already drifting off.

Quietly, he lets himself out of her room and walks out onto the dark London streets.

David stands at the window of his flat, looks out at the grey sky and listens.

The thud of a football hitting a concrete wall.

A baby crying.

Manic cartoon voices from a TV.

A mother calling her children in for tea.

It'll be noisy, the estate agent had warned David. *It's a family kind of place.*

When his mother went into The Birches and he sold the house he'd shared with her his whole life, he looked for a flat, and this is where he ended up.

The estate agent wanted David to buy an exclusive bachelor pad in Chelsea, the kind of place with an onsite gym and swimming pool, an immaculate courtyard garden and guarded gates.

But David had said no, he liked this better.

He passes his tongue over his lips to get the last bit of sticky jam and empties the crumbs from the packet of Jammie Dodgers onto the window ledge. He's snapped off the spikes that are meant to keep the pigeons away. He thinks back to his mother at the home and how she likes to watch the pigeons landing outside her window and pecking at the treats she leaves for them. She always liked birds; he supposes that kind of memory never goes.

David looks out at the city lights and thinks of Isabel and the man she brought into the hospital today.

Is it normal? she'd asked him. *That someone should forget his name?*

No . . . not normal, he'd answered. *But then, where the human mind is concerned, there is no normal.*

Well, we're going to have to find a way to help him remember, she'd said.

He sees her face in front of him. Her blue eyes shining with determination. Determination runs through everything Isabel does: the way she walks with her small, brisk steps through the hospital; how she cleans the ward with such care; and how, this morning, she'd knocked on the staffroom door, her head held high, and asked for him, because she believed he could help.

Right from her first day at the hospital, he noticed how Isabel would stop and listen when he was talking to patients. And then she started to ask him questions – medical questions, things that you wouldn't know to ask unless you had some training, or were really interested. Better questions than many of the interns asked.

He noticed, too, that she didn't ask the other doctors; maybe she was intimidated by them in a way that she wasn't with him. Much as he hates the way he looks – too short, too round, a facial expression that's never quite serious enough – he knows that these features make him more approachable.

One day, when they'd only known each other for a few weeks, they bumped into each other at the Get Well Soon Café. They sat down together and talked for an hour. Then they began making a habit of it – whenever their breaks coincided, they'd meet up at the café and talk.

Sometimes their conversations touch on their personal lives, but that's rare. Mostly they talk about patients and interesting cases on the ward.

They've worked together for ten years now and Isabel has come to understand how David works in a way that the other doctors and nurses never will.

They bathed an old homeless woman together once. She had Alzheimer's, like David's mother. Kept forgetting that she lived on the streets. Spent her days looking for a home that never existed. The dirt was so engrained in the folds of her skin and under her nails, her hair such a tangle of knots, that they thought they would never get her clean. But they did. With Isabel, they always made things work.

So he should have understood why she bathed the man today. But it made him feel flustered to see her in that bathroom, so close to the stranger.

David opens his eyes and goes over to his shelf of medical books. He pulls out the tomes on neurology that he studied as a medical student. Neurology, of course, is still a young and imprecise science; the brain, as compared to the rest of the body, a relatively unchartered territory.

And the lines between the conscious and the subconscious brain, between remembering and forgetting, are so blurred that David wonders whether he'll ever be able to untangle them.

The problem with cases like that of the man Isabel had brought in today is that the brain shows no physical signs of trauma: the scans came out clear. Besides his pneumonia, and the battering his body has taken from living rough, he's in good shape.

But psychological trauma is subtle in its manifestations.

He closes his eyes and lets out a long breath.

Somewhere, in a flat below him, a child starts to play scales on a piano. David's mother and father used to play the piano in their small terraced house in East London: they would sit side by side on a small stool, their bodies pressed together, their hands criss-crossing.

There could be any number of reasons for why the man had forgotten, David thinks. Either he's still in shock, or he doesn't want to allow himself to remember. Or, of course, he's hiding something. Because that too is the problem with the human brain – unlike the body, its responses are not purely reflexive. The mind has a way of shaping its own course.

Dr Reed has intimated as much. Fresh out of medical school, she thinks she has all the answers.

What puzzles David is that without damage to the frontal cortex, it's unusual for memory loss to last long – and the man seems to have been in this fog of forgetfulness for weeks.

Another thing that troubles David is the man's accent. He doesn't seem to have any recollection of his native tongue and yet he doesn't sound English. And it isn't easily identifiable, either, as though it's been eroded over time. Another anomaly: language, like music, goes deep. Long after the deepest memories have vanished, it's one of the things that stays.

David sits down, settles the books beside him and takes out his phone. He has a friend from university, a linguistics specialist. Maybe this is the place to start.

He dials the number and waits for Alex to answer.

'Hello?'

'I'm sorry to disturb you—' He glances at his watch and realises that it's nearly eleven. 'So late.'

'Who is this?'

David clears his throat. 'It's me. I mean, it's David. Your friend . . . '

The word *friend* hangs between them. They were best friends at Hull university. Spent all their time together. Alex was as obsessed with language as David was with human anatomy. They shared a flat for a couple of years. Neither of them really had any other friends – certainly not girlfriends. And then David came back to London to work and to be close to his mum. And, of course, Alex met a girl and fell in love and got married and had kids, and did all the normal things everyone does in the end – even people who, when they're younger, aren't good at socialising or making friends.

Everyone, it seems, except David.

Once a year, Alex sends David a Christmas card with a picture of his family on the front; David hasn't been so good at staying in touch.

'Deardorff? Christ, I haven't heard from you in years,' says Alex.

Years? Had it really been that long?

Sometimes, David feels that the days he spends at the hospital are somehow outside time, the time that other people experience, anyway.

'I'm sorry,' David stutters.

He doesn't understand how anyone has the time for anything other than what's right in front of them. Between the hospital and his mother, he just doesn't have anything left to give.

'There's a patient I'd like you to take a look at.'

'A patient?'

'On my ward. He's an unusual case.'

'Now why doesn't that surprise me?'

David remembers how, in Hull, they'd sit together in the library, studying, and how he'd share interesting medical scenarios with Alex and how Alex would reciprocate with the strange ways in which human beings used language. They were both drawn to odd cases.

'A friend of mine brought him into the hospital. She—'

'She?'

David can hear a smile in Alex's voice. It's like all the years they've been out of touch folded in on themselves and they're students again. David sometimes developed crushes on girls – a medical student, someone working in a café or behind the desk at the library. Usually people he didn't know at all. Girls who he knew were out of his league. So, obviously, he never plucked up the courage to talk to them.

'She works at the hospital,' David goes on. 'She found him sitting outside London Zoo.'

'London Zoo?'

'It's near the hospital.'

'Right.'

'No papers. No memory of who he is or where he's come from. And he must have been living rough for a while. He's got pneumonia—'

'And I fit in how?'

'He's got an unusual accent.'

'What kind of unusual accent?'

They'd test each other before exams: Alex learnt about medicine, David about linguistics. They imagined careers in which they could work alongside each other.

'At a guess, I'd say Eastern European. But beyond that, I don't know. Anyway, he's a really interesting case.'

'You said that already.'

And then there's a pause.

David knows no matter how married Alex is and how many kids he has and how much of a suburban life he's adopted, he'll be intrigued.

'And he needs our help,' David adds. 'He doesn't have anyone.' David clears his throat. 'I thought you could have a listen—'

'I live in Hull, David.'

David scratches his head. 'Could you get a train?'

Alex laughs down the line. 'You haven't changed a bit.'

'You could stay with me,' David suggests.

'I'll check my diary and get back to you—' Alex says.

'There's a degree of urgency.'

Alex laughs again. 'There is, is there?'

'He's not well.' He clears his throat. 'And I'm not sure how long I can keep him at the hospital.'

'Why's that?'

Alex knows exactly why that is: he specialises in the study of language change in immigrants. And you don't need a degree in linguistics – or medicine – to know that immigrants don't get to stay in hospitals, not without papers.

'He doesn't even remember his name, Alex. We didn't find any identification on him. Not a thing.'

'I see.'

'So you'll come?'

'You want me to cancel my lectures and my classes, leave my wife and kids, all at a moment's notice, and get the train down to London – for this patient of yours?'

'That would be very much appreciated.' There's a pause. David holds his mobile phone closer to his ear. 'Alex?'

'Still not living in the real world, then, mate?'

'Sorry?'

Alex laughs again. 'You'll owe me.'

David doesn't understand what this means or what he could possibly give Alex that he doesn't have already.

'Of course.' David waits a beat. 'When can you come down?'

'I'm afraid I can't just up and leave. I'll have to clear my schedule.'

'I said that this was urgent ...' David's voice breaks. He

knows he's sounding unhinged. He thinks about the comments he's been getting from colleagues, and Reed's probing. 'Without papers or a name or an address or any family to speak of, it's just a matter of time before the police get involved. And then he'll get taken into the care of immigration services. Put in some kind of detention camp. Eventually, they'll work out where he's from and he'll get deported. And God knows what will happen then.'

'What do you mean, what will happen?'

David takes a breath. 'I don't know, I've just got this feeling . . .'

'A *feeling*?'

David knows how foolish he sounds – and how unlike himself. Even as students, all those years ago, Alex and David prided themselves on how they worked with facts and evidence. No conjecture. No gut feelings.

David swallows his pride. 'Yes, a feeling. That something's not right. That he's vulnerable somehow. And that he needs help. Medical help. Psychiatric help. If we can work out where he's from and why he's here, maybe it will buy us some time – or a reason to keep him here.'

Another long pause.

'Look, I'll come when I can,' Alex says. 'Until then, I'm sure that you'll work something out. You always do.' He pauses. 'Gather some facts and send me some sound files to listen to in advance.'

'Thanks, Alex.' David hangs up quickly before Alex has the chance to change his mind or, worse, start asking personal questions.

David sits back in his chair. Calling Alex was the right thing to do, he tells himself. And yet there's another part of him that remembers what one of his old neurology professors said: *Sometimes*

remembering can be worse than forgetting, David. Sometimes, remem-
bering can do more damage than good.

David had been shocked by his professor's words: it had felt as though he was undermining his life's work. If forgetting was a good thing, if it was best to ignore a damaged mind, what was the point of the work they did? But over time, he'd come to understand what his professor was doing: he was warning him. The mind is fragile – it has to be treated with care.

Nevertheless, if there's something he is sure of in this case, it's that this man Isabel brought in this morning can't afford to stay lost.

River

River walks ahead of Mum up the narrow stairway to their flat, dragging a red bucket and mop behind her. Mum's carrying the hoover and keeps bashing the sides of the walls, which means she's tired: leaving marks on the wall is usually something she tells River off for.

River knows it took it out of Mum – looking after Reg all day and then doing all that extra cleaning at the hospital – so River said she'd help her clean the restaurant tonight. Plus, there's no school in the morning, so it doesn't matter if she goes to bed late.

'Isabella!' Grumpy Gabs stands at the bottom of the stairs, holding a plate of biscotti up to them.

Grumpy Gabs is grumpy with everyone except Mum.

'We're fine, thank you,' Mum says. She doesn't like to take favours from people, even if it's only a silly plate of biscuits.

'Well, I don't want them.' He shrugs and places them on the bottom step.

Every month his family in Naples send him Italian treats. And every time he tries to palm them off on Mum. Either that, or River finds them in the bin when she takes out the rubbish. Jules, who always knows what's going on with everyone, says that Grumpy Gabs doesn't get on with his family. Something about his brother getting the family restaurant back in Italy and marrying the girl Gabs has loved for like his whole life. Which is probably why Gabs makes fry-ups and fish and chips rather than proper Italian food – like he wants to make some kind of statement against his parents or something.

River puts down the mop and the bucket, runs down, past Mum, takes the plate of biscotti and gives Grumpy Gabs a kiss by the side of his grizzly, grey beard.

Grumpy Gabs grunts and kind of half smiles.

'Thank you, Gabino!' River calls over her shoulder, and carries the biscuits upstairs.

Mum gives Gabs a bow, too tired even to say thank you. He shrugs again and goes back into the restaurant.

'Poor Gabs,' River says. 'He really likes you, Mum.'

River reckons that if Mum paid Gabs more attention, then maybe he'll get over what his brother and his parents did to him. And she's seen how Gabs looks at Mum. She's the only thing that takes a bit of the grump out of him. But then most guys like Mum, it's getting her to like them back that's the problem. She keeps saying that she doesn't need a man in her life. That she's happy with things as they are, living with Jules and River. Which would be fine if she actually *looked* happy.

'You sure you don't fancy him, Mum?' River asks. 'Even a little bit?'

'River ...' Mum says. 'Don't start.'

'Well, I think he's sweet.'

'You think every man who crosses my path is sweet.'

River shrugs. 'I just think it's good to explore your options.'

Mum laughs. 'My options?'

River nods.

'Come on.' Mum heaves the hoover up to the door of their flat. Then she says: 'If I had a relationship with Gabino and it all went wrong, we wouldn't have a place to live.'

He hasn't put the rent up since they moved in when River was born. And with all the cleaning Mum does for him, he doesn't ask for much. Mum says that if it weren't for Gabs, they'd have to live miles and miles out of town.

'And anyway, he's not my type,' Mum adds.

'Who is your type, then?'

'Not Gabino,' Mum says.

'Not anyone . . .' River says under her breath, following Mum into their bedsit.

Not anyone except Dad. Dad must have been Mum's type otherwise they wouldn't have had River together. Jules has hinted a few times that Mum still loves him, though River doesn't understand how you can love someone who's been away for like a whole lifetime.

River shoves the mop and the bucket in the cupboard by the fridge.

'Shush, you'll wake Jules.'

'Sorry.' River closes the door quietly.

Jules goes to bed really early because she wakes up at five every morning so that she can pick up the triplets and Nula before their parents go to work. Some days, Jules goes to bed and wakes up so early that River and Mum don't see her at all.

Jules and Mum share a room. They've been friends since they were eleven years old and they found themselves sitting next to each other on the first day of school. Finding a friend like Jules is the only thing that gives River the teeniest bit of hope that secondary school might be okay.

'We're fine as we are.' Mum puts her arm around River. 'Aren't we?'

River's lost count of the number of times Mum's said this. And the number of times she's nodded and said, 'Of course we are.'

Like she does now. Even though she's not sure it's true. Because whatever Mum says, she looks kind of lonely. Which means that being with River isn't enough.

'Hot chocolate?' Mum asks.

River nods. If there's one thing better than biscotti, it's biscotti dipped in hot chocolate. They were back so late from the hospital that they didn't have time to make tea: River's tummy's been rumbling for hours.

On her way to the kitchen, Mum takes a pound coin out of her purse and slots it into River's piggy bank. River's told Mum that she doesn't need to give her money when she helps with the cleaning, that she likes to do it, but then if she hadn't had any pocket money today then she wouldn't have been able to get the grapes for Reg.

'Thanks, Mum,' River says.

Mum gives her a wink and disappears into the kitchen.

River curls up on the sofa and thinks about everything that's happened today: meeting Reg in the park; her last day at primary school; and then spending hours at the hospital trying to help Reg remember who he is and where he's from.

Mum comes back and hands River a mug of cocoa.

'So, can I spend the day with Reg tomorrow?'

Mum still hasn't given her a definitive answer.

Mum slumps down beside her, grabs a biscotti and bites off a huge chunk. River wouldn't be surprised if Mum forgot to have lunch as well.

'Mum?'

'I don't want you to get too attached.'

'He's nice . . . '

'He's a stranger, River, we don't know anything about him.'

'Well, he doesn't know who he is either, so that makes us even. And we know he's nice – isn't that the only thing that matters?'

Mum swallows another bit of biscotti and brushes some crumbs off the sofa. 'It doesn't make him less of a stranger.' Mum puts down her mug. 'Come on, let's get your bed ready.'

River sleeps on the sofa bed. She likes sleeping out here: the space, being able to look out of the big lounge window (especially when Pablo comes to visit), listening to the sounds of the street below.

As Mum folds out the bed and gets River's duvet and pillows from behind one of the armchairs, River takes the biscotti crumbs, opens the window and puts them on the windowsill.

'You shouldn't be encouraging him,' Mum says.

'He's hungry.'

'London pigeons are the most overfed pigeons in the world.'

'Not any more they're not. They're being banned from all sorts of places where people used to feed them.'

Mum sucks on her teeth and shakes out the duvet. 'They're not clean.'

Not being clean is one of Mum's bugbears. Which kind of makes sense, with her job, but still, it makes her kind of exhausting to live with.

River gets into her rainbow pyjamas, brushes her teeth, snuggles up on the sofa and pulls the duvet up to her chin.

'I think I could help Reg,' she says. 'And you're always saying we should help people, if we can.'

Mum sits on the side of the sofa and strokes River's head. 'He's very sick, River. And he's in hospital, he's getting all the help he needs.'

'But he likes me – that's what Dr Deardorff says, so he might tell me stuff that he won't tell anyone else. That's why I have to spend more time with him, Mum. He's starting to open up, I can feel it. And he's scared.' River pauses. 'He tried to run away.'

Mum's head jolts up.

'He did what?'

River feels guilty for breaking her promise to Reg but she has to get Mum on side.

'He didn't get very far. I just saw him climbing out of bed. I think he's worried that he's not allowed to be in the hospital. But I told him that if you're sick, the hospital is where you're meant to be.'

Mum goes very quiet. 'It was good of you to stop him, River.'

'You see, Mum, he listens to me – he trusts me.'

'I just don't want you to get your hopes up. Reg has been through a lot.'

River grins. 'You called him Reg.'

'I did?'

River nods really fast. Her grin spreads wider. 'You did, and that means he's not a stranger. Not any more.'

Mum leans over and kisses River's head and then ruffles her straggly brown hair. 'You're impossible, River.'

'Does that mean I can spend tomorrow at the hospital?'

Mum gently pushes River's shoulders down until she's lying back on her pillow. Mum's mouth is fixed, her teeth biting into her bottom lip in that determined expression she gets when she's working out how to pay the electricity bills for the flat or how to get River to like school more. But her eyes are soft and kind of faraway, like when she speaks about Venice and the gondolas.

Mum tucks the duvet around River's body.

'Mum – you didn't answer, about going to the hospital, tomorrow?'

Mum's eyes focus in on River – and they're still soft. 'Yes, you can go and see Reg.'

Reg

That night, Reg drifts in and out of sleep. And three times already, he's woken up with a start, sweat running down his spine.

He keeps having the same dream.

It starts with him in the bath again, like this afternoon. Her hand draws circles on his back as she washes his body. His fingers move up to the nick by his ear – and then he feels her fingers there too, touching the small scar as though she thinks she can heal it. And then he's jolted into another dream – and he's in water again, but this water is cold and dark and so deep that he can't find his footing.

At the end of one of these cycles of dreams, he slipped so far down into the water that he never found his way up again.

And down there, in the dark water, he sees her, her long, dark plait hanging down her back, and he's calling to her but the water muffles his voice and she doesn't turn round.

His knee throbs, startling him awake.

The moon shines through the hospital blinds.

The nurses' feet scritch, scritch on the linoleum, as they walk past.

A new patient snores beside him.

Reg's mouth is dry, his tongue heavy. As he picks up a cup of water on his bedside table, he sees the rainbow the little girl drew for him, the grapes, the red flowers from the park, and his eyes fill with tears. Why can't he stop himself from crying? It's as though his body is filled with water that keeps trying to get out.

Is this the kind of man he is? A man who cries at a child's rainbow?

Forcing as much strength as he can into his legs, he lifts them over the side of the bed and walks, one slow step at a time, to the window.

It's raining again.

Who was it that had teased him about the rain in England? That it never stops, even in summer. That it came in a thousand forms. He'd wondered whether the English had different names for it, like the Eskimos' fifty words for snow.

He watches the drops slide down the window and notices a pigeon sheltering on the windowsill.

Reg walks over to his bedside table, picks up a bread roll that has gone dry, and brings it back over to the pigeon. Then he tries to open the glass but it won't move. At first, he thinks that it's because he's grown weak. But then he realises that it's been painted shut: there's no way to get the bread to the pigeon.

'I'm sorry,' he says, tracing his fingers along the glass.

When the medicine starts working and his lungs are healed, when the swelling in his knee goes down and he can walk better, he'll go back to the zoo. He'll sit under the open sky and feel the air on his face, no windows or doors or drips or pills. And he'll feed all the birds that come to him.

A while later he wakes with a start and looks into the face of the young nurse.

'You were having a bad dream,' the nurse says.

His head pounds. He blinks and looks at him again.

'Would you like to tell me what you dreamt about?' He reaches for a small notepad in the pocket of his blue uniform. 'Dr Deardorff says that dreams can help retrieve memories.'

Everyone is asking him questions. Too many questions.

'I don't remember,' he says.

The nurse sighs and puts the pad away. He's disappointed him. But disappointment is safer than giving answers to strangers.

'There's water in my ears,' he says.

'You keep saying that. But we've checked, your ears are fine.'

He shakes his head. 'I can feel it . . . '

The nurse sighs. 'Okay.' He picks up a small white tube on the bedside table and eases Reg onto his side. 'This should help.'

Reg waits for the cool drops to trickle down his ear canal.

'Now the other one,' the nurse says.

Reg heaves himself over and offers him his other ear.

He can smell the red flowers on his bedside table: that thick, rich scent just before the leaves turn and drop.

When the nurse has gone, he takes a pen from the pencil case River left for him and opens the red exercise book with the torn pages. He draws a tree, as big as a giant. Then he draws a swing: long pieces of rope from its branches, a plank of wood. And then the sea, big waves crashing over the roots of the tree, the swing, the branches—

His fingers grow weak and he lets the pen drop out of his hand; the exercise book falls to the floor.

Isabel

Isabel stands in the corridor, watching her little girl perched on the edge of a stranger's bed. River and Reg's heads are bent towards each other, so close that it's difficult to tell where one tangle of brown curls begins and the other ends.

Isabel's breath catches. It's as though she remembers this scene from somewhere.

She looks at the man's hands guiding River's, the delicate joins along each finger, the down of dark hair on his knuckles.

Isabel tugs at the collar of her uniform. Her mouth feels dry. She swallows hard and takes a breath.

She looks back at him. He raises his eyes for a second, as dark as his hair.

You come from another place, she thinks. *Somewhere far away from this small life of ours.*

She holds his gaze for a second and then looks away. She still feels him looking at her so she goes over to the window and tries to open it and then remembers that they painted them shut last year when they set up a climate control system throughout the hospital.

When she turns back, his attention is back with River and the drawing. They're sketching something with some stubby coloured pencils from River's pencil case.

And then the worry about River floods in again.

If she could learn to sit still long enough to observe her subject, she could be a good artist, one of River's reports had once said. Isabel remembers her hackles rising: one rare compliment, and even that had an exception clause.

Perhaps River was right – that school isn't the place for her. But what choice does Isabel have? If River doesn't go to school, she won't have a future.

And then she realises that she sounds exactly like her parents. The parents who'd helped her prepare for nursing school, the parents who'd been so disappointed when she said she wasn't going; that she was going to have a baby instead.

A disappointment so great that Isabel knew she had to move out of home.

A disappointment so great that she's never had the courage to go back or to introduce them to their grandchild.

River asks about them sometimes: her grandma and grandpa, she calls them, using familiar names even though she's never met them. And there are days when Isabel thinks that maybe she should get in touch. But it's been over ten years since they last spoke: they wouldn't even recognise each other any more.

Thinking about her parents and River not wanting to go to school makes Isabel's heart sink into her stomach.

'Looks like they've known each other their whole lives.'

A voice comes in from behind her.

She jumps and then turns to see David.

'Their whole lives?'

David frowns at her for a second. 'River and our guest. Don't you think?'

'River . . . yes, of course, yes.' She smiles but her lips feel strained and shaky. She takes a breath and tries again. 'Our guest – I like that.'

David has a way of making it sound like it's a privilege to look after the patients on the ward, like he really is a host and these are the rooms of his house – and he's invited them to stay.

David is balancing a cup of coffee in one hand and a packet

of Jammie Dodgers in the other. There are crumbs on his grey tie.

'Would you like one?' David holds out the packet of biscuits.

She pictures him at school, holding out his lunchbox with his chubby arms and fingers, in the hope of making a new friend. She's lost count of the number of times he's offered her a Jammie Dodger.

'Thank you.' She takes one, even though she doesn't feel in the least bit hungry.

He stares at her, waiting for a response. The jam is cloyingly sweet, but she takes another bite.

He smiles and his ears go pink. Beads of sweat sit along his hairline. He stares at the biscuits for a moment and then shoves another one into his mouth.

'Is he starting to remember things?' Isabel asks.

David gulps down another bit of the biscuit.

'No, not yet. Though if anyone's going to get anything out of him, it's River. She'd make a good doctor, you know?'

Isabel laughs.

'What's funny?' David asks.

'Years of study – of sitting still with books and passing exams?'

She'd mentioned it to David a few times, her worries about River. How her teachers complained about her not being able to sit still and concentrate. How she was always forgetting things and losing things and giving her attention to just about everything *except* what was going on in the classroom. That she was only barely scraping through primary school. That the thought of secondary school, without the same support structures in place, with all the demands of the curriculum and exams, made Isabel panic. She didn't know how River was going to survive the next few years.

David mops his brow, pushes his glasses up his nose and gives her the same kind of look as when he's explaining the diagnosis for a patient. 'Don't underestimate her, Isabel. She'll come good.'

Isabel's teeth clench in the back of her mouth. How easy it is for him to say that. He has a stable career. A good income. No family to worry about. David doesn't have the first clue as to what it's like being a parent.

'I'm not underestimating her,' Isabel says. 'I just know the system.'

A system that doesn't like kids like River.

Isabel turns back to look at her little girl. She's drawing an enormous rainbow in the exercise book she gave Reg. If only rainbows were an academic subject. If only there was a place that could understand how amazing she was.

Reg is smiling. He hands River different coloured pencils as she gets to each new layer of the rainbow. All the rain in England wouldn't account for the thousands of rainbows River has drawn in her life.

'What if he doesn't remember?' Isabel asks David.

'That's unlikely.'

'But it happens, right?'

'We're a long way from that.'

'Well, how long do we have?'

David finishes the last bit of his Jammie Dodger, swallows hard and brushes down his shirt, smudging a bit of jam into the white fabric.

He sighs under his breath.

'I imagine we have a few days.'

'And then?' Isabel asks.

'Let's cross that bridge when we come to it.'

Isabel recognises the doctor-speak a mile off.

'And what will that bridge be, exactly?'

David smiles at her. 'We'll work it out when we get there.'

Isabel wants to help Reg, of course she does. But she's scared of how River will feel if he suddenly disappears from their lives. If there's one thing Isabel can't bear, it's mopping up River's disappointment.

Dr Reed sweeps in, a cloud of perfume preceding her. She stands next to David and nods at River.

'Who is that?'

'She's my daughter,' Isabel says.

Dr Reed sighs. 'Well, that's a shame.'

Isabel raises her eyebrows. 'A shame?'

'That they're not related.' She tilts her head to one side. 'They could be, you know?'

'Excuse me?' Isabel asks.

'I'm just saying that our patient could do with having a relative – if he wants to stay in the country.'

'We don't know where he's from,' David says quickly. 'He might be a Londoner for all we know.'

Dr Reed shrugs. 'But that's not likely, is it?'

David doesn't answer.

'Could I sit in on some of your assessments?' Dr Reed asks David. 'I haven't come across a case like this before – prolonged amnesia with no damage to the frontal cortex.'

Tell her no, Isabel thinks. *Tell her to get lost and find some other consultant to follow around.* She doesn't want this woman anywhere near Reg.

'It's a delicate case.' David pulls a cloth handkerchief from out of his pocket and mops his brow.

'I'll be discreet,' Dr Reed says, tapping her nose.

David keeps mopping his brow. 'Well, maybe something could be arranged.'

'Mind if I take a look at his notes? And his MRI scans?'

David clears his throat. 'I can't see any harm—'

'Good, good.' Dr Reed smiles, revealing a row of neat, white teeth, and strides off towards Reg and River.

'Can't turn down a keen new doctor,' David says.

Isabel likes that David looks for the good in people: if he didn't, he wouldn't give her the time of day. And he would never have taken Reg on as a patient. But sometimes she wonders how an intelligent man could be so undiscerning: the last thing they need is an upstart young doctor snooping around Reg's case.

If only Reg could remember where he came from. He can't have just appeared on that bench outside London Zoo out of thin air.

Together they walk over to Reg's bed.

Isabel kisses the top of River's head. 'Time to go home, darling.'

'Can't I stay a bit longer?'

'It's late.'

'But I can come back tomorrow, can't I?' She looks up at Isabel, her eyes pleading.

Isabel feels Dr Reed's eyes on her, waiting for a reaction.

'We'll see,' she says.

River turns to Reg. '"We'll see" means I've still got some per-suading to do, but I'll be here, I promise.'

Reg smiles at her, his big brown eyes so soft and kind that, for a moment, Isabel forgets that they're in a hospital and that Reg is a stranger and that at any moment now he might disappear from their lives.

River jumps off the bed. 'Can I take these home?' she asks, looking at the stack of drawings they've done together. Alongside

River's rainbows and flowers and suns and rainclouds, there are small pen drawings: the outlines of animals; people walking along the pavement outside London Zoo; the view across a bridge, the river under it churned up and full of waves, like the sea.

'It would be my honour.' Reg tears a few of the pictures out of the exercise book and hands them to River.

River clutches the papers to her chest. 'I'll put them up in my room!'

Isabel hears Dr Reed whispering to David. 'Couldn't those pictures be useful?'

David pretends not to hear.

'You can keep my pencil case.' River places it on Reg's lap. 'In case you feel inspired. I always get my best ideas at night time.'

Isabel's heart contracts. Her dear little girl, always so willing to help.

Please may this not end badly, she thinks.

River

River sits in the Get Well Soon Café, sketching on a piece of printer paper Norma, the waitress, gave her. She's waiting for Reg to finish his physio session so that she can go back up to the ward. Maybe if she shows him that she's practised her drawing, he'll give her another lesson.

'Wow, you're good,' a voice says from above her.

River looks up. It's Dr Reed, the new doctor who keeps hanging around Reg.

River feels herself blush. 'Really?'

Dr Reed nods. 'You've captured how tall and gangly he is – and his big eyes.'

One of the things that River's learnt from Reg is that you don't have to draw exact copies of what you see in front of you for the picture to be good. When he draws, he plays around, making things bigger and smaller and different shapes.

Just focus on a few key things you want to bring across, like someone's ears or their mouth or their tie, and the rest will fall into place, he explained to her.

'Reg has been teaching me,' River says. 'He's really good at drawing.'

Dr Reed pulls up a chair and sits next to River. 'He is, isn't he? Why do you think that is?'

'What do you mean?'

'Don't you think it's strange – that he remembers how to draw and yet doesn't remember anything else?'

'Dr Deardorff said that it's normal – it's muscle memory. Like learning to ride a bike. You never forget.'

Dr Reed smiles. She wears this really bright pink lipstick, which looks kind of strange on a doctor – like she's going to a party rather than working with sick people.

'Yes, I suppose he's right.' Dr Reed pauses. 'Is there anything else Reg can do – anything you've noticed?'

River feels a prickling on the back of her neck. She doesn't understand why Dr Reed is quizzing her so much about Reg.

'You probably know more about him than I do,' River says. 'You're a doctor, aren't you?'

Dr Reed blinks. 'I suppose I am.' She looks over to the counter. 'How about a hot chocolate?'

River's tummy's been rumbling and she hasn't had any money to buy anything and Norma's been too busy serving other people to notice. And anyway, Mum's told River a million times that you shouldn't ask favours from someone if you can't pay them back straight away and that Norma will get in trouble if she keeps taking things out of the stock for River without it going through the till.

River nods. 'Yes, please.'

Dr Reed flicks her blonde hair out of her eyes and clicks her fingers in the air. For a second, River doesn't understand what she's doing, and then she realises that she's trying to get Norma's attention. Which is kind of cool and kind of doesn't feel right at the same time.

'Hey, Norma, how about two hot chocolates?' Her voice rings across the café.

Customers from neighbouring tables look up.

Norma doesn't reply.

'Norma!' She calls out again. 'Your two favourite customers

95

need you.' Dr Reed smiles at River. River notices a bit of lipstick smeared across her front teeth.

Norma's known River since she was a baby: Mum would bring her in when Jules couldn't watch her. So Dr Reed is right: River is one of Norma's favourites. But Dr Reed's only been here for a few weeks – how can *she* be one of Norma's favourites? Though, from the way the nurses and the doctors look at her, River supposes that she's the kind of person who can become someone's favourite pretty fast. Like the pretty girls at school: the ones who have straight, untangled hair and sit still and get good marks.

Norma lifts her head from the customer she's serving, an old man with a Zimmer frame, sticking-up grey hair and big black glasses. She remembers Mum describing him once. Apparently, he used to be a Physics professor and now he can barely remember what day of the week it is. Mum says he can still talk to her about gravity and do really complicated sums though. Weird, how memory works.

'Cream and marshmallows, River?' Dr Reed winks at her: her long, black eyelashes brush her skin. She doesn't wait for River to answer before turning back to Norma. 'Give us the works, Norm!'

Norm? No one calls her Norm.

Norma doesn't answer but a few minutes later she turns up with the hot chocolates anyway. She thumps Dr Reed's mug down in front of her, which makes the hot chocolate spill a bit over the rim. And she doesn't apologise or mop it up.

Maybe River was right first time: maybe Dr Reed went a bit far, calling herself one of Norma's favourites.

Dr Reed puts a ten-pound note in the pocket of Norma's uniform and says, 'Keep the change.'

Norma ignores that too and comes back with a pile of pound coins on a saucer.

'I like a woman with spirit,' Dr Reed whispers. 'We girls need to be strong.'

Dr Reed takes a sip of her hot chocolate and then leans back and crosses her legs.

'So, what do you two talk about?'

'Who?'

'You and Reg.'

It feels weird, hearing her call him Reg.

'Just stuff,' River says. 'Nothing specific really.'

'But you spend ages together. You must talk about something?'

River thinks about the long silences that hang between her and Reg when she's sitting on the side of his bed, especially when they're both drawing. And how it feels comfortable and not like they have to fill up the space with words. And how, when they do talk, she feels like he listens to her – properly, even when she goes off on tangents about Pablo the pigeon or rainbows.

'He talks quite a bit about the zoo,' River says.

'The zoo?'

'Where we found him. And I think he likes elephants too,' River says.

'Elephants?' Dr Reed laughs in a way that River doesn't like. Like she doesn't get that even if it sounds silly out loud, it's important to him.

Then she feels bad for saying anything to Dr Reed: maybe liking elephants is something special that Reg wouldn't want her to share.

'Why did he want to see them, do you think?' Dr Reed asks.

River shrugs. 'I guess he likes them.' River picks a pink marshmallow off the top of her hot chocolate and pops it in her mouth.

It tastes too sweet and sticky. 'I think Reg is still very confused. I don't think he really knows what he's saying. I guess we'll have to wait for his memory to come back.'

River hopes this will make Dr Reed stop asking questions.

'That's assuming it's gone,' Dr Reed says under her breath and then takes a long slurp from her hot chocolate.

'What do you mean – "assuming it's gone"?' River asks.

Dr Reed wipes her mouth. 'Oh, nothing. Memory is a complicated science.'

'That's what Dr Deardorff says.'

'Well, Dr Deardorff's right about most things, isn't he?' she says.

'I suppose so.'

'Though it never hurts to ask questions.'

From what River's seen, no one's *stopped* asking poor Reg questions.

'You're a good detective, I'm sure you're helping a great deal.'

She leans over and brushes a strand of hair out of River's eyes. Which makes River feel about two years old.

River doesn't get it: one minute Dr Reed is treating her like a grown-up who might have important information about Reg and the next she's treating her like a kid.

'Well, he obviously talks more to you than to anyone else,' Dr Reed says.

That makes River feel a bit better, like someone's noticed the trouble she's gone to in trying to get to know Reg.

'I think he likes talking to me because I'm a kid.'

Dr Reed nods and looks at her like she wants her to go on.

'I suppose because I don't make things complicated.'

'Like we doctors do?'

'I guess so.'

'You're a wise girl, River,' Dr Reed says.

Which makes River feel better. Maybe Dr Reed's not so bad after all.

Dr Reed leans in towards River. 'If there's ever anything Reg says that makes you wonder – you know, sit up and scratch your head, something odd, something that jars, you know you can always talk to us.'

'Us?'

'To Dr Deardorff or Nurse Green.' She pauses. 'Or me.'

'Okay,' River says, but she's not sure.

'Thank you, River, you've been most helpful.' Dr Reed stands up, leans over the table, pats River's head – which, this time, makes her feel like she's Dr Reed's pet dog – and then, a second later, she's on the other side of the café, talking to Mr Long, the manager whose office Mum cleans.

Isabel

Isabel opens her eyes to see her best friend stabbing at the light switch on her bedside lamp.

'Stupid fuse has tripped again,' Jules says. 'We really should get out of this dump.'

Rain falls hard against the window. Sometimes, Isabel dreams that it rains so hard that the whole street floods and they can't get out of the house. That the restaurant and the bedsit just floats off down the road and makes its way to the Thames and then out to sea. And then what? Maybe if the wind was blowing in the right direction, they could get swept around the world. Maybe this little bedsit of theirs could end up floating down a canal in Venice.

Isabel rubs her eyes. 'We don't have anywhere else to go.'

Jules shrugs. She knows as well as Isabel that their joint salaries barely cover the rent and that Gabs gives them an amazing deal. Unless one of them wins the lottery, this is where they're staying.

Isabel flicks on her phone: 11:39 p.m. She rubs her eyes.

'You're doing another night shift, Jules?'

'It pays double. And we need the cash.'

Jules specialises in nannying multiples – because they pay more. And she works as a night nanny, even if she's been working all day, because that pays more too. While Isabel stayed at school to finish her A-levels, Jules did a nannying qualification. She's been working ever since. By the time she was seventeen, she'd saved so much money from looking after people's kids that she paid for both their flights to Venice.

Isabel watches Jules pulling on her jeans, her baggy man's shirt, so big that she doesn't need to undo the buttons, the sleeves already rolled up. She passes a comb through her short tufts of hair.

Through the bedroom window, the red, green and white Gabino's sign flickers.

Isabel gets out of bed.

'Why are you getting up?' Jules asks.

'Can't sleep.'

Jules sighs. 'You can't let the patients get to you like this, they don't pay you enough to care that much.'

'Do they pay you enough to care that much?' Isabel asks. Jules would do anything for the kids she looks after.

Jules rolls her eyes and walks out of the bedroom.

Isabel pulls on a jumper and follows her into the lounge. For a moment, they both stand side by side, looking at River sleeping on the sofa bed. She's curled up, facing the wall, her long, knotty hair spread across her pillow.

Isabel thinks back to when River was a baby and they had her in a cot with them in the bedroom. They'd spend hours watching her sleep.

'What's with the map?' Jules whispers, looking at the piece of paper sellotaped to the wall above River's bed. 'And all the pictures.'

'They're from Reg.'

'Your new patient?'

Isabel sighs. '*The* new patient, yes.'

Isabel hears a low coo coming from outside the lounge window. She's shooed that stupid pigeon away more times than she can remember but he just won't get the message.

Jules goes over to the fuse box and starts flipping the switches. Through the open bedroom door, Isabel sees the bedside lamp flick on.

'Thanks,' Isabel says.

Jules is the only one who ever fixes anything around here: broken doorknobs, blocked sinks, dripping taps.

Jules walks over to the kitchen table and looks down at the medical books Isabel's been studying.

'It's a bit convenient, don't you think?' Jules sits down and pulls out a bag of Haribo: she took up eating them five years ago, when she quit smoking.

'What's convenient?' Isabel asks.

'That this new patient of yours has forgotten everything.'

'It's a medical condition.'

'Yeah – but how can you prove it?' Jules puts a fistful of gummy sweets into her mouth and starts chewing.

Isabel thinks about how she bathed him and then shaved his face. How she nicked the side of his ear. How she drew circles on his back with a sponge, and it felt like she was painting on skin. What would Jules say if she knew about all of that?

'He's miserable, Jules, he has no one. He doesn't even remember who he is. Believe me, if he could remember, he would.'

Jules swallows what's left of the sweets, scrunches up the bag.

'You sure about that?'

'About what?'

'That he'd remember if he could? I mean, how can you be sure that he's actually forgotten? You said yourself that he doesn't have a brain injury. Everyone's just taking his word for it.'

'Why are you doing this?' Isabel asks.

'Because it's my job.'

'Your job?'

Jules rolls her eyes. 'To make sure you and River don't get yourselves mixed up in some shit I'll have to get you out of.'

And she's right. Jules has been looking after Isabel since they started secondary school together. They were River's age. None of the other kids talked to them: Isabel, because she was small and shy and couldn't catch a ball and Jules because she had short hair like a boy and a loud voice and because her mum had died, which they found embarrassing.

'He's just a patient,' Isabel says.

A bolt of lightning cracks outside the window and rain crashes against the glass. In the shadows, Isabel can see the pigeon shifting on the windowsill.

'A patient River won't shut up about,' Jules adds. 'A patient she's chosen to spend the summer with over me.'

Isabel smiles. 'You're jealous.'

Jules lets out a snort.

River stirs in her bed.

'Shh!' Isabel hisses.

'I don't do jealous,' Jules says. She grabs her mac and heads to the door. 'I just don't think it's a good idea to get River involved with a man who's so . . . '

'Mucked up?'

Jules nods.

'We're all mucked up, Jules. And she's involved already. River's the one who found him, remember?' Isabel pauses. 'And it's making her happy. There's nothing to worry about, Jules, really.'

Jules doesn't say anything. Which makes Isabel feel worse than if she'd cracked some joke or made a sarcastic comment. When Jules goes quiet, it means she *really* disagrees.

Jules pulls on her Doc Marten boots, grabs her bag and heads to the door.

'Get some sleep,' she throws over her shoulder.

And then she's gone.

River

River wakes to the sound of thunder. She loves storms, how they bring the dark sky to life with sound and colour.

Gabs has a TV in the restaurant so sometimes, when there aren't any customers, River gets to watch. She knows it's kind of weird, but she loves the weather forecast, especially when there's an extended edition and they talk about why it's so rainy or sunny or stormy – how sometimes, a weather pattern can start one way on the other side of the globe, like a big tropical storm in Hawaii or something, and then, as it travels it loses its grumpiness so that by the time it gets to England, all that's left is a bit of warm drizzle.

She got into it because, after work, Mum wanted to watch the news and River wanted to be with Mum so she'd sit on her lap and look at the screen and not really understand what anyone was going on about – until they got to the weather. The picture of the map and the cloud and rain and sun symbols, they made sense.

Mum still watches the news and River still watches the weather forecast but they rarely do it together any more.

Anyway, one time, she saw a programme about how thunder is made: that the heat produced by lightning creates this column of air, which vibrates like a drum and then cracks and echoes and rumbles. It's like the sky turns into an orchestra.

It hasn't stopped raining since they found Reg. It's like the weather's decided that until they work out the puzzle of where he comes from, it's going to keep moaning and grumbling and making everything wet.

A flash lights up the room, followed by a crack and boom.

River looks out of the window, hoping that Pablo is sheltering somewhere safe and warm.

Then she hears a rustle of paper and notices that there's more light in the room than usual. She flips over in the sofa bed and sees Mum sitting at the kitchen table, a headlamp clamped to her forehead. She bought it because their fuse box keeps tripping. And because she doesn't want to wake River by turning on the main light.

Mum's head is bent over a pile of books. River knows exactly what she's doing. Whenever Mum gets curious about a case at the hospital, or when River's got something wrong with her like a rash or tonsillitis, or sometimes when she just can't sleep and needs to stop her brain from buzzing around all over the place, Mum sits at the kitchen table and reads medical textbooks. It's how Mum worked out that River has ADHD.

The books are thick and heavy and the print is really small and every time River tries to read them, her brain hurts. But there are cool pictures too, which Mum sometimes explains to her. Mum traces the pictures sometimes, to help herself learn them. And when she knows them really well, she draws them out freehand. Pictures of hearts and lungs and the brain and the human eye. They're tucked between the pages of her books.

The books sit on a shelf in the kitchen where most people's cookery books would go. Mum's always been interested in medical stuff, which River supposes is why she decided to be a cleaner in a hospital rather than in a school or an office. The textbooks get left behind when the trainee doctors and nurses move on to a new hospital. River and Jules have also found a few for Mum in the charity shops around Regent's Hospital.

River swings her legs out of bed and rubs her eyes. 'What are you reading about, Mum?'

Mum looks up and blinds River with her headlamp. She takes it off and puts it on the table.

'Amnesia.'

River comes and looks over her shoulder.

The thunder and lightning have stopped now; it's just raining really hard again.

River looks at the page Mum is reading. It's got the picture of a human brain with all the bits parcelled out and labelled.

River smiles. 'You're reading up on Reg?'

'I'm just trying to understand ...'

'So you *are* interested?'

'I'm interested in his case, yes.'

River rolls her eyes. She wishes Mum would admit that she likes Reg just as much as she does.

'What's amnesia, then?' River asks, sitting on the chair next to Mum.

'It's a whole load of things. It basically means memory loss. It's a condition that can have lots of different origins.'

'Like what?'

'Well, brain injury is the obvious one.'

'But Dr Deardorff said that Reg's brain wasn't injured.'

'The scans don't show any sign of damage, no.'

'So, what caused it?'

'That's what I'm reading up on.'

'And – what do *you* think, Mum?'

Mum always has theories about things, sometimes better theories than the doctors and nurses. River's always encouraging Mum to tell them what she thinks, in case it helps them find a better treatment for the patients, but Mum says that people don't like cleaners to be clever clogs. Which River thinks is just stupid: if you've got the answer to a problem, then you should share it.

River reckons that Mum would give any doctor a run for his money when it comes to diagnosing patients. Anyone except maybe Dr Deardorff who has the biggest brain in the world. What's more, Mum never went to university – she's taught herself everything she knows, which must make her especially clever.

Mum having taught herself is one of the top arguments River has for not going to school in September: if Mum can learn how to be a doctor, which takes most people years and years, then surely River can teach herself the stuff they learn at school.

'But I'm *not* a doctor, am I, River?' Mum says. 'For that, I would've had to go to university and study.'

But River thinks Mum's missing the point – which is that she knows stuff, really important stuff, and that no one ever taught her.

River's got six weeks before school starts to talk Mum round to the idea of not going back to school.

Mum yawns. She's got bags under her eyes.

'Why don't we cuddle up in my bed and you can tell me more about it?' River suggests.

Mum closes the textbook. 'Okay, but only for a little while. It's late.'

Cuddling with Mum on the sofa bed is one of River's favourite things. It reminds her of when she was little and they'd sleep together in Mum's bed and Jules would be in her bed and they'd chat and laugh, even if it was really late.

That was a nice time. A time when River and Mum didn't bash heads so often.

It'll get better again, Jules said to her once. *Most mums and daughters tend to fall out for a few years.*

River wasn't sure. She and Mum are turning into such totally different people she doubts they'll ever see eye to eye again.

River pushes away the thought and pulls the duvet over them both. She snuggles in, putting her head in the crook between Mum's head and her shoulder.

'So – what do you think made Reg forget?' River asks.

'I'm not sure . . .'

'But you have a hunch, right?'

Mum always has a hunch.

'PTSD.'

'What's that?'

It doesn't sound good. It sounds like the kind of thing that the Ed Psychs at school are always telling River she has: ADHD.

'Post-Traumatic Stress Disorder. Something must have happened to jolt his brain. Not his physical brain, but . . .' She hesitates. 'His mind, I suppose. His thoughts and his emotions. A shock that made him want to forget.'

River looks up, startled. 'So, he *is* pretending?'

Mum strokes River's head. 'No. He's not pretending. Or I don't think he is. His mind wants him to forget, so that it can protect him from having to think about what happened – because the memory is too painful. It doesn't mean that Reg knows what it is, or that he's consciously choosing to forget.'

Mum's told River about the conscious and subconscious brain before. How sometimes the two parts don't talk to each other properly. And how a lot of the time the subconscious brain plays tricks on the conscious brain but because you can't see it and because it's kind of secret and sneaky, it's impossible to stop it from happening.

'If it's a really bad thing, maybe we shouldn't be trying to help him remember,' River says.

Mum smiles. 'There's the dilemma.'

River likes it when she gets something right with Mum.

'We want him to remember because remembering will help him work out who he is and where he's from but that means jolting his brain back to remembering the bad stuff too,' River says.

'Exactly.'

'So, what do we do?'

Mum leans back against River's pillow and stares at the ceiling. 'I guess we wait and see.'

'That doesn't sound like a solution.'

And it doesn't sound like Mum. Mum's always fixing things and cleaning things up and making things okay again: she never just sits back and waits.

'Sometimes the brain remembers all by itself, when it's ready to confront what happened.'

'How long will that take?'

'No one knows.'

When River was little, she always thought that medicine was pretty simple: someone had a broken leg or a bad cut or a disease or something and, with a bit of stitching up, a few plasters and some medicine, they could be made better. But when River got older and Mum began to tell her about the patients on the neuropsychiatry ward where she cleans, River realised that being sick could be a whole lot more complicated than that, especially when you were sick in your head rather than in your body.

Mum closes her eyes and River can feel her drifting off. She pulls the duvet over Mum so she doesn't get cold.

Maybe what they need to do is find out what happened to Reg before he remembers anything for himself. Then they can work out whether it's something he should know or whether it's something that is best left forgotten.

If River *really* listens – and if she does some investigations of her own – she could work it out. It's worth a try.

AUGUST

David

David sends Alex, his linguist friend, the latest sound file of Reg's voice, hoping that it might inspire him to come to London. It's been ten days since they talked on the phone.

Ten days. David shakes his head: it's a miracle he's managed to keep Reg at the hospital this long.

David closes his laptop and looks over at Reg and River, drawing together.

He wouldn't ever admit this out loud, but a small part of him hopes that Alex doesn't find anything. Sometimes, he even allows himself to hope that Reg's memory doesn't come back – or not for a while, anyway. Because if it does, all this will change: River and Isabel coming into the hospital for long visits; Isabel staying on after her shifts; River sitting on Reg's bed, drawing with him and making jokes; David finding excuses to check up on his patient so that he can hang out with them for a bit longer.

Being here with them makes him happy, happier than he's been in a long time.

I'm so glad you're enjoying school, David, his mother said when he visited her last night.

Even she'd noticed.

'Look, Dr Deardorff!' River holds up the red exercise book she gave Reg for his drawing. 'Reg drew a picture of you!'

David looks at his face peering out at him: chubby, Santa-Claus cheeks; thinning hair; round glasses with so many reflections that you can't make out his eyes; an oversized stethoscope around his neck.

David gulps.

He knows this is how others see him – the same him that he sees in the mirror when he wakes up every morning. There's no escaping himself. And he knows, too, that it shouldn't bother him. But it still takes him by surprise: how silly he looks, how large, how unlikely to ever attract anyone, let alone anyone as beautiful and lovely as Isabel.

'Isn't it brilliant?' River says.

David nods and smiles. 'It's a good likeness.'

He'd thought that Dr Reed might be right and that all this drawing would jog Reg's memory, or offer them some clues about his identity. But the things Reg draws are mostly present observations. Pictures of River and Isabel, of the nurses on the ward, the bench by the entrance to London Zoo where Isabel and River found him.

In fact, he won't stop drawing. Whenever he's not sleeping, he has a pen in his hand.

David understands, now, how Reg got that ink stain on his forefinger: he holds the biro so low that it smears right onto his skin; as he sweeps the pen over the paper and as he draws, the stain spreads and gets darker.

It's as though Reg is trying to pin down his present memories before they slip away.

'You don't need to worry,' David has told him. 'You're able to form new memories, memories that will stay.'

But still, there seems to be an urgency to the drawing, as though he needs it, somehow.

David has read studies of patients, some of them with the most severe cases of amnesia, who could still undertake muscle-memory tasks. One man, the worst case of amnesia ever identified, had no ability to remember at all: the moment he experienced something, it disappeared. And yet he could play a full Bach Sonata – because even when our minds let us down, our bodies remember. And something deeper than our bodies too. Maybe that's what's happening with Reg when he draws.

Of course, there are a few oddities in the drawings, things that can't immediately be explained or related to what Reg sees in the present. He likes to draw big oak trees. One of them, which he spent longer on than the others, has a long rope-swing hanging from its branches. And there are often waves lapping along the bottom edge of his pieces of paper. When David asks Reg about these, he shrugs and says he's just teaching River to draw.

And he's getting through to her. From what Isabel has told David, Reg has been more of a teacher to River these last ten days than anyone at her primary school ever was.

His eyes prick with tears. He rubs them behind his glasses and then looks back at River.

Yes, Reg has made the little girl happy, and that's made Isabel happy – he's seen it, how it's lifted something in her.

He wishes he were creative and inspiring, that he could offer River and Isabel something more than himself.

'Ah, our mystery patient.' A voice booms across the ward.

David's muscles tense.

Mr Long, the hospital manager, strides towards them, followed by Nurse Green and Dr Reed. Nurse Green is holding a camera up, snapping pictures as he goes.

'Don't mind us,' Long says. 'We're just getting some images for the hospital Instagram account.'

'You're putting the hospital on Instagram?'

David gets visions of confused-looking patients in hospital gowns being photographed, their images cropped and filtered.

'Have to keep up with the times.' Long slaps him on the back.

David coughs.

If Long spent as much time understanding medical procedures as he does on publicising the hospital, they could start tackling the long waiting lists and staffing issues.

'Mind if we take a picture of you with … what do you call him?'

'Reg!' River says. 'He's called Reg.'

Mr Long raises his eyebrows. 'And you are?'

'Reg's friend.'

The manager looks over to David, waiting for an explanation.

'Ms Rushworth and her daughter found Reg and brought him in. They're an important anchor for him,' David says.

The manager doesn't even listen to the answer. He's already instructing Nurse Green to come closer with the phone. Then he leans in towards Reg and smiles.

Reg frowns. He doesn't like what's happening, and he's right: patients shouldn't be subjected to this kind of thing.

The manager goes to the foot of the bed and picks up Reg's chart. David hopes to God that he's as clueless as he thinks he is.

On the day Reg was admitted, when Long asked about the patient with no ID, no home address and no memory of anything that happened before he was brought in, David gave him the impression that he was going through the proper procedures: contacting the relevant authorities, processing the paperwork. But it won't be long before Long questions why no one has been in to see Reg.

Long looks up from the chart.

'So, what's the prognosis, doc?' he asks David.

Which means he couldn't make sense of what he just read. Where does the board get these managers from?

'His knee is healing well,' David says. 'He's doing physio every day, and he's on antibiotics for the pneumonia—'

'And up here?' Long taps his head.

God, what an oaf.

'We're working on it.'

'Hmmm.' Long looks around the room. His eyes fall on the drawings. 'What's all this?' He picks up a sketch of Isabel, only she's wearing a doctor's coat rather than her usual maroon cleaner's outfit.

David takes the drawing out of the manager's hands. 'Art therapy.'

The manager's face stretches into a smile again. 'Progressive practices, that's what I like to see.' He claps David on the back again. Then he leans in and whispers in his ear: 'Can I have a quick word?'

Sweat runs down David's spine. Long has the particular skill of seesawing from nonchalance to searing criticism.

'Of course.' David follows him out into the corridor.

Nurse Green hangs back to give Reg what David knows to be some perfunctory checks, all for the benefit of the manager. Dr Reed, however, follows them out.

Long smiles at her.

'Good to have such fresh blood on board, don't you think, Dr Deardorff?'

He's brought him out here to praise Dr Reed?

David nods. 'She's certainly made an impression.'

'Keen mind. Picks things up that we oldies miss.'

Or rather, looks the part for your Instagram account, David thinks. Because Dr Reed is exactly the kind of appointment Long likes to make: young and pretty, perfect for his publicity shots.

'You'll take good care of her, won't you David? Show her the ropes, mentor her.'

'Of course.'

'Good, good.' Then he bows his head and motions for David to come closer.

Dr Reed steps closer too: her perfume, something dark and musky, is so strong that it makes David feel dizzy.

'Now, about this case.' Long jerks his head towards Reg's cubicle. 'His papers – they're all in order?'

David knew this was too good to last: Long never leaves anything alone.

David rubs his brow. 'Yes, it's all in hand.'

David prides himself on his honesty, but there are some people who make truth-telling impossible.

Out of the corner of his eye, he notices Dr Reed raising her eyebrows.

David doesn't like her hanging around this case. He doesn't like her hanging around full stop.

'Good, good.' Long slaps David on the back again.

David's not a violent man but one of these days he's going to slap him right back.

'Just have to check these things,' Long goes on. 'You know how it is. We're so pressed for beds. And the budget is squeezed as it is. We can't be looking after any Tom, Dick or Harry.'

Looking after any Tom, Dick or Harry is exactly what they should be doing, thinks David. If you're a doctor – a hospital – your job is to take care of people who are sick, wherever they're from.

'Well, keep up the good work,' Long says.

There's a crash at the bottom of the corridor.

Long looks up. 'What on earth?'

118

A young woman pushes a triple buggy towards them. Her eyes are frantic, her face pale.

A toddler skips beside her. The woman has a diamond nose stud, a ring in her eyebrow, and tattoos cover her bare arms.

She seems oddly familiar, though he's certain they've never met.

'Oh dear,' Long says, looking her up and down.

David knows that this woman is most definitely *not* the kind of person that would look good in one of Long's Instagram shots. Which makes him like her.

'Right, I'll be off,' Long says.

Reed trots after him.

'What a buffoon,' David says under his breath.

He feels a sharp jab in the back of his shins.

'Excuse me.'

He looks up just in time to see the tattooed mother powering past him with her buggy. The little girl turns around and gives him a smile. Then the woman stops and looks around her. She squints at one of the signs and bites her lip; her hands are shaking. It's odd, David thinks, on the one hand she seems bulldozer confident, but there's clearly something bothering her too.

'Can I help you?' David asks.

The woman looks past him, shakes her head and walks on – so fast that he struggles to keep up.

'Are you all right? You don't seem well . . .' he calls after her.

'I don't like hospitals,' she calls over her shoulder.

Which strikes him as an odd thing to say.

A moment later, the woman, the little girl and the triple buggy are stationed next to Reg's bed.

'Jules! You're here!' River gives the woman a massive grin.

Jules. It clicks into place now. He's heard her name a thousand times: she's Isabel's best friend. The woman who lives with her and takes care of River.

'I thought I should come in and see what the fuss was about.' Jules ruffles River's hair. 'Considering you've abandoned me for the summer.'

River jumps off the bed and stretches her arm out to Reg.

'Reg, meet Jules – Jules, meet Reg.'

Reg and Jules look at each other and smile.

Jules inspects Reg for a second. 'The mystery man Isabel can't stay away from.'

David's heart sinks.

'Jules!' Isabel hisses. Her cheeks go a bright pink.

'Well, he is, isn't he?' Jules says.

Jules's eyes start darting around again, like she's looking for the nearest exit.

Her jitteriness makes him nervous.

She gets out a bag of sweets and starts munching on them faster than David's ever seen anyone eat sweets – faster even than him.

The little girl accompanying Jules jumps onto Reg's bed. 'Mystery man, mystery man!' she chants.

River goes over to hug the little girl. 'And this is Nula, Reg. I've told you about Nula. She's like my little sister.'

Nula grins.

Jules scrunches up her bag of gummy bears, shoves it in her pocket and picks up one of Reg's drawings.

She tilts her head to one side. 'I like your artwork, Reg.'

Reg touches a tattoo on her arm. 'I like yours.'

Jules smiles and seems to relax a bit.

'He's been teaching me to draw, Jules!' River says. She holds up a picture of a pigeon.

Jules nods at the drawing. 'Ah, Pablo. That is a good likeness.'

'It's not finished yet,' River says. 'I need to capture his spirit.'

'His spirit? Well, there's a challenge,' Jules says.

River nods and frowns and looks back at her drawing. Then Jules's head snaps up. 'What are you staring at?' she asks David.

It takes David a moment to realise she's speaking to him.

'Um . . .'

She looks at him, her pierced eyebrow raised.

'I was just checking that you were all right. You still look very pale.' He tries to put on his professional doctor voice.

'I am?' she asks, still staring at him.

He doesn't know whether he's said the right thing or the wrong thing.

'It's okay, Jules, Dr Deardorff's one of the good guys,' River says.

'I know who Dr Deardorff is,' Jules says.

She does? So Isabel speaks of him too?

'And I'm not questioning whether he's a good guy, I was just asking why he was staring.'

You were staring too, David thinks.

River shrugs. 'He's a doctor,' she says, as though that explains everything.

'Jules,' Isabel says. 'Come on, let's get you out of here.' She walks towards her and takes her arm.

Nula starts playing with the remote next to Reg's bed. The bottom half lifts. Jules takes the remote out of her hands and sets it straight again.

'You can't touch stuff here, Nula. They're not toys.'

The way she says it makes him feel like he's been told off. Like the whole world has been told off and needs to stand to attention. She's terrifying. And thrilling.

He looks her up and down. Her Doc Marten boots. Her

short hair with all its colours and its Elvis quiff at the front. The diamond nose stud that keeps catching the light.

Looking at her is like looking into fire or at the sea – your eyes get lost and you forget to turn away.

'I'm sorry,' David says. 'I'll leave you to it.'

'Don't worry,' Jules says. 'You were right – about the pale thing. If I stay here any longer, I'm going to puke.'

'She's phobic,' River explains.

For a second, David thinks she's talking about him – that this Jules woman has some kind of physical aversion to him. And then he remembers that they've only just met.

A moment later, Jules sweeps past him again with her buggy and the little girl.

He steps out of her way.

River

River sits on her bed, balancing a piece of paper on one of Mum's medical books: she's drawing a picture with an old biro she found in one of the kitchen drawers. River always thought that, to do good drawings, you had to have proper art supplies, like charcoal pencils and expensive oil paints and thick creamy paper and easels. But Reg just draws a few squiggles with any old pen and paper and it looks amazing.

Maybe if she keeps practising really hard, one day she'll be able to draw as well as him.

She's trying to get Pablo just right. Reg says it's a good idea to draw things that you love or that you're really interested in, because that's how you *capture their spirit*. When she asked what that meant, he said that loving what you draw makes it come to life.

River hopes that, if she draws a really good picture of Pablo, one that makes him come alive, Mum will see him like River does, as the amazing and beautiful bird that he is.

'River – we've got to get going!' Mum's stressed voice rings out from her bedroom.

Jules left about an hour ago to get Nula and the triplets. River wishes Jules were still here to defend her, not that she takes her side about school stuff.

They're going to visit Downside Academy, River's new secondary school. More precisely, they're going to visit the Learning Support teacher who'll be in charge of keeping River *on track*. Like River's some kind of train or something.

A moment later Mum's standing in the kitchen. River shoves her drawing under her pillow. She doesn't want Mum to see it: she'll just make a comment about what she could do to make it better and then River won't feel like finishing it.

From the corner of her eye River sees a flap of wings at the window: Pablo's clocked on to Mum being there and has made a quick exit.

Mum comes over, puts a glass of water down on River's bedside table and opens the palm of her hand. River looks down at the two white pills sitting there. She wishes she didn't have to take them – they make her brain and her limbs go numb.

'It's the holidays, Mum – it doesn't matter if I'm distracted.'

Mum keeps holding out the pills.

'*Please?*' River asks.

Mum shakes her head. 'We have to be consistent with this, River, it's important. You know that.'

River picks up the pills, shoves them in her mouth and takes a big gulp of water.

Mum keeps standing over her.

'What?' River asks.

'You can't wear that, darling.'

River looks down at her stripy dress and her stripy tights and the rainbow trainers Jules gave her for her last birthday.

'Why not?'

'Because we have to make a good impression.'

River doesn't understand why being dressed colourfully should make a bad impression.

'I'm allowed to wear what I want in the holidays,' River says. 'Mrs whatshername should understand.'

'Mrs Endicott.'

What kind of a name is Endicott?

'Okay, *Mrs Endicott* will understand that it's the holidays and that in the holidays we get to wear our home clothes.'

Now it's River's turn to notice what *Mum's* wearing – and it makes her stomach seize up: it's The Suit. Mum's one and only smart bit of clothing. When it was new (Mum never had it new, she got it from a charity shop), it was probably black, but now it's all faded and dusty-looking, like a blackboard that's been written on and rubbed clean too many times.

Mum wears The Suit when she gets invited to funerals of patients from the hospital – which is actually much more often than you'd think, considering she's only a cleaner. And she wears it to the hospital Christmas party every year, because it's the only going-out kind of thing she has to wear. She puts a red scarf over it to make it look Christmassy. She also wears The Suit when she has her reviews with Stingy Simon. And she wore it whenever she got called in to speak to the Head at Caius Primary about River *not* being on track.

Jules says Mum could wear a bin liner and still look pretty, and she's totally right. But still, River thinks Mum would look good with a bit more colour.

And The Suit doesn't have good vibes.

Nothing about this day has good vibes.

Mum marches across the lounge and throws open the small wardrobe next to River's bed.

Even before Mum opens the door, River can feel it waiting for her. She's felt it hanging there like some kind of limp ghost, ever since Mum bought it from some online second-hand uniform place.

The uniform is old and smelly and has a stain on the back of the skirt and it's way too big for River. But River could just about cope with all that. The thing that really gets to her is that it's grey. Not a magical, pigeon-grey with hidden colours that shimmer in the sun, but proper, sooty, burnt-to-ash grey.

River folds her arms. 'I'm not wearing it.'

'Wearing what?' Mum brushes her fingers along the hangers in the wardrobe, making them clang.

River's head hurts.

'The uniform,' River says.

Mum laughs. 'You don't have to wear the uniform, not today.'

Not ever, thinks River.

'I'm just looking for something a bit more neutral,' Mum goes on.

River doesn't do neutral. And nor do her clothes. And she likes it that way.

Mum pulls out a navy jumper: it's the jumper from her primary-school uniform. Mum picked the crest off so that River could wear it like a normal piece of clothing, *because it still fits and it would be a waste to get rid of it.*

It's the ugliest jumper in the entire universe. Plus, River's had to live inside that jumper for too long already. If she could burn it right here and now, she would.

'Just put it over your dress,' Mum says. 'It will smarten you up.'

Before River has the time to protest, Mum's yanking the jumper over her head like she's some kind of toddler who can't dress herself.

Mum smiles. 'There, that's much better.'

River grunts. But she doesn't say anything because at least Mum hasn't made her wear that stupid grey uniform.

'We need to stop by the hospital on the way,' Mum says. 'Just so I can make sure Ash understands what he has to do.'

Mum asked Stingy Simon to move her shifts around so she could take River to visit her new school. Mum *never* moves her shifts around, not even when she's sick.

Which means that today is a big deal. A really big deal.

River's stomach clenches up even more.

'I thought you called Ash last night?' River says.

'I did.'

'So why do you have to go over things again?'

'Oh, you know Ash.'

River does know Ash: he's cool and relaxed and he'll be just fine doing Mum's shift. It's Mum who thinks she's the only one in the world who can ever do things properly.

'Can I see Reg, then?' River asks. 'While you're talking to Ash?'

Mum sighs.

'Please?'

If they find Reg not feeling very well, Mum will feel sorry for him and decide that they should stay and look after him and then she'll call the teacher to cancel and they won't have to go.

'Okay, but only for a few minutes,' Mum says. 'We have to be on time for Mrs Endicott.'

Endicott. River shudders.

She grabs the drawing she started from under her pillow and stuffs it under her ugly navy jumper. At least seeing Reg will make this day a bit better.

'You have to capture his spirit,' Reg says again. He traces the outline of Pablo's body with his forefinger.

River stares down at her drawing. Back home, she'd thought it was okay, but looking at it now, she's embarrassed she even brought it in.

'I'm still not sure what you mean about spirit,' River says. 'I mean, I did what you said – I drew something I love ...'

'This is about *his* spirit, River. You need to ask yourself what he's thinking and feeling.' He pauses. 'Imagine you're him. Think about how he's different from all the other pigeons you've ever seen, about what makes him special.' Reg puts a hand over his heart. 'You must capture how he makes you feel, too.' He pauses and catches her eye. 'Then you'll have his spirit.'

River's art teacher at Caius Primary never talked about spirits. She just said you had to focus really hard and make sure you copied down exactly what you saw in front of you. Which River had never managed to do.

Reg puts a hand on River's shoulder. 'You'll get there. Just keep watching him. And not just with your eyes.'

'How can you watch without your eyes?'

Reg smiles. 'You use all your senses.'

River remembers how her English teacher taught them about writing poems using different senses. 'You mean like, smell and taste and touch and sound?'

'Exactly. And your sixth sense too.'

'My sixth sense?'

River's English teacher hadn't mentioned that. She's beginning to wonder whether her teachers at Caius Primary made her feel stupid because they were scared she'd find out the truth: that they didn't have a clue about the stuff they were teaching. Or no more clues than the pupils, anyway.

'It's your intuition,' Reg says. 'Your gut instinct.' He puts his hand on his skinny stomach. 'What you feel about something: something that you can't always explain.'

River's teachers definitely wouldn't get that.

She thinks about Pablo and how he makes her feel and how she knows that he can read her thoughts and how he understands about Mum not liking him but still comes back to visit River.

'Your sixth sense is the magic you bring to your drawings,' Reg adds.

'The magic?'

'Like the spirit.'

128

River looks again at the drawing. He's right, all she's done is try to copy what she sees with her eyes: it could be any pigeon in the world.

'Will you help me?' River asks.

Reg puts his hand over hers. 'Of course.'

Then River folds the piece of paper with the picture of Pablo and puts it in the pocket of her dress.

'I wish I could stay here with you,' she says. 'Rather than going to visit my horrible new school.'

He laughs. 'How do you know it's going to be horrible?'

'Because all schools are horrible.'

'They are?'

River nods. 'All the ones I've ever known, anyway.'

'This one will be different.'

She shakes her head. 'It's got a grey uniform.'

'Oh.'

'You see?'

'You can wear a little colour elsewhere,' Reg suggests. 'Like in your socks – or a ribbon in your hair?'

'I tried that at Caius and it got me in trouble. They're really strict about uniforms.' River glances at the door to make sure Mum's not in earshot. 'Anyway, it doesn't matter – I've decided that I'm not going.'

Reg's brow gets knotty. 'I don't understand.'

'I mean, I have to go today – to make it look like I'm going along with things – but I'm not going in September.' River gulps. 'I've decided.' It's the first time she's said it out loud. 'I've got four weeks to talk Mum round.'

River waits for Reg to say something encouraging, like he understands and that he's on her side, but he just looks at her with his big sad eyes.

'Maybe this new school will be better.'

River shakes her head. 'It'll be worse.'

'How do you know?'

'Secondary school means even more sitting still and even more exams and tests and even less playtime outside. It's going to be horrible.'

Before River has the time to explain any further, she hears Mum's voice out in the corridor saying goodbye to Ash.

A moment later Ash pokes his head round the door and gives her a goofy grin and good luck thumbs-up sign. He knows River doesn't like school. She bets he didn't like school either when he was a kid. He's always getting in trouble with Stingy Simon, and River's sure that if Stingy Simon weren't ordering the cleaners around he'd be a horrible teacher in a horrible school ordering kids around. He's that kind of person.

'Come on, River,' Mum says, walking over to the bed. 'Time to go.'

Reg sits up straighter and gives Mum a smile. Whenever she's around his eyes are brighter and his skin loses its tired, grey look. But then Mum has that effect on most patients. It's why they love her so much.

Sometimes, River wishes Mum would make her feel like that; sometimes, she thinks that Mum likes the patients and her job at the hospital more than she likes River.

'I'll come by later,' Mum says to Reg.

When Mum says that, Reg's eyes go brighter too. River's so glad they found him that day. Everything's been better since Reg has been around.

Reg turns to River. 'I want to hear all about how it goes.' He gives her a kind smile. 'And remember to look past the grey.'

'Past the grey?' Mum asks.

'Oh, it's just a little joke between us,' Reg says.

Which makes Mum smile and look a bit hurt at the same time, like she does when Jules and River share secrets.

River tries to give Reg a smile back but her mouth and her cheeks feel strained. She wants to believe him that Downside Academy might be okay, she really does, but deep down she knows that that's just not possible, that she and school just don't mix.

The bus takes an hour to get from the stop outside the hospital to the Academy. Mum and River hardly exchange a word. By the time they get to the front gates of the school, River feels like she's going to be sick from all the lurching.

Mum couldn't get River into any of the local schools. The posh clever kids who live in the big houses around Acacia Road got places first. The ones who don't have lots of bad notes on their behaviour records. So Mum extended her search, and still couldn't find River a place. River thinks Mum should have taken this as a sign and given up. Only Mum doesn't do signs. She just kept looking until she found Downside. It was the only school in a twenty-mile radius that accepted River's application. Which, from where River's standing, is a big red flag signalling that it's going to be rubbish. If River were a school, she wouldn't give herself a place.

River looks through the school gates. The buildings match the uniform: grey concrete blocks, piled on top of each other like rabbit hutches.

It's the first time they've seen Downside Academy in real life, rather than on the computer or in the brochure they sent Mum, and River can tell that Mum's disappointed too.

She hopes Mum gets it now: why coming here is a bad idea.

River looks at the lights shining inside the school. Without any kids, it's like a weird ghost town.

Please may I never have to come here, she prays.

Mum gets out a small mirror and rubs some blusher into her cheeks, which makes her look like she's just swallowed a ton of fresh air. She only ever wears blusher with The Suit.

Mum's cheekbones shimmer.

'What are you smiling at?' Mum asks.

'You look pretty, Mum.'

Mum gives River a sideways smile. Which makes her look even prettier – but kind of sad at the same time. Pretty and sad: that basically sums Mum up.

River knows that this is all about Mum wanting to make a good impression, so they take her seriously – rather than just seeing her as a cleaner. Which River thinks is totally stupid. Mum's cleverer than all the teachers in the world put together.

'Why is Mrs Endicott in school over the holidays?' River asks.

'She's probably meeting people like us,' Mum says. 'And planning. Teachers have to do planning. For the new term.'

'But the new term's ages away – school's only just finished.'

'It's good to be organised, River.'

River doesn't get the point of being organised: you spend so much time sorting stuff out for later that you miss the good things happening right now.

'Mum?' River asks.

Mum stops walking. 'Yes?'

'Did your parents want you to go to university?'

Mum's cheeks flush as pink as her lipstick.

'I mean, you're always going on about how important it is to go to school and to go to university and to get a good degree. But you didn't. And I bet your parents wanted you to go.'

Mum looks down at her shiny black shoes, the ones that go with The Suit.

'Yes, they did.'

'And were they cross, when you didn't?'

'Yes.'

'But you still didn't go?'

'I've told you before, River, I wanted to look after you. That was more important.'

'Did *they* think it was more important?'

River knows that talking to Mum about this stuff is out of bounds, but she wants her to understand that you can't make someone do something that they don't want to do. That she got to decide, so River should get to decide too.

'Come on, River.' Mum starts walking again.

River hangs her head and follows Mum to the main doors.

Inside, everything smells of disinfectant, even worse than at the hospital. The display boards on the walls are blank. The classrooms empty.

River and Mum's footsteps echo along the corridors.

Mrs Endicott welcomes them into a room the size of a broom cupboard. She's wearing purple-rimmed glasses and red tights: in theory, these colours should give River some hope that Mrs Endicott might be okay after all. But River has come across enough teachers like Mrs Endicott to know that it's all a show. It's not that they like bright colours, not in the way that River does – they just wear loud clothes to make themselves seem fun and approachable and like they're going to play games with you instead of what they're really going to do which is force you to sit still and work.

River's suspicions are confirmed when Mrs Endicott spends the whole meeting flipping through bits of paper. They're probably the reports from her old school, which means that Mrs Endicott will have made up her mind about River already: that she's *difficult*. And if there's one thing teachers don't like, it's difficult.

River's leg starts jiggling.

Mum puts her hand on it.

River forces herself to stop the jiggle and takes a strand of her hair to chew instead.

Mum takes the strand out of River's mouth.

Mrs Endicott looks up at them.

And when she talks, she only talks to Mum, as if River's not even there.

So River puts on a fake smile and pretends like she's listening but really, she goes into a totally different zone.

She's practised this technique a million times.

For the next half hour, as Mum and Mrs Endicott's voices drone on, River plans what she's going to do in the next few weeks to make sure she never has to come here:

1. Write to the Prime Minister and ask her to change the law about kids having to go to school. Prime Ministers take big, life-changing decisions all the time, like going to war for example, which is a much bigger deal than making school optional.
2. Find ways to show Mum that she can learn all kinds of stuff without having to go to school.
3. Persuade Jules to take her side. Jules hated school: she kept getting in trouble for having tattoos and stuff. She should be the first one to understand why River doesn't want to go.
4. If Jules won't budge, River will get Reg on side. Maybe once she's explained it all properly to him he'll find a

way to make Mum understand. He always has this way of making things sound really calm and sensible. And River's noticed how Mum listens to him.

5. Get Pablo to rally his troops and invade Downside Academy. If all the pigeons in London take up residence in the school, then they'll close it and no one will have to go there.

River finds herself laughing at the thought of pigeon poop dropping all over those grey concrete buildings.

Mum and Mrs Endicott look up and frown. It obviously wasn't a funny bit in their conversation.

'Is everything all right, River?' Mrs Endicott asks.

'Yes,' River smiles. 'Everything's just fine.'

'She seemed nice,' Mum says as they sit in the bus on the way home.

River doesn't answer.

'She's certainly done her homework,' Mum adds.

'You mean, she's read up on what a hopeless case I am?'

'You're not a hopeless case.'

River looks at Mum. She should just tell her straight out that she's not setting foot in that school again. No silly plans and schemes. No campaigns to get her to agree. Just tell her how every time she thinks about going to school, she feels so sick she thinks she's going to die.

'I don't want to go to Downside,' River says, her voice quiet and steady. 'I don't want to go to any school.'

'We've talked about this already, River.'

'We haven't. Not properly,' River says.

'Going to school isn't optional.'

'It should be.'

'You have to have an education.'

'Why?'

'Because that's how life works. You have to go to school and work hard and get good marks so that you can go to a good university and get a good job—'

'You didn't.'

Mum closes her mouth and swallows hard.

'I mean – you didn't go to university, and look how clever you are. You're always working out what's wrong with patients and you learn stuff from reading books. I could read books on my own and listen to them on audio and use the internet and TV. There are lots of ways I can learn. I can teach myself, like you do. And I can get good at stuff. Going to school isn't the only way, Mum. You proved that.'

Mum grips the bars of the seat in front of her. Her knuckles go white. She looks down into the lap of her black skirt.

'I'm a cleaner, River.'

'No you're not – not *really*. You're—'

'I'm what?'

River goes quiet.

Mum's eyes go glassy. 'Life's not all silly rainbows, River.'

Silly rainbows? Mum's never said anything mean about River's rainbows; she knows they're the one thing that makes River happy.

River feels like she's been punched in the stomach.

'We're poor,' Mum goes on.

'No, we're not.' There's a bitter taste in River's mouth.

'We are, love. We live in a run-down bedsit above a smelly Italian restaurant. You sleep on a sofa, for Christ's sake – in the lounge. You don't even have your own room. And I share a tiny room with Jules. We can't afford decent clothes. Or food. We don't have a car. We barely manage to pay the bills. If it weren't for Jules, God knows where we'd be.'

'It's not like that, Mum. It's fine—'

'It's not fine, River. You may think it is now, because you're still young and because you're used to it, but soon you'll grow up and then you'll see what it's really like, and it'll make you angry – like it makes me angry – that anyone should have to live like this. And if I haven't done something to help you make a better life for yourself, you'll resent me.' Tears drop down Mum's cheeks. Her lips look blurry from the smudged lipstick. 'School's your way out, River. It's your only way out.' She wipes her tears on the back of her hand. 'My parents were right: I should have gone to university. And I should have listened to them, River.'

River's body slumps down into the seat.

Did Mum really see their lives like this? Did she really think they were *poor*?

Mum and River have always struggled to see things the same way. Jules explained it once by saying that it was like they were looking at the same world but through different glasses. That it's just something that happens when two people are different. But this takes things to a whole new level. Mum and River aren't wearing different glasses – they're looking at totally different worlds.

As Mum and River sit beside each other, Mum's words hang between them like lead weights.

When the bus lurches to the stop at the end of Acacia Road, Mum gets out a hanky, blows her nose hard, mops at her eyes and then gets up and starts walking down the aisle.

A moment later they're both standing outside Gabino's. River always thought that Mum found it fun living above an Italian restaurant. She's never called it smelly before.

But now, as River looks up at their flat, she can't stop Mum's words crashing around in her head.

We're poor.

Smelly restaurant.

Bills.

Mum looks at her watch and bites her lip. River knows that she has to get back to the hospital if she's not going to be late for her shift.

They go inside and River sits on her sofa bed while Mum gets changed into her work clothes. She keeps looking at the window, hoping that Pablo might show up, but the window ledge stays empty.

And then she wishes Jules would crash in and take up loads of space and make loads of noise like she always does, so that River doesn't have to listen to the thoughts in her head.

River gets it now, why Mum doesn't like Pablo: why would she? She doesn't like anything about their lives.

'Jules will be here soon.' Mum kisses River's forehead.

River doesn't move.

'She'll give you tea.'

River doesn't say anything.

'I shouldn't be too long.'

River nods, staring at the floor. She notices how the carpet doesn't quite reach the edges of the wall.

She feels Mum hovering over her, waiting for her to say something, but River doesn't have any words.

'Bye, then.' Mum grabs her handbag, walks to the door of the flat, turns around one last time and, when River doesn't respond, she leaves.

Isabel

Isabel rubs her eyes and looks at the alarm blinking next to Jules's bed: 3.14 a.m.

It's been hours now that she's been trying to sleep: her body is heavy and desperate for rest but her mind won't stop whirring.

She swings her legs over the edge of the bed, pulls on a pair of jeans and a T-shirt, slips her feet into a pair of trainers, grabs her phone and goes out into the kitchen.

Before she leaves the flat, she stops and looks at River: a thick tangle of brown curls the only part of her visible under the duvet. She goes over, kisses the top of her head and, for a second, she closes her eyes and breathes in every part of her little girl.

They've been fighting recently, mainly about school, but this, the smell of River's hair, the feel of it under her lips, her sleeping warmth, makes it all melt away. River, more than any other place Isabel has ever been, feels like home.

Her mind flickers to the man lying alone in the hospital bed of Regent's Hospital. Who is *his* home? she wonders. And will he ever find them again?

She picks up the keys to the flat, runs down the stairs, through the restaurant, out into the street and looks down Acacia Road.

A car drives past. At the end of the road, a white van rattles over a manhole. On the other side of the road, a couple walks arm in arm. They keep tripping over each other, wobbling off the pavement and laughing.

She looks up: a grey haze, no stars.

As she stares at the sky, Isabel remembers walking through the streets of Venice. No one slept there either, but it was different. People walked slowly, as though the night would go on for ever. She remembers the millions of stars, how the moon bounced off the water. The night was generous – a secret pocket of time, a place where you could live, for a while, and let the world fall away.

Maybe that's why she'd taken him home with her that night: because she thought that the moment they shared would be protected, that whatever they did wouldn't spill out into the light of day.

And that's all they shared: a moment. One that will never be repeated. One that, she is beginning to realise, has been holding her back for too long. From living. From falling in love.

Without the shortcut through Regent's Park, it takes a long time to walk to the hospital. When she gets to the ward, her eyes are burning with tiredness.

As Reg sleeps, she takes in the outline of his body under the hospital sheet. She imagines the network of organs and arteries, the tissue and muscle and bone, the blood that pumps through his body. No different, she thinks, from any other human body. No different from her or Jules or River or David – or the patients on the ward. He's made of the same parts as the rest of them, and yet everyone treats him as though he doesn't belong here, as though he's not allowed to occupy the same space as they do. Why? Because he speaks differently? Because his eyes and his hair and the tone of his skin suggest that he's from somewhere else? Because he doesn't carry the right papers in his pocket? Because he can't remember?

You belong here, she wants to tell him. *With us.*

She scans the room for what needs doing. She empties the bin, folds a blanket that's fallen off the end of the bed, fills a jug with water and gets a clean glass. Then she tidies the papers and pens scattered on his bedside table. He must have been drawing for hours. There are sketches on paper napkins, in the margins of the newspapers she brought for him. River's exercise book lies open on the drawing of a wild sea, a small fishing boat lost in the waves. She wonders whether that's where his home was, a house by the sea. She'd like that, maybe as much as living in a small flat overlooking the water in Venice.

She gets a picture of River running along a beach. Of walking behind her with this man who has so unexpectedly come into their life.

And then she checks herself.

Is she thinking of him like this because she knows that he's as inaccessible as the man she knew for only one night in Italy? So it's safe to think of him – and to come and see him? Because nothing will ever come of it.

Or is it more than that? Is it possible that, when his past has been untangled, when he does remember, he might really be able to stay?

She feels foolish for allowing her mind to wander like this, but, tonight, with no one watching or listening, she doesn't care.

Isabel looks over to him again; he's in a deep sleep, his body heavy on the sheets.

She sits beside him, picks up a biro and River's exercise book and starts drawing his body – the parts you'd see if you shone a torch under the skin, the parts she understands, that she's learnt about from her medical textbooks.

There's so much that makes up a person, she thinks, *it's a miracle that not more goes wrong.*

She keeps sketching. His ribcage and under it, his heart and his lungs, lungs inflamed with pneumonia.

'I didn't know you could draw.'

She jumps.

His eyes are wide open, as though he's never been asleep.

'Let me see.' He holds out his hand. The ink stain on his left forefinger has grown. All that drawing with River.

Isabel covers the picture with her hand; her fingers are shaking.

'It's nothing,' she says, blushing.

'It doesn't look like nothing.'

He lifts himself up and pulls the exercise book out of her hands.

'It's beautiful.'

She shakes her head. 'It's just technical – anatomy. And not very good anatomy at that.'

'You draw what the human eye can't see.' He pauses. 'That's beautiful.'

She looks back at the picture she drew. She's always found the human body amazing – and beautiful. She loves how intricate and complicated and connected it is. But she never thought her pictures were art.

He looks up at her. 'Is it me?'

She laughs nervously. 'Kind of.'

'Well, I look very handsome.' He smiles at her and, for a second, she gets that same feeling that she gets when she kisses River's head: like she's come home.

'Do you draw all your patients?'

She stares at him.

'My patients?'

'Was it part of your training, to become a nurse?' He laughs.

He thinks that she's a nurse?

'Oh ... no ...' She realises her mistake. That no one has told him. 'I mean, I'm not ...' She gulps.

'Not what?'

She takes a breath. 'I'm a cleaner.'

His eyebrows shoot up. 'A cleaner?'

She bows her head, thinking of all the times she's had to write down her job on forms, or to explain it to River's teachers or other parents at pick-up. And how, once they know, they look at her differently. It's not a job anyone ever aspires to.

He leans over, places his fingers under her chin and lifts her head until she looks at him.

'It is a noble profession.'

She blinks. '*Noble?*'

He nods. 'Imagine what the world would be like without you? Hospitals especially.'

'I suppose cleaners are necessary.'

'You make our world more beautiful.'

Beautiful, that word again, in such an unexpected context.

'And you care for us – is that not true?' he adds.

'Perhaps.'

'So we *are* your patients after all.'

It's how Jules and River refer to the people on the ward too: *your* patients.

'Yes.'

Isabel glances over at the bits of paper on his bedside table. 'You've been busy, all those pictures.'

He follows her gaze.

'It helps.'

'To remember?'

He keeps staring at the pictures. 'It just helps.'

She nods.

'Would you show me how to draw? A real picture?' she asks suddenly, not sure where the words – or the desire – came from.

And then a memory comes back to her: she used to do art, at school. It's what took her to Italy.

She realises that everything that happened that night in Venice, with River's father, made her forget the rest of her life. Like that there was a time when she loved to draw.

She wonders what else she has forgotten.

Without answering, he pulls the rolling table over him and motions for her to sit closer. Then he takes the picture she was drawing and places it between them.

'What do you see?' he asks.

'See?' She stares at her drawing. 'I don't understand.'

'Look at me.'

She looks up.

'What do you see on the surface of my body? Above what you drew here?' He passes his long fingers over the paper.

Her stomach clenches. 'I don't know . . .'

He picks up the biro and holds it out to her.

'Try,' he says.

She shakes her head. 'I can't draw, not properly. Not any more.'

'Is a face so different from a heart?'

She looks at him, at the deep hollows of his eyes, the curve of his jaw, his smile lines, his dark hair falling over his forehead. Maybe he was right, maybe it wasn't so different after all.

'Try,' he says again.

She leans over the paper and starts drawing the outline of his face, then his hair, his long neck, the sharp line of his nose. And she keeps drawing, looking up at him and back down at the paper, losing herself in the movement of her hand and the face coming to life in front of her. Something in her is coming loose.

'You have made me look younger,' he says, smiling.

She stares at the picture for a moment. And then she starts drawing again.

Someone coughs behind her.

She drops her pen.

'You're visiting early.' It's Nurse Green.

Isabel stands up, brushes her hand through her hair and looks down at her jeans and trainers. She's not meant to be here.

'My daughter forgot something.' Isabel grabs the red exercise book.

Nurse Green looks from Isabel to Reg. He knows Isabel's not meant to be here, not at this time.

He goes over to check Reg's IV drip. Reg's eyes have become agitated again, his breathing ragged. She's noticed how he doesn't like it when the doctors and nurses are around. Except for David, but he's different.

I shouldn't have come, she says to herself again. *He's in a fragile state of mind; he doesn't need me coming in and making problems for him.*

Except she wanted to come. And she wanted to stay.

'My son's always leaving things behind too,' Nurse Green says.

Isabel snaps her head up.

'Spend my life retracing his steps,' Nurse Green goes on. 'It's exhausting, right?'

Nurse Green turns around and, for a second, he holds Isabel's gaze.

'You have a son?' Isabel asks.

He's older than Isabel was when she had River, but not by much.

Nurse Green nods. 'I'd better get back to him now.' He looks at his watch. 'My shift ended an hour ago and even a grandparent's goodwill runs out sometime, hey?'

Isabel's chest contracts. She thinks of all these years when her parents could have helped with River; how, even though they disagreed with her decision to keep her, they would have loved her.

How little we ever really know about anyone, Isabel thinks as she watches Nurse Green walk away down the corridor.

She sits back down and looks at Reg. He seems calmer again.

He picks up her drawing and holds it up.

'You did it,' he says. 'You're an artist.'

She looks at the picture she drew. It's not good, not in the sense of a true artistic representation of another person. But it's him – the him lying here beside her, and maybe, in some small way, it's the other him too, the one he can't remember, the one that he might be again one day.

Maybe that's what art does, she thinks. Not a tracing of a heart or a lung but something that you create from what you feel as much as from what you see. A drawing that touches on something from elsewhere.

'Can I ask you a question?' Isabel says quietly.

He nods.

'You're scared, aren't you?'

He bows his head.

'I mean, I can tell that something's worrying you. About being here. About people asking so many questions.'

His head drops further.

'It must be overwhelming, not to remember. But it's more than that, isn't it?'

He looks up at her. 'More than what?'

'What is it that you're *really* frightened of?' She looks right into his huge brown eyes. 'Maybe I could help.'

Reg goes quiet for a really long time. Then he says:

'I am frightened, yes. It is a terrible thing, not to know what

146

one is frightened of. Worse, I think, than knowing.' He swallows, hard. 'If I knew, I could . . .' He hesitates.

'You could?' Isabel prompts, her heart hammering.

'I could try and escape it.'

Isabel sees it now. How awful it must be not to know whether, by trying to remember, you're running right into the thing that you fear most. Maybe forgetting is easier.

'Do you want to remember?' she asks.

His eyes widen and then he sinks back into himself. His hands move back up to his ears, like he wants to block out the question.

'I'm sorry,' she says. 'I shouldn't have asked that.'

He looks at her and lowers his hands. Then he takes a breath.

'It's okay. I understand your question.'

He goes quiet and looks over to the small window to the right of his bed. It's getting lighter; soon it will be morning.

It's not worth going all the way home – her shift is going to start in a few hours. She gets her phone out of her jeans pocket and texts Jules to say she came in early and to give River breakfast.

Then she pushes away the rolling table and gets up off the bed.

'I'm sorry I woke you, I should let you get some rest,' she says.

He frowns, those knots she's come to know, pushing up into his brow.

'You look tired too,' he says.

Hearing him say the words makes it come back, the exhaustion in her body, how her mind hasn't rested in days – not since she brought him into the hospital.

And how she hasn't been able to forget him, not for a second.

'Why don't you stay for a bit.'

She looks at him, her heart hammering.

'Just rest a little, here, with me,' he adds. 'Unless you need to get back to River?'

She hasn't felt like this in years. She hasn't felt like this since that night, in Venice. It's like a part of her body is coming back to life – a limb that's been numb, an organ that, for a while, had failed.

'Are you sure?' she asks.

'I feel better when you're here,' he says.

'You do?'

Her heart is hammering so hard she can barely hear her own thoughts.

'Yes, I do.'

She looks at the picture again, the one she drew of him. How it's just a picture but it feels more significant and concrete than anything she's done for years.

'Okay,' she says.

And then, without even thinking, she pulls up one of the visitor chairs to the bed, slumps her body down into the padded seat, places her arms on the bed and lowers her head.

As she closes her eyes, his voice drifts towards her. She can feel his breath, warm against her arm.

'You are right – the question you asked,' he says after a while.

She keeps her eyes closed, her eyelids heavy, her body already given up to sleep yet longing to stay here with him, just a bit more.

'I don't know if I want to remember,' he says.

Reg

A week later, Nurse Green pushes Reg's wheelchair out into the hospital garden.

'The fresh air will do you good,' he says. 'Doctor's orders.'

It's finally stopped raining. Out here, everything gleams and drips: the grass and the bushes and the flowers and the outdoor furniture.

Reg can't believe that he hasn't been outside since Isabel brought him into the hospital; it feels like a lifetime since his lungs have breathed in fresh air.

He was a little scared of going outside, of whether he was ready to be part of the world again. But as soon as Nurse Green opened the door that leads into the small walled garden, the sweet, damp air ran at him and he felt alive again.

'Can I walk from here?' he asks. 'I'd like to be on my own for a bit.'

'Are you sure you're strong enough, Reg?'

He nods.

Funny, how everyone has taken to calling him Reg. He's beginning to grow into the name — for the first time in a long while, he feels rooted here, amongst these people.

'Well, take it gently.' Nurse Green lifts a plate of sandwiches off Reg's lap and helps him up to standing.

His legs are weak and his knee is already aching, but he wants to do this.

'Dr Reed will be along soon, she has someone who'd like to ask you a few questions.'

He hopes Dr Reed doesn't come too soon; he wants to be out here alone for a while. And anyway, he's tired of questions – all they do is remind him how little he remembers.

Nurse Green runs ahead of him down the path and leaves the plate of sandwiches on a small steel table in a corner of the garden. Then he comes back, grabs Reg's stick from where he'd balanced it on the handlebars of the wheelchair, and says:

'Yell if you need me.' He places the wheelchair by the door.

Nurse Green is better when he's on his own, Reg thinks. And he remembers the other morning, when he found him with Isabel, how he said he had a son.

When Nurse Green has left, Reg steps forward.

Everything rushes at him at once. The brilliance of the sun; the smell of wet grass and flowers and fumes from the cars on the other side of the wall; birdsong and traffic and a low cooing fill his ears.

He thinks about how much more life there is beyond the hospital walls and how living inside for what feels like months rather than days has made him numb.

As he breathes in and out, he tilts his head to the sun, letting it warm his face. Then he eases his feet out of his hospital slippers, places them by his chair and walks off the path and onto the grass. The wet grass squeezes up between his toes and his heels sink into the rain-softened earth. He turns his palms up to the cool, morning air, closes his eyes and feels his body coming back to life.

When his knee starts throbbing again, he walks slowly over to the table where Nurse Green put his sandwiches. It's the first time in days that he's felt hungry.

He sits down, picks up a sandwich and takes a bite.

'Reg!'

Rapid, clicking footsteps.

A hand squeezes his shoulder.

He coughs and puts down the sandwich. His body tenses up.

'Nurse Green said we'd find you out here.'

It's Dr Reed. And she's brought someone with her: a man in a brown suit and a thick yellow tie. The man doesn't look like a doctor.

Reg's lungs contract.

'This is my friend, Mr Boswell.'

Dr Reed and the man sit on either side of Reg.

'He's going to ask you a few questions, hope that's okay.' Dr Reed touches his arm. 'You're used to questions by now, aren't you, Reg?' She turns to Mr Boswell and smiles: her straight, white teeth catch the sunlight. 'My friend's done a great deal of research into situations like yours. He could be a great help to us.'

Maybe Mr Boswell is the friend that Dr Deardorff mentioned: the one who specialises in reading voices, who might be able to trace his words back to where they came from.

Only he doesn't look like a professor either.

Mr Boswell takes out his phone and starts typing on the screen. Without looking up, he says:

'I thought he didn't know his name.'

Dr Reed laughs. 'Oh – Reg? That's just a nickname. A kid gave it to him. It's because we found him in Regent's Park.'

We? Reg is certain that Dr Reed hadn't been there on the day River and Isabel had found him. But perhaps he's forgotten that too.

'Regent's Park, eh?' Mr Boswell keeps typing into his phone.

'Quite the story, isn't it?' Dr Reed says.

'Indeed,' says Mr Boswell.

Sometimes, Reg thinks that the questions and answers would happen regardless of him being there or not.

He could slip away and they wouldn't notice.

'So, Reg, are you ready for a few more questions?'

Reg rubs his eyes. 'I'm a little tired . . .'

'Oh, we won't be long, Mr Boswell's efficient, aren't you?'

Mr Boswell shrugs.

Reg feels bile rise into his throat. The man reminds Reg of someone. Not a specific person, exactly. Rather a type of someone.

'Are you a doctor?' Reg asks him.

Mr Boswell looks up at him, then glances at Dr Reed.

'A doctor of sorts,' Dr Reed says.

Mr Boswell clears his throat. 'So, tell me a bit more about your, eh, situation. It's a strange thing, to forget your own name.'

The words hit Reg like an accusation. He doesn't want to answer Mr Boswell's questions any more.

'I mean, you can forget just about everything,' the man goes on. 'But your name, that stays with you, doesn't it?' He laughs, exposing his tobacco-stained teeth. 'Even an animal knows his name.'

'An animal?' Reg asks.

Dr Reed leans forward and touches his knee. 'What Mr Boswell means is that our names are primal, that even a dog remembers his name.'

Reg blinks at her.

'No clue at all?' Mr Boswell asks.

Reg stares at him, not knowing what to say.

'Let's talk about your English,' Mr Boswell says. 'You have an accent, of course.' He turns to Dr Reed. 'One that hasn't been identified, is that right?'

'We're working on it,' Dr Reed says.

Reg feels sick. He doesn't like the thought of Dr Reed – or her friend – working on anything that concerns him.

'But your English is very good,' Mr Boswell goes on.

'Thank you.'

'Why is that, do you think? That your English is so good, considering you're foreign.'

'English is important,' Reg says.

It just comes out. He's not sure how he knows this, but he believes it's true. That the words that come to him are the right ones, in the right language.

Mr Boswell looks into Reg's eyes. 'English is important? Why's that?'

Reg looks at him blankly.

Mr Boswell scans Reg's body and then points at the stick resting beside him.

'A recent injury or a chronic condition?'

'We think it's a recent injury. It's been twisted out of shape, somehow.'

There. Answers provided for him. He needn't be here at all.

'What happened to your knee?' Dr Reed asks. 'You can tell us, Reg.'

Something flashes across Reg's eyes. A table under his body, hard as metal. Something pulling at his arms and his legs. He can't move. A tearing through every cell of his body.

And after that, darkness.

The sea is rising again; water crashes in his head.

He closes his eyes and presses his hands to his ears.

'Everything okay?' Mr Boswell asks.

'He's fine. It's just something he does.' Dr Reed lowers her voice. 'A tic, you know.' Reg feels someone yanking at his arms.

'It's okay, you can take your hands off your ears, Reg. There's nothing to worry about, we're here to help.'

Reg looks from Dr Reed to Mr Boswell. He tugs at his hospital gown. His knee throbs. He doesn't want to be here.

'Can't remember where you injured yourself, then?' Mr Boswell asks.

Reg looks down at his hands. At the ink stain on his finger. He shakes his head. 'No.'

'So your memory loss dates from before the injury?' Mr Boswell asks.

Reg doesn't answer.

'Reg?' Mr Boswell says. 'Reg?'

Reg puts his hands down on his lap and looks into his palms.

'I don't know ... I'm very tired ...'

'Reg! You're outside!' A voice floats across the garden.

He hears her footsteps, strong and solid against the earth.

He opens his eyes and smiles at River.

River comes up to him and kisses his cheek. 'I hope you haven't been overdoing it, Reg; remember what Dr Deardorff said – plenty of rest.'

She sounds like her mother.

River notices Dr Reed and Mr Boswell.

'Who are you?' River asks, looking at the man in the brown suit.

Dr Reed crosses her legs. 'We're doing some important work, River.'

'Well, I think Reg looks a bit tired,' River says.

'I have a few more questions—' Mr Boswell says.

'Well, you could come back another day,' River suggests.

She definitely sounds like Isabel.

'I'm not sure that'll be possible,' Mr Boswell says.

Dr Reed fixes her eyes on River, smiles and then turns to her friend.

'Come on, I'll fill you in on the rest.' Dr Reed uncrosses her legs, stands up and pushes her chair into the table.

Mr Boswell follows.

Before he goes back inside, Reg notices Mr Boswell stop, turn around and hold his phone up in his and River's direction. Then he puts the phone back in his pocket and follows Dr Reed.

River

'It's cool that you're outside,' River says.

He doesn't answer.

'Reg?'

His eyes are wide and he looks lost, like that first day on the bench.

She leans in towards him. 'You okay, Reg?'

He's staring at the door Dr Reed just went through with her friend.

'It's okay, they're just busybodies,' River says. 'If they annoy you again, you can call Dr Deardorff, he'll help.'

He smiles at her but she knows he's still feeling stressed out by them. River wishes that everyone would just leave him alone for a bit. It's obvious that he doesn't want to be poked at.

'Anyway, that guy was weird,' River says. 'But then there are loads of weird people around here, right, Reg?'

'Like me?' he asks.

He says it like it makes him sad, like when people make River feel like she's a freak because she has ADHD.

'You're one of the sanest people I've met. Apart from the memory thing, but then that's not your fault.'

River's hung around the neuropsychiatry ward long enough to know what *really* weird looks like. And from her experience, the patients are the sanest of the lot. The surgeons, they're the really odd ones, but then you'd have to be odd to want to spend hours cooped up in a dark room cutting people up – especially those who poke around in people's brains.

She looks at the plate next to Reg. He's only taken a small bite out of one of his sandwiches.

'You need to keep your strength up, Reg.'

She thinks about how Mum hardly eats anything either.

'I don't have much appetite,' he says.

'Is it because of the pills?' River asks.

He shrugs. 'I don't know.'

'I have to take pills too and they're horrible and they make my tummy feel all full and bloated, which means I'm basically never hungry, but then, if I don't eat, I feel worse.'

His eyebrows knit together. 'You are sick?'

'Not really. Well, yeah, kind of, but that's not how I see it. I find it hard to concentrate and to read and to sit still for long periods of time.'

His eyebrows scrunch up even more.

'And you take medicine for that?'

River nods. 'It can get really bad. When I get super hyper. And it annoys people, especially teachers.'

'So you take medicine because other people don't want to be inconvenienced by you?'

'I'd never thought of it that way.' It's the first time anyone's told her anything other than that her Dex tablets are the best invention ever. 'I wouldn't be able to focus on our drawing if I didn't take my meds. And maybe you wouldn't like me – I can get totally hyper.'

He shakes his head. 'I would always like you, Miss River.'

River jumps off her chair and gives Reg a big hug. She feels the top half of his body stoop down until his head rests against her shoulder. She wishes she could make him feel better.

River looks back at the plate of sandwiches. Maybe, if she can work out what Reg's favourite food is, then she could find it and bring it to him. No one forgets what they like to eat, do they?

'When you were a kid, what did you ask your mum to make, on your birthday, or for special?'

For River, it's lasagne. It's the only thing Mum knows how to cook. And it takes her like three days to make, but she makes it every single birthday.

Reg looks at River blankly.

'Your favourite food,' River prompts.

Reg's shoulders drop. 'I don't remember.'

'Well, we can try some things out until you do.'

River thinks back to the hot chocolate she shared with Dr Reed and how she told her that she'd do anything to help Reg get better and how she was so glad that she was helping too. She should suggest the food thing to her.

'We'll find something, I promise.'

She decides to add that to her Help Reg Remember list.

River eases her backpack off her shoulders.

'I've got some stuff for you.' She unzips the top of her backpack and pulls out a bag. 'It's your suit, Mum had it cleaned. It might have got a bit crinkled, sorry.' She looks up at him and bites her lip. 'Don't tell Mum.'

Reg looks at the bag, confused.

'They're the clothes we found you in,' River says.

He nods. 'Thank you.'

Then she pulls something else out of her backpack. 'And I went into the art shop on our road and asked if they had any ink drawing pens that they couldn't sell or didn't need any more, you know, like the ones people try out before they buy, and the guy gave me this.' She places a pen onto his lap. 'The nib's a bit wonky, but it's a proper artist one.' She grins. 'Do you like it?'

Reg takes the pen, unscrews the lid and touches the nib with the pad of his thumb.

He presses the nib to his lips and closes his eyes.

'So you like it then?' she prompts again.

He puts the pen down on the red exercise book he carries with him everywhere now, reaches for her hand and looks her in the eye and says: 'You've brought me a piece of home, dear River.'

River's eyes go wide. 'So I guessed right?' Electricity rushes through her body. She wants to jump around the room. 'You had a pen – like this one – back at home? In your old life?'

'I think so.'

Her heart does a leap.

She knew she could help him remember.

And then her heart sinks a little too.

She wants to help him, really she does. She doesn't want him to be sad any more. She wants him to be with the people who love him, his friends and his family – because someone like Reg is bound to have people out there who love him very much.

But River also knows that if he does work out where home is, it means she might not be able to hang around with him any more. Because the likelihood of him being from around here is like zero: he's probably from miles and miles away, which means that when he does remember, he'll go away and they'll never see each other again. And that would suck. Reg is the best thing to have happened to her in ages. He gets her. And he makes her feel like she can do something – more than that, like she's *good* at something. Something that involves sitting still and concentrating, which she usually hates. And Mum's been in a better mood too. And the hospital feels nicer for him being here, too. Even Jules said he was cool, and she hardly says that of anyone.

'The pen could help you draw more things,' River says. 'Things from your memory.'

Reg looks back down at the pen. And then he frowns and his eyes go sad and she's worried he's going to cry again.

River doesn't understand how he can go from happy to sad in the time it takes to blink.

'Reg? Are you okay?'

A flock of birds fly overhead in a V-formation. They both look up at the brilliant blue sky.

'Could we go for a walk?' he asks.

'Around the garden?' River asks, already picking up his stick.

For a long time, Reg doesn't say anything, he just keeps staring at the sky. Then he looks back down at her:

'I'd like to go back to the zoo.' His eyes are bright.

Now it's River's turn to go quiet. Part of her wants to march him right out of this horrid hospital – and she loves going to the zoo, even just the outside of it. But there's an ache at the base of her skull, like another voice is trying to get in: a voice that says it's not a good idea.

But what harm can a little walk do? Everyone's been telling her about how she's helping Reg get better; well, part of getting better is making him happy and finding things he loves to do. And just the thought of going to the zoo is making his eyes sparkle. So, who knows, he might even remember something when he's there. And then everyone will be proud of River for taking him.

Her leg starts jiggling up and down with excitement.

'Are you allowed?' River asks Reg.

Reg gives her a small smile. 'No one said I couldn't.'

River grins: she knows this line of reasoning well. She's used it a million times with Mum.

'Are you well enough, though? I mean, your knee – and your cough?'

He nods again.

River looks at her watch. Mum's working in the basement of the hospital for at least another hour. Stingy Simon is making her catch up some hours she missed and he's giving her all the horrible jobs. No one likes working in the basement: it doesn't have any windows and it smells of chemicals.

'If you don't want to come, I can try to find it on my own,' Reg says.

'No, you can't go on your own – you'll get lost. And anyway, I want to come. I'm just trying to work out how we're going to do it.'

They can't very well just stroll out past reception; someone will see them and try to stop them.

River flutters her fingers by her side as she works out what to do. Then she grins. 'I know a way out.'

She takes Reg's elbow, helps him out of his chair and hands him his stick. And then she looks him up and down and realises that he can't possibly walk through London in a hospital gown.

'We'll stop by the loos for you to get changed.' She picks up the bag with Reg's suit and puts his new pen and the exercise book in her backpack. Maybe he'll feel inspired to draw something in the park and it'll jog his memory.

Before they leave the hospital garden, Reg takes her hand and gives it a squeeze.

'Thank you, Miss River,' he says.

And, for just a moment, the sadness in his eyes dissolves.

River stands outside the gents, trying not to look suspicious. Reg has been ages – and she can't very well go in after him.

Then it gets worse.

Dr Deardorff walks towards her down the corridor, munching

on a Jammie Dodger. When he gets to her, he wipes some crumbs off his lip and says:

'Is your mother still working?'

She nods. *Please may he not need a wee*, she thinks. *Please.*

'I thought you'd be with Reg,' Dr Deardorff says.

'He's just having some physio.'

Reg has loads of physio for his knee, so it's a safe one to go with, but then Dr Deardorff is his doctor and he probably knows his schedule. And he's probably wondering why River is hanging around outside the gents.

Only Dr Deardorff doesn't seem to twig that anything's wrong.

'Good, good,' he says. 'Reg needs to get that knee moving. Good to see you, River. Thank you for all the work you're doing with him.'

Dr Deardorff smiles at her and begins to walk away.

Phew.

Then he turns around.

'Could I ask you a question, River?'

River hears shuffling behind the door of the gents. *Wait, Reg*, she thinks. *Just a few more seconds.*

'Does your mother like chocolates?'

'Chocolates? No, not really. I mean, she doesn't eat much of anything really.'

His shoulders drop.

'Why?' River asks.

Dr Deardorff pushes his glasses up his nose. 'I just wanted to thank her, you know, for all the hard work she does on the ward.'

The hand dryer is going now. River has to find a way to get Dr Deardorff to leave – and fast.

'Something Italian,' she says. 'She'll like that. But proper Italian – not like microwaved or deep-fried Italian.'

Dr Deardorff frowns. 'Microwaved Italian?'

'Oh, it's just what Gabino makes.' She glances at the bathroom door. 'As long as it's proper Italian, she'll like it.'

Dr Deardorff smiles. 'Thank you, River.'

God knows what he'll come up with.

'I'd better go,' River says, hoping that it will prompt him to turn back round and leave too.

'Righty-ho.' He looks confused for a while and then takes another bite of his biscuit and heads off.

Thank God.

The door to the gents swings open.

River's heart is beating so hard it feels like it's going to leap right out of her chest.

Then she sees Reg and bursts out laughing and all the tension whooshes out of her body.

Reg stands in front of her in his faded black suit with his white shirt and his black tie, and everything looks creased and shrunk like he's had a growth spurt since he last put his things on. And he's still wearing his hospital slippers.

'I'll go and get your shoes,' she says.

He shakes his head. 'We don't have much time.'

Her heart starts racing again. River's nervous enough about this whole going to the zoo thing without Reg being antsy about it too.

'You sure you can walk in those?' she asks.

They're white and flimsy – definitely not made for going outside.

'I'll be fine.'

She nods. 'Okay. Let's go.'

If they don't leave now, she's going to lose her nerve.

*

River guides Reg to a little corridor that shoots off the side of the ward. There's nothing there except a fire exit. She knows it's not alarmed because Ash, Mum's cleaner friend, comes out here to smoke on his breaks. It's right at the back of the hospital too, the ugly bit where all the pipes and bins are, so they're less likely to be seen.

As Reg stands at the top of the fire escape, he takes in a deep breath and looks out across London. From up here they can see the network of roads and taxis and buses and cars. They can see Regent's Park too, and the zoo.

'It's beautiful,' Reg says.

She's never really thought of London as beautiful. She often thinks she'd be happier in the countryside, with tall trees and puddles and long grass, which is why she loves the park so much.

'Come on, we don't have long,' River says.

It takes them ages to get to the zoo. Reg needs to stop every few minutes to catch his breath and to cough and because his knee is creaky and because he keeps getting his floppy hospital slippers caught on uneven bits of the pavement.

But they make it. Within twenty minutes, they're standing in front of the entrance to the zoo. People keep sweeping past them. River wishes she had the money to take him inside. Maybe she could ask Dr Deardorff whether, one day, they could take him inside to see the animals. Maybe it would help him get better.

Reg rubs his eyes. His shoulders are stooped and his breath is wheezy.

River looks over at the bench where she first found him.

'Maybe we should go and sit down,' she suggests.

He shakes his head. 'I need to stay here.'

She doesn't understand why he just wants to stand here on the pavement.

'The bench isn't far,' she says.

He shakes his head.

'Would you like to hold my arm?' she asks.

He nods. 'Thank you.'

She takes his arm and tries to carry his weight a bit. She can feel his legs wobbling under him. She wishes he'd sit down.

'You don't like it much at the hospital, do you?' River says.

He shakes his head slowly, his eyes still closed.

'You won't have to be there long,' she says. And then she feels guilty because she doesn't know that. What happens if his knee and his pneumonia and his not remembering take a really long time to heal? What if he's like one of those patients Mum talks about who live in the hospital for years?

'I mean, as soon as you're better, you can come back here more often. Or even better, to the places you remember.' River feels her words getting all tangled up. Sometimes she wishes her mouth were zipped permanently shut.

Reg opens his eyes and stares at the posters advertising the animals at the zoo. His eyes look sad and confused again, which wasn't the point of coming here. And they're going to have to get back to the hospital soon if they don't want anyone to find out that they've escaped. She doesn't want to waste a minute.

'Why don't you draw something?' she asks. 'Before we head back?'

The pen made him so happy that she hopes this will get him back on track.

'Here?' Reg asks.

She nods. 'It's nice to draw outside, don't you think?'

Back at Caius Primary, River was always trying to persuade

the teachers to let them have their lessons outside. And they always said the same thing: *you won't be able to concentrate.* They didn't get that she'd concentrate a million times better out in the fresh air than cooped up inside.

She hands him the exercise book and the pens. 'We could go to the bench and you could sit down and take a break and draw something.'

He really should sit down.

'Draw something?' he asks.

'Your favourite animal – how about that?'

He looks from the entrance of the zoo to the bench like he's measuring the distance with his eyes and weighing up whether it's okay.

Then he nods. 'Okay, just for a little while.'

They walk over to the bench and Reg sits down. He leans back and closes his eyes and relaxes. River supposes that, for a while, this was his home. Or as close as he's got to home since he forgot where his real home is.

Then Reg picks up his pen and uses it to scratch behind his ear. 'My favourite animal?'

River nods. 'You must have a favourite animal. You know what mine are already.'

He smiles. 'Pigeons.'

She nods. 'I like hummingbirds too, but I've never seen one so it doesn't count.'

River saw hummingbirds on *Animal Planet* on Gabs's TV and she loved how their feathers were like rainbows and how they moved all the time. The presenter said that hummingbirds can beat their wings fifty times a second. River thought about how unfair it is that she always gets in trouble for moving around too much while hummingbirds get to flutter and fidget as much as they like and people don't criticise them – they just think they're beautiful.

'You can love something you've never seen,' Reg says.

'You can?'

He nods.

'Okay, well then I love hummingbirds. But I love pigeons more, because they're just as beautiful but people don't see it straight away, they have to really pay attention, and I think that's kind of cool. I'd still like to see a hummingbird one day though. And I'd love to find a dress that made me look like them. I'd get married in it – if I ever get married.'

River can't imagine ever living with anyone other than Mum and Jules.

'You'd like to get married?' Reg asks.

'Maybe. He'd have to like rainbows though. And pigeons. And not sitting in the same place all the time.'

'Your mama never got married?'

River shakes her head.

Reg's eyes go sad again, like a cloud has swept over them.

'Anyway,' she says quickly, to stop him getting down in the dumps again, 'I'm going to go over to the information desk to ask if they have any leaflets on Whipsnade so we can look up the opening times. Then we can try and persuade Mum and Dr Deardorff to let you go and see the elephants. In the meantime, you draw me your favourite animal – it can be a surprise.'

River stands in the queue for ages. And then, when she gets to the information person, he says that they've run out of Whipsnade leaflets.

There were so many people milling around that her view of the bench was blocked; she hopes that Reg was okay without her.

She runs back to find him.

And then her heart stops.

The bench is empty.

She stands there, blinking, as though, if she stares hard enough, Reg might magically appear. And then it begins to sink in: he's gone.

She looks around. She can't see Reg anywhere.

Her heart starts beating again – really fast. As fast as a hummingbird's wings.

Where is he?

And then she spots her exercise book lying open on the bench. He's drawn a picture of an elephant. He's drawn elephants for her before, but this one is different: its legs are buckling under the weight of a huge, fat man with a moustache. The man's bigger than the elephant, like the elephant is a dwarf and the man is a giant. The man's got a megaphone in his hand and a stretched smile that sends a shudder up River's spine. There's a blindfold tied around the elephant's eyes and his ears are sewn shut to the sides of his head and his legs are tied up with thick rope.

In his other hand, the man holds a whip, which he's about to bring down on the elephant's back.

Her heart goes still, but not in a good way: something's not right. This picture. And Reg disappearing.

River grabs the exercise book, shoves it into her backpack and scans the area around the bench.

She should never have taken Reg out of the hospital.

River cups her hands around her mouth and calls out: 'Reg!'

People standing around the entrance to London Zoo look round at River.

Mum's definitely not going to let River hang out with Reg after this.

River tries to think logically. Where would Reg have wanted to go?

'Reg!' she calls again.

And then she hears the screeching of tyres.

And someone shouting: 'Bloody idiot!'

And other cars honking and braking.

Something makes River start running.

She pushes past the people on the pavement and looks up and down the road.

And that's when she sees him, standing in the middle of the road, cars and buses and taxis stopped at angles around him, drivers poking their heads out of their windows and shouting at him to get out of the way.

People have gathered on the pavements on either side of the road: they're staring and pointing.

Reg is holding his hands over his ears and his hair's sticking up in all directions and, somewhere along the way, he's lost his hospital slippers.

'Reg!' River runs into the middle of the road. 'Reg!'

He doesn't move.

'Reg! What are you doing?'

She grabs his arm and tries to yank him towards the pavement, but he won't budge.

His eyes are fixed on a spot across the road.

'Come on, we need to get out of the way. You could have got yourself killed out here.' He still won't move.

River's seen Reg do this a few times before: freezing, like he's seen a ghost or something. Dr Deardorff calls them *Reg's episodes*. He thinks that it's when he sees something and it jogs some deep memory inside him but he can't quite work it out so it upsets him.

Only, having episodes in hospital is fine. Loads of people on the neuropsychiatry ward have episodes. Having them in the middle of a busy road, on the other hand, is totally dangerous.

River wishes she'd listened to that voice in her head back at the hospital, the one that said that it wasn't such a good idea taking Reg out here.

River's head thumps so loud she can't get her thoughts straight. This day couldn't get any worse.

'Come on, Reg, we've got to get out of the road.' River takes his hand.

With his other hand he points across the road. 'I saw her.'

'Who?'

'Over there.'

River squints and tries to follow his gaze.

'The woman ... with the dark hair.'

There are loads of people around and just about half of them have dark hair. But for some reason River's eyes focus on a young woman with a long, black plait swinging down her back. Like the one Reg drew in the picture that first day in the hospital.

The woman's walking away from them.

'Her?' River says. 'With the plait?'

He nods. And then says: 'But it's not her.'

'Not who?'

Maybe things might turn out okay. Maybe, rather than being traumatised, all of this will have jogged him into remembering something important.

He shakes his head and looks down at his bare feet. 'No one.'

River lets out a long breath.

'Come on, Reg,' River says gently. 'Let's get you back to the hospital.'

And that's when she sees Mum standing on the pavement in her cleaner's uniform, staring at them both.

Isabel

'We never have breakfast,' River says to Isabel. 'Not together. Not sitting down.'

Isabel clears the junk mail, bills, bank statements and medical textbooks off the rickety kitchen table, sprays the surface with kitchen cleaner and wipes it down with a paper towel.

'Well, today we are.' Isabel dumps the kitchen paper in the bin and then comes over and pulls out a chair. 'Sit down, River.'

Isabel was planning to talk to River last night but then Stingy Simon called her in to cover a late shift on the ward. By the time she came home, River was asleep.

And then Isabel spent the night tossing and turning, thinking about what she knows she has to say to River: that things have to change; that Isabel should never have allowed them to get mixed up in all this.

'But you don't like breakfast,' River says, still standing.

Isabel doesn't answer.

'And there's nothing to eat,' River points out.

There's a dull thumping at the back of Isabel's skull. She goes to the fridge and, for a second, she stares at a Post-it with a phone number scrawled across it. She did some digging and found her parents' contact details. They've downsized but they're still living in Enfield.

She's been thinking about calling them. Seeing Reg having lost everyone like that has made her think that maybe she should get in touch. River has no one except her and Jules. And River's getting to be such a handful: maybe they could help. Maybe, now that so much time has passed, they'll be ready to forgive her for not making anything of the life they gave her.

But she doesn't have the energy to think about that right now. She needs to deal with River before she gets totally out of hand.

Isabel rubs the back of her skull, trying to push away the headache. And if she hadn't got there in time, God knows what could have happened to River. Her chest contracts.

She yanks open the fridge.

Breakfast, Isabel thinks. River needs a proper breakfast. Not just those cereal bars she eats on her way to school every day.

She scans the shelves of the fridge.

An orange with a bloom of white mould sits on the middle shelf.

Under it, a limp iceberg lettuce.

In the fridge door, an upturned bottle of ketchup.

Isabel can feel River's stare pressing into her back.

She slams shut the fridge and opens the kitchen cupboards until she finds a box of Cheerios that she doesn't remember buying. Jules probably put it in there; she's the only one who ever does any food shopping.

Isabel wishes Jules were here now. She'd know what to say to River.

She brings the box over to the table, along with a bowl and a spoon, and thumps them down in front of River. 'There.'

Then she shakes the Cheerio hoops into the bowl and grabs one and eats it to show that she's willing to join in. It's so soft it feels like paper dissolving in her mouth.

'We don't have any milk,' River says.

'They're better without milk.' Isabel grabs another fistful of Cheerios and shoves them in her mouth.

River stares at her, wide-eyed.

Isabel swallows hard and tries to push the *I'm the world's worst mum* thought to the back of her mind.

'Okay, then let's go downstairs,' Isabel says. 'We'll have breakfast at Gabs's.'

'You're taking me to eat at *Gabs's?*' River asks, her brown eyes wide. 'You're always going on about how unhealthy his food is.'

'We're having breakfast.' Isabel grabs her handbag and heads to the door.

'Don't you have to go to work?'

'I've taken the day off sick.'

River screws up her face. 'You've never called in sick. Stingy Simon is going to flip out.'

'I'll make up the time.' Isabel is Simon's best cleaner: he's not going to fire her. If she upsets him, he'll make her life hell, but she can deal with that. 'It's fine, come on.' Isabel holds the door open for River.

'And Reg will miss you,' River says, her voice meek.

Isabel stares at her for a second and blinks. 'Come *on*, River.'

They walk down the back stairs to the café and sit at one of the small booths by the window.

'Special occasion?' Grumpy Gabs asks. His bald head shines under the bright strip lights. Mum's been trying to persuade him to get softer lighting for years.

River grins. 'No, Mum's just cross at me. And we don't have any food.'

'Scrambled eggs on toast,' Isabel says, without looking at River. 'And an espresso for me.'

'With ketchup,' River adds.

Gabs nods and gives Mum a smile but she doesn't notice so he walks away again.

They sit in silence for what feels like an age. The weather report on the BBC News rumbles on a TV screen in the corner. More rain forecast, the wettest summer on record. How many times have they said that now?

'Why don't you tell me off and get it over with,' River says eventually.

'It's not about telling you off.'

Gabs comes over with Isabel's espresso. She takes a quick sip and burns her tongue. 'Damn it.'

'You always do that,' River says.

Isabel puts down her cup of espresso and catches River's eye. 'How am I meant to trust you, River?'

'We didn't do anything wrong.'

Isabel raises her eyebrows. 'We?'

River bows her head. '*I* didn't do anything wrong.'

'You have to start making more sensible decisions, River.'

Isabel feels like her voice is coming from outside her body, that she's some kind of ventriloquist's dummy that's using the words a mother's meant to use. But she has to let River know how serious this is.

She takes a breath and keeps going.

'You need to grow up a bit – you're going to secondary school in September . . . '

River rolls her eyes.

'Don't do that. It's rude.'

'Jules does it all the time.'

'Jules is a grown-up.'

'You just said you wanted me to act more grown up.'

The pounding in Isabel's head gets worse. She closes her eyes. She thought she'd be able to keep a grip on the conversation but it keeps slipping away from her.

Gabs brings the scrambled eggs. They look dry and greasy all at the same time. River pushes them away.

'You have to eat something, River.'

River raises her eyebrows. 'Like you, you mean?'

Isabel wonders when her eleven-year-old daughter suddenly turned into a teenager. She takes a breath.

'What were you thinking, taking Reg out of the hospital like that?'

'What was I *thinking*?' River's voice trails off and she clamps shut her mouth, like she's changed her mind about what she wants to say. 'I was thinking that it might be nice for him to go for a walk. He's been cooped up in there for weeks.'

The pounding in Isabel's head has turned into a full-blown migraine. She takes another sip of coffee.

'You should have asked someone,' Isabel says.

River looks down at the table and fiddles with the toothpicks in their little paper wrappers. 'If he hadn't walked off, it would have been fine.'

'That's the point, River. He's really sick. His behaviour is going to be unpredictable, he can't help it.'

River unwraps one of the toothpicks and stabs it into the grooves of the wooden table. 'He really wanted to go to the zoo. He said it would make him feel better.'

Isabel massages her temples. This is harder than she thought it would be. She thinks again about how much better Jules would be handling this.

She steadies her breath and says:

'I don't want you to see Reg any more.' The words thump around in Isabel's head. All she can think is that if River doesn't see him any more then she shouldn't see him any more either.

She swallows hard.

'Did you hear me, River?'

River doesn't respond.

Isabel realises that River's looking over her shoulder, her eyes fixed on the TV screen. All the blood's drained out of her rosy cheeks. Gabs has stopped rubbing down the counter too – he's holding his cloth in mid-air, staring at the screen, like River.

Slowly, Isabel turns around.

Behind the newsreader, there's a blurry photograph of Reg. River's sitting beside him. They're in the hospital garden.

Isabel stands up and presses her hands into the table. 'What on earth?'

The camera swivels to a man in a brown suit and yellow tie being interviewed by the newsreader.

'That's the guy!' River stands up, her chair screeches behind her. She points at the screen. 'The guy who came to the hospital to talk to Reg.' She gulps. 'Dr Reed's friend.'

David

David steps out of the Tube and blinks at the grey sky. He takes off his glasses, wipes his forehead and pinches the bridge of his nose. Another thirty minutes pressed up against someone's armpit. He can't do this any more.

I should learn to drive, he tells himself. But then it comes back to him: the ten failed driving tests.

You're a liability, the last examiner told him.

David was training to be a doctor – his job was to save lives, for goodness' sake – and he'd nearly run over an old lady as he tried to parallel park. The back wheel had flipped onto the kerb; she'd barely got out of the way in time. All he could think was that it could have been his mother.

And that was that: he never went for another test.

I should walk, he thinks. *Or cycle.* People walk and cycle for miles around London. It would be good for him. And then he gets a vision of himself in trainers and Lycra, arriving at the hospital door red-faced and sweating, in need of a shower, and every bit of his body feels ashamed. Some people are just not made for physical activity.

No, the Tube will have to do.

He takes a sausage roll out of his satchel, bites into the thick, salty pastry and, for a moment, he forgets the jolting and shoving and sweaty armpits of the Tube.

When he gets to the hospital, there's a commotion in front of the main entrance. A medical emergency, he thinks at first. But then they'd have gone to A&E. And there aren't any paramedics or ambulances – or injured patients. Just men in suits with heavy black cameras strapped round their necks and microphones and notepads.

What the hell?

He walks towards them, wondering how he's going to get through, when he spots one of the security guards standing by the glass doors, along with Norma, barring the way to a couple of particularly persistent-looking reporters.

'Excuse me, please,' David says as he weaves through them.

And that's when he catches wind of it.

'I'm reporting live from outside Regent's Hospital where we believe they're harbouring an illegal immigrant.'

David instantly feels sick.

A woman grabs the cuff of David's blazer. 'Are you a doctor?' She shoves a mobile phone to his mouth, like a microphone.

Oh, Christ.

'Do you know anything about the amnesiac?' the woman asks.

'Um ... no comment,' David says, feeling how stilted his words are.

'Is it true that he's forgotten his name?' the woman asks.

David bows his head and ploughs on.

Another reporter stands in front of him with a camera. 'How much is he costing the NHS?'

David looks up. 'Excuse me?'

'If he's an immigrant and he doesn't have the papers to be here and he's not working, he's not paying his taxes, is he? Which means he's scrounging off our services,' the young reporter goes on.

David shakes his head, pushes past the man and his camera,

and finds himself standing in front of a young woman with frizzy brown hair and chapped lips.

'Is he a terrorist?' she asks.

David grinds his teeth and looks around at the reporters. *Idiots.*

'No, he's not a terrorist.'

'So you *do* know him then?' The woman with the hair shifts her weight from one heel to the other.

'Are you his doctor?' someone else calls over to him.

David lifts his satchel to his face and uses it as a shield to push through the last few reporters.

The security guard quickly opens the doors for him.

Norma runs towards him. 'They've been there for hours. It was on the news first thing.'

David loosens his tie. His shirt is drenched in sweat. The sausage roll feels like a brick in his stomach.

He'd been stupid to think that he could keep Reg here for so long. Someone was bound to say something. But he'd been careful. And everyone seemed to have warmed to him – the nurses, the other doctors. Even Long didn't seem to mind.

And then he thinks of Reg, sitting in his hospital bed alone. Does he know what's going on? If he does, he must be feeling more confused than ever. David feels acid pushing up his throat. They'd been making such progress.

Within a few minutes, he's standing at the foot of Reg's bed, staring at two police officers.

Dr Reed is there too.

Nurse Green cowers behind her.

David looks at Reg. His dark eyebrows are sloped down so low, they seem to shield his eyes. He's rubbing and rubbing at the ink stain on his forefinger. His whole body is shaking.

'What's going on?' David asks the female police officer.

'Well, that's what we'd like to ask you. I gather you're the consultant taking care of Mr . . . ' She looks at her notes.

'He's got amnesia, he doesn't remember his name,' David snaps.

Reg closes his eyes and brings his hands to his ears.

'A bit odd, don't you think? To forget your name?' the male police officer butts in.

David ignores his question. 'You need to clear the reporters from the hospital entrance. They're blocking the way for patients.'

The police officers shoot each other a glance.

'The officers came to ask a few questions,' Dr Reed says.

'Thank you, Dr Reed, I'm sure I can handle it from here.'

'Dr Reed has been most helpful,' the female police officer says.

And that's when it clicks. Of course. The one person who, right from the outset, challenged David's decision to take Reg on as a patient. And then all her snooping around, pretending she wanted to learn from him.

David looks at Nurse Green, whose cheeks are aflame. David thought he was beginning to understand Reg's condition, that he might turn into a half decent nurse.

'We'd like to take your patient in for questioning,' the female police officer says.

David looks over at Reg again: his eyes are still closed, his hands still clamped over his ears.

'He's not well enough.' David's almost shouting now. He's not going to let them do this.

'That's not what we were led to believe.' The woman looks at her notes again.

'He has pneumonia, a knee injury – and severe amnesia. Moving him now could cause him both physical and mental distress.'

'I gather he took a long walk yesterday.' The woman locks eyes with David. 'Your colleagues informed us . . .' She keeps pointing at her pad. 'London Zoo, it says here.'

What is the woman talking about?

'He hasn't left his bed,' David says. 'Except for his physiotherapy sessions.'

The woman tilts her head to one side. 'Were you on duty yesterday afternoon, Dr Deardorff?'

He'd clocked off early. The hospital was quiet and after he bumped into River, he wanted to go out and find a gift for Isabel. And then he went to see his mother.

'He can't have gone for a walk,' David says. 'We wouldn't have allowed it.'

The male police officer clears his throat. 'I'm afraid there's photographic evidence. A CCTV camera from the front of the hospital. He was with a young girl. I gather he caused quite a disturbance.'

'A disturbance? What on earth are you talking about?'

'We believe he was trying to abduct the young girl.'

'Abduct? What? What young girl?'

And then it begins to dawn on him: River. Something must have happened with River.

'You obviously have to get up to speed with the details of your patient's case,' the female police officer says.

David's blood pressure shoots up.

'Excuse me?'

'The point is,' she goes on, 'he was clearly well enough to walk quite a distance. Which means he's well enough to come with us.'

'Then I'm coming with you, too,' David says. 'And I'm calling a lawyer.'

There's a lawyer who's worked with the hospital before; he'll get in touch with him. God knows if he can do anything but it will buy them some time.

He turns to look at Reg: all this is about him and through this whole inane discussion, he's been lying there silent.

As he looks into Reg's sad, confused face, David feels like he's failed him. Any light that had come back into his eyes over the past week, any improvement at all in his state of mind, has been snatched away from him in the last hour.

He looks so lost, thinks David. And, right then and there, he decides that he's not going to give up without a fight.

A terrorist? For God's sake.

'Help me get him dressed,' David says to Nurse Green. 'And you can take the rest of the day off,' he says to Dr Reed.

'The day off?' she repeats, holding out her palms in protest.

'Yes, I think that would be the best for everyone.'

David knows that she hasn't committed a dismissible offence, not in the eyes of the hospital authorities. In fact, they may well pat her on the back – which is no doubt why she's done this. A quick promotion. Maybe she's even after David's job. But for now, he's her supervisor and he wants her as far away from his patient as possible.

'What about Nurse Green?' Dr Reed says.

Nurse Green looks at Dr Reed with wide eyes; he'd trusted her too.

'Nurse Green is needed here,' David says. 'I'd like you to go. Now.'

Dr Reed looks at the police officers as if expecting them to come to her rescue, but they're busy filling out paperwork and talking on their phones.

She stumbles out of the cubicle and down the ward corridor.

David turns to Reg. 'It's all going to be okay.'

But Reg just looks at him, bewildered.

'Please get Reg's clothes, Nurse Green,' David says.

He nods and goes over to the cupboard.

They lift Reg to sitting and put on his shirt and jacket and then ease on his trousers. He feels limp as a rag doll.

And don't you give up either, David wants to tell him. *We're going to work this out, together.*

'A wheelchair, please,' David instructs Nurse Green.

If they're going to force this poor man out of bed and drag him to a police station, they're certainly not going to make him walk.

'We'll meet you round the back,' he says to the police officers. 'The last thing my patient needs is to be wheeled through a throng of reporters.'

'I'm afraid that's not possible,' the female police officer says. 'The car's at the front.'

Reg looks up, startled.

David puts his hand on Reg's shoulder. 'It'll be okay,' he says again.

Though, right now, nothing feels even close to okay.

The lift doors open and David wheels Reg out into the hospital lobby. Reg's hands are clamped to the arm rests, the bones of his knuckles pushing through his skin. The police officers walk in front of them. He feels Nurse Green by his side, sucking in his breath as he sees how many people are standing in the car park.

David takes off his glasses and rubs his eyes. When he puts them back on again, he looks out at the blur of faces. He feels dizzy.

There have been controversial cases at the hospital before which have attracted media attention. That's the nature of psychiatric wards. But David had managed to stay well away from them: had kept his head down, focused on his job and let management deal with it.

But this time it's different. They've come so far. He and Isabel are Reg's only hope.

Isabel and River would never forgive him if he let something happen to Reg. He wouldn't forgive himself.

When they get to the doors, he turns to Nurse Green. 'Thank you for your help. You'd better get back to your duties on the ward.'

'I could come with you?' he says. 'I'd like to help.'

'That won't be necessary, thank you.'

He bows his head. 'I'm sorry,' he mumbles.

'Your patients need you,' David says. 'Back to work.'

The nurse steps back.

David takes a deep breath. The police officers ask the security guy to open the doors, and he wheels Reg out under a blindingly grey sky.

Reg

Reg stares out of the car window and watches the world rush by. He's been here before, watching the world recede behind him, not knowing whether he'll ever be back.

He should have walked away when he had the chance. That was his intention when he left the zoo. He'd caused enough problems already. River and Isabel and Dr Deardorff and all the others who'd helped him didn't need any more trouble. But then, as he crossed the road outside the park gate, he saw her – and he hadn't been able to move.

And then River came and dragged him back to the hospital.

'It'll be all right,' Dr Deardorff whispers beside him.

The car radio crackles with news of incidents being handled by other police officers around London.

The female police officer is driving.

The man calls the station about preparing an interview room. 'We have him,' he says.

He remembers those words too. Maybe he is coming back to where he was meant to be all along.

Dr Deardorff is on his phone, talking to someone back at the hospital, explaining what happened. 'I'm sorry about all this,' he says. 'Yes, I'll make sure I sort it out.'

Reg closes his eyes and allows the sounds to wash over him. The traffic outside. The radio. Dr Deardorff talking into his phone. The rain beating against the windows of the car.

Yes, maybe this is where it was all meant to end.

The car brakes and his body jolts forward. The seatbelt digs into his chest. He feels the pressure of Dr Deardorff's body slamming against his.

He opens his eyes.

'Idiot!' the female officer says, thumping her hands on the steering wheel. 'Stopping like that without warning.'

She's cursing at a car in front of them.

'You all right?' Dr Deardorff asks, rubbing his neck.

He nods.

The woman unbuckles her seatbelt, gets out of the car and goes to talk to the driver in the car in front of them.

Reg looks through the open driver's door. He scans the gates of a park he recognises.

And that's when he sees them, standing in the rain.

River, jumping up and down, waving and pointing and tugging at Isabel's arm.

Isabel looks up, transparent against the grey sky, her palm held over her eyes to shield her face from the rain. She's looking right through him.

She doesn't belong to the earth, he thinks. She's more air than flesh, so light on the pavement she might fly away.

He raises his hand to wave back and then he remembers. They must not see him, not any more. They must not know where he is going. He has to keep them safe.

The policewoman settles back into the driving seat and slams shut her door.

'I've given them a caution,' she mumbles to her partner. And then she puts the car back into gear and they drive off.

Reg closes his eyes once more, forcing himself not to turn his head and look back to the place where River and Isabel were standing.

*

For a long time, Reg sits alone in the room with the steel table and chairs nailed to the floor.

Dr Deardorff is outside, still on his phone.

Footsteps along the corridor.

Voices.

The slamming of doors.

His body tenses at the familiarity of being in a place like this.

At last, the door swings open.

A man comes in wearing a navy pinstriped suit and shiny black shoes. He's carrying a briefcase. Beside him stands Mr Long, the hospital manager.

Dr Deardorff walks in behind them, rubbing his temples.

'Let's get you out of here,' the man with the briefcase says.

Reg looks up at Dr Deardorff. 'I don't understand.'

'Mr Long has petitioned for your bail.' The man puts his briefcase down on the table. 'There's a great deal we're going to have to sort out, but for now, they're letting you go.'

Reg doesn't understand why a hospital manager would want to help him.

'I don't have money for a lawyer,' he says.

'Dr Deardorff said he would take care of it.'

Reg stares at the man who has done so much for him already. And now he's spending money on him too. It's not right.

Reg sits back in his chair. 'I think it would be better for me to stay here,' he says.

The lawyer's eyes widen.

'What do you mean?' He turns to Dr Deardorff. 'Is he confused, or what?'

Dr Deardorff comes to sit next to Reg. 'I know this has been a very hard day, Reg. But we're here to help you.'

Reg shakes his head. 'I'm not confused. It's better for me to stay here.'

The three men stare at him blankly. Mr Long drums his fingers on the steel table like he's trying to work something out.

For a long time, no one says anything. Dr Deardorff sits back, takes off his glasses and rubs his eyes.

Then Reg hears light, rapid footsteps coming down the corridor.

'Reg!' River's voice comes through the open door of the interview room.

'You're not allowed back here.' He recognises the voice of the policewoman who brought him here.

River's voice again. 'He's my friend, I have to see him,' she says. 'And he hasn't done anything wrong! Reg! Reg! Are you there?'

He hears more footsteps.

The door to the interview room slams shut. He thinks of River standing behind the steel door, Isabel a few paces behind.

'It looks like someone wants you to come with us.' Dr Deardorff opens the door.

At the end of the corridor, Reg sees them, standing side by side, their eyes wide. Different as the two of them are, for a moment they look like one person.

Isabel strokes the back of River's hair in a long, slow rhythm.

Reg swallows hard. They shouldn't be here.

'We just want to talk to him,' River blurts out. 'Make sure he's okay.'

'That might not be advisable,' the lawyer says. 'Considering the news coverage. And the impact this has had on the hospital.'

Dr Deardorff stands up and walks past the lawyer. 'Of course you can talk to him, River.'

River

River sits between Mum and Reg in the back of Ash's car. It was Ash who drove them from the hospital to the police station.

She hasn't stopped holding Reg's hand since they found him; she's decided that she's not going to let him go ever again.

Reg's skin is clammy and he keeps trying to rub at the stain on his finger, like he did in those first days after they found him. Anger burns in River's throat: she doesn't understand why the police would do this to Reg. Aren't they meant to protect people?

Dr Deardorff said that Reg could stay with him while the lawyers and the police and everyone sorted things out, so Ash drives them all to his flat. Then Ash says he has to get back to his family. Which is weird – River had never thought of Ash having a family. But then everything about tonight is weird.

Mum, Reg and River follow Dr Deardorff through a big entrance lobby and into a lift. River keeps hold of Reg's hand the whole time.

As they step out of the lift, River yawns and rubs her eyes. And then she notices that someone's standing there with an umbrella and a small suitcase. He has large, dark-rimmed glasses and he looks tired.

'Who are you?' River asks, tilting her head to one side and examining him. She feels Reg's hand tense up in hers.

'It's okay,' she whispers to him. Though she isn't sure it is.

'Alex!' Dr Deardorff pushes past River and gives the man a hug and slaps him on the back. 'You came!'

That's weird too. Dr Deardorff doesn't hug people or slap them on the back or act this excited.

'Alex?' River asks. 'Who's Alex?'

Dr Deardorff turns round. 'Alex is an old university friend. He might just be able to help us.'

Isabel

Isabel stands in David's flat watching River, curled up, asleep next to Reg. It's nearly midnight, she should take River home, there's nothing more they can do here tonight. And yet she doesn't feel able to disturb the picture in front of her. River pressed up against him, like a small animal seeking comfort. His head is bowed over her, deep furrows in his brow. Pens and paper lie scattered around them. River carried them in her backpack and handed them to Reg as soon as they got to David's flat, as though she knew that this was the one thing he needed.

When she saw Reg at the police station, he looked grey with exhaustion. She was worried that those few hours had undone weeks of work. But with every moment that River sat beside him, Isabel felt Reg's mind and body settling again.

River. She'd refused to let it alone.

We can't just leave him, she had told Isabel as they stood on the pavement outside the park, watching the police car driving him away. *He'll be expecting us to help. He won't understand.*

And even though Isabel had told River, only an hour before, that she couldn't see Reg again, she knew River was right. They're as close a thing as he has to family right now.

God knows what he's been through in the last few hours.

As though he senses her watching him, Reg looks up, his face grey with exhaustion. He offers her a small smile. She thinks of that time when she went to see him in the middle of the night, how he'd encouraged her to draw him. How, in that moment, it felt like no one in the whole world existed but them.

Careful not to disturb River, he edges his body along the sofa, places his hand on the cushion beside him and waits for her to sit down.

As she sits beside him, she feels the warmth of his body next to hers.

'I like the outfit.' She smiles and nods at the flannel pyjamas David lent him: they're both too wide and too short on him. For a moment, she sees a small boy rather than a man.

Perhaps that's what happens when you lose any sense of who you are and where you're from, when the slate is wiped clean: you become a child again.

He blushes. And then his eyes cloud over. 'I'm sorry, Isabel. For all this. I've been such a burden.'

She puts her hand on his arm. 'You've made River happy, that's not a burden.'

He holds her gaze. 'You have both made me happy.'

Isabel isn't sure what happiness looks like for a man who's lost everything, but it makes her glad that she and River have helped in some small way.

Isabel hears Alex and David's muffled voices from the study. David is briefing Alex on the details of Reg's case. They've decided to interview Reg first thing in the morning. Alex has made it clear that he has to go back to his family in Hull tomorrow; he's booked a train for the end of the day. This, him being here to help with Reg, is a favour to David.

A linguistics specialist, that's what David called him, someone who would listen, not only to Reg's words but to the music of his voice – a music which might lead them back to where Reg comes from.

It all feels too simple, Isabel thinks, and too definite. What if Alex gets it wrong? And what if whatever it is he finds out turns out to be something none of them wants to know?

Like that he comes from so far away that they'll never see him again.

Like that the police are right and he's an illegal immigrant and could be deported?

Isabel knows that it's only been a few weeks, but Reg is the closest River has ever had to a father. It would break her heart to lose him.

She turns to Reg. 'I told River I didn't want her to see you any more.'

Reg nods gently.

'Why are you nodding?' She realises that she'd expected him to object. To talk her out of it, even.

'You're right.'

Isabel looks up. 'I am?'

'I would do the same.' He hesitates. 'If she were my child, I mean. I would protect her too.'

They hold each other's gaze again. And then, at the same moment, they look down at River, sleeping.

The point is, River is still here, next to Reg; Isabel wasn't able to keep her away from him.

'River didn't agree,' Isabel says. 'She thought it was her fault that you got arrested. I couldn't stop her going to you.'

When River saw Reg on the news, she ran straight out of the café. And she didn't stop running until she saw the police car outside the hospital.

'She refuses to let you go,' Isabel says. 'And you know River, she's stubborn.'

There's a pause. Then, his voice so quiet she nearly misses it, Reg says, 'And you?'

Isabel's cheeks grow hot. 'Me?' She laughs nervously. 'Yes, I suppose I'm stubborn too.'

'I meant, would it not be easier for you to let me go?'

'Easier?' *Easier?* she thinks. God no, not easier. She shakes her head. 'Wiser, perhaps, but not easier.'

He smiles at her and his eyes brighten for a moment.

Reg gently takes River's hand out of his and folds his fingers around Isabel's instead.

'Thank you,' he whispers.

She should pull away.

She should ask David to call a cab and take River home.

She should tell Reg that it's time to say goodbye, for good this time.

But instead, she lowers her head onto his shoulder and closes her eyes.

They sit like this for a while, listening to the traffic rushing past outside, to a pigeon cooing on the windowsill, to River's slow, deep breathing.

'Can I ask a question?' she says gently.

'Another one?' There's a smile in his voice.

She nods, her head brushing his shoulder.

He opens his palms in front of her, inviting the question.

'Are you very unhappy?' she asks.

He looks down into his palms.

'I have moments of great happiness. With you and River—'

'But on the whole – you're sad. I can see it.'

He nods slowly. 'Yes.'

'So this is my question: I don't understand how it's possible to be so sad – and not know what it is that makes you unhappy? I mean, if you don't remember, surely you shouldn't have those feelings?'

He looks up at her, his eyes wounded.

'That came out wrong,' she says quickly. 'I know that you can't remember, I just don't understand how it works.'

194

'I do not understand it either,' he says. 'But I feel it. Here.' He touches his heart. 'And here.' He moves his hand to his forehead. 'It is a knowledge I can't put into words, but it's there.' He pauses. 'And I know it's my fault.'

'Your fault?'

He nods. 'The sadness.'

'I'm sorry,' she says. 'For everything you're going through.'

He raises and lowers his shoulders in a light shrug as if to suggest that this is how it was always going to be. Then he takes her hand.

'So, tell me, Isabel, do you remember what made *you* unhappy?'

Isabel swallows, her throat thick.

'Was it River's father?'

She can't answer that. She doesn't know any more what it is that's made her sad all this time. Whether it was River's father, a man she spent a few hours with when she was too young to realise that she was changing the course of her life for ever – or the fact that she's spent years refusing to let it go, barricading herself in so that no one can get that close again.

'Was he your first love?'

My only love, she thinks. But she wouldn't ever say that out loud: it makes her feel foolish. That she's wasted so much. That she's hidden behind an idea of love that, if it existed at all, only lived for a few hours.

'What made you think he was my first love?' she asks.

'You are young to be River's mother.'

'Young?' Isabel feels a hundred years old. A hundred years of persuading herself not to fall in love again.

But of course she knows what he means about how young she was, back then. It's why her parents reacted so badly. And why she'd left home, abandoned her studies and moved to London with Jules. Jules knew that she could make more money from nannying in London, enough money to look after both of them.

She found them the flat above Gabino's, got Isabel the job interview at the hospital – *just until you get back on track*, she'd said.

Only, eleven years had gone by and there wasn't even a sign of Isabel getting back on track.

How had she let that happen? And why had it taken this stranger to make it so clear to her that she should have let go of the past?

She thinks about how, yesterday, she'd come close to calling her parents again and how things had felt like they were moving forward: she was putting hers and River's life back together again. And then all of this happened.

'How did you lose him?' Reg asks.

'We didn't really know each other.' Isabel lifts her head from his shoulder. She realises how strange this sounds. 'It was complicated.'

'I understand,' he says.

They catch each other's eye and she believes he does, in his own way.

Isabel looks out through the open window of the lounge and notices a pigeon sitting on the ledge. An old impulse shoots through her limbs, willing her to go over and shoo it away, but she stays sitting next to Reg and looks at the bird.

She wonders whether it's River's pigeon, the one who's always bothering them. It would be just like him to have followed River all the way here. Maybe that wretched, noisy bird keeps watch on her. That's how River would explain it.

The bird tilts its head to one side and stares at her with its small black eyes.

Does he recognise her? Is he thinking, *What on earth are you and River doing in this flat?*

Her head hurts. She shakes off the thought, blinks, and when she looks again, the pigeon is gone.

She keeps staring out of the window; the night sky is so dark, it's like it's sinking into itself.

'I was travelling in Italy,' Isabel says. 'The summer before university. In September, I was going to go home to train as a nurse. This was a last-minute holiday – my friend, Jules, got us a deal.'

'Venice?' Reg asks.

'Yes, Venice. Jules went off one night to find an Italian tattoo parlour – she has a tattoo from every place she's ever visited. It's her way of keeping memories, I suppose. Anyway, it was such a beautiful night that I decided to go for a walk. I kept walking for hours.'

Isabel feels like part of her is still that teenager, walking the streets of Venice, hoping she'll see his face again.

'You met him there?'

She nods. 'I got lost. So lost I couldn't find my way back to the hotel.'

If only she'd ignored him and kept walking. If only she hadn't let a stranger step into her life. But then there wouldn't have been River. And River was everything to her.

'He found you?'

'I suppose he did, yes.'

It all sounds like a terrible cliché now, but at the time, it had felt like the most surprising thing in the world. She was standing under a street lamp, studying her tourist map, her feet aching, and all of a sudden, there he was, ready to guide her back home.

River shifts in her sleep and rearranges her body until her limbs are spread across both Reg and Isabel.

'She never stops moving,' says Isabel. 'Even in her sleep.' She strokes her little girl's hair. 'She's been like that since the day she was born.'

'What happened then,' Reg asks. 'When he found you?'

'You ask a lot of questions,' she says.

He smiles. 'It feels good not to have to be answering them.'

It must have been terrible, all these days of being interrogated and feeling like you never had the right answer: like you were failing the test over and over, and that even if you did find an answer, it might not do you any good.

'He walked me home.' Isabel pauses. 'And I invited him up.'

Isabel remembers him walking behind her up the stone steps to the hotel room she shared with Jules – for a drink, she'd told him – a thank you for guiding her home.

She'd never done anything like that before. It felt like she was in a film: brave and impulsive and glamorous. She couldn't wait to tell Jules how her sensible best friend was letting her hair down at last.

'We talked all night. It was like we'd known each other for a lifetime – longer than a lifetime.'

She feels herself blush. Not that long ago, she'd talked to Reg too, at night, lying beside him in his hospital bed.

Is the feeling she has when she's with him as much of a fiction as the feeling she had that night in Venice? Or is this real? She has so little experience of love, she hardly knows.

'You fell in love,' Reg says gently.

'I thought I did.'

'You *thought* you did?' He smiles. 'The heart doesn't think.'

'I don't know any more. Like you said, I was so young.'

'And he left you?'

'Not exactly.'

Reg waits for her to continue.

'I never asked him to stay. There were so few words said between us. No promises. No expectations.'

She feels it again – how foolish it was to invest so much in those few hours, most of which they were asleep.

'But he left?' he says again.

She wishes she could find a way to explain that it wasn't like that. But then maybe it was. Maybe, this whole time, she's been justifying what he did because she wants to believe that what they had meant more than his actions suggested. And because she wanted to protect herself, and River, from getting things wrong again. From being impulsive and falling in love and turning their lives upside down. Because that's what love did – it took everything you thought was safe and familiar and threw it out of the window. And she couldn't afford for that to happen again.

'Yes,' Isabel says. 'When I woke up the next morning, he was gone.'

She remembers the sunlight falling through the shutters, lighting up the space beside her on the bed.

'I'm sorry,' Reg says.

'I suppose he was like River: didn't like to stay in one place for too long. Happier on the go. Or that's what I tell myself.'

'Did you look for him?'

'Not at first. He'd have stayed if he wanted to; going after him would have spoilt things.'

'And then?'

'I went back to England.' She pauses. 'To my parents.'

'And you found out you were carrying River.'

Carrying River. Yes, that was the right way to put it.

'I realised that I loved him, that I missed him. And then, a few weeks later, yes, I found out I was pregnant.'

Isabel wanted to be clear about this: she didn't love him or miss him *because* she was pregnant. She would have gone back to look for him, even if there hadn't been a River. Wouldn't she?

Maybe not. Maybe that too had been a fiction. How easy it is to deceive oneself, Isabel thinks. And how long it takes to admit to it.

'You said that you didn't look for him *at first*?'

'No, not at first. My parents were so disappointed in me. It was all so complicated. They wanted to know who the father was so that they could force him to take responsibility, to marry me – or even just to have someone to blame. And when that wasn't an option, they wanted me to terminate the pregnancy. They said that if I threw everything away on having a child, I'd regret it for the rest of my life.' Isabel pauses. 'They didn't understand.' She gulps, her throat tight, tears pushing into the backs of her eyes. 'River is the one thing I've done in my life that I don't regret.'

He rests his hand on hers. 'I understand.' She feels the warmth of his palm on her skin. 'So what did you do?' he asks.

'I moved to London. I pretended that I was going to do it all: have River and keep up with my studies. That I could make it work.' Isabel shakes her head. 'I didn't have a clue.' She pauses. 'Motherhood consumes everything.'

'I meant about the man you loved, River's father.'

Isabel looks back out of the window. The sky seems lighter. She wonders when the switch happens between night and dawn, the exact moment when one becomes the other.

'I never found him.'

Very gently, Reg takes her hand and kisses it. She holds his gaze and then leans in and kisses him, his lips as warm as his palm.

For a moment, everything goes still.

And then a voice rings through the flat.

'Hey – David, any chance of a coffee?'

Isabel and Reg pull apart.

River stirs beside them and starts rubbing her eyes.

'What's going on?' She looks from Isabel to Reg.

Isabel looks over and sees David's friend, Alex, by the study door. David stands a few paces in front of him. In his hands, David cradles a small package wrapped in tissue paper, the colours of the Italian flag. And he's staring right at her.

David

The next morning, David stands in front of the mirror behind his bedroom door and forces himself to look.

The mirror stares back at him, its surface too bright. He shifts his glasses down his nose and rubs his eyes so hard they feel raw.

It's his birthday today. Forty. And not a soul knows.

He thought he might have told her how he felt by now. That for some reason, by the time he turned forty, things would be different between them.

And instead, she'd brought him a stranger to look after, a man who didn't know his name or where he was from. Penniless. Lungs inflamed with pneumonia. And David had said yes, of course he'd help. Because he's never said no to her, not once.

And then she'd fallen in love with him, the stranger. Of course she had.

What an idiot.

David pushes his glasses back up his nose and refocuses his gaze on his reflection in the mirror. He decides it's time he made an inventory – faced the fleshy bulk of his body head-on. He starts at the bottom and moves his way up:

Flat, white feet.

Fleshy ankles.

Thick shins.

Dimpled knees. 'Dimple Dave' the boys would chant as he got into his PE kit at school. Dimples in his knees. Dimples in his knuckles. Dimples in his elbows. Dimples in his chubby cheeks.

Dense thighs, no daylight between them as he stands here.

A wobbly bulk of a stomach spilling over the band of his boxer shorts.

His chest, a fat casing of flesh.

Hairy, sloping shoulders.

Long, gorilla-awkward arms.

A short neck.

Too many chins.

A stub of a nose.

Thick lips, too pink for a man.

Sunken, grey eyes.

A high, bulbous forehead.

A receding hairline.

I'm a cartoon, he thinks.

His heart races. He wipes his brow with the back of his hand.

The full force of it hits him now: there's no hope.

He blinks and looks away.

You look reassuring, Norma had told him once. *That's why the patients love you so much.* She'd pinched a wad of fat at his waist. *That's why I love you.*

Norma, the kind, grey-haired waitress in the hospital café, working well past her retirement. A widow. A woman who would take him home in a heartbeat.

But *reassuring* wasn't a type that women fell in love with. Not women like Isabel, anyway.

David gulps down his breath. None of this matters any more, he thinks. No one need ever see him like this. At least there's some relief in that.

He puts on his white shirt and one of his grey suits and goes to the kitchen.

Alex looks up from the coffee machine.

'You okay, mate?' he asks.

David nods.

'Sure?' His eyebrows come together. 'You look, I don't know – kind of frayed.'

Frayed. Yes, that was a good word for how he felt. Loose threads trailing behind him, catching and pulling into big, gaping holes.

'I didn't sleep well,' David says.

'Too much excitement, eh?' Alex smiles.

'Something like that,' David says.

Alex, as oblivious as ever to the lives of everyone but his own. He could pin down a person's accent to within a mile of their hometown and yet he couldn't see that his friend's heart had been broken right in front of his eyes. Too much time had passed between them.

Alex sits down and holds up a box of Coco Pops. 'Okay to help myself?'

David nods.

As Alex pours himself a bowl of cereal, he shakes his head and smiles.

'I looked through your cupboards,' he said. 'You still eat like a kid.'

David shrugs. When Isabel had walked into the flat yesterday, he'd thought of clearing out the whole place. He'd thought of a million things he'd do to make the place more welcoming. He'd allowed himself, for a second, to entertain the thought that she might help him – that they could make this their home.

But none of that matters now.

'Want some?' Alex asks, a mouth full of soggy, milky-brown cereal.

David shakes his head and mumbles, 'Not hungry.'

'*Not hungry*, seriously?'

David presses his fingers to his temples. He needs to get out of here.

Alex jerks his head towards the bathroom door. 'Reg is having a shower. We'll get to work as soon as he's ready.'

The sound of rushing water comes through the bathroom door.

'I'm going out,' David says.

'Out? Where?'

'To work.'

'I thought you'd want to stay – that you were desperate to find out where Reg was from?'

He can't stay here, not today.

'I'm needed at the hospital.' David walks to the front door. 'Call me when you have a result.' He shoves his feet into his shoes without bothering to open the laces. He hesitates and turns round. 'Thanks for doing this, Alex. I'll make it up to you, I promise.'

'You sure you're okay?' Alex asks.

The shower in the bathroom stops running. Any minute now, Reg will step out, and then David will have to look at him. And remember last night.

'I'm fine,' David says and disappears into the hallway.

David stands on the pavement, shielding his eyes from the glare of the sun.

Why, today of all days, does it have to be so damn bright? Why can't it be raining like it has been every other day this summer?

There's a cooing at his feet. He looks down at a pigeon strutting around in front of him. The pigeon comes to a stop, flaps its wings, settles into its fat body and looks up at David.

He tries to shoo him away with his foot.

The pigeon stumbles back, startled, but then regains his footing, fluffs up his feathers and looks up at him again.

'Sorry, mate, I don't have anything for you.'

The pigeon cocks his head to one side, one black, beady eye fixed on David. A shaft of light falls on his breast and lights up his feathers, green and blue, like an oil slick. He thinks of the pictures River's been drawing. She's right – there's a whole load of colours in those feathers besides grey. Reg had helped her to see that; of course Isabel would fall in love with him.

David kneels down and strokes the pigeon's back. The pigeon flinches a little but doesn't move.

On the Tube, David gets lost in the rhythm of the train. Today, he doesn't care about the bodies pressing into his or about armpits and sweat and people treading on his feet. He just stands there, watching the stations come and go.

Then, he walks up the escalators until he's back under a bright sky.

And then he heads to the hospital.

Norma stands at the door of the Get Well Soon Café and grins at him, holding out a small plate with a chocolate muffin. She's stuck a birthday candle in the middle.

Of course Norma remembered, she has a chart up in her kitchen to help her remember the birthday of every doctor and nurse and cleaner in her wing of the hospital. *It's the little things that make you want to keep living*, she'd said to him once. And he'd realised that, even though her husband had been gone for five years, she was still learning to put one foot in front of the other without him at her side. *At least I've been spared that kind of love*, thinks David.

'Thank you, Norma,' he says, taking the plate.

She leans in and gives him a kiss on the cheek. Then she stands back and waits.

'Go on then,' she says. 'Blow out the candle – and don't forget to make a wish.'

He blows hard but doesn't wish, he's done with wishing.

They both cough at the acrid smoke that rises from the candle.

Norma waves away the smoke and says, 'Asked her yet?'

David shakes his head.

Only three people know about his feelings for Isabel. He's only actually told two: his mum and Milek from the post office, mainly because they're unlikely to ever tell Isabel. Norma worked it out all by herself.

'Well, maybe today would be a good day.' She smiles.

He wants to tell her that there's no point putting any more energy into hoping that he and Isabel will get together. Last night put an end to any crazy idea he ever had about them being together.

She frowns. 'You feeling okay, Dr Deardorff?'

He forces a smile. 'I'm fine, Norma, thank you.'

She keeps frowning and he can feel her eyes on him as he walks away from her, balancing the muffin on the plate.

When he gets to the neurology ward, he pulls the candle out of the muffin and puts it on the table in the staff room. Someone will eat it.

Then he stands in the corridor, watching.

Nurses rush by, patients sit propped up in their beds, having their breakfasts. An old woman with yellow hair lies in the bed that Reg occupied until just a few hours ago.

And then he hears her: the squeak of her trolley at the far end of the corridor; her light, plimsolled tread.

Taking a step to the side, he presses himself against the wall, longing to be invisible.

After such a late night, he hadn't thought she'd be here. But then Isabel's always here.

She's talking to Ash; there's laughter in her voice and her head is thrown back. Light from a window haloes her hair.

She's happy, David thinks. For the first time since he can remember, Isabel looks really happy.

Blood rushes in his ears.

'David?' A slap on the back. 'What are you doing here?'

Long's voice is so loud that, in the periphery of his vision, David notices Isabel and Ash looking up.

And behind him, he sees Dr Reed leaning over a patient. So they let her come back.

'Maybe you should take a holiday,' Long says. 'You're over-due.'

He's standing too close.

David steps back and says, 'I don't need a holiday.'

'I wasn't really asking, David.' He gives him a forced smile.

'Excuse me?'

'You've just been at the heart of a major news story, a story that's already done the hospital trust a great deal of damage.' He leans in. 'You need to lie low for a while.'

Everyone on the ward is staring now. Most of all, David can feel Isabel's eyes on him.

'I was putting my patient first,' David says. 'That's my job.'

'He might be an illegal immigrant—'

'We don't know that.'

Long sighs and puts his hand on David's arm. 'You look tired. Take a few days.'

The hand on his arm tightens to a grip and David realises that this is a last warning: that he's being told to leave the only place where he knows how to function.

He looks at Long for a moment and considers challenging him. *You need to speak up more*, his father used to say when he was a child. *You won't get anywhere in life by staying quiet*. When his father got stabbed doing exactly what he'd tried to drill into David – speaking up – David had allowed himself to keep quiet. And he had got somewhere in life – wasn't he a doctor?

But maybe his father was right. Perhaps if he had spoken up more he'd have told Isabel how he felt by now, and he'd be able to hang onto this job.

'Good man.' The manager slaps him again, this time on the chest. David feels the vibration through his whole body. 'I knew you'd understand.'

Before David has the chance to say anything, Mr Long is walking away from him down the corridor.

David bows his head and goes over to the lift.

'David?'

He feels her hand.

'David – you okay?' She's out of breath.

He turns round and, for a second, he looks right into her blue, dancing eyes. Yes, she's happy. Of course she is.

Slowly, David nods. 'I'm fine, Isabel,' he says. 'Just fine.'

The lift pings, the doors open and he steps inside, hoping that this small, metal cave will close and swallow him up.

David sits next to his mother, a packet of Jammie Dodgers between them.

'You're back from school early today,' she says.

'Yes.'

A weight presses down on his chest. He knows she can't

remember – that he shouldn't expect her to – but there's something about a mother not knowing that today is the day she gave birth to her only child that strikes him as unbearably sad.

'Maybe you could go out and play with the other boys for a bit – while it's still light?' she says.

He nods.

Through the window of his mother's small nursing room, he sees an old man sitting on a bench.

He thinks of the place where River and Isabel found Reg. Maybe if he found a bench somewhere and sat there and waited for the rain to drench him, for a beard to grow, for his clothes to fray, maybe if he waited long enough for his mind to dissolve, maybe then someone would notice him.

He nearly laughs out loud: an illegal immigrant with amnesia has more of a chance with Isabel than he does.

'I've got to go, Mum,' he says, standing up.

'Have fun,' she says.

He kisses the top of her head. 'I will.'

He's lost count of the number of times he's been tempted to walk her home. He wanted to know everything about her, to learn the route she and River took through the park each morning. To see the road she walked along every day, the building she lived in, the colour of her front door, the Italian restaurant with the bad food and the grumpy owner that River joked about.

He's grown fond of River, the little girl who dresses like a rainbow. David realises he's never articulated these ideas to himself before, not so precisely anyway, but it's what he's felt all along: he'd actually believed that, one day, they could be a family.

He remembers the first time he saw them: they were running hand in hand across the road in front of the hospital. It was raining then too, but it didn't seem to bother them. At first, he'd thought they were both children, Isabel barely taller than her little girl.

The next day, he found Isabel mopping the floor in the gents. *I'm nearly done in here*, she'd said. *I'll be out in a minute.* He remembers thinking, right at that moment, that he didn't want her to go anywhere. *I want you to stay*, he'd thought. *Now. Always. Right here, with me.*

David looks up at the flickering red, white and green sign: *Gabino's.*

Every time David had felt the urge to come here, he talked himself out of it. He thought about what she'd see: a big, clumsy, lumbering man, standing outside her bedroom window. In his head, he was Romeo. But that's not what she'd see. She'd think that the man she'd come to trust was in fact a stalker. She'd call the police and then put in a complaint at the hospital.

So, time and again, he talked himself out of coming here. It was best to keep their lives beyond the hospital separate.

But now there was nothing left to lose. Not a job. Not her.

David takes the silk scarf out of his jacket pocket and lets the cool fabric fall between his fingers. It's how he imagined Isabel's skin would feel if he touched it.

Sitting on his bed late last night, he'd opened the package, knowing that he would never give it to her now. Italian silk, cornflower blue to go with her eyes.

What a fool, he thinks, and shoves the silk scarf back in his pocket. His stomach groans; he can't remember the last time he's gone so long without eating.

Damn it, he thinks, *I'm hungry. And if there's one thing that's never let me down, it's food.*

He walks into the restaurant.

*

'The Full Italio-English, please.' David reads from the laminated menu.

Beans, chips, Italian sausage, fried eggs.

He thinks about what River said the other day: *Something Italian ... But proper Italian – not like microwaved or deep-fried Italian.*

He gets it now.

As he pictures the greasy food on his plate he thinks about his dimply knees and his big belly, but he shrugs off the thought. *None of it matters now*, he says to himself again.

The man, who must be the restaurant owner, the infamous Grumpy Gabs, scribbles the order on the back of an envelope.

The television blares behind them.

'To drink?' Gabs asks.

'Filter coffee. With sugar.' He takes a breath. 'And cream.'

The man nods.

When Gabs disappears behind the counter, David looks around.

There's no one else in the restaurant. Faded black and white film posters cover the walls: *Cinema Paradiso. Il Postino. La Dolce Vita.* The place smells of old cooking oil. The laminated floor curls in the corners. The only redeeming feature about Gabino's is that it's spotless: no trails of grease on the checked oil-clothed table; no crumbs or coffee stains or clumps of dust under the heaters.

The door swings open. River skips in, holding the hand of the little girl called Nula. Nula's sobbing, her cheeks red and tear-stained. Behind her, the nanny, Isabel's best friend, shoves her three-seater pushchair over the step, cursing.

'Dr Deardorff!' River cries. 'You're here!'

He'd thought he could avoid them, that River would be

out having fun somewhere. Isabel at work. That he could just sit here a while, in the place Isabel called home, and then disappear.

At that moment, Gabino comes out carrying an enormous plate, dripping with fried food.

'Hi, Gabs!' River cries.

Gabino looks at her, nods, grunts, and puts the plate down in front of David.

Nula, the little girl, tugs at River's rainbow dress. She's still sniffing. David notices that her tights are torn open at the knees and that a flower of blood has spread on the pink fabric.

'She fell in the park,' River says. 'I'm going to take her upstairs and find her a plaster.'

David kneels down in front of Nula and holds her knee. 'It looks like you took quite a tumble.'

Nula sniffs and nods.

'She's fine,' Jules says, coming up behind them. She grabs a soggy chip off David's plate. 'You need to cook these longer, Gabs!' she calls over to the bar. 'And make the oil hotter.' She takes another bite. 'And they're still frozen inside. Christ, Gabs, a soggy *and* frozen chip, how do you do it?'

'Jules grew up in a pub – her mum ran the bar,' River whispers. 'So she's an expert chip-maker.'

Expert chip-maker, he likes that.

'Ach! Mind your own business.' Gabino swats her words away and disappears into the kitchen.

Then it comes back to him: Jules.

David stands up and holds out his hand. 'Nice to meet you again, Jules.'

Jules blushes. Then she takes his hand.

He notices a small bird, like a sparrow, on the inside of her arm. The weight that's been pressing down on his chest ever since he visited his mother lifts for a moment.

'You're staring again,' Jules says.

'I'm sorry.' He looks her in the eye. 'I have a tattoo,' David says. Then he realises that she's the first person in the world he's admitted this to.

'You *WHAT*?' River's eyes pop. 'Show me!'

David takes off his grey blazer and rolls up his shirtsleeves. On the inside of his flabby white bicep there's a smudged tattoo. It's a jagged green line, surrounded by a black frame. A heart monitor.

Jules looks closer and squints. 'Weird.'

'Initiation rites. Med school. I woke up with it one morning with no memory whatsoever as to how it got there.'

'Wow, they still do that stuff?' Jules asks.

'Well, they did. It was a long time ago.'

'I would've beat the shit out of anyone that did that to me,' Jules says.

Thinking back to the medical students at Hull, he smiles: she'd probably have been able to take them on.

'Jules only pretends to be scary,' River says. 'She's a softie inside, aren't you, Jules?'

Jules rolls her eyes. 'I need a cigarette.' She rifles through her bag and, oddly, pulls out a bag of Haribo. 'Will you watch them, River?' She nods at the triplets and starts shoving the sweets into her mouth.

River nods. 'Dr Deardorff will help me. And he can put a plaster on Nula's knee too.'

'Sure,' Jules says, already striding out through the door.

There's something solid about her, he thinks. Bold. Rooted. He likes it.

'Does she smoke?' David asks River.

'No. She used to. Now she eats sweets instead – and goes for walks, to make the craving go away.'

'Sounds like a good plan.'

'Yeah. She said she had to quit otherwise she'd get lung cancer and that couldn't happen because she needs to look after me and Mum.'

'She's a good person,' David says.

'Yeah. Like I said – she's a softie underneath.' River looks across the restaurant. 'Right, let's go upstairs,' River says. 'You carry Millie and Maisie,' she starts to unstrap the babies from the buggy. 'I'll take Mabel and Nula.'

Before he has time to protest, River's thrust two babies into his arms and is guiding him up the narrow back stairs to the flat she shares with Isabel.

'What about your breakfast?' Gabino calls after him, gruffly. 'It's going to go cold.'

He thinks about making a joke about the frozen chips. If Jules had been here, maybe he would have. But then he feels sorry for the grumpy Italian man.

'You can wrap it up for me. I'll take it home.'

Gabino grunts and then plods away.

Reg

Reg stands in the shower cubicle, water crashing over his shoulders and down his back. He's so tired he hardly has the strength to stand up. And his knee's throbbing again.

All night he kept trying to picture Isabel's face. He could feel the individual parts: her blue eyes, her hair like feathers, brushing his skin – the lips he kissed. But whenever he tried to see her whole, she slipped away from him.

She felt like someone that he'd kissed a thousand times. And like someone completely new too. How could those two things be possible at once?

He's scared that the sea is coming again and that it will wash everything away, not just what came before but all the good things that he's stored up these last few weeks.

When he kissed her, he felt like he'd reached some kind of home that he'd been searching for for months. For a moment, he didn't feel so alone.

But at the same time, he knew he should pull back, that by holding her so close, he was hurting her in some way.

His throat tightens. His ears fill with the sound of crashing water.

The sea keeps rising.

He sits down in the cubicle, drops his head over his bent knees and clamps his hands over his ears.

A fist bashes on the bathroom door.

Sparks fly behind his eyelids.

There's too much noise.

More bashing. The shower cubicle shakes from the force of it.

'Hey, mate – you okay in there?'

A muffled voice comes through the door. Alex, Dr Deardorff's friend.

'You've been in there for a while,' Alex goes on.

Reg presses his hands harder over his ears. Why is everything so loud?

'You okay?' Alex asks again.

He opens his mouth to speak but his voice is stuck somewhere deep in his body. Maybe he's forgotten how to form words. Maybe that would be easier, he thinks, not to be able to say anything ever again.

'Reg?'

'I'm . . . ' he croaks. 'I'm fine.' He pulls himself up and fumbles at the button to turn off the water. 'I'll be out in a minute.'

'Cool – I'll just be out here. Whenever you're ready.'

He's going to help you remember, River said, late last night just before she and Isabel left. *I hate tests too*, she'd whispered. *But you'll be just fine, I know you will.*

So this meeting, with Dr Deardorff's friend, was a test.

The problem is, he hasn't got a clue what passing the test looks like – or whether getting the answers right is a good thing.

What if, after all of Alex's questions, after he's examined the shape of his vowels and consonants, his pronunciation and into-nation, his word choices, he uncovers what Reg has suspected all along? That he's done something wrong, terribly wrong. That the police should have kept him locked up.

He has to get out of this flat and be alone again, then he won't be able to hurt anyone any more.

He looks down at his hands.

He picks up a piece of soap from the holder on the wall and rubs at the ink stain on his finger; he keeps rubbing until his skin goes raw and red.

He's shivering now. Goosebumps rise along his arms and his hair drips down his face.

He closes his eyes and tries to still his mind.

Dr Deardorff's friend will help you, Isabel said before she took River home last night. *You don't need to worry.*

Another bash on the door, followed by Alex's voice:

'Coffee's ready.'

Reg steps out of the shower cubicle and looks at himself in the steamed-up bathroom mirror, the outline of his face barely discernible in the mist.

He doesn't remember where his clothes are so he puts the pyjamas David lent him back on and steps out into the flat.

Alex is sitting on the sofa, his head bent over his laptop. No one else seems to be here.

On the other side of the room, the television is on. A presenter sits behind a desk, looking into the camera.

The migrant crisis has reached new heights ... In the light of Brexit, borders into the UK are bound to be tightened ... There are more people on the seas than ever. The Mediterranean. The Channel. Unprecedented risks are being taken.

Reg holds onto the doorframe of the bathroom to steady himself.

He closes his eyes.

And a picture flashes in front of him: it's of the girl again, with the long plait hung over her shoulder. She's got her back turned to him so he can't see her face, but he knows it's her. And she's walking away.

He reaches out and grasps at thin air.

A moment later Alex is at his side, grabbing his arm and steadying him.

'You okay?'

Reg opens his eyes and stares at Alex.

He has to get to her, quickly, and he has to get away from these people.

'You're not going to pass out on me, are you?' Alex laughs nervously.

Reg shakes his head, but he's not sure. His head feels light, his legs like they're going to buckle.

The voices keep blaring out from the television. He raises his hands to his ears, but the words still come through.

Why would people leave their home, if it weren't for a better life?

'Oh Christ – I'm sorry.'

Alex spins round, looking for something, then he grabs the television controller from the coffee table and switches it off.

'So used to having the news on, I don't even hear it any more,' Alex says.

Slowly, Reg takes his hands from his ears.

'I thought we'd make it casual, start with a chat . . . ' Alex says. 'Why don't you join me on the sofa? We can start with some easy questions.' Alex holds his hand out to the place where, only a few hours ago, Reg sat with Isabel and River.

The voices from the television still ring in his head.

Alex pats the seat beside him.

Reg sits beside Alex and looks down into his palms.

Alex puts a hand on his shoulder. 'You ready for this?'

'I'm a little tired.'

'What, David's old couch didn't work its magic?'

Reg looks at him blankly.

'Not one for small talk, eh, Reg?' Alex slaps him on the back.

Reg coughs. Then he asks, 'Where's Dr Deardorff?'

'David's gone out for a bit,' Alex says. 'Here, have some coffee, it will wake you up a bit.'

Alex places a mug of steaming black coffee in Reg's hands and then reaches for his laptop, flips open the lid and opens a new screen.

'Okay if I ask you some questions now?'

Reg nods.

'Good.'

Reg notices a tremor in his fingers; he's worried he's going to drop the mug. He clenches his hands together and looks back at the front door. *I have to find her,* he tells himself. *She's been waiting for me this whole time.*

Alex starts speaking. The questions crash into each other:

'Are there any words you find yourself repeating? Are there times when you feel like no one understands what you're saying – any words in particular? Could you give me a description of a place you've visited in London? Could you say this sentence very slowly . . . ?'

Alex stops speaking.

'Reg – are you listening?'

Reg nods but he keeps staring at the door.

Alex tilts the screen towards Reg. 'Okay, here, let's start with this.' He clicks on a sound file. 'Have you met anyone here whose voice sounds similar?'

He opens some more screens. Images flash up in front of them.

Reg interrupts. 'You know already, don't you?'

Alex looks up. 'Know what?'

'Where I'm from. You don't need to do these tests. You've been listening to me since last night and Dr Deardorff sent you the recordings he took of my voice. You're an expert.' Reg pauses. 'So you know.'

Maybe he can help me find her, thinks Reg. *If he knows enough.*

Alex shakes his head. 'I don't like guesswork. I'm on the scientific end of the linguistics field: I like to gather hard evidence before drawing conclusions. Yours is a complicated case.' He threads his fingers through his hair and avoids Reg's gaze. 'I'm not sure it's helpful to speculate.'

'But you know.' Reg stares at Alex, waiting for an answer.

Alex scratches his chin. 'Dr Deardorff said to take things slowly. You've been through a lot.'

'I want you to tell me.'

Alex sits back and sighs.

'I suppose it's your choice.'

Reg nods, waiting for him to go on.

'My guess? A border town in Eastern Europe. There are several influences in your voice – they'll take a while to untangle.'

'A border?' Reg asks.

Alex nods. 'Probably.'

Borders, thinks Reg. The seams of countries that don't belong either to one side or to another. Nowhere places for people like him. Yes, that would make sense.

Alex looks back at his computer. 'I think we should continue with the questions.' He angles the screen towards Reg. 'I'm going to play some sound clips of people speaking in different languages. Tell me if one of them resonates.'

Reg tries to concentrate but the voices blur into one.

He can't stay here any longer.

He covers his ears with his hands and shuts his eyes.

'Reg?' Alex's voice comes to him from what feels like a thousand miles away. 'Reg – everything okay?'

The water laps over his feet. It's coming up over his ankles, his shins, above his knees.

He has to get to her.

'Reg?'

He feels Alex's hand on his arm.

'Let's take a break,' Alex says.

Reg opens his eyes. It's so bright in the room that he struggles to keep them open. He stares through the window of David's lounge. The flat is so high up that all he can see is sky. It's blue for once, not a cloud. He hears the low coo of a pigeon from under the roof.

'I shouldn't have . . . ' Reg starts. 'I shouldn't have left.'

'Left? Where?' Alex asks.

Reg keeps shaking his head.

Alex rubs his back. 'Maybe all this was too soon. None of this is your fault, Reg. And we want to help you – if you'll let us.'

Reg screws shut his eyes. Of course it's his fault. Everything's his fault. He doesn't deserve their help, not Isabel's or River's or David's or Alex's. He's got distracted. He was meant to wait for her, at the entrance to London Zoo. And if she didn't come, he was meant to go looking for her.

'Why don't you take a moment,' Alex says. 'Then we can have another go, a little more slowly this time.'

Reg nods, still not opening his eyes.

Reg hears Alex stand up, gather the mugs, and walk into the kitchen. More footsteps and then the bathroom door slams shut.

He puts his hand in his pocket, reaches for the elephant charm, and turns it round between his fingers.

When you're feeling better, we'll go to see the elephants at Whipsnade, River promised him. *It's not far. We can take the train. Or Jules can drive us.*

His heart feels heavy.

He looks back down at Alex's computer screen and clicks through the pages.

If Alex knows where he comes from, then he must have done some research – and made some notes.

A picture flashes up in front of him. It's from a newspaper, a pen and ink drawing of an elephant, his feet bound, his ears stitched shut, a blindfold over his eyes.

His throat goes dry. He swallows so hard his eyes water. He blinks and looks again.

It's the picture he drew for River.

And there's a headshot beside it, the artist who drew it.

His hands shake.

Cold sweat runs down his back.

His breath goes shallow.

He has to get out of this flat. He's not meant to be here.

He stands up and walks to the bathroom door. Alex is humming, then the sound of a tap running, of water in the pipes, so loud, it's like the water is running down the walls.

And that's when it hits him.

I'm going to find you, he whispers to himself, realising that he's been looking in the wrong place all this time.

The sea, that's where she was. She wouldn't have been able to get any further, not without him.

He stumbles to the front door, reaches for the nearest coat, pushes his feet into his shoes and walks out into the hallway.

*

223

'How's it going?'

The security guard's voice follows him as he walks out through the glass doors of the lobby.

He pretends not to hear.

He stops on the pavement for a moment. Sharp pain stabs at his knee. He's forgotten his stick upstairs. Looking down, he realises that he's still wearing David's pyjamas and that he's taken David's raincoat.

But he can't go back.

The morning air washes over him; he breathes in and fills his lungs.

Cars rush past him.

'Watch where you're standing.' A woman with too many bags swings past him.

'Sorry . . . ' Reg stumbles back. 'I'm so sorry . . . '

The woman stops for a second and looks down at his raincoat; Reg realises that the hems of David's pyjamas are poking out.

She shakes her head and turns her back on him.

And then he starts walking.

Isabel

'If you check that clock one more time it's going to fall off the wall.' Ash grins at Isabel.

'I shouldn't have told you.' Isabel's cheeks burn.

'Just be careful,' Ash says, pulling his Henry vacuum cleaner behind him.

She didn't expect this from Ash. Ash is a throw-caution-to-the-wind kind of guy, which is the reason she told him rather than Jules, who would have rolled her eyes like she does every time Isabel mentions Reg. Not because she has anything against Reg, but because she knows Isabel. She can hear Jules's voice, loud and clear: *Look at yourself, Isabel, you've spent over a decade pining after a ghost and now you're falling in love with an amnesiac illegal immigrant?*

'Be careful? You're the one who's always telling me to go out on dates. To take more risks . . . '

'This one's complicated,' Ash says.

Of course Ash knows all about Reg. He watched him lying in that hospital bed, and, just like everyone else, he wondered who he was and where he was from and why he'd forgotten even his name. And he saw what happened when the newspapers got hold of his story. And the police.

And Ash is right, just like Jules is right: by even giving the kiss a second thought, Isabel is risking having her heart broken by a man who, at any moment, could disappear from her life.

But Isabel's not ready to hear the lecture, not yet. She wants this feeling – her whole body being on springs, her heart light as air – to keep going, just for a little longer.

'It might not mean anything,' Isabel says.

'A kiss never means nothing,' Ash says.

'No, I guess not.'

Ash is right. She thinks about how David stared at them last night, and the heavy silence that followed.

'Which is why you're going to speak to him, right?' Ash says. 'Sort all this out?'

'Right.'

'Good.'

It's what she'd been debating in her head all day. Whether she should just let last night go, wait to see what happens – how Reg behaves when they next meet – or whether she should confront Reg head on.

Ash leans over his trolley. 'So run it by me again: did he kiss you or did you kiss him?'

Isabel plays the events of last night back through her mind. She was tired, it was late, they were sitting so close on that sofa – she doesn't even remember who leaned in first.

'I'm not sure.'

Ash raises his eyebrows.

'Okay – I think it was me.'

'You think?'

'It wasn't that clear cut.'

Ash widens his eyes. 'You sure?'

'Whatever happens, he kissed me back, so we kissed each other. That's what matters, isn't it – more than who started it?' Though now Ash has put the thought in her head Isabel's beginning to wonder whether maybe she dreamt that he kissed her back. It was all over so quickly. If David hadn't interrupted them – if River hadn't woken up – would Reg have pulled away?

Or maybe the kiss was part of his amnesia, maybe he forgot, for a moment, who she was and who he was kissing.

Or maybe he was just overwhelmed by the events of the day.

The more she thinks about it, the more Isabel realises that, whatever happened last night, it was a mistake, a stupid mistake.

'I'll sort it out,' Isabel says.

She checks the clock again and watches the hands click to 5 p.m.

'At last.' She sighs. 'Will you put away my trolley?'

'Sure.'

She kisses Ash on the cheek. 'You're the best.'

'Yeah, yeah.' He grins. 'Just let me know what happens.'

She gives him a wave and, as she heads to the cleaners' locker room to grab her things, she sends Jules a text.

Could you keep River until 6?

Why? Jules texts back – too fast. She knows something's up.

Isabel mentally crosses her fingers behind her back and taps a reply into her phone:

Extra shift at the hospital. Won't be long.

Jules responds:

Left River with Dave back home. She said she wanted to stay with him. Thought you'd be okay with that.

Dave? Isabel replies.

Your doctor friend, Jules texts back.

David? Since when was he called Dave?

And then it hits her: Isabel left River with David, David who saw the kiss last night. What's he doing at their flat?

Sweat gathers along her hairline. Would he say anything to River about the kiss? At first, Isabel was worried that River had seen the kiss, but she never mentioned it.

Isabel puts away her phone.

And why isn't David with Reg? Reg was meant to have his interview with Alex today and David was going to give him moral support; he was worried that the interview would stir up all kinds of emotions that could upset him. David never leaves his patients when they need him.

She bats away all the questions and focuses on what she originally set out to do: to go and speak to Reg and find out what really happened between them last night.

Isabel slips her bag over her shoulder and heads towards the lifts.

'Isabel!'

She freezes. It's Simon.

Isabel turns around slowly.

'Heading home?' he asks.

She nods.

'I need you to do one last job,' he says.

'I have to pick River up.'

'Call your child minder.'

'Excuse me?'

'I need you to give Mr Long's office an extra polish.'

'It's on the schedule for tomorrow.'

'I said an *extra* polish. After what happened yesterday, we have to keep him happy. He's been to see me about your involvement.' Simon straightens his horrible, shiny purple tie. 'I've been asked to keep a closer eye on my cleaners.'

A *closer* eye? Isabel shudders.

'It's my duty to know what my cleaners are up to.'

Isabel had wondered when Simon would catch wind of what happened. And when he'd learn that she was involved – and then blame her. And she knows that he couldn't care less about Reg or her involvement with him – what he cares about is that she made him look bad. And that he was out of the loop.

'I'm not "up to" anything.'

He looks at her and blinks.

'Mr Long's been talking about staffing cuts. The budget needs a trim.' Simon snips the air with pretend scissors. 'We don't want him making any rash decisions.'

'You can't afford to lose me,' Isabel says under her breath.

'What was that?'

'Nothing.'

'Nothing?'

'I'll get right to it,' Isabel says.

'Good, good.' Simon turns on his heel and walks back down the corridor.

Isabel looks at her watch. If she doesn't hurry, she'll run out of time to go and speak to Reg before needing to be back at the flat. She goes to the cleaning cupboard, fills a bucket with a few basic products, and heads to the management suite.

She lets herself into Mr Long's office, empties the bins, polishes the desk, tidies his papers, gives the computer screen a wipe, rearranges the cushions on his sofa, picks up a few stray bits of fluff off the floor and takes the back stairs out of the hospital.

Within fifteen minutes she's in a cab heading to David's flat.

Isabel never takes cabs. Not when it's pouring with rain. Not even when her feet are killing her after a long shift at the hospital and River's moaning about the long walk home. Not even in emergencies. A short cab ride through London eats up a week's grocery budget.

But today's different.

Only, she hadn't banked on rush hour traffic. Or the taximeter shooting up as they sit in a queue.

'How much longer will it take?' Her voice wobbles, she's losing her nerve.

The taxi driver shrugs. He shifts his piece of gum to the side of his mouth. 'No telling with this traffic.'

She doesn't have time for this. She thrusts a ten-pound note at the driver: 'I'll walk from here.'

She opens the door and steps out onto the pavement.

'Hey!' he calls after her.

But she doesn't turn round. She has to get to David's flat.

Isabel stands at the security desk at the bottom of David's apartment block, red-faced and out of breath.

'You been for a jog?' The security guy smiles.

She shakes her head and prepares herself for another delay. What reason could she possibly give this guy for letting her go up to David's flat when he's not here?

'I'm ... I'm ...'

'Isabel.' He smiles. 'He's gone out for a while but his friend's still up there. You can go on up.'

'You know who I am?'

He winks. 'Sure I do, you were here last night.'

Thank God. One hurdle dodged. After a day like today, she deserves a break.

'And he talks about you,' he calls after her.

She stops walking but doesn't turn round.

'He's a good guy. You should give him a chance,' the security man adds.

Isabel can't take this in. She's holding enough in her head already.

She takes the lift to David's flat. The door is open a crack, so she lets herself in. Reg's stick stands propped against the wall, where he left it last night.

'Hello?' she calls out.

No one answers.

'Anyone home?' she calls out again.

She walks into the lounge and finds Alex sitting on the couch, his head in his hands. When he hears her walk in, he stands up. His skin looks grey. He clenches and unclenches his fingers.

Isabel's heart thumps. The flat feels too empty.

'Alex – where's Reg?'

Alex shakes his head.

She steps forward and holds out her hands. 'Alex? What is it?'

Alex keeps shaking his head. 'I'm sorry . . .'

'Sorry about what?'

He looks up at her, his skin pale, his eyes glassy.

'He left.' He holds out his hands. 'He just left.'

River

'You sure you're okay – you look like you're over-heating.' River stares at the beads of sweat shooting down Dr Deardorff's brow.

River and Dr Deardorff have been walking for over half an hour now. She's sure he could afford for them to take a taxi.

'It'll do me good,' he says, patting his belly. 'And anyway, we're nearly there.' He's so out of breath he has to pause between each word.

Although Mum's taught River first aid, she really hopes that Dr Deardorff doesn't pass out – having to put her mouth over Dr Deardorff's mouth and press her hands down on his man boobs would totally freak her out.

'Did Mum answer your text about us coming over to yours?'

He shakes his head. 'Not yet. But she'll be there anyway.'

'How do you know that she'll be there anyway?'

'She just will.'

This strikes River as an odd thing to say. The plan was for Jules to take River home, make her some tea and they'd wait for Mum to get back from the hospital. Why would she be at Dr Deardorff's?

They walk on and River forces herself to go slower so that Dr Deardorff can catch his breath.

'Mum's right,' River says. 'You're nice.'

'Nice?' The word sits like a brick in his stomach. Does anyone ever want to be *nice*?

River nods. 'Really nice. You totally made Nula feel better.

When she gets upset it usually takes ages to calm her down and you just did it in a second.'

'I'm a doctor.'

'Yeah, but there are loads of doctors who make you feel worse.'

He laughs again. 'I suppose there are.'

'And you make the best eggy bread ever!'

'I'm glad you liked it.'

'You should teach Mum, she can't cook to save her life. Except lasagne and even then, she uses jar sauce. You could come round and give her a lesson.'

'Maybe.'

He blushes – his skin goes even redder than it was from being out of breath.

'No, seriously, she needs lessons. Even Gabino is better than she is.'

They walk on a bit in silence. River's beginning to recognise the roads from when Ash drove them here yesterday afternoon.

'And Jules thought it was cool that you got a tattoo – and Jules's cool bar is *really* high.'

'I didn't choose to get a tattoo.'

'Still, you should tell people about it.' River pauses. 'And you should wear more colour.'

'Colour?'

'You only wear grey suits and grey ties and grey socks and grey shoes.'

He looks down at his shoes. 'They're black.'

'They're scuffed, which makes them look grey. Looking at you is like watching TV with the colour broken.' River bites her lip. He's been really nice to her and she's just made him feel really bad about his clothes. 'Sorry.'

'It's okay.'

They walk on for a while in silence. Then he says:

'I like grey.'

'You do?'

He stops walking, bends over, presses a hand into his waist. 'Sorry – a stitch.'

River *really* hopes he doesn't pass out.

'Actually, it's not that I *like* grey,' he says after a while. 'Not in and of itself.' He stands up straight all of a sudden. 'I suppose I'm a bit scared of colour.'

'Scared of colour?' River laughs. 'That's the silliest thing I've ever heard.'

'No one's ever taught me how to match them. I'm worried I'd get it wrong and end up looking foolish.'

River puts her hands on her hips. 'Who told you colours had to match?'

'Isn't that just one of those rules that everyone accepts is true?'

'Rules?' River rolls her eyes. 'Well, I don't follow that rule and look at me.' She does a twirl. 'I make colours not match on purpose. It's more fun.'

'I'm not sure I could get away with it.'

'It would cheer your patients up.'

'Perhaps.'

'Even just a colourful tie . . . or socks or something.'

'I'll give it some thought.'

'We could go shopping. I know some great charity shops near our house. Jules and I go all the time. You'd get a bargain.' And then River feels herself blush. Dr Deardorff wouldn't need to go to a charity shop. He's a doctor, he's probably got loads of money.

'Thank you for the offer, River, that's very kind.'

By some miracle they find themselves standing outside Dr Deardorff's block of flats. River scans the building. It was so dark last night that she hadn't realised quite how different it looked from their flat on Acacia Road, like how much posher it was. As she thinks about Dr Deardorff standing at their old rusty hob making eggy bread, she suddenly feels embarrassed.

'Can I ask you a question, Dr Deardorff?'

'Just one?' He smiles.

River nods.

'Fire away.'

'Why were you at our house? I mean, why were you eating at Gabino's – when you could have been eating anywhere? And why weren't you at work?'

'Well, there's more than one question there.'

'I know, but they're connected, right?'

'You're a bright spark, River, you know that?'

No one had ever told River that she was bright. She feels herself smile.

'I suppose they are connected,' Dr Deardorff says. 'I wasn't at work because my boss doesn't want me at work.'

'Mr Long?'

He nods.

'Why not?'

'Because he's unhappy that I looked after Reg.'

'Well, that's just stupid.'

'Decisions grown-ups make don't always make sense.'

'You're the best doctor in the whole hospital. That's what Mum says.'

Dr Deardorff pushes his glasses up his nose. That was one step up from nice, wasn't it?

'She does?' he asks.

'Yep. And you're definitely better than Dr Reed. She's the one who brought the reporter onto the ward. I thought she was nice

235

but she's just mean and sneaky. She should be the one that Mr Long tells not to come to work.'

Dr Deardorff gives her a sad smile. 'Like I said, these decisions don't always make sense.'

They walk into the lobby and the security guard winks at Dr Deardorff and says, 'She's already here.'

Dr Deardorff mops the beads of sweat off his brow with a hankie.

'Who?'

'The girl you're always moping over.'

Dr Deardorff's face goes even redder than it is already from all the walking and sweating – his cheeks have almost turned purple.

'You've got a *girlfriend*?' River asks. 'Mum said you were a bat-something.' River scratches her head. 'One of those bat men who don't have anyone. I mean anyone special.' River wishes she hadn't said anything, it's come out all wrong. 'Mum's kind of a bat too. She hasn't got anyone special either.' River hopes that the last bit will make Dr Deardorff feel better.

At that moment, there's a flapping noise and then there are wings beating overhead, flapping at the big chandelier in the entrance lobby.

The pigeon swoops above them, finds a ledge and starts cooing.

He must have slipped in through the open door.

'Not again!' the security guard sighs. 'He's always trying to sneak in.' He comes out from behind his desk and starts shooing the pigeon.

'That's not going to work,' River says. 'Here, let me have a go.' She grabs a doughnut from the box on the security guard's desk.

'Hey!' the security guard says.

River ignores him, goes to the door, crouches down and holds out the doughnut in an open palm. Then she makes a very gentle whistling sound through her teeth and then follows this with a low coo which she pushes out from the back of her throat. Pablo likes it when she does that.

The pigeon stops flapping and looks at her.

'Come on, silly thing, you'll be happier outside.' She breaks off a piece of doughnut and throws it out through the front door.

The pigeon cocks his head to one side. And stays put.

'Come on,' she says and throws another piece of doughnut out.

The pigeon lifts his feet, seems to hesitate for a second and then swoops out of the front door.

'A pigeon charmer, hey?' the security guard says.

'I think it was the doughnut.' River smiles. 'It's probably what he comes in for.'

'Maybe,' the security guy says.

'All this walking and pigeon chasing has exhausted me,' Dr Deardorff says. 'Let's go up to the flat.'

Dr Deardorff's face is a bit less red than before; she hopes the pigeon has helped him forget her bat man comment.

They step into the lift and Dr Deardorff says:

'You acted like you knew the pigeon.'

'I know pigeons in general.'

'Like the one who comes to visit you at your flat.'

'How do you know about Pablo?'

Dr Deardorff smiles. 'Reg told me. He showed me your pictures.'

'He did?'

Dr Deardorff nods. 'I do have a question, though. How do you know it's always the same one who goes to your flat? Aren't there thousands of pigeons in London?'

'87,000,' River says. 'And I know Pablo's Pablo because of the colour of his feathers. And because he's got a special coo.'

Dr Deardorff laughs, which means he must definitely be feeling better.

'A special coo?' he says. 'You should become a linguist, like Alex.'

River chuckles. 'A linguist? Like, someone who works with words?'

'Yes,' Dr Deardorff says.

'Hasn't Mum told you? I have ADHD.'

'I don't think that matters.'

River juts out her chin. 'I'm not good at sitting still and learning things.'

Dr Deardorff presses the button for the top floor.

'If you're interested in something, you'll find a way. It might be a good thing.'

'ADHD – a *good* thing?'

'Well, sometimes, finding something a struggle – something that you really care about – makes you more determined than people who find it easy.'

The lift jolts and starts shooting up the building.

River had never thought that her ADHD could be good for anything.

'You *are* cool,' she says, tucking her arm under his.

The door to the lift pings open and they step into the corridor that leads to Dr Deardorff's front door. Which is open. There are voices coming from inside. Mum's voice. And that linguistics guy's voice.

River and Dr Deardorff walk into his flat. Mum and Alex stare at River and Dr Deardorff, looking really guilty for some reason. Mum looks tired. Tired and sad and worried. She hadn't looked like that this morning. In fact, this morning Mum had looked happier than she had in ages.

'Where's Reg?' River asks, looking around.

David

David scans his flat.

For the last hour, Isabel hasn't stopped crashing around the kitchen. Filling up the kettle, yanking open and then slamming shut the cupboard doors, pulling out mugs and then thumping them down on the counter, reaching into a box of teabags, grabbing a fistful of teaspoons from a cutlery drawer, spilling a bag of caster sugar, opening the fridge, sniffing at the milk. She won't stop moving. It's like if she forces herself to keep going as normal – if she pushes herself even harder than she usually does – it's all going to be okay: Reg is going to come back.

Every few seconds Isabel looks over at River, as if she's going to disappear too.

If Isabel's gone into manic mode, River's gone still and quiet. Too still and quiet. The only bit of her that's moving are her fingers, tap, tap, tapping on the windowsill. She's looking out at the grey sky. Occasionally, she turns to look at the front door and then looks back out of the window and starts tapping again, as if she's worried that Reg might suddenly show up and that she might miss it.

All the light and colour has seeped out of her and her shoulders are stooped, like she's sunk into herself.

As for David, he feels sick. Sick like he couldn't eat anything ever again. Like every Jammie Dodger he's ever wolfed down is pushing up into his throat. He feels his body: a big, fat, clumsy lump that's taking up too much space – space that Reg should be taking up.

He pulls his packet of Rennies out from his pocket and shoves a couple in his mouth.

A nice guy? A good doctor? If what River said was true, if Isabel did say those things about him, she wouldn't think them ever again, not after this.

He bites down on the chalky tablets and then swallows hard.

He knew that Reg was vulnerable; he should never have left him alone with Alex. He should never have asked Alex to come in the first place. What good was it, digging into Reg's past? He'd remember when was ready. And if he didn't – so what? They'd work it out.

Alex. Ever since David came back, his friend's head has been stuck in that laptop of his, as if that's where Reg is going to turn up. He's been biting so hard at the fingernails on his right hand that one of them is starting to bleed. The only time he takes his fingers out of his mouth is when he taps manically on his keyboard. Then he sighs and shakes his head, like it's his computer that's to blame for all this. No, he definitely shouldn't have asked Alex to come. He should have dealt with Reg on his own.

A loud bubbling sound suddenly fills the room – steam swirls around the kitchen. Christ – Isabel left the kettle lid open.

He looks over at her: she's staring at River again – she hasn't even noticed the kettle, which is boiling over now.

He lurches over and slams the lid shut then flips the switch off by the socket.

Isabel spins round and claps her hand over her mouth. 'Oh, I'm sorry.'

And then she bursts into tears and buries her face in her hands.

He goes over and, without processing what he's doing, puts his arm around her and draws her in close. Her shoulders heave against his chest. He feels the wet patches from her tears seeping through his shirt.

'It's okay.' He rubs her back in gentle circles. 'It's okay.'

Her head shakes from side to side against his chest.

'It's all my fault,' she says.

'No.'

She stands back, her face a beautiful, blubbery mess. She sniffs and wipes the back of her hand across her eyes.

'Nothing's your fault,' David says. 'Nothing.'

River suddenly spins round and looks at them.

'We should be out there looking for him. The longer we wait, the further he'll get.'

Alex looks up from his laptop.

'It's London, he could be anywhere,' he says.

David clenches his jaw. 'Tell me again what happened?'

He still can't believe that Alex just let Reg go.

Alex stands up and comes over to the kitchen counter.

'We made some good headway. I'd started asking him questions. I'd made some notes . . . '

River comes over too. 'So you found out where he was from?'

'I got close. He probably lives in a border town somewhere near Poland. There's a real melting pot of influences in his accent and vocabulary. I was going to send the recordings to a friend at Hull, a specialist in Eastern European dialects.'

'Did you tell Reg?' River asked. 'I mean, did you tell him where you thought he was from – Poland or wherever?'

'He was desperate to know . . . ' Alex starts.

David clenches his fist. 'We'd agreed that you shouldn't say anything until you were certain.'

'Why?' River asks. 'Why shouldn't Reg know where he's from?'

'He should know. We just have to tread carefully. Be sure of our facts. And of the impact the information will have on him. He's very fragile, River, you know that.'

River chews her lip. Her eyes go watery. 'I think I'd like to know where I was from – even if I was fragile.'

David feels a thud in his chest. She's right.

'So how much did you tell him?' David asks.

Alex sits back and sighs. 'I'm sorry, David, he just wouldn't stop asking me and looking over at the notes on my laptop . . .'

God, he really doesn't know anything about how to handle patients.

He waits for Alex to go on.

'I gave him what I had. I made clear that nothing was certain. That his was a complex case. That at best, it was a guess.'

'Tell me exactly what you told him,' David says.

'Like I said, I wasn't specific. I told him as much as I've told you.'

'But you know more?' David says.

Alex doesn't answer.

'Alex?' David stares at him and waits for him to continue.

Alex clears his throat. 'Belarus. But I didn't tell him that.'

'Belarus? Where's that?' River asks.

'A country right in the middle of Eastern Europe,' Isabel says.

Everyone turns to look at her. She hasn't spoken in ages.

'How do you know that?' River asks.

'Your mum knows everything, River.'

Isabel stares at David for a moment and blushes.

'Is it a nice place?' River asks.

'Look, I don't even know if I'm right,' Alex says. 'Not a hundred per cent.'

'And you're sure you didn't tell him?' David clenches his jaw. Alex might be a damn good linguist but he sure as hell isn't a psychologist. He should never have left him alone with Reg.

Alex nods. 'Yeah, I'm sure.'

'Was he happy, though, when he found out what bit of the world he was from – even if he didn't know where exactly?' River asks.

Alex shakes his head. 'He looked shocked for a bit. And then got agitated, started coughing – found it hard to catch his breath, you know? I thought he was tired from all the questions, that it had taken too much out of him, so I suggested we take a break. I went to the loo—'

'You left him alone?' David asks.

'For Christ's sake, David, I went to the toilet. So yeah, I left him alone – for a minute – *in your flat*. He was fine. He's a grown man.'

It's not as simple as that, thinks David. Considering what he's been through, his current state of mind, his lack of recollection about who he is and what brought him here – added to the shock of finding out something so important about his life – he may as well be a child.

'What happened then?' River asks.

Alex pulls at his collar and looks towards the door. 'When I came back, he was gone.'

'Just like that?' River asks.

He nods. 'Just like that.'

'Didn't you go after him?' River asks.

Alex nods. 'I ran down the street but there wasn't a trace of him.'

For a while, the four of them sit in silence. Dusk has turned to night. David closes his eyes and listens to the sound of the London traffic. He hears a pigeon cooing and, despite the mess of the situation, he smiles. That pigeon probably knows more about where Reg is than all of them put together.

Isabel's head is hung low. He can't bear to look at her.

River jumps down off her stool.

'When you went to the loo, did he look like he was going to make a run for it?' she asks Alex.

Alex shakes his head. 'No, he just seemed tired.'

River looks around the flat. 'Something must have happened – between when you went to the loo and when you came back. Something that made him want to leave.'

'His behaviour's unpredictable, River,' David says. 'You've seen that. It's part of his condition.'

'But still, something must have made him take off like that.'

David has worked long enough as a neurological psychiatrist to know that even though there might be logical triggers to someone's behaviour, they often remain a mystery to even the patient.

River goes over to the coffee table and looks around.

'This was where you saw him last?' she asks Alex.

'Come on, River,' Isabel says. 'I know you mean well, but it's late and we're all tired.'

River pretends not to hear. 'Alex?'

Alex nods.

River scans the sofa and the carpet and the coffee table, as though she's looking for fingerprints. David is touched by her seriousness, by how committed she is to finding an answer in all this chaos.

'River, come on.' Isabel gets off her stool, and picks up her and River's raincoats from the back of a dining room chair. 'Enough's enough.'

River continues to ignore Isabel. 'Is this your computer, Alex?' River points to the laptop sitting on the coffee table.

'Yeah.'

'The one where you made notes about him?'

Alex nods.

The one you shouldn't have had open anywhere near Reg, David thinks.

River picks up the laptop, sits down on the sofa and opens up the screen.

'I don't think you should be doing that, River,' Isabel says.

River doesn't answer.

'River?' Isabel says, louder.

'You don't understand, Mum,' River snaps back.

Isabel takes a breath and comes to sit next to River. She puts her arm around River's shoulders. 'I know you're upset—'

River shakes her off and stares at the screen.

Alex and David go over to the sofa and stand over her. David watches her opening a series of tabs. Sound files. Articles. Pictures of Alex's wife and children. And then River points at the screen and gasps.

'Look! Look, it's him! It's Reg!'

Everyone leans in.

River turns to Alex. 'Did Reg see this?'

Alex shakes his head but then he stops. 'I don't know. No. I don't think so. I didn't show it to him.' He pauses. 'But he saw me use the computer, so I suppose . . . ' His voice trails off.

'But you left him alone.' David pushes his glasses up his nose and stares at his friend. 'And, judging from this article, you knew exactly who he was – and you didn't tell me?'

'You rushed off so quickly this morning. And I wasn't sure.' His voice is shaky. 'I only found the article last night. I couldn't get to sleep so I did some research. From the sound files you sent me and from meeting him yesterday, I thought I'd roughly worked out where his accent was from. So I started googling news items related to Belarus – in case there was something about a guy going missing. I didn't think I was going to come up with anything – I mean, what are the chances, right? And then I found this article and I remembered something you said about him drawing all the time and it seemed like it could be a match. But I wanted to check my facts—'

'*Your facts?* That's him – his face is on that article. What more facts do you need?'

David feels dizzy. He should have been more careful. Reg is his patient; it's his job to make sure that all this goes smoothly. Running out on him had been thoughtless and selfish. God knows where the poor man is now, or what he's thinking.

Everyone goes quiet and stares at the newspaper article and the grainy photo.

'Constantin Novak,' River says. 'Is that his name?'

Alex nods.

'He found out his name!' River says, her voice fizzing. 'He found out who he was. And that triggered a whole load of memories and he worked out where he was from. Maybe he's gone off to find it!'

She scrolls down and another picture emerges.

'And look – it's one of his drawings,' River says. 'I've seen it.' She gulps. 'I mean, he's drawn it for me before.' Her cheeks flush red.

'He's drawn it for you?' Isabel asks.

River nods. 'In my exercise book. He drew it that day when he walked off.'

They stare at the sketch of an elephant, blindfolded, its ears pinned down, its legs bound by ropes, draped in the green and red Belarusian flag. A man with a moustache, the upward curl of a lip, dressed like a circus master, sits on the elephant, a whip in his hand.

'Oh my God . . . ' Alex says.

'What?' River asks.

David shakes his head.

'What do the words mean?' Isabel asks, squinting at the screen.

Alex takes the laptop from River and clicks onto a Google translate screen and starts to enter some key words from the article.

'What does "agitator" mean?' River asks.

No one answers.

Alex enters some more words. David can see where this is heading, and it's not good. *Dangerous . . . Criminal . . . Reward . . . Police . . .*

He looks up at Isabel for a second. All the blood's drained from her face.

'I don't understand,' River says. 'Reg isn't a criminal. He can't be.' She gulps. 'Can he, Mum?'

Isabel strokes the back of River's head. 'No, he's not a criminal, my love.'

'So what did he do wrong?'

'It looks like he drew pictures people didn't like,' she says.

'What's so wrong about drawing a picture? And who cares if people don't like them? I don't understand.'

'It's not that simple, River,' says Isabel.

River turns to David. 'Dr Deardorff, what is it? What's wrong? Why are there all those bad words in the article?'

David doesn't know what to say.

'Because some people feel threatened by the truth,' Isabel blurts out. 'Because some countries are ruled by people who like their citizens to be silent.' Her voice is shaking. 'And if people speak out, they say bad things about them. Bad things that aren't true.'

They all look up at her and, for a while, no one speaks.

David was right, Isabel does know everything. Everything that's worth knowing, anyway.

'I think we should go to the police,' Alex says.

'No,' Isabel says, almost as soon as the words come out of Alex's mouth.

David sees it, clear as day: Reg leaving hasn't changed Isabel's feelings for him one bit. If anything, it's made them stronger.

'Mum's right, we can't go to the police. From what the article says, the police are the problem.'

'Not our police,' says Alex.

River frowns at him, confused.

'Constantin is out on bail, there are conditions,' David says gently. 'Like that he's meant to stay here, in my flat. River's right, if we go to the police – even our police – he could get in trouble.'

Isabel looks at him gratefully.

'So what do we do?' River asks.

'We find him,' Isabel says, as though it's the simplest thing in the world. 'Don't we, David?' She looks at him, her eyes searching his.

He holds her gaze and, very slowly, he nods. 'Yes, we'll find him.'

David

At 3 a.m., David sits alone in his flat, rubbing his eyes and staring at his computer screen. He's spent hours looking up articles about Constantin Novak, the censored, satirical cartoonist wanted for treason by Belarus's president.

He keeps wondering what Constantin must have thought when he read the article and when he saw the picture he'd drawn that got him into so much trouble. Did his memories come back? Was this hounding by the police responsible for causing him such stress that he forgot who he was and where he was from? Or had it all been an act? Did he keep his identity secret because he knew that it was his name that would land him in prison?

David had put River and Isabel in a taxi and persuaded Alex to go back to his family in Hull. There was no more his friend could do here.

He needs the space and the time to think about what to do next.

If they leave Constantin roaming around London on his own, God knows what will happen to him. River thought he might find his way back to London Zoo, but that's miles away from David's flat. And God knows what state Constantin's in: he's probably in shock, his knee will be giving him trouble, especially without his stick, and his pneumonia has only just cleared up – the last thing he needs is a relapse. Reg should be staying warm and calm and resting. And taking his medication.

Once again, David realises how much he's failed his patient. He won't ever let that happen again.

He rubs his brow.

Oh Christ, the police. He'd forgotten that, only a few hours ago, Reg had been taken in for questioning. Reg was meant to check in at the police station every few days. They were right after all: he was a flight risk.

David's chest pulls tight. He tries to breathe to ease away the pain but breathing hurts too.

Should he do what Alex suggested? Phone the police and tell them that Constantin has gone missing? He could explain to them that they'd made progress in identifying him, be up front about Constantin running away because he was scared and shocked. Perhaps they'd understand.

But that doesn't feel right. Once Constantin is in police custody again, God knows what will happen to him.

David gets up and paces around his flat.

If only he could find a way for the police to support Constantin, to see him as a cause of some kind – a figure for the British establishment to get behind. He was an artist, censored and persecuted by his country. The British believe in freedom of speech and expression, don't they? Surely Constantin has a case?

Then he has an idea.

He goes back to his computer and calls up one of the articles he found about Constantin: the only one from the English-speaking press.

It was by Clem McKee, Eastern European correspondent for *The London Chronicle*. The article is a year old.

At the centre of the piece stands a grainy headshot of Constantin: clean-shaven, the angles of his jaw softer than now, but his dark hair still has that untamed quality David recognises straight away. And those eyes, large and brown and unfathomable. The eyes that made Isabel and River stop and talk to him that day outside London Zoo. The eyes that, Constantin is certain, made Isabel fall in love with him.

David scans the headline: *The World's Deadliest Cartoons*. It's a summary of censored artists from around the world. Constantin's picture of the elephant lies at the centre of the piece.

David does a search on Clem McKee. It seems he specialises in exposing censorship.

Making contact with him would be a risk: even if he does take up Constantin's case, as soon as Constantin's story hits the papers, the police will be alerted. But it's worth a shot. The journalist obviously thinks a great deal of Constantin. Maybe, if he gets behind his cause, the police will think twice about sending him back to Belarus.

David looks up McKee's email address on *The London Chronicle*'s website and writes him a short message, not giving too much away. He wants to see how McKee responds, whether he's interested – and whether he's likely to help rather than hinder their case.

When the email is sent, David goes over to his window and looks out across London. There's a hint of colour in the night sky, as if dawn is already pushing through.

He opens his window and hears the ruffle of feathers, the scratch of feet adjusting themselves on the concrete ledge above his head. He looks up, past the ledge, at the shadow of a moon, thin as tissue paper in the brightening sky.

Where are you, Constantin? David whispers into the morning sky.

Isabel

Isabel switches on the lights of Gabino's café. It's 4 a.m. on Sunday morning; he won't be coming in to open for a few hours yet.

She gets the mop from behind the bar, fills the bucket up with soap and water and scrubs the floor. It doesn't need cleaning, but it's the only thing she can think to do. And the only way she can stop the thought of Constantin's disappearance from driving her crazy.

She and River spent yesterday walking up and down the road outside London Zoo. They didn't leave until it got dark. River was certain that he would go back; Isabel knew that finding him wouldn't be that easy, but she went along with it – she understood that River needed to feel like she was doing something to help.

Isabel has decided that today is going to be different. No more looking for Reg. She'd take River out to the cinema, something to get her mind off it all – to hell with the cost. They'd do normal mother and daughter things, have a day just the two of them, and tomorrow Isabel would go back to work and River would be with Jules and Nula and the triplets and, with every day that passed, Isabel would try to press a bit more normality into their lives.

She should never have let herself get so close to Constantin. She knew it would end badly. Why had she gone looking for more? Her life was enough. More than enough.

Yes, it was time to get back to how things were meant to be. To her life with River and Jules and her job at the hospital.

And then, maybe one day, they could forget that they had ever stumbled into the life of Constantin Novak.

Isabel switches on the TV for company but a news item on migrants crossing the Mediterranean flashes onto the screen, and her mind goes back to Constantin.

She'd read up about Belarus on Gabs's old PC in the office. Everyone knows about Syria and other famous extremist regimes in the world. But what about this European country with a dictatorship, a country that still has capital punishment and that persecutes its artists? Why does no one speak out about that?

She turns down the volume on the TV, walks over to the bar to switch on the espresso machine and goes back to scrubbing the floor, focusing all her energy on a stain in the corner that she's been fighting for years. She notices a trail of ants creeping up a curl in the linoleum and dumps an extra lot of water on top of them and squashes the mop onto the gap in the wall through which she suspects they're coming.

There's a thud on the mat outside the restaurant. She looks up to catch a wave and a smile from the Sunday paperboy. They're often up at the same time.

Isabel puts away the mop, goes out and picks up the Sunday papers and brings them inside. Then she makes herself an espresso and sits down at a table. As she sips at the hot bitter liquid, she pulls the cellophane off the papers.

It takes her brain a moment to register the face staring up at her from the front page because it's not in her head but right here, in front of her, in print, in a national newspaper.

'Mum?'

Isabel spins round. River's standing at the back door of the restaurant, by the stairs that lead to their flat. She's in her rainbow pyjamas and there are dark smudges under her eyes.

'What are you doing, Mum?' River asks, looking around.

Isabel wants to go over and hold River – she wants to wrap her up, like she did when she was a baby, to block out the world, to keep her from all those loud, ugly things. But before she has the chance to move, River is skipping over to her. And then she stops and stares. She's seen it too.

River picks up the newspaper and starts reading random phrases from the article under the picture of Constantin:

Missing: talented artist . . . political refugee . . . censorship . . . needs to be found urgently . . .

Her eyes scan down the article.

Dr David Deardorff, MD, has been treating Constantin Novak . . . he says that it's vital that we find his patient . . . Novak's safety is at stake.

River looks up from the paper, her eyes wide.

'Dr Deardorff told the papers about Reg?'

Isabel keeps staring at the words: they swim in front of her, blurring in and out of focus.

'Mum?'

'It looks like it, River.'

'But that's crazy! He was so cross when the other journalist printed all that stuff.'

'I know.'

'So why did he do it? Now the police are going to find him and drag him back to prison and everything is going to be much, much worse.'

Isabel folds her hands on the table. The lack of sleep and the espresso have sent a headache pounding at the back of her skull.

'I'm sorry, River, I don't know. I just don't know.'

River

River walks right past the security guy in the lobby of Dr Dear-dorff's flat and bangs on the button to the lift.

Isabel follows behind.

The lift doors open and River jumps inside.

'He's not here,' the security guy calls after them.

River spins round. 'Well, where is he?'

'Probably looking for that Russian bloke, like the rest of the country.'

River steps out of the lift and walks towards him.

'He's not Russian. He's from Belarus!' River's voice is nearly hysterical. 'It's a *completely* different country.'

Mum had shown her on a map: Belarus is a country right in the middle of Eastern Europe.

'And what do you mean – "the rest of the country"?'

'Well, that's the campaign, isn't it? To find him.' He holds up his phone. 'There have been two hundred messages on the Facebook page already.'

River comes over and grabs the phone. 'What Facebook page?'

Mum says she's never going to let River have a Facebook profile, even when she's thirteen. They don't even have their own computer – when River has to use the internet for homework, she has to go down to Gabs's office and borrow his.

'I didn't think Dr Deardorff would know about Facebook,' River mumbles, staring at the screen.

The page is headed: *Find Constantin Novak!* And there's a

picture of him, an old one from one of the websites they looked at on the night he ran away.

There are over 500 Likes already. And lots of people have commented. River looks through the messages. Mostly, they're nice comments, like that people think Constantin is a hero and deserves the protection of the British government, that a man of his talent should be celebrated and not hunted down. A few idiots have posted messages saying he should go back to where he came from.

Constantin Novak. She can't get her head around that name. To River, he'll always be Reg.

River gives the security guy back his phone and looks at Mum.

'Mum?' She chews her lip. 'Dr Deardorff's done all this because he thinks it can help us find Reg, hasn't he?'

River's never been able to work out whether Dr Deardorff likes Reg. He helped him, like a doctor is meant to help a patient, and he was interested in his case – but then he's always really interested in his patients, especially ones with unusual conditions. River had noticed how sometimes Dr Deardorff looked at Reg a bit suspiciously, especially when Mum was around. Maybe he thought there was something bad about Reg, like the people who wrote about him in the articles on Alex's computer. But if he didn't like him, he wouldn't be doing all this, would he?

'Yes,' Mum says. 'David's done this because he wants us to find Constantin.'

Mum and River stand on the pavement outside Dr Deardorff's flat. Pigeons coo overhead. River looks up and wonders whether Pablo is up there with the others. Last night, as she was falling asleep, she asked Pablo to rally the troops and help them find Reg. River did a project at school on carrier pigeons in the Second

World War and how they saved millions of lives – they even got medals for their bravery. It was the only project she ever got a good mark for.

Maybe that's what Pablo is doing now: telling all the pigeons who live near Dr Deardorff's flat to help with the search.

River looks back at Mum.

'Could you call Dr Deardorff and ask him if we can help him with the search?'

Mum gives River a weary smile. 'We should leave it to David, River. We'll just complicate things . . . '

Mum's been really quiet ever since they left the security guy in the lobby.

River fixes Mum with her gaze. 'It's not complicating things. The more people that are out there looking for Reg, the better. Dr Deardorff understands that – its why he's doing all this Facebook stuff.'

'It's upsetting you, love,' Mum says. 'We should never have—'

'What?' River interrupts. Her cheeks burn. 'We should never have what? Found Reg? Helped him? You know that's rubbish. We were *meant* to find him that day. And we're *meant* to look for him now.' River gulps. 'And I'm upset already. I'm upset that he's missing.' She gulps. 'And I won't stop being upset until we find him.'

Mum leans in and kisses River's forehead. For a moment, she holds River and they stand in silence, listening to the sound of the pigeons and the traffic.

'You're not going to let this go, are you, River?' Mum says eventually.

River pulls away from Mum's arms and smiles. 'Nope.'

Mum sighs, takes out her phone and dials Dr Deardorff's number.

River

Early on Monday morning, Jules crashes into Gabino's with the triplets; Nula trails behind but as soon as she sees River she runs into her arms.

Mum gives Jules a hug.

'Thanks for taking River,' Mum says as she gets her bag and her raincoat.

'Jules says we're going on a treasure hunt,' Nula blurts out. 'But that the treasure's a person.'

Mum exchanges a look with Jules.

'You're okay with us looking for Reg?' River asks Jules.

River had thought that Jules would roll her eyes and say that looking for Reg was asking for trouble and that they should stay out of it.

'Sure,' Jules says. 'Just don't blame me if it all backfires.'

Mum looks away.

'How could it backfire?' River asks.

Jules shrugs. 'I'm just saying.'

Mum opens the door. 'I've got to run.'

Stingy Simon gave Mum all the early shifts this week. It's because she was involved in the whole Reg thing – everyone's getting in trouble for helping Reg. Which doesn't make any sense at all. Surely helping people who really need it, like Reg, is what you're meant to do when you work for a hospital. River wonders how people like Stingy Simon and Dr Reed and Mr Long ever get hired in the first place.

'Be good, River,' Mum throws over her shoulder.

'*Be good!*' Nula giggles. She knows that being good isn't one of River's strong points.

They all stand by the steamed-up restaurant window and watch Mum walk down the road.

'Asking to have her heart broken, that one,' Jules mutters.

Which is a weird thing to say.

'What do you mean?' River asks.

Jules doesn't answer. Instead, she takes out three tissues and wipes each of the triplets' noses like they're on a processing line. Then she looks up at River. 'No luck finding him yesterday, then?'

River shakes her head. 'And Dr Deardorff didn't answer any of Mum's calls.'

Mum said he was probably too busy dealing with all the messages on the Facebook page but River still found it strange that he didn't call back. Dr Deardorff never ignores Mum.

So, because there wasn't anything else to do, Mum and River went back to the bench outside London Zoo and then they walked round and round Regent's Park until River thought her legs would drop off. It felt like lots of the other people outside the zoo and in the park were looking for Reg too. Something about the way they were glancing around and whispering made her think that they'd seen Dr Deardorff's Facebook page and were trying to help. Mum said River was probably imagining it, that there are always loads of people out walking on Sundays. But the point was that River *wanted* to believe that the whole of London was looking for Reg. And that they'd find him soon.

Jules sits down at one of the restaurant tables and takes out her phone.

'I'll give him a call.'

'Give who a call?'

'Dave.'

'Dave who?'

Jules looks up at River and raises her pierced eyebrow. 'Dave Who?' she rolls her eyes. 'Dr Deardorff, you muppet,' she says in that *Duh!* way that boys use at school when River gets a really easy answer wrong in class because she wasn't paying attention.

'Why are you calling him *Dave*?'

Dr Deardorff is the least Dave-looking David River can think of.

Jules shrugs. 'He didn't correct me.'

'You talked to him – without anyone else there?'

'I didn't know I needed permission.'

'You don't. It's just – weird.'

River goes to sit on the chair beside Jules and settles Nula on her knee. Nula tries to grab at Jules's phone but Jules whips it away to the side.

'We met, remember?' Jules says. 'That day he babysat you.'

'*Babysat* me?'

'Okay, on the day he was hanging out with you until your mum got home.'

'I didn't think you'd swapped numbers.' River's sure she would have noticed.

Jules shrugs again. 'Well, we did. Dave thought it would be a good idea. In case anything happened.' One of the triplets drops her dummy and starts crying. Jules picks it up, gets out a disinfectant wipe, cleans the dummy and slots it back in. 'And he needed some help with setting up his Facebook page.'

'So you're the one who helped him?'

Jules nods.

None of this makes any sense. Jules and Dr Deardorff having each other's phone numbers and spending time helping each other? Totally weird.

'When did you help him?' River asks.

'On Friday night.'

Jules holds up her hand because Dr Deardorff has answered his phone. A moment later, they're nattering away to each other like they've known each other for years.

And a few minutes after that, Jules, the triplets, Nula and River are traipsing across town to his flat.

Only, before they get to the end of Acacia Road, Dr Deardorff calls Jules again and asks if they can meet at the London Eye instead: he's just got a tip-off from someone on Facebook that Reg might be there.

'Probably just a hoax,' Jules says to River. 'But I guess it doesn't hurt to check.'

'What's a hoax?' River asks as she helps Jules carry the triplet buggy down the Underground steps.

'A trick.'

'Why would it be a trick?'

'People like to get involved in stuff like this – nutters. Time-wasters.'

'*Nutters! Nutters!*' Nula sings out, jumping down two stairs at a time.

'Why?' River asks.

'Because they've got nothing better to do.'

Jules crashes the buggy down the last step, jolting the triplets in their seats. Millie starts crying; Jules lifts her out of the buggy, gives her a few firm rubs on the back, kisses one of her chubby cheeks and then slots her back. Then she pushes the buggy onto the Tube.

Sometimes, Jules makes River think of a big, colourful, tattooed octopus – with piercings. It's like she never runs out of arms to do anything. And she's always got everything under control.

That's how Reg would draw her, anyway.

'Mum says that mean people are unhappy people,' River says as they sit down in the train.

'That's because your mum's a softie,' Jules says.

River isn't sure that's true, Mum's one of the toughest people she knows. Not as tough as Jules, but still.

The doors shut and, for a while, the train doesn't move.

'Can I look at your phone?' River asks, hoping that there's still WiFi down here.

Jules hands it over.

There are two bars of reception, enough to get her onto the Find Reg Facebook page. Hundreds of people have signed up. One of the small icons catches her eye. She clicks on it. It's Dr Reed, her hair all fluttery around her face, her lips really red. River scans down her profile page. There aren't any pictures of the doctor with her friends or family or pets or where she's been on holiday. There are just loads of selfies, most of them pretty bad, taken with her looking in a bedroom mirror.

Although River's angry at Dr Reed for involving that reporter and getting Reg arrested, she still feels sad for her. It doesn't look like anyone wants to be Dr Reed's friend.

As the train jolts into motion, River hands Jules back her phone. The train sways them back and forth and everything goes quiet. Even Nula and the triplets go kind of trancey and still.

After a while, River asks:

'Jules – why are you helping Reg?'

Jules sniffs and raises her chin. 'I'm not.'

'You're not?'

'I'm helping you. And your mum.' She pauses. 'And protecting you – or trying to.'

River thinks back to Jules's comment about things backfiring.

'Protecting us from what?'

'From yourselves, mostly.'

'From *ourselves*? I don't understand.'

'You will. One day.'

'*One day* . . . ' Nula echoes.

One day is one of Jules's most annoying phrases. Like she's the one with all the answers and no one's old enough or clever enough to get it. Even Mum.

When they're on the train, River turns to Jules and says, 'Is that why you said that thing to Mum this morning – about her getting herself in a mess?'

Mabel spits her dummy out again and starts crying. Jules picks up the dummy, puts it in her pocket and bounces Mabel on her knee.

'Sort of,' Jules says.

'Explain.'

'You really need me to explain?'

River nods.

'Your mum likes Reg, right?'

'Reg?' River nods. 'Yeah, we all do.'

Jules rolls her eyes again. If there were eye-rolling competitions, she'd definitely win.

'I mean, *like*-like.'

River feels dizzy. '*Like*-like? I don't get it.'

'Well, your mum's obviously got herself in a situation.'

'A situation?'

'I'm beginning to feel like there's an echo in here,' Jules says. 'Look River, in case you haven't noticed the blindingly obvious, your mum likes Reg or Constantin or whatever he's called. And he's done a runner.'

So River hadn't dreamt it. That night, when she woke up in David's flat, she *thought* that she saw Mum and Reg kissing but then she told herself that her mind must have been playing tricks on her – that she was imagining it because she *wanted* to see it.

Because though it's fine living with Mum and Jules, River's always kind of hoped she might have a dad one day.

And she's hoped, too, that Mum might find someone to love her; not in the way that Jules and River love her but in a way that makes her feel glowy and special.

'And Dave's looking for him because he likes your mum,' Jules goes on. 'Which makes it a situation.'

River's head hurts.

River knows that lots of the guys Mum works with have a crush on her, but she's never thought it was serious. Plus, Mum's always saying that doctors don't have time for cleaners, not really, even the ones who try to be nice like Dr Deardorff.

And then she thinks back to that first drawing of Reg's she ever saw – and how, even though the hair was all wrong, it looked like Mum.

'Dr Deardorff *like*-likes Mum? Properly? More than just fancying her because she's pretty?'

'I think it's more than fancying.'

'Since when?'

Jules nods. 'Since for ever.'

River sits back. 'Wow.'

'He thinks he likes her, anyway,' Jules adds.

'How can you *think* you like someone?'

'You build up a picture in your head of what you like about them and it might not be them at all, not really, it's just this perfect person you've made up. And even if that person existed, they'd probably be rubbish for you. People rarely know what's good for them. Best to stay well clear of all that stuff.'

'You mean love?'

The tops of Jules's cheeks flush pink. 'Yeah. Love.'

River's head hurts even more now.

'Anyway,' Jules goes on. 'I don't trust your mum to sort out this mess. That's why I'm helping.'

Thoughts crash around in River's head. She doesn't get it. Mum *loves* Reg? And Dr Deardorff *loves* Mum? Or they *think* they do?

'So that's why the security guard at Dr Deardorff's flat winked at Mum,' River says.

'Probably, Neville's pretty sharp.'

'Neville?'

'The security guy.'

River's mouth drops open. 'You've been to Dr Deardorff's flat?'

'No – just the lobby. Neville called him down.'

River tries to imagine Jules sitting next to Dr Deardorff on the posh leather sofas in the lobby of his block of flats. The picture in her head doesn't look right.

'Why did you go there?' River asks.

Jules rolls her eyes again. 'How else was I meant to show him how Facebook works?'

River looks out of the dark train windows. Everything feels like it's shifting – and like she can't keep hold of it.

'Have you ever loved anyone, Jules?' River asks.

Jules lets out a burst of air through her lips. 'Me?'

'Yep.'

'Maybe.' She flicks her head to get her fringe out of her eyes. 'But like I said, it's not worth the trouble.'

Mabel has fallen asleep against Jules's chest; Jules kisses the top of her head. Babies and small children are the only people Jules doesn't mind giving hugs and kisses to. Come to think of it, maybe the reason Jules likes to spend her whole time being a nanny is because babies and small children are less messy to love than grown-ups.

'What's your type?' River asks, because she's not going to let it drop, not now that she's got Jules to talk.

Jules sniffs. 'I don't have a type.'

'Do you like someone right now?'

Jules doesn't answer. Which usually means that she doesn't *want* to answer. Which is weird considering she just said to stay away from all that love stuff because it leads to trouble.

Nothing about this day is making any sense.

'You said you didn't believe in love stuff.'

'I don't.'

'So why didn't you answer just now?'

Jules shrugs but her cheeks go pink again.

'Who is it?' River asks.

Only before Jules has the chance to answer, the train jolts to a stop and they've got to Waterloo.

Jules stands up, puts Mabel back into the buggy and heads to the doors of the train.

River scoops Nula up and follows her out.

Constantin

Constantin looks up and down the road. Cars screech. Buses lurch towards the pavement, disgorge passengers, let more in and then lurch off again.

A hundred footsteps march past him, bodies with heads bent low, their eyes on their feet.

Above him, the grey clouds thicken.

And as he stands there, lost in noise and movement, he feels the sea again, rising up his body.

He holds his hands over his ears.

Concentrate, he says to himself. *Or you'll never get there.*

When he saw the picture of his face in the newspaper, flashes of memory came back to him. Images mostly. And one keeps coming back over and over again: the sea. He's been feeling it all this time, pulling at him. And it scared him. But now he realises that that's where he should be: not standing on a pavement outside the entrance to a zoo, surrounded by strangers, but by the sea. It's where he'll find her.

He rubs his eyes and looks again at the map, pinned behind the sheet of scratched plastic.

'You lost?'

A voice rises from below him. He looks down.

She's young, too young to be sitting here with long, knotted hair and dirty fingernails and eyes that look ready to strike a deal.

'I know this city like the back of my hand.' She grins and holds up her hand for him to inspect.

He looks down: dirt traces the lines of her skin.

'So do you, eh, Gus?' She takes her hand back and pats the dog sitting beside her on the nose. 'Better than a satnav, this one.' She puts an arm around the black dog and draws his greying muzzle towards her.

He's so thin that his ribcage pushes through his skin like an accordion. She kisses the top of his nose. He licks her face.

Why is she sitting on the street? She's no more than a child, Constantin thinks.

'I've got these.' She reaches into her waterproof jacket. 'A quid each or two for a quid fifty.' She holds up a handful of maps and fans them out like a deck of cards.

When Constantin doesn't respond, she tilts her head, looks him up and down and gives him a sideways smile.

'You're not a tourist, are you?'

'No . . . not really.'

'Escaped from a loony bin, then?' She grins and looks down at the hem of his pyjamas, trailing the ground.

He suddenly feels tired. Too tired to move on and too tired to explain either. His knee aches, and so do his lungs.

'I don't mind,' the girl adds. 'Most of us are a bit doolally.' She taps her head. 'Nothing to be ashamed of.'

Eventually, Constantin sits down beside her on the pavement, wincing with pain as he bends his knee. He was stupid to have left like that, without taking his stick. But after seeing those pictures on the computer, his head was in such a fog – all he could think about was that he needed to leave the flat. To find her.

'You're new to this, aren't you?' she asks.

'To what?' He looks into her eyes, clear as water.

She sticks her nose in the air. 'To "being one of no fixed abode".' She's changed the tone of her voice; she sounds more like Dr Deardorff, slow and articulate.

'I'm just on my way to somewhere . . .' He stops. How can he explain it to her?

'Aren't we all.' She gives him a wink. 'But while you're at it, here's some advice from a seasoned traveller.'

A seasoned traveller? She can't be much older than River.

He feels a stab in his chest: someone should be looking after this young girl. And she shouldn't be talking to someone like him.

'Get some waterproof clothes,' the girl says. 'Buy, borrow, steal, or, more likely, rifle through a bin or two. Rich houses, they're the ones to look out for – throw good stuff out all the time, just because it's the wrong colour or last season or whatever.' She pauses. 'Seriously, mate, you need to stay dry.' She looks up at the sky. The light bounces off her blue eyes. 'The rain, it gets into your bones.' She looks back at him. 'And find yourself a dog – for company, warmth and because it will make people give you more money. And find something to sell.' She holds up the maps. 'Or to play.' She points at a battered guitar propped up against the wall next to her. 'Or mime or sing or something.' She looks at him thoughtfully. 'Do you have a talent?'

He thinks of his drawings. Of the elephant, his eyes bound, his ears stitched shut. His drawing wasn't a talent: it was a curse.

'No, I don't.'

'Well, I'm sure you can find something.'

He rubs his knee. He's worried that if he stops for too long he won't be able to get going again.

'I'm looking for the sea,' he says.

'Come again?'

'The river that leads to the sea.'

'You're speaking in riddles, mate.'

He stands up, brushes down the front of the raincoat he bor-rowed from Dr Deardorff, and looks again at the map on the

269

noticeboard. He needs to get going; he's wasted enough time already.

The girl tugs on the hem of his coat. 'Look, I didn't mean to be rude. It's probably your accent or something. You said you want to find the river?'

He looks at her and nods.

'You mean the Thames?'

'Maybe. Is there a bridge there?'

She laughs. 'A bridge on the Thames?'

He nods.

He'd worked out that if he could find a bridge, he could stand on the middle of it and look down the river, as far as it went – maybe he'd even get a glimpse of the sea.

'There's a hell of a lot of bridges in London, you're going to have to be more specific.'

'The nearest one.'

She takes out one of the maps she tried to sell him. When she notices him watching, she smiles and cups her hand over her mouth.

'They give them out free at the tourist information office. This guy gets them for me. But don't tell anyone – they're my best seller.'

She holds up the map and, with a dirty fingernail, she points at a long, snake of water weaving its way through London.

'That's the Thames. And that there is Westminster Bridge. It'll take you about an hour from here – longer if you limp all the way.' She glances at his knee.

He nods. 'Thank you.'

'Here, take this – no charge.' She hands him the map. 'Just a word of advice: I wouldn't try and compete for a spot near the river. It's saturated.'

'Saturated?'

'Crammed. Filled up. With people like us.' She pauses. 'It's because tourists like the river. It makes them go all soppy and romantic and that loosens their purse strings, if you know what I mean. That's why it's a good spot.'

'Thank you,' he says. 'But I won't be staying.'

'Staying where?'

'By the river. I've got to go to the sea.'

She smiles and he can feel that she feels sorry for him.

'Well, remember to keep dry,' she says. 'That's the main thing.'

'Thank you,' he says again and leans down to stroke the top of the dog's head. His fur feels thin over his skull.

The dog licks his hand and he turns to go.

'Hope you find it,' she calls after him. 'Whatever it is you're looking for.'

A few moments later he hears her plucking at the guitar strings. And then stopping to sell one of her maps to another passer-by. 'One for a pound. Two for a quid fifty.'

Constantin walks for what feels like hours before he hears it: the rush and pull of the water; the smell of damp rising over the city.

And that's when he realises that he's not ready to see it yet.

Gongs ring from somewhere overhead; they vibrate in his skull.

He looks round and notices a clock: a tall, brick tower reaching up to the sky, its hands thick and black. He narrows his eyes and tries to make sense of the hands, to work out what time it is, but they just blur in and out of focus.

Behind it, more bells join in, higher pitched, several of them crashing into each other.

He feels dizzy. Stars dance behind his eyes.

He holds his hands over his ears again, but he can still hear the bells ringing.

He widens his eyes and looks at the spires in the distance, dozens of them, piercing the sky.

Although his legs are weak from walking, his feet take him away from the river, past the big clock and towards the sound of those bells.

For a while, he stands in the cool, dark church, willing his mind to still.

Diamonds of light push through the stained-glass window. Cold marble presses in from all sides: it rises through his feet, pushes into his body, and goes right to his bones.

The church smells of candles and old incense and musty books and the damp of people's rain-wet clothes.

Somewhere, an organ is playing.

He stumbles towards one of the rows of chairs and sits down.

This is a holy place, someone whispers in his head.

A young girl in a red raincoat walks down the aisle. His head throbs. He blinks again. A long plait hangs down her back.

His heart jolts.

The sea, soon it will be at his neck. Soon, it will be over his head and pull him under. He has to push it down, long enough to get to her.

His eyes blur again.

The girl flicks her plait over her shoulder and keeps walking.

He shudders.

He forces himself to stand, to place one foot in front of the other on the marble slabs.

He reaches her by the candles. From behind, he can see the underside of her cheek, lit up by their flame.

He touches her shoulder and she turns round.

Her eyes are pale – a watery grey – her skin is wrinkled, and her hair isn't dark, it's white.

She's an old woman.

He swallows hard.

Whoever he's looking for, it's not her.

'Are you all right?' Her words come to him as if at the end of a long tunnel.

Again, he feels time slipping.

He can't hold it back any longer. A wave crashes over his head and pulls him back down into the dark waters. And then everything goes black.

David

Sweat runs along David's forehead and down the back of his shirt. The box he's carrying slips in his palms.

His phone buzzes again.

He was used to getting a message or a call once a week, usually from work. Now, his phone won't stop ringing; he's suddenly the most popular guy in London.

He balances the box on his hip and fishes his phone from his pocket. A message from Clem McKee comes up on the screen:

My editor loved the piece. Hundreds of emails. Writing another article for tomorrow. Send me a quotation.

It hadn't been easy to find the British journalist who'd written about Constantin Novak. It turns out that Clem McKee is working as a Middle East correspondent now, chasing dictatorships and censorship further from home. Which explains why he's missed all the tabloid stories about Reg: the amnesiac with a talent for drawing cartoons who was wandering lost around London.

But as soon as David got hold of him, he showed interest in Constantin's case. He was due to come back from Syria for a few weeks' leave and said he'd take the story to his editor right away.

'One moment Constantin and I were in touch,' Clem explained in the first of many phone conversations they'd had – a crackly line from Aleppo. 'Albeit on a rather ad hoc basis, and the next – nothing. Not a word. We'd built up a good rapport. And this was unlike him. Constantin wasn't one of those flimsy sources that backed out on you for no good reason: he wanted the British people to hear his story. He joked about us working together in London one day. He was desperate to come to England.' There'd been a long pause. 'I spent weeks searching for leads. I even went out there. But nothing. I thought they'd done away with him and buried the evidence. They're good at that.'

It was listening to Clem McKee that really made it sink in: the seriousness of Constantin Novak's situation, how much of an enemy he was to the Belarusian regime. How it was a miracle that he'd made it to England at all. And that it wasn't surprising that he'd lost his memory. God knows what the man had been through.

Of course, David isn't kidding himself about the nature of Clem's involvement. He seems like a good guy, and he's obviously taken Constantin's story to heart. But still, there's something about the whole newspaper industry that makes David nervous.

'Over here, Dr Deardorff!'

He spots River in an oversized rainbow T-shirt jumping up and down, the London Eye spinning slowly behind her.

A moment later Jules is taking the box out of his arms, balancing it effortlessly while she pushes her enormous buggy. David is struck again by her strength and efficiency: you'd never feel lost with Jules around.

On the phone, Jules had said River wanted to help and asked whether they could get together. Jules being with River meant that Isabel wouldn't be there, which was why David had agreed to this. He didn't want to have her in front of him every two seconds, being reminded of that night when she kissed Constantin and why it was that she was so desperate to find him.

'That's the man we're looking for!' Nula points at David's chest.

River laughs. 'No, Nula. This is Dave, remember? The one who put a plaster on your knee. He's helping us to look for Reg. He's not the one who's lost.'

Nula shakes her head. Her curls swing around her face. 'He is the man.'

'These the badges?' Jules asks, ripping open the tape on the box.

David nods. The badges had been Jules's idea. Everything had been Jules's idea: the Facebook page, the Twitter feed; the posters; the photo of Constantin in *Metro*. And the badges: white circles with Constantin's famous sketch in the middle: the bound and blindfolded elephant. Underneath it, the words: *Find Constantin*.

'It will make people feel part of the cause,' she'd said. 'Like those ribbons people wear.'

Jules pins a badge onto each of the triplets, hands one to River and Nula and then comes over to David and grabs the lapel of his suit. He suddenly feels foolish for wearing something so formal. But what else was he meant to wear? His life consisted of changing between his grey suits and flannel pyjamas.

Jules pricks the needle through his lapel to his shirt and right into his chest.

'Ow!' David yelps.

'Don't be a baby.' Jules smiles and pats the badge. 'There. Perfect.' Her cheeks flush pink.

Behind all those tattoos and piercings, she's got a nice smile, he thinks. *And kind eyes.*

Jules gives a fistful of badges to Nula and to River and the three of them start handing them out.

David's surprised at how willing people are to accept the badges. He's been surprised, too, by how many strangers have taken on Constantin's cause, people who, only twenty-four hours ago, didn't know that this man existed.

'So, what did the guy say?' Jules asks. 'About where he saw Constantin.' She scans the South Bank.

'There were a few sightings,' David says. 'One by the National Theatre, another near Westminster Bridge. They said he looked confused, that he was kind of ambling around. I thought it was worth coming over.'

For a few minutes, all of them – David, Jules, River, Nula, even the triplets – look up and down the river.

And then the back of David's neck prickles and his eyes burn.

Further up the South Bank, a man walks away from them wearing a long, navy raincoat. *His* raincoat.

He rubs his eyes and looks again.

Dishevelled, curly brown hair.

A limp. The man has a definite limp.

David lurches forward.

'Dave – everything okay?' Jules asks.

'I . . .' He points ahead of him at the man and starts walking.

He feels Jules at his side, swift as a bird.

A moment later they're running down the South Bank, Jules calling over to River to mind Nula and the triplets.

Considering he's limping, Constantin is walking fast.

'Come on!' Jules takes David's hand and drags him along.

She's seen him too, he thinks. It must be him.

David doesn't have the energy to run any faster but he takes a breath and pushes into his heels.

His shoes squeak.

Why doesn't he own trainers? he thinks. Why, when he's with Jules, does nothing in his life seem to fit?

The man is about to climb the stairs to Waterloo Bridge when David calls out.

'Constantin!'

The man stops in his tracks. Very slowly, he turns around.

David's head drops and he feels Jules's hand on his shoulder blades.

The man smiles. 'Hello?' His eyes are blue, his eyebrows thin. It's not Constantin.

Jules goes up to him and says something to him. She takes some pound coins out of her purse and presses them into the man's palm, then she comes back to where David is standing.

'It's okay,' she says gently.

David is breathing heavily. There's a pressure in his chest. He takes out his packet of Rennies and puts two in his mouth.

'No, it's not.' He chews hard on the tablets. 'I'm an idiot.'

'You're not an idiot, you got a tip-off that he might be here and you were right, that guy did look like him.'

David shoves another Rennie in his mouth and then looks up at this woman who, only a week ago, was nothing more than a name on Isabel's lips.

'And you shouldn't take too many of those,' Jules says, nodding at the box of Rennies.

Only Jules would have the balls to lecture a doctor on how many tablets he should be taking.

He puts the packet back in his pocket and drops his shoulders. He looks at the ground.

'What am I doing?' he asks.

She lifts his chin. 'You're trying to help.'

He looks her in the eye. 'And what good does that do?'

She lets go of his chin and tilts her head to one side. 'It's not about that.' She smiles at him. 'Helping's who you are. You've got to do it.'

He feels an echo of familiarity in her voice.

'That's what my mum says.'

Jules raises her eyebrows. 'Your mum? She's still around?'

He nods. 'Sort of. She lives in a nursing home.'

Jules touches his arm. 'I'd like to meet her someday.'

He looks up at her. 'You would?'

'The woman who raised Dr Dave Deardorff?' She smiles. 'Of course.'

He knows she's just trying to be kind – to cheer him up. But he likes that she said it. He's never taken anyone to see his mum.

David hears footsteps behind him and wheels clattering against the paving stones.

'What happened?' River comes up to them, out of breath, pushing the triplets. She found a way to get Nula to stand on a small platform on the back of the buggy. For a second, she reminds him more of Jules than Isabel.

'Sorry, guys,' Jules says. 'False alarm. We'll keep looking, but for now, I think we need a break.'

Jules sits them all down on a bench opposite an ice-cream stall.

'Dave, you watch the triplets and Nula. River, you come with me.'

It should irritate him, the way she calls him Dave, but it doesn't. It's as if Jules sees someone in him that no one else does. He likes that.

'Dave – did you hear what I said? Okay to watch the triplets?'

Before he has the chance to explain that he hasn't got a clue how to look after babies, Jules is walking over to the ice-cream stall with River, and David's left sitting with four children under the age of five. They look up at him with wide eyes.

He thinks about what a Monday would usually look like for him: ward rounds, meetings, paperwork. Instead, he's running around after strangers and sitting on a bench on the South Bank in the company of five children and their strangely wonderful tattooed nanny.

And the funny thing is, despite the craziness of all this, despite how foolish he feels right now, he doesn't miss the hospital, not one bit.

One of the triplets starts dribbling some milk. He takes a linen handkerchief out of his pocket and mops at her mouth. Another one grins at him. The third one lets out a fart.

'They like you,' Nula says, swinging her legs.

'They do?'

'Yep.'

They sit there for the next half hour, eating their ice creams. Jules even lets the triplets lick a bit of her cone. Passers-by must think them the strangest family in the world.

He laughs, spitting out a blob of ice cream onto his grey suit trousers.

'Sorry,' he mops at his thigh.

'What was so funny?' River asks.

'Oh, just this whole thing,' David says.

'Dave's wondering what it would be like to be married to me and to have you all as kids.' Jules winks at him.

He stops rubbing at his thigh and stares at her. The tips of his ears burn.

Jules throws back her head and lets out a laugh. He notices a piercing on the little flap that attaches her tongue to the bottom of her mouth; it's beautiful.

'I'm right, aren't I?' Jules says.

He's never met anyone like her.

He laughs nervously. 'You got me.'

River starts giggling. Nula joins in. And then the triplets start gurgling and spitting too, until all seven of them are laughing and choking on their ice creams.

'Well, as this is a family outing, I think you should take us all on the London Eye,' River says. 'After all, it's the summer holidays.' She smiles at him and attempts a Jules-like wink. 'Isn't it, Dad?'

'Why not,' David says. 'I've never been.'

'You've never been on the London Eye?' River cries out.

David blushes. 'No.'

From suit to pyjamas. If only they knew that those two uniforms defined the pattern of his days: that besides work, sleep, food and visits to his mum, his life was empty.

'Well, let's go!'

He pays some ludicrous price to get them further ahead in the queue, and, fifteen minutes later, they're in a glass bubble being lifted into the sky.

Looking out at the grey London skyline, David feels free as a bird, freer than he's felt in a long, long time.

Jules takes two of the triplets out of the buggy and puts them on his lap.

'They should get to see the view, too,' she says.

Trying not to look completely inept, he tucks one girl under each arm and leans back.

Jules pulls the third triplet onto her lap.

'There he is! There he is!' Nula jumps up from beside River, goes to the edge of the bubble and pushes her palm against the glass.

'Come away from the window,' Jules says.

'But he's down there, look!'

They all look in the direction of her small palm. Westminster Bridge. The Houses of Parliament. Big Ben.

River goes over to Nula and takes her hand. 'I know you're trying to help, Nula, but we're all a bit tired of looking.' She lifts her up and brings her back to the bench and sits beside David. 'And he's probably miles from here by now.'

'But I *saw* him.' Nula kicks her legs against the side of the bench, getting David in the shins.

'Stop that!' Jules says, shooting Nula a stern look.

River puts her hand on Nula's knees to still them.

Nula scowls, sticks out her bottom lip and folds her arms over her chest.

The glass bubble takes them higher.

David rocks the two babies on his knees and feels their bodies go limp and sleepy against his stomach. He always thought babies were terrifying but there's something reassuring about the warmth and softness of their bodies leaning into his. He looks down at the river Thames and lets his eyes blur out of focus.

Then he takes Nula's little hand.

'You're right,' he whispers. 'He's out there somewhere, and we're going to find him.'

David

A week later, David looks down at the lobby of *The London Chronicle* headquarters. River and Nula are settling into some colourful chairs and Jules manoeuvres the pushchair with the triplets to face them.

For a second, Jules looks up at him and gives him a wink.

The tips of his ears burn.

'Nice family,' Clem McKee says.

'They're not . . . '

'Not what?'

David keeps looking at them. 'Never mind.'

'You don't look much like your picture,' Clem says as they reach the top of the escalator.

This is the first time he's meeting Clem McKee in person.

'My picture?'

'On the hospital website.'

Clem beeps him through a security door and they head towards a coffee shop.

'Must be your clothes.'

David looks down at his jeans and T-shirt and trainers. Two days ago, Jules and River took him shopping.

You can't go around in a suit, Jules had said.

Why not?

Because it puts people off. You need to look warm and approachable.

Jules was the brains behind the *Find Constantin* campaign. He doesn't know what he'd have done without her.

'They're not mine,' David says, pulling at the neck of his

T-shirt. 'Well, they're mine but they weren't – before. I mean, I haven't had them for very long.'

God, he sounds like an idiot.

Clem frowns. 'Your T-shirt wasn't yours before?'

'Yes. And the jeans. And the trainers.'

Clem laughs. 'Well, you look good.' He smiles. 'Younger.'

'Thanks.'

'Coffee – cake?' Clem asks, nodding his head at the counter.

'Just coffee.' David's been trying to be good. Or, in truth, he's been too embarrassed to eat at the rate he usually does with Jules watching. And he's been too busy to think much about food.

As Clem goes to get the coffees, David looks around. Young people sit hunched over laptops. They look like students, but he supposes they must be journalists.

'So, you work at Regent's Hospital?' Clem asks, putting down the coffees.

'I'm taking some time off.'

'Right.' Clem nods. 'I heard there was some trouble.'

'I suppose there was, yes.'

'Well, you've certainly been busy.'

'Are you going to help us?' David blurts out. And then he feels embarrassed. 'I'm sorry, I know you've only just got back . . . '

'Sure I'll help you. I've been itching to get back into Eastern Europe. And I've never stopped thinking about Constantin.' He shakes his head. 'I can't believe he actually made it to England. It was his dream, you know? To live here. To work where the press was free and he could draw pictures without his life being threatened.'

David nods.

Clem takes a sip of his coffee, wipes his mouth and then says, 'But something happened, right?'

'We're not sure. But he wasn't in a good state when he was brought into the hospital.'

'I can believe that.' He takes another gulp of coffee. 'You said his memory was affected?'

'He couldn't even remember his name.'

'Christ.'

'We were trying to help him—'

'And he disappeared?'

David nods.

'Like he did to me. And we'd made such progress on his story.'

'The censored cartoon?'

'Yes, and his other drawings. How he came to be such a critic of the current government's regime and the nature of the threats he'd received. We wanted to expose how his government was censoring artists like him.'

'And you say he disappeared?'

'Our meetings took place in a small flat in Minsk and then, one day, he was gone, the flat empty, nothing but a few old drawings pinned to the wall. The place had obviously been ransacked: drawers pulled open, beds upended, Sofia's clothes scattered everywhere.'

David's head jolts up. 'Sofia?'

'His wife.'

David's chest seizes up. 'His *wife*?'

'You didn't know he was married?'

'No.' His chest clenches so tight he struggles to breathe. 'No, I didn't.'

Clem pauses. 'Christ, he forgot that too?'

'I suppose so. Yes.'

David's beginning to doubt everything he thought he knew about Constantin. Perhaps Reed had been right and Constantin was pretending to forget. Perhaps he did remember Sofia. And his name. Perhaps the police were right when they said that forgetting was a convenient excuse to avoid the law. But that doesn't seem right, somehow.

And then he thinks of Isabel and that night when he saw them kissing. Would Constantin have done that if he remembered he had a wife?

David takes out a handkerchief and mops his brow.

'Everything okay?' Clem asks.

'I'm fine. Tell me what happened after you found the flat like that?'

'Nothing much. I kept going back, hoping they might be there or that I'd find some clues revealing what had happened to them. I interviewed the neighbours and the owner of the restaurant. No one had seen them. I thought they must have gone into hiding, because the pressure from the government was increasing – and Constantin was refusing to stop publishing his drawings. He once told me that he was so determined to let the world know what was going on in his country, that he'd print the pictures himself if he had to.'

'So, he was looking for trouble?' David asks.

Clem raises his eyebrows. 'Is there any way of telling the truth without getting into trouble?'

'No, I suppose not.'

'But you're right, he did appear to be pushing the boundaries. Sofia was nervous; she's probably the one who decided they should leave.'

'She didn't support the work he did?' David asks.

'I wouldn't go that far, but Sofia and Constantin came from different worlds. Her father is a well-connected businessman in Minsk who's friends with the president. And he's rich. She married below her status and not only that, she married a man who couldn't keep his mouth shut – or rather, who couldn't keep a lid on that pen of his. It didn't go down well with her father. As far as he was concerned, Constantin was an embarrassment.'

'But Sofia sided with her husband?'

'They didn't speak much about their personal lives, but Constantin once said that she'd accused him of not putting his family first.' Clem folds his hands on the table. 'That would have made a good article in itself – *Family versus Country* – but Constantin would never have allowed it: he made me promise to keep her out of anything I wrote.' He looks up at David. 'Marriage is complicated, eh?'

'I wouldn't know,' David says. He holds up his left hand as if to prove it and then blushes. 'Not married,' he clarifies.

Bat-something, wasn't that what River had called him?

'I'm sorry, I thought the woman in the lobby – the children,' Clem says.

David laughs. 'They're just friends.'

Clem looks confused for a moment; perhaps the term *friends* hadn't been the right one.

'Oh, I see. Well, I am – married that is. And my wife doesn't like my job much either.'

'It can't be easy for her,' David says. 'Your work takes you to dangerous places.'

He thinks about the crackly line to Syria when he first spoke to Clem.

'Yeah, I guess that's about the size of it.' Clem opens his palms. 'But she knew the man she married. That it's who I am.'

David nods. He wonders how he would feel if the person he loved most in the world told him to stop working. But then his job isn't exactly controversial, not like the work Clem and Constantin

287

do. And anyway, as things stand he doesn't even have a job. Oddly, he doesn't seem to mind all that much.

'But you think Sofia fled with him?' David asks. 'That they left together?'

'Yes, I do.'

So she had been loyal, even if she disagreed with his work.

'And you think she came to England with him?'

Clem sighs. 'I don't know, David, but she's not here, so something must have happened.' He pauses. 'I imagine her father made sure she was okay. He has connections, but the regime out there is fickle: Sofia's father might have the president's ear one moment but that can change on a penny.'

David feels dizzy. Constantin has a wife? And she's disappeared too? He tugs at the neck of his T-shirt again and tries to breathe.

'You should get some rest,' Clem says. 'Looks like you've been working flat out on this campaign of yours.'

'Did you try to look for Sofia?' David asks.

'Of course. I even went to see her father. As you can imagine, he was delighted to see me show up on his doorstep.'

'A journalist from a liberal English paper known for criticising the regime?'

Clem smiles. 'Precisely.'

'But he spoke to you.'

Clem nods. 'He was worried about his daughter – and furious at Constantin. They were sure he'd put her in some kind of danger.'

'So you gave up looking?'

'My funding ran out. Once the subject of my story had disappeared, there wasn't much I could do to persuade my editor to keep me in Belarus. Your email was the first I've heard of Constantin in over a year.'

David takes a breath. 'But you think we can find him?'

'There's more chance of us finding him in England than in Belarus, that's for sure. I still can't believe that he made it to London. It's a long journey – through Poland, Germany, the Netherlands and France – all the time looking over his shoulder, worried that he was being followed and that he'd be taken back and thrown in jail by the authorities.'

'And your editor is on board with all this?'

'As long as the story holds the public interest, yes, he's in. Just keep drumming up support through your channels, David, and I'll keep pushing Constantin's story in the paper and let's see if, between us, we can find him.'

Clem gets up, which David takes as a cue that the meeting's over. He stands up and they walk out of the café.

David stops walking and turns to Clem.

'Would it be okay if you didn't mention Sofia in your articles?'

Clem raises his eyebrows.

'I think it would be best to focus on Constantin,' David says quickly.

Clem shakes his head. 'It could help with the emotional edge – a husband and wife separated by a corrupt regime —'

'I understand,' David says. 'But maybe you could hold off on that angle, just for a while. Focus on Constantin the man: the lone figure.'

David realises he doesn't have a clue what he's talking about. And what's he trying to achieve. However this turns out, Isabel's going to end up finding out about Sofia.

'There's just someone I'd like to talk to first,' David says. 'If that's okay.'

If Isabel is going to find out, David thinks, it's not going to be through reading a newspaper article. He can do that for her, at least.

Clem nods. 'I can't make any promises, but I suppose we can keep back the wife angle for a bit. It might give the story an extra shot of adrenalin further down the line.'

Sweat gathers along David's hairline and drips down his brow. He takes a handkerchief out of his pocket and mops his face.

'Thank you,' David says.

But his heart's still racing.

What's he got himself into? A few weeks ago, he was a doctor. His life was structured and simple. And now he's standing in the headquarters of one of the country's leading newspapers.

'Find out anything interesting?' Jules asks him as they walk out of *The London Chronicle*'s big glass doors.

'Not really.' David looks down at his trainers.

Clem's words keep spinning round in his head: *as long as the story holds public interest ... keep drumming up support through your channels ... the wife angle ...*

He doesn't know if he can do this any more. He's a doctor, that's what he's trained to do – not this chasing around and investigating and talking to journalists and setting up Facebook pages.

River tugs on David's arm. 'But the journalist guy's going to help us, right?'

'Yes, I think he is.'

River takes David's hand and jumps up and down. 'Three cheers for Dr Deardorff!'

'Hip, hip, hooray!' Nula cries.

One of the triplets lets out a gurgle.

'Well, hopefully it will speed up the search,' Jules says.

Isabel. David's head pounds. He needs to sit down.

'You okay?' Jules asks, grabbing his arm.

David nods. 'I'm fine. I just need to sit down for a bit.'

They find a bench. Then Jules gets out her phone and starts dialling. 'We should tell Isabel the good news.' She puts the phone to her ear. 'Hey, it's me. Dave's been amazing. Again.' Jules pauses and then rolls her eyes. 'You should have seen him marching up to this journalist at *The London Chronicle*. Total legend.'

David looks down at the strange trainers on his feet. He can feel his ears heating up.

'We're going to find your guy, Isabel,' Jules goes on. 'I can feel it . . .'

Her voice trails away.

David leans over and buries his head in his hands. *Your guy.* He waits for the words to wound him but they stay floating in the air. Maybe he's beginning to let go, he thinks.

Constantin

Constantin stands by the River Thames, looking down at the steel structures straddling the dark water.

He feels like he's been walking for weeks but he knows that it's only been a few days.

He had thought that, perhaps, when he got to the Thames barrier, he might find the sea. But there's nothing here except the river and big silver machines that churn the water.

Maybe it's time to give up. He's been walking for so long now, he doesn't have the strength to continue.

He coughs. His throat feels raw. Every time he takes a step, there's a tearing at his knee. He lifts himself up onto a wall which divides the river from the bank, and looks down. It would feel good, he thinks, to let his body fall into the dark, swirling water and to become part of the river. Perhaps, with time, his body would find its way to the sea.

He closes his eyes and feels for the elephant charm in his pocket.

He lifts it to his lips and takes a step forward.

'Can I help you?' A voice comes to him out of nowhere.

Constantin's legs sway under him.

He opens his eyes and sees a man in blue overalls standing on the riverbank.

'I'm not sure it's very safe up there.' The man holds out his hand.

He feels the pull of the river. Beyond it, he can hear the sea.

'Sir?' The man's closer now. 'I really think you should come down.'

Before Constantin has the chance to answer, two hands grip his waist and pull him backwards.

'Here, have this.' The man in the blue overalls pours some tea from a thermos into a plastic cup and places it in Constantin's hands.

Constantin looks around. He's sitting in the passenger seat of a van. He's sat in one like this before, he thinks, but he doesn't remember where.

He's been trying to force his mind to retrieve what happened: what brought him from Belarus, the country the article said he's from, to London. But all he gets are flashes. The face of a young woman with dark hair, a plait over her shoulder. And the sea. He knows he must get back to the sea. That that's where he'll find her and so himself.

'Is there someone you'd like me to call?' the man asks.

Constantin shakes his head.

'Well, my name's Stephen.' He holds out his hand. Constantin takes it: a big, strong, calloused grip.

Stephen waits for a moment and then asks, 'So what's your name?'

A picture of the article flashes across his mind: *Constantin Novak*. It doesn't feel like his name any more.

'Reg,' he says.

'Reg?'

Constantin nods. 'After Regent's Park.'

Stephen frowns. 'I think you need some help, Reg. I could take you to see a doctor. Or to a hospital.'

Constantin thrashes his head from side to side. 'No hospitals.'

Stephen rubs his hands on his overalls and stares out through the dark windscreen of his van.

293

For a while, the two men sit in silence.

Constantin sips at the hot, sweet tea. She'd brought him tea too, at the hospital: the woman with the pale eyes and transparent skin and hair like feathers.

What was her name again?

Present memories have been slipping. He doesn't remember where he was yesterday, or how he got here.

Maybe his mind is giving up at last. Maybe soon he'll be free from it all.

He sinks back into the seat of the van. He likes it in here, no crowds, just the sound of the water swirling below.

'Thank you,' he says, 'for the tea.'

Stephen smiles. 'My wife makes it for me each morning; says she adds a magic ingredient.' He taps the thermos. 'I don't know about that – you know how women like to say these things – but her tea always does taste better than the one I make.'

Constantin drinks the tea and hands the cup back to Stephen.

Stephen screws the cup back on the thermos. Then he clears his throat.

'So, what were you doing up there?'

Constantin hears the rush of the water crossing the great barrier over the Thames.

'I was looking for the sea.'

The man's eyebrows shoot up. 'The sea?'

'Rivers lead to the sea,' Constantin says. 'Don't they?'

'Yes, yes, I suppose they do.'

'I thought that if I kept walking, then maybe—'

'You've been trying to find the sea on foot?'

'It seems so far away.'

'It sure is. My wife and I live on the coast, a place called Broadstairs. I commute to London every day. The sea is my home.'

Constantin's heart jumps. He turns and looks Stephen right in the eye. 'So you understand?'

Stephen laughs. 'You must be a seaside dweller too,' he says. 'It gets into your blood, doesn't it, the sea air? And once it's there, there's no turning away from it?'

Constantin nods.

'Liz and I live just off Botany Bay, we grew up there.' He gives Constantin a sideways smile. 'Childhood sweethearts.'

Even in the dark Constantin can see a blush in the man's cheeks.

'We've never had the heart to leave,' Stephen says.

'It sounds like a good place.'

'It is. And it's a hell of a lot cheaper than living in London.' Stephen whistles through his teeth. 'Daylight robbery, house prices out here. Mortgaged for life – and what do you get for it? A shoebox?' He shakes his head. 'I'd commute another hundred miles before I paid those prices.'

'Yes, it is better to live away from the city,' Constantin says.

'So, were you trying to walk home, is that it?' Stephen asks.

Constantin takes another sip of the tea. He closes his eyes.

'Yes, home.'

'Whereabouts? I could give you a lift?'

'Could you take me there – to your sea?' Constantin asks.

'*My* sea?' Stephen laughs.

Constantin nods.

Stephen's brow contracts. 'Are you sure you live near Broadstairs?'

Constantin nods.

'If you're sure you live nearby, I suppose it couldn't hurt to take you along.'

'Thank you,' Constantin says. 'That would be kind.'

Stephen shakes his head. 'Wait until the wife hears about this.' He turns on the ignition and laughs. 'Okay, let's hit the road, Reg.'

For a few miles, the two men sit side by side in silence. Road signs rush past, as do service stations, cars and lorries. The van is warm, soft music hums from the radio. Constantin's eyelids keep dropping closed. He could sleep for a lifetime, he thinks. But he keeps forcing himself awake, jolting his head up despite the burning in his eyes.

The man turns off the motorway into a small side road and asks, 'Do you have a specific address?'

Constantin shakes his head. 'I don't remember.'

'Um,' Stephen scratches his head. 'So where do you want me to drop you off?'

'Anywhere will be fine.'

'Hang on – you said you lived near here, that's why I brought you along. I can't have you wandering around getting lost.'

'I won't be lost.'

Stephen grips the steering wheel. 'It's dark out there, Reg. It would be good to have an address.'

'Do you live near a beach?' Constantin asks.

'Me? Yeah. But I don't know what that has to do with—'

'I'll go there.'

'You want me to take you to the beach?'

Constantin nods. 'Yes, the beach. To the sea.'

She wouldn't have made it to London Zoo, not without his help. He had to go back and get her.

Stephen scratches his head again. 'I don't know . . .'

'I'll be fine, really.'

Stephen looks at him for a moment and then nods.

'Okay, it's your call.'

Half an hour later they pull up in an empty car park behind some sand dunes. Even though the windows of the van are closed, the smell and the sound of the sea still push through.

Constantin lets out a breath. He's made it, at last.

Before Stephen has the time to turn off the ignition, Constantin stumbles out of the car.

He leans into the open window. 'Thank you.'

And then, before Stephen has the chance to say anything, Constantin walks off across the dunes. He breathes in hard, filling his lungs with sea air. His knee feels stronger. He thinks that maybe he could run.

A few minutes later, he sees Stephen's van turning out of the car park and then disappearing down the lane.

Although it's only late afternoon, the sky is so dark that it feels like night. Storm clouds hang low and heavy. Below the sky, the sea thrashes against the pale shore. White cliffs rise from the sand. They glow against the dark sky and the darker sea below.

He pulls off his shoes and socks and places them next to David's raincoat, hoping that, somehow, it will find its way back to him. Then he rolls up the trousers of his pyjamas and walks into the sea.

As the water washes over his feet, as the sand sinks under him, his mind stills.

This is where I'm meant to be, he thinks.

He closes his eyes and keeps walking until the cold water numbs his body.

When the sea reaches his collarbone, his feet begin to lose their grip on the sand.

And then the sea pulls him under – and he lets go.

Isabel

It's been a week since Reg left, and still there are no leads.

She's heard enough reports of missing people. Every day that goes by without any news means that either they'll never be found, or worse: that when they do, it'll be too late.

She can't keep going like this for much longer, not knowing either way.

Longing and fearing and being so angry all the time.

Which is stupid, she knows – the anger. He ran away when he saw those articles about himself, he was frightened. He probably felt like he didn't have any other choice but to go. But still, he left them without an explanation or saying goodbye or letting them know that, however fleetingly, they meant something to him.

And she's angry at David too. And Jules and River and everyone else who's set off on this wild goose chase. Because it means she can't move on. Every moment of every day, she's reminded of him. And whenever she's reminded of him, she feels him watching her as she draws him, the person beyond the network of bone and tissue and muscle that she'd learnt from her medical textbooks.

And she's as angry at Clem McKee, the journalist from *The London Chronicle*, who got everyone's hopes up. Because now he's saying that he won't be able to keep up interest in the story for much longer, not if there are no fresh leads. *Or a new angle to the story*. But what new angle could there be? Constantin's missing, that's all there is to it.

And the person who's going to get most hurt by all this is River. Because she'll never stop looking for him or wondering about him. River would never give up on anyone.

Most of all, Isabel is angry with herself. She wishes she could go back to that day in July and take a different path to school, avoid the entrance to London Zoo, tell River to leave the man alone – refuse to take Reg to the hospital. If she'd never brought him in that day, David would still be working at the hospital and she'd still be in Simon's good books rather than having to do crazy early mornings followed by late-night shifts because he wants to teach her a lesson about not being above her station and getting involved with the patients.

And if something has happened to Reg, goodness knows what it will do to River.

God, she'd do anything to turn back time.

But life doesn't work like that. Or that's what she's told herself, over and over.

The problem is, she's spent the last decade working out how life does work, and that hasn't got her any further.

Isabel pushes the anger back down her throat. Maybe she can't turn back time but she can get a grip. She can focus on the life they had before Constantin – and the life they're going to have to get back to when they all come to terms with the fact that they're not going to find him. In ten days' time, River will be starting secondary school. Every time Isabel brings it up, River insists that she's not going. As if it's an actual option. Isabel has to find a way to help her understand how important it is.

She takes her phone out of her pocket and looks at the number she stored there a few days ago: *Mum & Dad*.

It felt odd, typing those words after all this time.

Every day she gets a step closer to calling them, but then

something gets in the way. Usually the fear that, even after eleven years, they're still disappointed in her.

'Looking at your phone *again*?'

She jumps and looks up: Simon stands in front of her.

She remembers a picture Constantin drew of him: a tap-dancing rat, whiskers twitching, beady eyes, paws in the air.

She'd laughed and told him he was brilliant.

He hadn't taken the compliment.

Drawings can be dangerous . . . he'd said to her.

She hadn't understood what he meant, not then. Had he understood what he was saying? Did he remember the cartoon that got him into such trouble – the one he drew for River?

'I'm disappointed,' Simon says, shaking his head and sucking his teeth. 'I thought that after our little chat, you were going to prioritise your career.'

'I am,' Isabel says, shoving her phone back into her pocket.

'Well, every time you look at your phone rather than cleaning the ward, you're wasting taxpayers' money. I hope that sits well with your conscience.'

Blood rises to the surface of Isabel's skin.

What about all the money wasted on paying for paper-pushing managers like him?

'I'm sorry,' she mumbles and goes back to her trolley.

'I need you to work later tonight,' Simon calls after her.

Again? Surely someone else is due a late shift.

She grits her teeth. 'Sure.'

Simon gives her a sharp nod. 'Good, good.'

As he walks away, she feels her phone vibrate and, without thinking, she whips it out of her pocket.

She wakes up the screen. There's a long Facebook message on the Find Constantin page.

Don't look at it, she tells herself, *switch it off, leave it alone. We're not going to find him. It's all too late.*

But she can't look away.

She scrolls down and reads:

We live in Broadstairs, Kent . . . it's probably nothing but my husband drove someone home from London tonight . . . I read the news a lot . . . I've been following your campaign . . . I don't want to waste your time . . . like I said, it's probably nothing . . .

'Isabel?' Simon's voice echoes down the corridor.

Isabel looks up. He's glaring at her.

She ignores him and keeps reading the message.

He wanted to be left on the beach . . . it was dark . . . Stephen wasn't sure it was the right thing to do . . . He found him by the river, near where he works . . . he'd walked for miles . . .

Isabel's heart leaps into her mouth. The river, the sea, walking for miles, the strangeness of the story – it feels too familiar to ignore.

She hears the click of Simon's heels coming down the corridor. A moment later he's standing beside her, holding out his hand.

'How about I put that in the office until the end of your shift.' He nods at the phone.

Slowly, Isabel raises her eyes from the screen.

He's going to take away her phone? Is that even legal?

Isabel grips the phone hard and shakes her head.

'Let's not cause trouble, Isabel.'

Every sensible bone in her body tells her to back down, to bow her head and apologise, hand him the damn phone and get on with the cleaning.

But she can't, not this time.

Isabel pulls her NHS Staff lanyard over her head and thrusts it into Simon's open palm.

For a second, Simon looks at her, stunned.

'Isabel?'

'I'm leaving.'

He goes red, anger pushing up under his skin.

She's never answered back to him – not once in ten years.

'You might like to reconsider your actions, Isabel.'

She doesn't bother answering.

'You won't be able to come back. Your position will be filled.'

Isabel walks away from him.

'Isabel!' His voice is desperate now. 'Isabel!'

But she's already in the lift, dialling David's number.

Constantin

Down here, in the dark water, everything is still.

The storm and the waves are far above; all he needs to do is wait a little longer.

His mind floats and his limbs stretch out around him.

It won't be long now, he thinks.

And then he hears a loud thud a few yards away from him. An anchor sinking into sand. And without him willing it to, his body pushes back up to the surface.

He gasps at the damp air and coughs out water. His limbs thrash, like they're coming back to life. And through his blinking eyes, he sees a small fishing boat.

He blinks again. And then he sees her face, leaning over the railing, looking down at him.

His heart swells. He knew he'd find her here.

He reaches out a hand but another wave surges over him and when he comes back up for air, she's gone.

David

David sits in the taxi outside the hospital, watching the rain falling hard against the window.

Isabel opens the door and sits next to him; a rush of fresh air sweeps in with her.

Her cheeks are flushed, her eyes shining.

He was going to call her tonight, arrange a place to meet so that he could tell her about Sofia. But then she called first, breathless with excitement: *I think we might have found him*, she said.

'You think I'm crazy?' Isabel bites her lip.

He shakes his head. 'No, you were right to call. The tip-off sounds genuine.'

'It does, doesn't it? That stuff about the river and the sea – and the walking?'

David nods. 'It's definitely worth a shot.'

Isabel squeezes his hand. 'And the fact that the woman said she'd never posted a message on Facebook before – I looked up her profile and it's true, she doesn't even have a photo on her page. She must have started the account just to get in touch.' Her words tumble over each other. He can tell how, after all the disappointments, she longs for this to be the message that leads her back to Constantin.

'Where to?' the taxi driver looks over his shoulder.

'Botany Bay,' Isabel says.

The driver laughs. 'Not sure my old taxi will make it all the way to New Zealand.'

'Broadstairs. Kent,' Isabel says quickly.

'I think he was joking,' David whispers.

'Oh . . . I'm sorry.' She puts a hand to her mouth. 'It's just this message – I was ready to give it all up, you know?'

'I know. But let's take it a step at a time, eh?'

'Of course.' She nods and bites her lip. 'I know it's probably another loose end.'

He puts his hand over hers. 'Let's go and see.'

Things have been easier between them. Lighter. He doesn't feel as flustered any more. Or as scared that he'll do and say the wrong thing.

The taxi driver indicates and pulls out into the thick London traffic.

'What did you tell River?' she asks.

He'd spent the day with Jules and the kids, like he had every day in the last two weeks. Simon had Isabel working these crazy hours and without his job at the hospital to occupy his every waking hour, helping Jules out has given David some kind of purpose. He'd thought that maybe tomorrow, he might take them to see his mum. Jules keeps asking about her.

Isn't it strange, he thinks, *how it only takes two weeks to start a whole new life?*

'Jules and I discussed it—' he says.

Isabel smiles. 'You did?'

'She thought it was best not to tell River yet – about the sighting. Not until we were sure.'

'So, what did you tell River?'

'That the hospital needed me. An emergency. All hands on deck.' He pauses. 'Which isn't exactly a lie – I mean, this is an emergency, you called from the hospital and you need me, right?' He gives her a smile.

'*Constantin* needs you,' Isabel corrects.

'Right.'

'Good call, though – about not telling River.' Isabel looks out of the window. 'Jules is good at making decisions.'

'She is.' He feels the tips of his ears go hot. 'She is,' he says again, tugging at his T-shirt. 'She said she'd take Nula home and then go back to the flat with River and wait for us,' he goes on. 'She knows it's important.'

She knows, he thinks, *how much you care about Constantin.*

He'd thought about telling Jules about Sofia – maybe the news would be better coming from her. No one knows Isabel better. But it hadn't seemed fair to put that burden on her. Jules has done enough already. And more than that, he didn't want Jules to think he was a coward. He didn't want Jules to think anything bad about him.

They sit in silence as the taxi weaves in and out of the London traffic. Then, after what feels like hours, they pull out onto the motorway.

The rain falls harder.

David looks out of the window and feels a thud in his chest. He realises that if they do find Constantin, all this will end. There won't be any reason for him to spend time with River and Isabel – and Jules – any more.

Isabel leans her head against David's shoulder and sighs. He feels her warm breath on his neck.

'I got fired today.' She lets out a small laugh. 'I got *myself* fired.'

He smiles. 'Good.'

She sits up. 'Good?'

'You're wasting your time in that job.'

'Excuse me?'

He hesitates for a second, but then blurts it out. She's needed to hear this for a long time.

'You need to go back to nursing school. Or to apply to medical school.'

'*What?*'

'You're brilliant with patients. And Jules told me ...'

'She told you what?'

'That it was your dream, when you two were growing up.'

Isabel folds her arms over her chest. 'I like being a cleaner.'

He laughs.

'Don't laugh at me.' She crosses her arms. For a second, she makes him think of River.

'I'm not laughing at you, Isabel. I know you like working at the hospital. As far as I can see, you're the best cleaner in the country. The hospital is going to suffer for losing you. But it's not what you should be doing – and you know it.' He takes a breath. 'I could help you.'

For a long time, Isabel stares out of the window. Then she says, 'Let's focus on Constantin.'

The rain has turned to a thin drizzle. Mist rises over the sea. At the end of the car park, there's a white van with lights on inside. A man and a woman step out, the man holding a torch. He waves at them to come over.

David takes Isabel's hand. 'Come on.'

The couple have that fresh, rosy-cheeked look of people who live by the sea, like they've breathed in more air than other people.

'This is where Stephen last saw him,' Liz, the wife, says. 'Isn't it, love?'

'I shouldn't have left him,' Stephen says.

His wife takes his hand. 'It's okay, my love.'

The four of them look up across the dunes at the beach. The cliffs stand rooted in the dark sand, tall as ghosts.

'I suppose there hasn't been any sign of him?' Isabel says. 'Since you came back?'

Stephen shakes his head. 'We only just got here. And it's pretty dark out there.'

Isabel nods. 'Of course.'

The wind picks up. The rain lashes against them.

Liz tightens the toggle of her hood. 'It feels like it hasn't stopped raining all summer,' she says.

They all stand there and nod.

The wettest summer on record. How many times had they heard that? The only person who didn't seem to mind was River.

Liz looks from David to Isabel. 'I don't mean to interfere, but do you think we should call the police? Or an ambulance or something? As backup?'

'No,' Isabel says. 'Not yet.'

'It's just, the tide can be pretty brutal in this weather.'

'I understand,' Isabel says. 'But we're going to look first.'

Liz is about to say something when David notices Stephen pressing her arm.

'Come on, love, let's get back in the van and wait.' He looks at David. 'We're here if you need us.'

Before he turns to go, Stephen adds:

'I hope you find him.' He pauses. 'He seemed like a nice guy.'

David hears a small choke coming from Isabel. He tucks his arm under hers and nods at Stephen.

'Thanks,' he says to him.

And then David and Isabel walk up to the beach, their bodies pushing against the headwind.

*

'He liked walking. I mean, he wouldn't just have stopped here, near the car park – he would have gone further,' Isabel says, looking up and down the beach.

'Okay, so we'll walk too – until we find him.'

'I think we should separate,' she says. 'You go that way.' She points at the long stretch of beach that heads towards a cluster of houses. There's a sailing boat moored not too far from the shore being tossed up and down in the waves. 'I'll go this way.' She nods at the row of white cliffs in the distance.

Isabel knows that Constantin would have walked away from the houses, David thinks, and that those cliffs would have attracted him. She wants to find him first.

'We should stick together,' he says.

She shakes her head.

'No. It's better this way.'

He thinks of River again: that same stubbornness.

'Okay. Call me, though – if there's anything. Anything at all.'

She nods, her eyes wide and glassy. She might be stubborn; she might know exactly what she wants to do and whom she wants to find, but it doesn't mean she's not scared.

He steps forward and puts his arms around her and holds her in a way he's never allowed himself to do before.

'Isabel . . . ' he starts.

'Don't tell me it's going to be okay,' she whispers. 'I don't want to hear that.'

'I won't.' He pauses. 'Just look after yourself, all right?'

He feels her nod against his chest.

And then they move apart and with every step, he forces himself not to turn round and go after her.

River

Jules holds out her packet of Haribo Starmix.

They're lying side by side on the sofa bed and Jules is being totally weird.

'You're sharing your sweets?' River asks.

Jules never shares her sweets. First, because she panics when she runs out, and second, because River isn't allowed sweets – sugar and ADHD don't mix.

'It's the holidays,' Jules says.

'It's been the holidays for ages and you haven't let me have any of your sweets. What's changed?'

'Suit yourself.' Jules shrugs and shoves the packet of Haribo back in her pocket.

'Hey – I didn't mean I didn't want one.' River leans over and snatches at Jules's pocket.

Jules pushes her away. 'Too late. Offer's closed.'

River lies back against her pillow.

'That's not fair.'

'Life's not fair.'

For a while, they lie on the sofa bed, listening to the rain. It hasn't stopped all day. People on TV say it's global warming, that the whole earth is getting so hot that the weather's gone crazy.

After a while, River says, 'Something's happened, hasn't it, Jules?'

Jules doesn't answer.

'Jules?'

'Nothing's happened.'

'So why do you keep looking at your phone? And why's Mum not home? And why did Dr Deardorff rush off so fast?'

Most nights Dr Deardorff stays to eat at Gabino's and they basically have to kick him out to get him to go home. Even though his flat is a hundred times nicer, he prefers hanging out with River and Nula and the triplets – and Jules.

'It's like Dave said, the hospital needed him.'

River thought that was weird. He hadn't gone back to the hospital in ages. Why would they call him up now, out of the blue?

River sits up. 'Has there been another lead?'

Jules doesn't answer. If there's one thing about Jules, it's that she doesn't lie, so her going quiet can only mean one thing.

'There has, hasn't there? That's why he went off and Mum's not back? Why didn't they tell me?'

Jules sits up too and looks out of the window. Pablo lands on the windowsill and flaps his wings against the glass.

'They don't want to get your hopes up, River.'

'My hopes up?'

'They know how disappointed you've been – when we've had a tip-off and it hasn't led to anything.'

'I haven't been disappointed.'

Jules raises her eyebrows.

Of course she's right. It's been horrible, thinking that, at any moment, Reg is going to walk back into their lives and then finding out that it's another dead end and that with each dead end, Reg is probably getting even more lost.

Jules goes over to the window, opens it and holds out her hand.

'What are you doing?' River asks.

'He's getting wet.'

'He gets wet all the time and you don't let him in.'

Something's definitely up.

311

'Well, I won't tell your mum if you don't,' she says.

River jumps up and joins Jules by the window. Pablo stares at them for a moment, like he's worried it's a trick, but when River holds out her hand too, he flies into the room.

He lands on the kitchen table and looks around.

'Just no shitting inside, Pablo, that's the deal,' Jules says.

River goes over to the kitchen counter to get some bread and brings it over to the table. She looks at the medical textbook open on a section about amnesia that Mum was reading when they first met Reg. Then she sees a piece of paper poking out from the top of one of the pages. She eases it out and notices that it's the same paper as in the exercise book she gave Reg to draw in. And there's a picture of a man on it and it kind of looks like the pictures that Mum draws when she's testing herself on anatomy, only she's scribbled over the organs and tissues and muscles and bones and turned it into an actual person. River looks closer. Her heart does a somersault. It's Reg. Kind of. The man's got the same big eyes and he's tall and gangly and has messy hair. Only he looks younger than Reg, much younger.

River grabs the piece of paper, goes over to Jules by the window and shoves it in front of her face.

'What's this?'

Jules stares at it for a second and then shrugs. 'Nothing.'

Her eyes went wider when she looked at it: it definitely isn't nothing.

'Jules?' River prompts. 'Who's the picture of?'

'How am I supposed to know?'

'You know everything.'

She shrugs again.

'Well, I think Mum drew it – it was in her textbook. Only Mum doesn't draw, not like this.'

'She used to.'

'What do you mean?'

'She did art at school. Loved it.'

'What?'

'It's how her Italy obsession began. All the best art's over there.'

'Mum did art – like proper, artistic art?'

Jules laughs. '*Artistic* art?'

'You know what I mean. It's not Mum.'

'No, it hasn't been, not for a while.'

River thinks about the piece of paper again and how it comes from the exercise book she gave to Reg. Which means that he gave it to her. Maybe he gave her a drawing lesson too.

River doesn't know whether to feel happy or jealous.

'She drew it with Reg, didn't she?'

'I don't know, River.'

River holds the paper closer to Jules's face.

'Who is it, Jules, tell me?'

'Oh, for Christ's sake, River, this is starting to feel like the Spanish Inquisition.'

'The what?'

'You're asking too many questions.'

River squints at the paper again. Even if he's much younger, the guy definitely looks like Reg. River swallows hard. Mum's totally captured Reg's spirit.

River shakes her head. 'I can't believe that Mum used to do art.'

River thought that Mum only liked real stuff. Facts, like textbooks and the news – not stuff that came from your imagination.

A flapping of wings comes from the kitchen which reminds River that Pablo's in the flat and that she was going to feed him. She goes over, puts the picture back into Mum's textbook, picks up the piece of bread and crumbles it over the kitchen table for Pablo.

Pablo starts pecking at the bread.

Jules is still by the window, looking out at the rain.

'Do you think this is a proper lead?' River asks her.

Jules doesn't turn round.

'Dr Deardorff wouldn't have gone off with Mum if they didn't think there was a chance they could find Reg.'

Jules shrugs. 'We'll see.'

River comes and stands beside her and looks out at the dark, rainy night.

'Where do they think he is?'

'Kent.'

'They've gone all the way to Kent? But that's miles away.'

Jules nods.

River looks over at the map of London Reg gave her. She never thought he'd leave London. She thought that, if they found him anywhere, it would be next to one of the places he wanted to visit like Big Ben or Trafalgar Square or one of the bridges across the Thames.

'Why would Reg be in Kent?' River asks.

'Dave said something about the sea.'

At least that makes a bit of sense. River remembers how Reg used to talk about the sea and that he'd thought you might be able to see it from London. It was another thing he was sad about, like the elephants not being at London Zoo. She wishes they'd had the time to take him to Whipsnade; it makes her sad to know that he might never get to see them.

'Could we borrow Gabs's car and go after them?' River asks. 'They could do with our help.'

'No.'

'But—'

'I shouldn't even have told you about the lead, River.'

'Yes, you should. I've been looking for Reg as much as anyone else.'

Jules nods. 'I know, River. I know.'

Jules shuts the window and goes back to sit on the sofa bed. Pablo flies up to one of the bookshelves by the door and looks down at them.

River comes over and sits next to Jules. 'You've liked having him around, haven't you?'

'Pablo?'

River rolls her eyes.

'You shouldn't do that – your eyes will get stuck.'

'You do it all the time!'

'My eyes have had a lifetime of practice.'

River knows that Jules is just avoiding her question about Dr Deardorff.

'I think Dr Deardorff likes you.'

Jules doesn't say anything.

'We should get him some funky glasses – to go with his new clothes.'

Whenever River sees Dr Deardorff in his T-shirt and jeans and trainers he thinks of those before-and-after photos you see in magazines and how it feels like you're staring at two totally different people. That's what's happened with Dr Deardorff: he's turned into a completely new person this summer. And it's not just the clothes.

'You could take him glasses shopping,' River says.

Jules still doesn't answer.

She's changed too. Not so that it's visible on the outside, like with Dr Deardorff's clothes, but River's noticed it. She's got softer. Like this whole letting Pablo in from the rain.

'I think he'd like it,' River says.

Jules blushes. And she never blushes. Her skin's not the type to go red.

Jules stands up again. She can't stop moving: it's like she's caught River's ADHD or something.

'Time to go back out, buddy,' Jules calls up to Pablo.

'He's only just come in. And it's still raining.'

Jules picks up one of Mum's medical journals and swipes it at Pablo. Then she goes over and opens the window. River watches him flying out into the rainy night.

'He's not dead, is he?' River asks.

'Dead – who?'

'Reg. It's not a body they've found?'

Jules goes quiet again.

'Jules?'

'Look River, I don't know any more than you. All Dave said was that they had a lead and that it sounded serious.'

River nods but she doesn't like the fact that Jules didn't tell her, outright, that she was being stupid, that of course Reg wasn't dead, that everything was going to be fine.

'Let's just wait and see,' Jules says.

River looks past Jules through the dark window. *Go and find them, Pablo*, she whispers to herself. *And make sure Reg is okay.*

David

David gets out his phone. He's been walking for half an hour; his clothes are soaked through and he's shivering. And the wind is getting worse.

He wipes his glasses and squints down the beach. His chest tightens: he can't see her anywhere.

Why did he let her go off alone?

He looks towards the cluster of houses and the sailing boat. He was planning to go to the first house and knock on the door. Maybe the owners have seen someone walking down the beach alone.

Then he spots something near the water and breaks into a run.

By the time he gets to the raincoat – *his* raincoat – and the shoes, he's wheezing, his heart racing.

The waves lap at the coat, like they're trying to pull it in. By morning, the items would have been washed away and no one would have known that Constantin was even here.

Trying to phone Isabel at the same time, David runs towards the water, but his fingers are shaking too hard to function properly. He tosses the phone onto the sand and cups his hands over his mouth:

'Constantin!' he calls. 'Constantin!'

The wind swallows his words.

And then the sailing boat catches his attention again – how violently it's being tossed around by the waves, its white sails flapping at the wind like wings. He feels his pulse beating through his body. Red lights flash in front of his eyes.

He tries to steady his breath and to focus on the boat again.

Maybe that's why Constantin took off his raincoat and his shoes: he thought he could make it to the boat and sail back home.

David kneels down, unties his shoes and takes off his socks.

And then he stops.

A small voice creeps into his head.

This isn't you, David. Just be sensible and go and ask for help.

He closes his eyes and shakes his head to make the voice go away.

David knows that he's not the guy who rips off his shirt and dives in the icy water to save the world. No: he's the guy who stands under the bright hospital lights in scrubs over a grey suit waiting for the gurney to come in. Everything neat and clean and safe.

But he's not at the hospital any more. God, he probably doesn't even have a job any more.

And nothing he's done in the last few weeks resembles the old David.

And standing on a beach in the middle of the night with a storm coming, looking for an illegal immigrant, that's not him either.

But he's here, isn't he?

He opens his eyes and takes a breath.

I don't care any more about who I'm meant or not meant to be, he thinks. He promised Isabel and River that he'd help them find Constantin, and he's going to do whatever it takes to keep that promise.

So, knowing that the heavy fabric will weigh him down, he takes off his jeans, then he removes his glasses, folds them closed, places them on the pile of clothes – and wades in.

The pulse beating through his body is replaced by the sound of the waves, crashing around him.

He wades in further.

The cold water stings. Stabs of pain shoot up his torso and his arms.

An image flashes across his mind: he's ten years old, standing on the edge of the swimming pool at school. The summer term humiliation of having to get into his trunks, his heavy body pulling him down like a stone as the other boys shot through the water.

God, how they'd laugh if they could see him now: half blind, standing in the middle of a storm, shivering in his underpants.

He gulps down a big breath, throws himself at the sea and pushes his arms against the water.

A wave crashes over his head and pulls him under for a second. He kicks himself up to the surface and gasps at the air.

'Constantin!' His voice cracks but he lets out another strangled shout: 'Constantin!'

He turns his body round and round, treading water to see if he can spot anything, but the sea is so churned up that it's hopeless.

His heart beats faster. He feels lightheaded and dizzy. There's a searing pain in his chest. He doesn't know how much longer he can fight the waves.

David scans the coastline for Isabel and then he realises how stupid it is to even try to see her without his glasses. The shoreline blurs in and out of focus.

He closes his eyes for a second and allows himself to imagine her walking towards him: a small figure floating along the sand, the wind and the rain not even touching her.

He should have told her about Sofia, he thinks now, as though it's the one thing he's left undone.

He blinks salty water from his eyes and his mind flicks back to River and the triplets and Nula – and Jules. Jules looking at him, her eyes serious: *Don't do anything stupid, Dave*, she'd said.

And then a wave crashes over him and the world goes dark.

Constantin

One Hour Earlier

Constantin scrambles onto the shore, coughing up seawater. His heart pounds against his ribcage.

The rain has eased now. The wind too. For a little while, the world is still.

Once he's caught his breath, he looks up at a clearing in the clouds: a fingernail of moon slips through and then disappears again.

Then his eyes go back to the sailing boat. When he was in the sea, the boat swayed so hard that he thought it would capsize. Now, it seems suspended on the water.

Through the stillness, her words come back to him:

If anything happens, we'll meet by the elephants. We'll see them together.

His heart seizes up. His eyes fill with tears.

He screws them shut.

I'm coming, he whispers.

His knee burning with pain, Constantin walks back up the shoreline and looks for the car park. The rain has started again, heavier than before. He's shivering. He should have put his shoes and the raincoat back on.

Maybe Stephen came back, he thinks, *maybe he knew that I'd need him*. But the car park is empty. Deep puddles reflect the shifting clouds.

How far was the motorway from here? It shouldn't take long. He could find his way back.

The sky gets darker. Cuts sting his bare feet, but he keeps walking.

He has to keep his promise to her.

And then he sees it: a white car, blue lights flashing in the rain. It pulls up beside him.

Isabel

Every part of Isabel's body feels numb.

She's reached the cliffs but there's nothing here except miles of white chalk.

Just another dead end.

It was stupid to think that Constantin could have come this far, or that he even wanted to be found. Why were they all so desperate to find him? He chose to walk out on them, didn't he?

As she heads up the beach back to David, she gets out her phone to call him. There's only one bar of reception.

Then she notices a message from Jules sent half an hour ago.

There's a link to a news website. And Jules's words underneath: *Guess the search is over.*

Isabel's heart races.

The search is over? What does she mean?

She clicks on the link. It takes ages to load and she has to keep wiping rain off her screen to see clearly.

At last a headline flashes up:

REGENT'S PARK AMNESIAC PICKED UP BY POLICE.

Oh, God.

She tries to scan the article but the screen on her phone keeps freezing. She switches the phone off and waits for it to reload.

He's okay, that's the main thing, she tells herself. They always knew that the police might get to him first. They can handle this.

Now she has to get to David.

She breathes in and out a few times, trying to calm herself

down. Then she looks back at her phone. It's working again. She calls David but it goes straight to voicemail. Damn it.

He can't have got that far, maybe he's even turned back – realised, like her, that this is hopeless.

Isabel shoves her phone in the pocket of her dress and heads back up the beach.

'Isabel! Isabel!'

Liz, the woman who contacted her through Facebook, runs towards her, waving frantically.

When Liz gets to her, Isabel says, 'I know, I know, they've found him.'

'What? Found who?' Liz's eyes are wild. 'No. No, you have to come – it's David.'

'David?'

Isabel's head spins.

Liz takes her hand and drags her along the beach.

'When you guys took so long, Stephen got worried. He headed up the beach to find David . . . ' Her voice breaks.

Isabel stops walking, grabs Liz's shoulders and shakes her. 'And what?'

'I called an ambulance . . . '

Isabel's legs feel weak. 'An ambulance?'

She pauses. 'And the police.'

Oh, God.

'I thought it was the right thing to do. They're on their way.' She gulps. 'Stephen saw him struggling – in the water. That's when he decided to go after him. And there still wasn't any sign of your friend. We thought that maybe he'd taken off again. The police are looking for him now.'

Her words tumble over each other.

Liz grabs Isabel's hand again and drags her further. 'Come on, we have to go and help.'

As the two women run up the beach, Isabel shouts out against the wind:

'What was David doing in the water?'

'I don't know – maybe he saw something,' Liz calls back.

Isabel stares out at the waves, the water, black as ink.

Stephen rushes up to them.

'I pulled him out . . . ' he says, his voice shaky. 'But I don't know what to do . . . ' He takes a breath. 'He's not waking up.'

Isabel pushes past him and places two fingers on David's wrist. It's faint but it's there – just the feather of a pulse pushing through his skin.

'Are you a doctor? Can you help?' Liz asks, her voice desperate.

'Yes. No.' Isabel gulps. 'Close enough.'

She kneels down beside David and pushes her palms down on his chest: 'One . . . two . . . three . . . ' she counts with each compression. She presses her mouth to his and breathes out hard until his chest inflates. And then she presses his chest again: 'One . . . two . . . three . . . '

In the distance, she hears sirens.

She breathes into David's mouth once more and then he coughs.

Isabel leans back just in time for David to splutter out a whole load of water.

Her heart lifts.

She eases his head up so that he doesn't choke. For a second, he looks up at her and smiles weakly.

'I thought I'd lost you,' she says.

He blinks up at her. He looks like a child without his glasses.

'You're going to be okay . . . ' she says.

'Constantin?' David says, his voice raw from coughing.

'They've found him . . .' Isabel says.

David leans back, his eyes close, and then he goes limp.

'David?'

She puts her ear to his mouth. Nothing.

'David? Wake up!' She shakes him. He was okay, just a second ago, he was awake. He was fine. 'David!'

River

River presses down on her leg to stop it jiggling up and down but it won't stop. If she sits in this chair any longer, she's going to explode.

Everything feels wrong.

Dr Deardorff isn't meant to be in hospital – not the A&E department of some hospital miles away from London.

And not as a patient.

And not in a coma.

And Jules isn't meant to be sitting next to him, holding his hand so tight it's like she's scared he's going to slip away.

Jules hates hospitals, but, early this morning, as soon as River was awake, she threw a cereal bar at her and told her to get in the car.

She hasn't left his side since they got here, not even to go to the loo or something.

And her face is all wobbly, her mascara and eyeliner smudged around her eyes.

She called Nula and the triplets' parents to say she wasn't working today. And Jules is like Mum: she never misses a day's work.

And Mum's been pacing the room so hard it's starting to make River feel dizzy.

River gets up and shakes out her leg. It feels like there's electricity trapped in her body – and not good electricity.

And Reg. She thought she'd feel relieved when they found him. But now he's all alone at the police station back in London and no one's saying anything about what's going to happen to him.

No, nothing feels right.

River looks out of the window. It's going to be a sunny day for once, which doesn't feel right either, not with everything that's happened.

'Don't you think we should ask about Reg,' River asks Mum. 'Call the police station or go and visit him or something?'

Jules's head snaps up. Her eyes are glassy.

'No,' she says.

Mum stays quiet.

'But he's alone . . . ' River says.

'He brought this on himself,' Jules said. 'Dave nearly died helping him – he's the one that we should be concentrating on now.'

River hesitates. She knows Jules is upset, but she can't help saying it:

'Dr Deardorff didn't nearly die because of Reg. He had a heart attack. That could have happened anywhere.'

Jules rubs her eyes as if she's not quite sure that it's River standing there in front of her, saying those words.

They operated on his heart and, ever since, they've been waiting for him to wake up. The surgeon said that it wasn't uncommon: a coma after a heart attack, the body's way of coping with the shock.

Mum thinks that they should transfer Dr Deardorff back to their hospital in London because everyone there knows him and will do even more to make sure he's okay, but the doctor said that they have to wait until he's stable. Whatever that means.

'It wasn't Reg's fault,' River says again.

River feels Mum's hand on her shoulder. 'Leave it, River.'

Jules shakes her head and goes back to gripping Dr Deardorff's limp hand.

River knows she's upset but she still thinks it's unfair that they should be blaming this on Reg. But she feels guilty too, for upsetting Jules.

How are you meant to be there for everyone at the same time? River thinks. How are you meant to know who needs you most? Dr Deardorff's obviously really sick – and he's the one who's been helping them find Reg. But he's being looked after now. Reg has no one.

River looks over to Mum. She's walked over to the window. River wonders whether, for once, Mum agrees with her: that they can't just ignore what's happened to Reg.

River walks over to her.

'Mum?'

She doesn't answer.

'Mum? Could we have a chat?' River whispers. Then she jerks her head towards Jules and lowers her voice further. 'Outside?'

River knows that Jules would flip if she heard what she's got to say.

Mum nods, her eyes still in a daze, and follows River out of the room.

They sit on a couple of chairs in the corridor outside.

'I'm worried about him, Mum.'

Mum puts her hand on River's leg; it's started jiggling up and down again.

'Have you been taking your meds?' Mum asks.

River brushes Mum's hand away. 'I'll take them when we get home.'

You have to work with the medication, the consultant had told her and Mum. *Especially at times of stress. It's not magic. It won't work on its own.*

But River doesn't care about meds right now.

'He needs our help, Mum,' River blurts out.

'I know.'

'I mean Reg.'

'I know.'

'I really think we should go to the police station.'

Mum looks down at her hands and, very slowly, she nods.

They tell Jules that they're going to get a cab home so they can have a shower and get changed and get some rest. Mum's clothes are still damp from being on the beach, so it sounds like a good reason. River knows it's bad to lie, and usually, Mum would never agree to anything but telling the truth. And River doesn't remember them ever lying to Jules. But sometimes the wrong thing to do feels like the right thing too.

Anyway, Jules is barely registering what's going on, she's too busy focusing on Dr Deardorff.

When they get to the police station, they have to explain to the receptionist, over and over, why they're here. It's like he's deliberately trying not to understand them.

'Are you the next of kin?'

'No—' River says.

'Yes,' Mum says over her.

The man raises his skinny eyebrows.

'Which is it?'

'We're his closest living relatives.' Mum's voice is so clear and strong that for a second River believes her words: that Reg is part of their family. That they belong together and that they have a right to see him.

Maybe Mum's right: maybe they are the closest thing Reg has to family.

'What's his name again?' the man asks.

River sighs and does a Jules eyeroll, hoping it will make the man take more notice. They've told him a million times already.

And it's not like he wouldn't have noticed Reg coming in. The police have been looking for Constantin Novak for weeks. It was all over the news: finding him was a big deal for them.

'Constantin Novak,' Mum says, really slowly, so that he gets it.

'I'll go and find out if he's here.'

'He's here,' Mum says.

River likes this new confident Mum. How she seems willing to take anyone on who gets in her way. Maybe she's got more of Jules in her than she realises.

The man doesn't answer. Then he comes out from behind his desk – as slowly as physically possible – and walks down the corridor.

They're about to sit down in the waiting area when the glass doors swish open.

The first person they see is the journalist Dr Deardorff has been working with to promote Reg's case: Clem McKee. He came to have coffee at Gabino's once, while they were still looking for Reg. At least he's still focused on Reg.

River jumps up. 'You're here!'

Clem smiles and nods.

River feels Mum's body relaxing next to hers. Clem's got connections, they'll listen to him.

The doors at the bottom of the corridor open.

River lurches forward. 'Reg!'

A policeman walks beside him.

Reg is thin and pale and his beard has started growing again. He's hunched over a cane that's too small for him, but at least they gave him something to lean on. His stick, the one the dog brought him, must still be at Dr Deardorff's flat.

When he sees River, his eyes light up and he smiles.

But then River feels Mum's arm gripping hers, so tight it hurts.

She's looking at a woman who's just come in through the main entrance; a woman who's standing next to Clem. And her eyes are fixed on Reg.

Constantin

'So you remember who I am?' Sofia says.

They're sitting in the lobby of the hotel where Sofia's staying.

It's been over an hour since Clem drove them here, the two of them sitting in silence in the back as the car crawled through thick, rush-hour traffic.

Constantin thinks about Isabel dragging River out of the police station: she didn't even give him the chance to explain.

'Yes, I remember who you are, Sofia.' His throat feels dry, every word an effort.

'The journalist said that you'd forgotten—'

A waiter puts a coffee in front of her.

'Are you sure I can't get you anything, sir?' the waiter asks.

Constantin shakes his head.

They wait for the young man to leave.

Sofia stirs cream into her coffee, takes a sip, puts the cup back down. Her hands are shaking.

She looks up at him.

'So how much do you remember?' she asks. 'About coming here?'

'Things are coming back slowly,' he says.

Ever since that night on the beach, when he saw the sailing boat, fragments from the past have been falling back into his mind, but the bits don't fit together. And he knows that something's missing.

She stares at him, her face pale and drawn, her eyes wide. What's she trying to tell him?

Sofia looks down at Constantin's hands: he covers the ink stain with his right palm.

'You've been working,' she says.

He shakes his head. 'Not working, no.'

'But drawing?'

'Yes.'

With a little girl, he wants to tell her. *A little girl who loves rainbows. And her mother.*

'I'm glad,' she says.

He looks up and catches her eye. 'You are?'

She nods.

You're ruining our lives, Sofia had screamed at him back in their flat in Minsk. *And what? For a few stupid drawings?*

This is how the memories are coming back. Snatched conversations. Voices. Images.

Constantin knows that they'd had this argument, about his work, many, many times. That the arguments were the reason he was in England: that he'd chosen his work over her.

Sofia pushes a strand of dark hair out of her eyes, an action so familiar to him his breath catches in his throat.

'Do you love her?' Sofia asks him. 'The woman – the one with the girl?'

He saw how Sofia had looked at Isabel. And he remembers this too, that he's never been able to keep a thing from her, that she knew him better than anyone.

'I haven't been myself,' he says.

She lets out a small, cold laugh. 'You hate politicians, but you talk just like they do.' She leans in. 'You never could give a straight answer, could you?' She sits back and shakes her head. 'Only through your drawings.'

He doesn't know what to say to her. How to begin to explain.

She smiles at him and for a moment, he sees another face: hers but younger, a child, a girl, leaning over the railing of a fishing vessel. A girl standing at the bottom of the stairs in their cottage in the forest.

The girl's voice comes to him.

Please, Papa. Please. We'll have so much fun together. I want to be with you.

Their daughter.

'I'm sorry ...' he mumbles.

His eyes well up.

'I shouldn't have let her come with me.'

Isabel

Let him go.

Isabel lies on River's bed, staring at the ceiling, and repeats the words in her head: *Let him go.*

Maybe if she says the phrase to herself enough times, it might work: he'll fade out of her life and then she can go back to how things were before the summer.

She thinks of Jules's words. *Look at the men you fall for, Isabel? You're asking for trouble.*

A one-night stand with an Italian who didn't even give her his name.

A stolen kiss with an amnesiac refugee found on a bench outside London Zoo – who couldn't give her his name, even if he wanted to.

'Mum, you okay?' She feels River's hand slipping into hers.

They've been lying side by side all night, drifting in and out of sleep. Back at the hospital, she was worried that River wasn't coping. Her ADHD symptoms were flaring up again. But ever since they found Reg, she's been stiller and quieter than she's ever seen her.

The first light of morning is coming in through the window.

Isabel gives River's hand a squeeze. 'I'll be fine.'

On the way home from the police station, River asked who the woman was and Isabel said the words, as though they'd been waiting there, in her mouth, all along:

'Constantin's wife.'

And then River had gone quiet, like she knew that it wasn't time to talk about it.

Later that night, Clem called Isabel and explained. The woman was called Sofia; he'd located her a few days ago in a small cottage in a forest on the border between Belarus and Poland. When she heard about Constantin, she'd taken the first flight to London.

Isabel puts her arm around River. It feels good to have her next to her – to remember that this crazy, stubborn, wonderful little girl is the only one she was ever meant to love.

The sun lights up the wall by River's bed: her pictures of rainbows. And the pictures of elephants that Constantin drew for her.

'We're going to have an Indian summer, that's what they said on the weather forecast,' River says. 'Warm sunshine all autumn – isn't that weird, after all the rain?' She follows Isabel's gaze to the pictures of the elephants. 'Did you hear that a baby elephant's been born at Whipsnade?'

River's trying to cheer Isabel up. To take her mind off what happened last night.

Only, as her little girl speaks of elephants, Isabel's heart jolts. Even if she manages to let go of Constantin, how's she meant to help River do the same?

River sits up and pulls one of Constantin's elephant pictures off her wall – a baby elephant with her mother – and hands it to Isabel.

'Elephants can be sad, like people – did you know that?' River says.

'I can believe that.' Isabel looks at the mother elephant in the picture, her eyes so small but so full of love for her new little creature. You can't have that kind of love and not feel sadness too.

'If a baby or family member dies, elephants stay with the body for days, trying to bring it back to life.' Her voice breaks. 'I looked it up.'

'You looked it up?'

River nods. 'On Gabs's computer. When Reg kept drawing elephants all the time and after we saw that cartoon on Alex's laptop, I thought I'd try to find out more about them – to understand why he was so obsessed with them. He calls them his spirit animal.'

River really needs to go to school. Even if she finds it hard to sit still and to read, she has the instinct to learn. There must be a way to make her feel happy about getting an education.

'That's wonderful, River. That you did all that research.'

'You know the most incredible thing?' She can hear the excitement in River's voice, like when she talks about rainbows. 'If elephants pass by the same spot where a baby or family member died, even years and years later, they'll stand there really still and silent for several minutes. Like we do on Remembrance Day.'

'That's amazing.'

Isabel looks back at the mother elephant. If something were to happen to River, she doesn't think she'd ever be able to leave the place where she died. She doesn't think she could go on living at all.

'Mum?'

Isabel sits up and kisses the top of River's head. 'Yes, my love.'

'There's something I didn't tell you – about Reg.' She gulps. 'At the hospital, he showed me an elephant charm.'

Isabel breathes out. She remembers how she'd found it in his pocket and placed it on his bedside table that first day. She never saw it again.

'It's silver and it's got these precious stones all over its body,' River goes on. 'It's really small, like it's meant to go on a bracelet or a necklace or something. I feel like I should have told you – or Dr Deardorff. Because maybe it was a clue.'

'It's okay, River. I saw it too.'

'You did?'

'I found it in his pocket – when I was putting away his wet clothes. I was the one who put it on his bedside table.'

River lets out a big sigh. 'So you're not cross?'

Isabel kisses the top of River's head, the thick tangled hair so familiar against her lips.

'No, of course not, River.'

'Don't you think it's strange, Mum? That he should have a charm like that. It's not something a man would usually carry around.'

'I suppose not. Maybe someone special gave it to him.' Isabel gulps. 'Maybe Sofia did.'

'His wife?' River says.

Isabel nods.

'I suppose so,' River says. 'Only it doesn't look like something she'd wear – if you know what I mean.'

A picture of Sofia forms in front of Isabel. Although she wore a suit and heels, there was a simplicity to her. No make-up or jewellery. The long hair that swept down her back. River's right, it somehow doesn't seem to fit.

'All the elephants from Whipsnade are from India,' River goes on. 'So they'll like it – the warm weather.'

Isabel nods. 'I'm sure they will, my love.'

'When Reg was still at the hospital, he told me that he wanted to go to India someday – to see the elephants there. Real ones living free. He said that if he were ever to get married . . .'

River pauses. Isabel looks at her little girl, her eyes wide and her cheeks pink from the warm room.

'To get married?' Isabel asks.

River props herself up on her elbow. 'Did he forget he had a wife?'

Isabel sits up on the sofa bed and looks at a worn patch in the carpet.

'Maybe. I don't know.'

'Well, he said he'd take his wife to India for their honeymoon.' River leans her head on Isabel's shoulder. 'Mum?'

'Yes.'

'I don't think he was talking about Sofia.' She pauses. Isabel can feel River's breath against her neck. 'I think he meant he wanted to take you, Mum.'

Isabel closes her eyes and feels the sun from the window on her face.

She pulls River into her chest and folds her arms around her; she doesn't want her to see that she's had these thoughts too. Not about India or honeymoons. But that, one day, she and Constantin might be together. And that River might finally have a father.

'Mum?'

Isabel doesn't answer.

'I know he kissed you, Mum.'

Isabel keeps holding River tight.

'I thought I'd dreamt it. My mind was so fuzzy that night in Dr Deardorff's flat. But then Jules said some stuff.'

Isabel opens her eyes.

'Jules?'

River nods. 'About Reg *like*-liking you.'

Like-liking. How simple those feelings sound.

'And I found a picture – in your textbook. The one you drew of Reg.'

Isabel stares at her. She doesn't know what to say. *God, what a mess.*

'I'm sorry, Mum.'

Isabel releases River from her arms and looks her in the eye. 'You don't need to be sorry about a thing, River.'

'Do you like him more than you liked Dad?'

'Oh, River.'

They lie in silence for a while and then, in a small, quiet voice River says, 'You've never told me about him. Not properly.'

Isabel takes a breath.

'I know.'

'What was he like – *really* like?'

'He was Italian.'

'So it's true?'

'Why wouldn't it be true?'

'I thought you just said that . . . to make him sound – I don't know, nicer. Because you love Italy.'

'You thought I said it to make him sound *nicer*?' Isabel asks. 'Nicer than what?'

'Than the person he really is.'

Isabel sits up on the sofa bed.

'What do you mean, the person he *really* is?'

'It doesn't matter, Mum.'

Isabel puts her hands over River's. 'I need to know, River – what it is you've been thinking all this time?'

'I just reckoned that if he was a nice guy, you'd have told me about him. Or I'd have met him. Or he'd still be my dad. The fact that he isn't around means that either he wants to stay away or you want to keep him away.'

'Keep him away?'

'To protect me.' She pauses. 'Like you always do.'

'Do I do that?'

River rolls her eyes. 'Yeah, Mum, you do.'

'So what *did* you think about your dad?' Isabel asks. 'I mean, specifically?'

'You really want to know?'

Isabel nods.

'Well, I worked out there could be four options.'

Isabel's eyes go wide. *'Four?'*

'Yep.' River pulls her hands out from under Isabel's and counts off the options on her fingers. 'First: he was a murderer or a psychopath or something and he's in jail and you never want me to have anything to do with him.'

Mum sucks in her breath. 'You believed that?'

River smiles. 'Not really. But it would have been a good reason.'

'And the other options?'

'Second: he didn't like me when I came out so he ran away.'

'Didn't like you?'

'Maybe, when I was a baby, he saw ...'

'Saw what?'

'That I had all these things wrong with me.'

Isabel's heart sinks. 'Wrong with you?'

'Like my ADHD. And maybe he knew that I'd get in trouble at school. No parent really wants a kid like that, do they?'

Isabel's eyes well up. 'Oh, River ...'

River holds up her third finger. 'Option three: I'm adopted.'

Isabel sits back like something's hit her in the chest. *'Adopted?'*

'Well, it's not like we look very similar, is it, Mum?'

Isabel shakes her head. 'I suppose not.'

'And we don't have a very similar character.'

'We're more alike than you know, my love ...'

'That's what Reg said.'

'He did?'

River nods. 'Anyway, I thought the adoption was a good fit. I mean, you and Jules are always getting caught up in people's lives and feeling sorry for them and taking on their troubles. I thought that you found me at the hospital. That my real parents ran away or abandoned me or something and that you decided to take me home. Like you did with Reg – kind of.'

'You're not adopted, River. Not even close,' Isabel says. 'What's the fourth option?'

'That Dad's dead. Though I never really believed that.'

'Why not?'

'Because being dead is too easy.'

Isabel's breath catches in her throat. 'Too *easy*?'

'I'm sorry, I didn't mean it like that. Of course it would be sad, but you could just have told me that and we could have been sad about it together and you could have spoken to me about how much you loved him and then, after a while, we'd have moved on. It was obviously more complicated than that.'

More complicated than him being dead? Trust River to come out with something like that.

Isabel sits up straight and takes a breath. She knows that it's time to clear all this up.

'I did love your dad. Very much. But in a strange kind of way.'

'A strange way?'

'It wasn't real.' Isabel sighs. 'I only knew him for a few hours.'

'You had a one night stand?' River shakes her head. 'Wow.'

'You know what a one night stand is?'

River nods. 'Jules said I should never have one.'

'Oh.'

'You know Jules and I talk about that kind of stuff. The stuff that makes you embarrassed.'

'Right,' says Isabel. She supposes she knew that.

River gives Isabel a cheeky smile. 'So, you had a one night stand?'

Isabel laughs.

'Yes, I suppose I had a one night stand. Though that's not what I'd planned – or what I hoped for.'

'I thought the whole point about one night stands was that they weren't planned?'

Isabel laughs again. 'I guess you're right.'

'What *did* you hope for?' River asks.

'That he'd come back, I suppose.'

'When he found out about me?'

Isabel pauses.

'Mum?'

'He doesn't know about you.'

'You didn't tell him?'

'We never found him again, my love.'

'We?'

'Jules and me. But mainly Jules. She went back to Venice to look for him.'

'*Really?*'

'Yes. Really.'

'And she didn't find him?'

'We didn't even know his name.'

River's jaw drops open. 'You had a one night stand with someone and you didn't know his name?'

Isabel's cheeks flush. 'Yes.'

River looks at Isabel for a moment, her eyebrows scrunched together, chewing on her bottom lip, like she's taking it all in.

'I'm sorry, River.'

River looks Isabel in the eye and then, slowly, leans her head on her shoulder, like before.

'I suppose we didn't know Reg's name – his proper name,' River says. 'Not at first. So maybe names don't matter all that much in the end.'

Isabel kisses the top of River's head and lets out a breath.

'Mum?'

'Yes, my love.'

'Is that why we don't see Grandma and Grandpa? Because you had a one night stand and never found Dad?'

Isabel cases a tangle out of River's hair and then kisses her forehead.

'Sort of.'

'Were they angry at me?'

Isabel sits back, her eyes wide. 'Angry at *you*?'

'Because I came along and you were really young and didn't get to go to nursing school, because you had to look after me.'

'No, River, they weren't angry at you. They were just disappointed in me; I didn't turn out how they expected.'

'I'm not turning out how you expected, either,' River says, her voice small and quiet again.

Isabel puts her arms around River. 'Oh, River, you're more wonderful than anything I could ever have imagined.'

River raises her head. Her eyes are full of light.

'I am?'

Isabel nods. 'Much, much more.'

'Even though I don't like school?'

Isabel smiles. 'Even though you don't like school.'

'So why didn't Grandma and Grandpa ever want to meet me?'

Isabel takes a while to answer.

'Mum?' River prompts.

'I never gave them the chance.'

344

It's the first time she's admitted it to herself: that maybe she's to blame for the eleven years of silence between them.

'Do you want to see them, River?'

River nods. 'I think so.'

'Okay,' Isabel says. 'Okay.' She strokes River's hair again.

For a while, they sit next to each other in silence. Then River asks, 'What was Dad like? I mean, I know you didn't spend much time with him, but you must have got to know him a bit?'

Isabel thinks back to that night in Venice as he stood in front of her, offering to guide her back home.

'Very Italian. And very handsome. And very charming.' Isabel laughs nervously. 'And very young.'

'You were young too though, right?'

'I suppose I was. I just always think of him as really young – as if, even if I found him now, after all this time, he'd still be seventeen.' She shakes her head. 'It's silly, I know.'

'What did he look like?'

'Like you. Which is why you can rest assured that you're not adopted.'

River sits up. 'So I remind you of him?'

Mum looks at River and blinks. 'Every day.'

'Really?'

'Really.'

'That must be hard.'

'Hard and wonderful.'

River twirls a long, straggly bit of her hair between her fingers. 'Did he have my hair?'

'Yes. Dark brown. Kind of curly and scruffy – but beautiful.'

'And my eyes?' River makes her eyes go wide and leans in close to Isabel so she can see.

'Yes, your eyes too. Brown as chestnuts.'

'What else?'

'Your skin. A soft, olive colour. His was a bit darker because he lived in a hot country. But it was the same kind of skin.' Isabel chews her lip. 'And he was kind of bouncy, like you are.'

'Bouncy?'

'He wasn't good at sitting still. I remember how he walked – there was an extra skip in his step. And how he didn't like to sit down for too long. He was always pacing around, trying to find new things to look at, even in the tiny hotel room I shared with Jules.'

'Did he have ADHD, like me?'

'Maybe.'

'What else?'

'There's one more thing that's always made me think of him.' Isabel smiles. 'You've got the same cheeky mouth.' Isabel closes her eyes for a second. 'I should have known from that mouth . . .'

'Known what?'

'That things might not be straightforward.'

'That's a nice way of saying trouble, right?'

'No, not trouble. You just do things in your own way.'

'So you do remember lots of stuff about him, even though you only knew him for a night?'

Isabel nods. 'I've had eleven years to remember – or to imagine.'

'To imagine?'

'To create a picture in my mind – to fill the gaps.'

River holds her gaze and an understanding passes between them; River knows the need to imagine a different life.

'Did you ever try again – to find him?'

'Every now and then Jules would do a search on Facebook.

We'd look at Google images from Venice, that kind of thing. It was silly, really.'

'You never found anything?'

'Nothing.'

'And you're not angry at him?'

Isabel shakes her head. 'Sad, sometimes. But not angry. He gave me two very precious things. He showed me what love was – the love I had for him. But more than that, he gave me the most precious gift in the world.' Isabel touches River's hair lightly. 'You.'

River pulls away slightly. 'But he didn't know he was giving me to you, did he?'

'Maybe not, but I'm still grateful to him.'

River leans her back against the wall.

'And do you still love him now? Even if it is in that strange way you said?'

'I did love him. For a very long time.' Isabel shakes her head. 'For a stupidly long time. Or I loved the idea of him. Of that night and of what could have been. But no,' she pauses, 'not now.'

River takes a breath.

'Do you love Reg more?'

Isabel hesitates: what's the point in telling River about her feelings for Constantin when, soon, he'll be out of their lives for good? Maybe that's happened already. But this whole conversation has been about telling her the truth. She doesn't want any more secrets.

'I think I do, yes.'

River nods and takes Isabel's hand and then kisses her cheek.

For a long time, they sit in silence on the bed. And then River says, 'What do you think will happen now?'

'I don't know.' She sighs. 'I really don't know.'

'Is Sofia going to take him away from us?'

'She's his wife, River.'

'I know, but . . . ' River's voice trails off. She gets it, Isabel thinks.

Isabel kisses the top of River's head.

'But he likes being with us,' River says.

Isabel nods. 'I know, my love.' Isabel puts her arm around River's shoulders. 'But things are complicated.'

Just then Isabel's phone rings. It vibrates on the coffee table in front of them. Jules's name flashes up on the screen.

Isabel picks it up.

River leans in so she can hear.

'Dave's woken up,' Jules says, her voice wobbly.

Isabel hasn't heard her best friend cry in years. Not since the day River was born. She was the one who stayed with Isabel through those long hours of labour and she was the first to hold River. 'She's perfect,' Jules had said to her, as tears rolled down her face.

Now, Jules is crying again. And Isabel knows why.

River leaps up. 'Dr Deardorff's back!'

'Is he okay?' Isabel asks.

Jules sniffs. 'He's a bit confused but yeah, he's going to be fine. We've asked if he can be transferred to the cardiac unit at Regent's Hospital and they said it wasn't usual, to move a patient this soon after surgery, but he's got some contacts here so we managed to swing it. They've arranged an ambulance to take him. He should be back in London in a couple of hours.' She pauses. 'You know what the first thing he asked was?'

Isabel waits for her to continue.

'Whether *you* were okay.'

Isabel hears Jules blowing her nose.

'I filled him in on everything that's happened,' Jules says.

Isabel knows what her best friend means by *everything*. That Constantin was picked up by the police, walking along a motorway. That Clem managed to get him out of police custody. That today, they were all going to be together again.

But then it hits her. Jules doesn't know about Sofia – Isabel didn't contact her last night – which means that David doesn't know either.

'We'll meet you at the hospital,' Isabel says, and hangs up.

David

David's eyes burn. His head is filled with fog.

They've been giving him tests ever since he woke up.

He still doesn't understand what happened.

A heart attack?

Major surgery?

And a coma?

The last thing he remembers is the cold waves crashing around him as he searched for Constantin.

The nurse releases the blood pressure band from his arm and then puts a paper cup of pills on his bedside table.

'Take these. And then you should get some rest.'

Lead weights press on his chest; every breath is an effort.

'Let me know if the discomfort gets worse,' she says.

Discomfort. He'd used these words with patients a thousand times – what a stupid phrase. Bloody painful, that was what it was.

He looks around the room.

'Where's … ?'

The nurse smiles. 'She's outside making a call to your family – letting them know you're okay.' She puts her hand on his arm and smiles. 'You're lucky to have people who love you so much.'

Family? People who love me so much?

He feels like he's woken up in someone else's body.

He takes off his glasses and rubs his eyes.

The nurse leaves and a second later Jules crashes in.

He puts his glasses back on and she comes into focus.

She shoves her phone in the back pocket of her jeans and pulls out a bag of Haribo. It's coming back to him: this strange woman who whirled into his life like a tornado.

She sits down on the edge of his bed and digs her hand into the bag of sweets.

'I'd offer you one but you've got to stick to the healthy stuff for a while. We need to look after your ticker, Dave.' She leans forward, taps his chest gently and then pops a couple of gummy bears in her mouth.

Still chewing, she says, 'I got in touch with Isabel and River – and Clem. They're meeting us at Regent's Hospital. I'll call them as soon as we get there.' She pauses for a second and looks him right in the eye. 'You caused quite the drama, Dave.'

David feels a mismatch in his brain: he remembers Jules, of course he does, but the woman sitting beside him feels different. Closer.

'I thought you hated hospitals,' he says.

She looks down into her bag of sweets and picks out a red gummy bear. 'I do.'

'So why are you here?'

She pops the sweet into her mouth. 'I made an exception.'

He smiles. 'I didn't know phobias had exceptions.'

She looks up at him and they lock eyes again. *She's terrifying*, he thinks. *Terrifying and beautiful.*

'Well, I'm here, aren't I?' she says.

He nods. 'Yes. Yes you are.'

'You should rest. The transfer will be tiring. And then you need to brace yourself for visitors. You know what River's like – she'll wear you out before she gets through the door.'

He smiles. He's missed them. The nurse was right: they're his family.

351

His lids grow heavy, his body drowsy from the medication, and he feels himself drifting off.

David feels Jules taking off his glasses and hears her place them on his bedside table. Her hand sweeps over his brow. And then her voice, gentle and quiet: 'Rest now.'

He must have fallen asleep in the ambulance, on the way back to London, because when he wakes again, the room looks different. There's a pressure beside him on the bed. His arm is trapped under Jules's head; she's fallen asleep. He tries to move but she's pinned him down, her body heavy with sleep, so he rolls his body to the side and eases his arm out that way.

She said she'd follow the ambulance by car. That she'd make sure she was there as soon as he arrived.

The stitches pull along his chest, but he keeps moving, inch-by-inch, until he's facing her.

Her eyelids flutter. He notices freckles on her nose and cheeks.

Her fingers move lightly against the sheets as though she's playing out a beat in her sleep.

He looks down at her arms, her shirtsleeves rolled up. He squints: even without his glasses he can see them: the birds floating along her skin. He brings out his free arm and traces them with his fingers.

Her eyes open. For a second, they look at each other.

'I'm not Isabel . . .' she says, her voice sleepy.

'Isabel?'

She sits up and rubs her eyes.

'You asked for her.' She swallows hard. 'When you first came round.'

He doesn't remember asking for Isabel. The only person he wants beside him is Jules.

'How long did I sleep?' She glances at the door. 'I thought they'd be here already.'

He catches hold of her arm and traces the tattoo of a sparrow on the inside of her wrist.

'Doesn't it hurt?' he asks.

She looks at him. 'I have a high pain threshold.'

He laughs; his chest pulls again. 'I can believe that.'

'And it doesn't – not really. Not as much as other things.'

He wants to ask her what *other things* but doesn't have the courage. Instead, he says:

'What made you do it the first time? I mean, what made you wake up one day and think "I want to have a picture drawn on my skin"?'

She shrugs. 'I thought it would help me remember.'

He sits up a little and presses his back into the pillows. His breath catches from the effort.

'Hey – take it easy.' She leans him forward and adjusts the pillow behind his back to make him more comfortable. 'We can't have you snuffing it before they even get here.'

'Snuffing it?'

'You nearly died, Dave.'

None of this seems real.

He looks down at the wing of a crow at the bend of her elbow. 'What do they help you remember?'

She looks out of the window.

'My mum.'

'Your mother had tattoos?'

She raises her pierced eyebrow and gives him a sideways smile. '*Mum* – a tattoo? God no.' And then she looks down at her arms and her cheeks flush pink. 'She was classier than that.'

'Classier than you?'

'Yeah.'

She doesn't see herself, he thinks. Not like he does.

'So what was it? About your mum?'

'She was a bird lover, totally nuts over them. Always had her head tilted up to the sky, to rooftops and trees. Worse than River and her pigeons.' Her voice goes quiet. 'She worked in a pub. We lived there. She put millions of bird feeders in the garden. People thought she was crazy, but I loved it.' She closes her eyes. 'I remember hearing them, through my bedroom window, early in the morning.'

David looks at Jules, and, for the first time since he met her, she looks like a little girl rather than the strong, competent woman who'd stormed into his world and made him feel alive again.

'When she passed away, the birds left too.'

'You were worried you'd forget that?'

'It's the only thing I remember about her,' Jules says. 'I wanted to make sure it didn't slip away.'

All at once, he remembers Constantin: the man he was looking for on the beach. And his drawings. When David woke up, Jules filled him in on what happened. How the police found Constantin walking along a motorway in the rain. How Clem's been fighting to get him out of custody.

He focuses on Jules again.

'What happened to your mum?' he asks.

'She died when I was five. Ovarian cancer. Went from fine to dead within a few months.' She takes a breath. 'Even when she was really sick, she'd take me to the park and point out the birds and tell me their names.' Jules pauses. 'They made her happy, I remember that.'

'You could have got a book, or a painting. To remember her by, I mean.'

Jules looks down at her arm. 'I wanted to feel it on my skin.' She traces the line of the crow's back. 'For her to be part of me. Something permanent, you know?'

He nods. 'You loved her.'

Jules looks at him and blinks. 'Yeah, I did.'

'And your father?'

'Raised by a single mum – can't you tell?'

Of course, he thinks. *No wonder she protects Isabel so fiercely.*

'So, when your mum died?'

'I went into foster care.' She looks up at him and gives him her sideways smile again. 'Too much of a handful for anyone to want to adopt.'

'I'm sorry.' He looks at the hollow of skin at the base of her throat, at her collarbone, just visible through her shirt and, above it, the thin, blue line of a tattoo.

He holds her hand. 'Would you come with me to see my mother?'

He remembers telling Jules about his mother being in a nursing home, that he went there every day. That she was all he had. When Jules had said that she wanted to meet her, he'd thought she was just being polite. But he knows Jules better now.

'I'd like you to meet her. When all this is over,' he adds. 'When I get out of here.'

She nods. 'Okay.'

He keeps hold of her hand and looks up her arm. 'I think they're beautiful,' he says.

She doesn't move.

He moves his fingers up along her hands, her wrists, her arms.

'The birds – the tattoos – they're beautiful.'

You're beautiful, he wants to tell her. And you make me happy, like those birds made your mother happy. I want to feel you on my skin too. I want to remember you for ever.

Jules moves his hand from her arm, places it down on the bed sheet and stands up.

'I should probably go.' She scrunches up the packet of Haribo and throws it in the bin by the bedside table.

'Stay – please.' He leans towards her and stretches out his hand. The effort makes him cough. His head spins.

Her brow creases. 'I told you to take it easy.'

He coughs again. 'I don't understand why you're going.'

'Like I said, they'll be here soon. You'll have more than enough visitors.' She picks her bag off the floor. 'You don't need me.'

'You've been here this whole time, haven't you?' he says.

She rifles through her bag. 'Where did I put my keys?'

'You're the only one who stayed,' he says. 'Even though you hate it here.'

She's on her hands and knees now, crawling under the bed. 'Got them.' As she comes back out she bangs her head on the side of the bedframe.

He feels a jolt and puts out his hand. 'Careful there . . .'

She rubs her head and walks towards the door.

'Did you hear what I said?' he calls after her.

She looks back. 'Yeah, I've been here.'

'Why?'

She shrugs. 'I guess because I wanted to.'

'You wanted to sit next to a guy in a coma?'

'It was a good break,' she says. She looks around the room. 'It was kind of peaceful in here.'

He wants to hold onto the hem of her T-shirt, her arm, her hand – any part of her.

'Please don't go.'

'Come on, Dave, it's for the best.'

'Whose best?'

She hesitates for a beat.

'Whose best?' he asks again.

She still doesn't answer.

He looks over at the chair beside his bed, the one she's sat in for hours.

'Why don't you wait a little longer. River and Isabel will want to see you.'

'I can see them any time.'

'But I want you here.' He feels the childishness of this request, but he doesn't care. She can't go. 'And I want to say thank you.'

'You don't need to thank me.'

'Yes I do, Juliet.'

Her face goes red. 'Juliet?'

'River told me.'

She juts out her chin. 'I'm going to kill her.'

'It's a beautiful name.'

She tugs at a tuft of hair behind her ear.

'Anyway, I'd like to thank you for being here this whole time. And I'd like you to stay, just a little bit longer.'

She looks at him and shakes her head and rolls her eyes and then, very slowly, walks back to the chair and sits down.

Constantin

Constantin and Sofia sit on a bench in the hospital garden under an old oak tree. He holds her, her head tucked under his chin, like when they were young.

'I let her go too,' Sofia says, her voice thick. 'It wasn't just you. That morning, I let her go.'

A piece of stitching pulls two fragments of memory together and it comes back to him whole: the morning he and Clara left the forest.

Two Months Earlier, Belarus

Constantin gets dressed in the dark: a suit Sofia makes him wear for special occasions – for her father's functions – but he's glad he's got it now. He wants to make a good impression when he gets to London.

He looks over to the bed where Sofia is sleeping. They had a farewell meal last night. And after that, he'd sat on Clara's bed, stroking her long, dark hair until she fell asleep.

It had been Sofia's idea that he should leave early and quietly, avoiding all the emotions of saying goodbye all over again.

You need to save your strength for the journey, she'd said.

He picks up his cane, goes over to the bed and kisses Sofia's forehead. And then her lips.

They'd drifted so far apart these past few months, that

sometimes it felt like they no longer recognised each other. But when he touches her skin, when he kisses her, the familiarity comes back. Sometimes, he's taken back to their first kiss, when they were students at the university in Minsk. She was a sculptor, he drew silly cartoons in pen and ink. And for some reason, she'd fallen in love with him.

Sofia opens her eyes for a second. 'Let us know when you get there,' she says. 'Promise?'

He nods. 'I promise.'

Then he hitches his backpack onto his shoulders and walks out onto the landing. With every step, he presses heavily onto his cane. It's been months now, and still it's not getting any better. As long as it gets him to England, he thinks. The hospitals there will be safe for him.

For a second, he stands outside Clara's bedroom and holds his palm to the wooden door. He wants to go in and hold her one last time, but she's a light sleeper – she'll hear his tread on the floorboards and wake. And then he won't be able to go.

He touches his lips to the door and whispers, *I love you, Clara.*

In the kitchen, he wraps a bread roll and some cheese in a piece of foil, takes an apple from the bowl on the kitchen table, and puts them in his bag. He stops for a moment and looks out through the window: the tall, dark trees sway in the morning breeze, as ancient as the world, he thinks.

After the arrest, the days in prison, and then the release, negotiated by Sofia's father, they ran away from Minsk and came to live here, in this small cottage hidden under the trees of a primeval forest on the border between Belarus and Poland. They took Clara out of the boarding school her grandfather paid for and brought her to live with them. Constantin could teach her everything she needed to know. And he promised Sofia that he'd stop drawing. They'd be a family.

But then, one day, when Sofia and Clara were out for a walk, he'd picked up his pen again: he hadn't been able to help himself. That's when he and Sofia knew that he had to leave.

Constantin walks to the front door.

He doesn't see her at first; the hallway is dark, and she's so still.

'Clara? Is that you?' He rubs his eyes.

She looks up and smiles at him.

'What are you doing up?' he asks her.

She's sitting with her back pressed to the front door. Dressed. Her backpack beside her.

'I'm going with you,' she says.

He shakes his head. 'No, Clara, we've talked about this.'

She gets to her feet and hitches her bag onto her shoulders.

'*You and Mama* have talked about this. *I* never got to decide.'

'It's too dangerous.'

'You've always said I should make my own decisions. Take responsibility.'

'This is different.'

'Why?'

'Because it's a long journey. And a dangerous one. Because I don't know whether I'll make it without being caught. Because, when I get to London, I don't how long it will take before I find a job or somewhere to live. I won't be able to look after you.' He pauses. 'And your grandfather—'

'Wouldn't like it?' Clara sighs. 'You've said all this stuff before, Papa. And Grandpapa doesn't like anything.'

'He likes you. And your mother. He'll keep you safe.'

'Why?' Clara says. 'Why should he protect us when other people aren't safe? You've said it yourself, Papa, Belarus is hurting its own people. People with talent and imagination, people who want to think for themselves. I'm going to be one of those people – like you, Papa.' Her words tumble over each other.

So she understood what had happened to him.

Sofia had been right: standing here with Clara, going through it all again, having to fight against his longing to take her with him – it was taking all the strength he had.

Clara takes a breath and looks him straight in the eye. 'Why do you want me to stay in a country you hate?'

For a while, as Clara's words settle between them, neither of them say anything.

And she's right. This country no longer has the space or the tolerance for people like him. He makes the authorities angry. People like him fill the country's jails. Some never come out. And yes: she is an artist too. Who knows what form it will take but she will want her voice to be heard. And she, like him, will refuse to be silenced.

Sofia has such trust that her father can protect them. But how long before his money is no longer enough to appease the authorities? Constantin has seen it before: how easily a person can fall out of favour under a brutal and unpredictable regime.

And what will happen to them then?

But he's promised Sofia that he'll leave alone. That Clara will stay here, in her homeland.

Out, in the still dark morning, an owl hoots from one of the ancient trees.

'I need to go now.' Constantin steps forward and tries to kiss Clara's cheek but she turns her face away. And she doesn't move from the door.

He's taller than her, and stronger, but he would never use force to assert his will. There's too much of that in this country already.

'Once I'm settled, you can come and visit,' he says.

Even though it's dark, he sees her eyes fill with tears.

The sound of an engine rumbles outside. The van's here to pick him up.

'I don't want to visit,' Clara says. 'I want to come with you.' Tears drop down her cheeks. 'And I've thought over all the things you and Mama have said to me. All the reasons and arguments for me staying and you going alone. I haven't stopped thinking of them all night.' She wipes her eyes on her sleeve. 'And I still think it's better if I come with you.'

'Why, Clara?'

She lets out a gulp and wipes her eyes again. Then she looks back at him. 'Because I'm meant to be with you, Papa.'

There's a creaking on the stairs. Constantin turns around to see Sofia standing in her nightgown, looking at them.

'You need to let your father go,' she says to Clara.

'No,' Clara says.

'You're putting his life in danger by going with him.'

Clara steps forward. 'You're just saying that to make me stay.'

'No, no I'm not.'

'I don't want to live here with you—'

'Clara.' Constantin turns back round and touches her shoulder.

'I love you Mama, I do.' She pauses. 'But I need to be with Papa.'

Constantin doesn't dare to look at Sofia. He's tried to protect her from this, but he knows she's felt it: how Clara always turns to him.

There are footsteps on the gravel. In a moment, the man they've paid to take him to the border will be at the door.

Clara looks up the stairs at Sofia, waiting for her to speak.

After a while, Sofia's shoulders drop and she says, 'It's your father's decision.'

Clara spins round and grabs Constantin's hand. 'Papa?'

Constantin knows what Sofia wants him to say. They haven't talked of anything else these past few weeks. That Clara should stay in Belarus, go back to boarding school, wait until they know Constantin is safe. He knew it was the right decision.

But he thinks about the life she'd have if they made it to London. A life of freedom, the chance of an education unsullied by the influence of a corrupt government, a life without fear. He longs to give her that.

He looks up at Sofia. She stares at him, her gaze level.

He bows his head.

It used to be so easy between them – when had that changed?

There's a knock on the door.

'Papa?'

He looks up at Sofia.

'Please?' Clara begs.

And then, something in him snaps loose, he can't fight any more. Very slowly, he nods.

'I can come?' Her face beams.

Clara runs past him up the stairs and takes Sofia in her arms. 'It'll be okay, Mama, you'll see. And maybe you can come too, once we're there.'

But even Clara knows that will never happen. Sofia sees this country as her home and, more than that, she loves her father. She'll never leave.

There's another knock on the door.

Clara turns away from Sofia and skips down the stairs. But then she turns to look at her one last time.

'You won't tell Grandpapa, will you? Not until we've got there?'

Sofia stares at her daughter as if she's a stranger. Constantin wishes that he could erase Clara's last words. In so many ways she is wise beyond her years, but she's still too much of a child to understand the tightrope that Sofia walks between her father and her husband, that her mother has it harder than any of them – and that she'll never betray her husband or her daughter.

Sofia climbs back to the top of the stairs. Then she stops and, without turning around, she says, 'Keep her safe, Constantin.'

And then, before he has the chance to answer, she walks back to their bedroom and closes the door.

Constantin

Sofia and Constantin are still sitting next to each other on the bench, but they're no longer touching.

'She was meant to turn fifteen in July,' Sofia says.

Constantin's throat tightens. He can't breathe. 'Yes, she was.' He pushes out the words.

On the journey from Belarus to Calais, he and Clara had planned how they'd celebrate her first birthday in London. He sees her face now, her eyes bright with excitement. They'd go for tea and cake in an old-fashioned English tea shop. Then they'd walk along the river Thames, across the famous bridges. And they'd keep walking all day around the streets of their new home.

A picture of Clara, walking through the streets of London, the streets he's come to know over the last few months, flashes in front of him and it feels so real his heart stops.

Clara had drawn a picture of London on the back of an envelope, all the things she wanted to see. Then she'd put it in the pocket of his jacket.

In case you ever get lost, Papa, she'd joked.

She was meant to be here. With him. She's meant to be here now, with all of them.

Blood rushes in his ears.

And it's all his fault.

The fact that she's gone.

That she's never coming back.

Constantin turns to Sofia, tears dropping down his cheeks and into his lap.

'I should have sent her back. I'm sorry. I'm so, so sorry.'

Sofia looks up at him. Her eyes are swimming with tears too.

'What happened?' she asks. 'I need to know.'

He swallows hard. A stone is lodged in his throat.

'When we got to Calais,' he says. 'The captain didn't want to take her.' His voice chokes up. 'I had the chance to send her back.'

Two Months Earlier

Constantin catches the arm of one of the crew.

'What's the delay?' he asks him.

They were meant to leave port half an hour ago.

So far, the journey had gone well. A twenty-three-hour drive in the back of a white truck from the Belarus-Polish border to Calais, without a single stop and search. It was a miracle.

And now that they've nearly made it to England, only a matter of miles away from his destination, the boat isn't moving.

After years of being hounded by the authorities, Constantin has learnt that paranoia is a valid reaction to most anomalies.

'Is there a problem?' Constantin asks, scanning the dock for police. He wouldn't put it past the Belarusian government to track him all the way to France.

The young fisherman shakes his head. 'The captain's a bit rattled about you bringing your daughter. That wasn't the plan, he never takes two.' The fisherman pauses. 'And he doesn't take children.'

This was why Constantin had chosen this boat over a cheaper seat on a crammed commercial cargo ship with dozens of other Eastern European migrants: the captain didn't take unnecessary risks.

The only reason the captain took anyone at all was because the fishing industry, on this scale at least, was dying. He needed to find an alternative source of income. And Constantin knew that there was a steady flow of migrants from Eastern Europe, desperate to start a new life in England, no matter what the cost.

Clara runs up to him. She's been doing a tour of the small sailing boat, as excited as him that, in a few hours, they'll be in England.

'What's wrong, Papa?' Clara asks.

He looks at her, standing in front of him, her hair in a tight plait, swung over her shoulder.

I should have left her with her mother, he thinks.

'The captain doesn't want to take you,' the fisherman says to Clara.

Clara's face drops. 'What?'

Constantin takes his daughter's hand. 'Are you sure you want to come, Clara? You can still go back. We can find a way to get you home safely.'

On the journey from Belarus to Calais, they'd been dizzy with excitement. He'd forgotten, for a while, to worry. But now that she's with him on the boat, on the most dangerous part of the journey, he realises how foolish he's been.

What if they don't make it to the other side?

And even if they do, how will he be able to look after them both? He barely has enough money to get from Folkestone to London. And what then? Where is Clara meant to go to school? What kind of life is there going to be for her out there? And what if his contact at the English newspaper comes to nothing? What if he can't find even a basic job?

She pulls her hand out of Constantin's. 'No! I'm coming with you, Papa. It's decided.'

Choice was one of the parenting tenets Constantin and Sofia had agreed on. That even though the government had tried, time and again, to take away the choice of the Belarusian people, they wanted their child to grow up believing that she had the freedom to choose her own way.

They also wanted Clara to know that with freedom of choice came the need for courage to face the consequences of her decisions.

And here she was: she'd chosen.

'It's dangerous,' Constantin says. 'We talked about this at home.'

Clara spins round and juts out her chin. 'Let me talk to the captain.'

Had he been this defiant at fourteen? Of course he had. But not as clever or resourceful, she had that from her mother.

'Time to go!' the captain calls from behind them. 'You'll need to pay extra for her passage,' he mumbles as he sweeps past.

Constantin doesn't know whether to be relieved: had a part of him wanted the captain to stand firm? To order Clara off the boat?

Clara beams and throws her arms around him. 'We're off, Papa, we're off!'

A moment later, the boat pulls away from the dock.

Constantin

'She was as stubborn as you,' Constantin says.

He reaches for a strand of hair resting on Sofia's shoulder, but she flinches, turns away and closes her eyes.

Constantin needs to understand what happened that night, the last fragment which will make sense of all this and help him understand why, that night on the beach at Broadstairs, he saw the figure of a young girl leaning over the railing of the fishing boat.

But every time his mind tries to go back to that time, it shuts down.

'I'm going home tomorrow afternoon,' Sofia says.

His heart jolts. 'Tomorrow?'

'My father doesn't know that I'm here.' She takes a sharp breath. 'After everything that's happened, he wouldn't understand.'

'You live with him now?'

She nods. 'It's for the best.'

The glass doors leading to the hospital café open. They both look up.

Clem walks towards them.

Not now, thinks Constantin. Whatever it is, it can wait. He needs to be with Sofia. And he needs to understand what happened to Clara.

But a second later, Clem's standing over them.

'David's woken up,' he says. 'I thought you'd like to see him. I've got the car outside.'

Constantin hesitates. He knows that it's his fault that David ended up in the hospital, that if he and Isabel hadn't come looking for him that night, he might be okay. And that this isn't the right time to leave the conversation with Sofia. But he has to go to him.

Sofia turns round. 'Who's David?'

'The man who saved my life.'

David

David looks up at the strip light and blinks. Everything's too bright and too loud.

He feels a hand gripping his. He turns his head and sees Jules.

'They're here.' She puts his glasses back on.

The door bangs open.

River jumps on his bed. 'You're back!' She throws her arms around him.

Jules puts her hand on River's shoulder. 'Gently, River, Dave's still very tired.'

'It's okay,' David says. He looks at River. 'Thank you for coming.'

'Reg got out of prison,' River says.

'Custody,' Jules corrects.

'Well, he's free. And . . . ' Then she looks over to Isabel, who slipped in behind River and is still closer to the door than to David's bed. 'Can we tell him the other thing, Mum?'

Before she has the chance to answer, the door opens again. Clem strides in, grabs David's hand and shakes it hard. 'Good to have you back, mate. You gave us a scare.'

Constantin walks in after him, the limp bad again. A few steps behind, he's followed by a woman with large, sad eyes. Long dark hair tumbles over her shoulders.

Sofia.

He looks over to Clem, who gives him a smile and shrugs. David doesn't even need to ask him, he knows already that Clem must have found her and brought her here.

David sits up a little straighter. 'It's good to see you both,' he says.

River jumps up from the bed. 'You knew about Sofia?'

'Yes, I did.'

David looks over to where Isabel is standing, by the door, and tries to catch her eye. *I'm sorry*, he wants to tell her. *I'm sorry I didn't tell you sooner and that you had to find out this way.*

But Isabel's gaze is down.

Constantin hobbles over to the bed. Jules steps to the side to make space for him.

'I'm so sorry for all the trouble I've caused you. I'm sorry that it's because of me that you are here, in hospital.'

David places his hand over Constantin's. 'It's not because of you.'

For a moment, the two men lock eyes.

'I would like Sofia to meet you,' Constantin says.

'I would like that too.'

Sofia steps forward and holds out a hand. When he first met Constantin, David thought that he'd never seen such sadness in a person's eyes. But looking at Sofia now, he realises that he'd only seen the half of it.

'I still can't believe you knew and didn't tell us!' River says.

David's chest burns.

There's a buzzing in his head. Something's not right. He looks back over to the door: she's not there any more.

He sits up, wincing at the pain in his chest.

'Your mother . . . ' he mumbles to River. 'Where's your mother?'

Everyone looks round. Isabel must have slipped out without them noticing.

Constantin picks up his cane.

'I'll go and find her.'

Isabel

Isabel stands on the pavement outside the hospital watching the cars and the people blur in and out of focus.

She knows she has to go somewhere, far away from here, but her feet won't move.

She feels a hand on her shoulder.

'Isabel?'

She tries to pull away from him but she doesn't have the strength.

'You have a wife.' She wants to shout the words at him but they come out quiet and broken.

He takes his hand from her shoulder.

'Will you let me talk to you?'

No, she wants to scream at him. *I don't care if you forgot or whether you knew all along. I just can't do this.*

'Please, Isabel.'

She looks at him: his eyebrows slope down and knots push up against his forehead.

'Please,' he says again.

They stand on Westminster Bridge, the sun low in the sky.

She looks away from him and stares at the river, willing her tears back into her eyes.

Constantin takes her hand. She pulls it away.

Why did he drag her all the way out here? Was it just to tell her that he was sorry that he'd kissed her? That it had all been a terrible mistake? He could have done that back at the hospital.

Then it hits her. Maybe he wants to make sure she keeps the kiss to herself – that she doesn't upset Sofia.

Though he doesn't need to ask her that either. She understands.

The sun hovers over the water, an orange ball of fire.

'It's beautiful, don't you think, Isabel?' he says, looking out at the river.

'Why did you bring me here, Constantin?'

'I needed to speak to you. Alone.'

'You don't have to explain, I understand.'

He opens his eyes and stares at her. 'You do?'

'Of course.'

Though a part of her still wonders how he could have forgotten that he had a wife: a warm, intelligent, beautiful wife. Surely no one would forget that.

'You could have worn a ring, given me a warning.'

He looks down at his left hand and rubs the place on his ring finger where a wedding band should have been.

'I threw it into the sea.' His brow contracts as though the memory comes back to him just as he says it.

'Why did you throw it away?' Her voice is shaky.

He looks back at her again.

'I knew that I didn't deserve to be married any more.'

'What do you mean?'

'I did something terrible, Isabel.'

'I know that you got into trouble for your drawings, that you came into conflict with your government, the police. David found the articles – and Clem filled us in on the rest.'

Constantin shakes his head. 'It wasn't that. That's not what I need to tell you.' He pauses. 'I brought you to the river, because it's where I came when I left David's flat. I didn't remember what happened when I travelled here from Belarus, not in a concrete way. But I knew I had to find my way back to the sea.'

'Why the sea?'

He closes his eyes and thinks back to that night and he sees the face again, a young girl leaning over the railing of the fishing boat. And then the memories rush in, clearer than ever.

He opens his eyes and looks at Isabel. 'I need to tell you about Clara.'

Two Months Earlier

'You jump first,' she says. 'Steady the lifeboat. Then I'll join you.'

He looks into her wide, bright eyes. She thinks this is all an adventure.

Torches scan the back of the fishing boat. In a few seconds, the guards will be here.

They'd fallen asleep. They were a few hours from the shore. And then they'd heard the fishermen shouting at them to move. And Constantin knew that everything was about to fall apart, that he should never have let her come – that he should have sent her back when had the chance.

But now it was too late.

Clara clicks the elephant charm off her bracelet and presses it into his hand. 'To give you courage,' she says.

They'd talked about elephants: how noble they were. And brave.

He puts the charm in his pocket.

The captain stands a few yards off. 'You need to hurry up,' he grumbles.

He's scared of getting caught too. If the Channel Patrol Officers find out that he's let them on board, they'll take away his licence.

'If anything happens, I'll see you at the zoo. We'll go and see the elephants together.'

If anything happens? He feels so sick he can't move.

She squeezes his hand. 'Jump, Papa!'

Keep her safe. Sofia's words ring in his ears.

He takes Clara's head between his hands and kisses the parting in her hair. It smells of the forest where they lived: of rich earth and sun-warmed leaves.

'Go!' she says. 'Quick!'

He jumps.

'Papa! Your cane – you forgot!' She throws it after him, but it misses. It clangs against the side of the boat and sinks into the dark water. 'Oh Papa, I'm sorry!'

The wind snatches at her words.

'It's okay!' he calls back to her. 'Just hurry up.'

The lifeboat sways under his legs. His knee hurts from the jump. He needs to sit down to ease the pain but he can't, not until she's beside him.

He thinks back to those days in prison. The long nights when they kept them awake, bright lamps shining into their faces, drilling sounds blasted through a speaker beside them, a sound so loud he thought it would stay in his head for ever. They tied their hands so that they couldn't shield their ears. The long days without food. And then the attacks on the body. They thought that by making them blind and deaf, by stretching their bodies in vices until their limbs were so damaged that they could never run again, they would break them.

But they didn't succeed.

Because here he is, with his little girl. And soon, they'll be safe.

The storm's got worse through the night. Waves crash around

the small lifeboat. Pools of water gather at his feet. The water rises around him.

We're not far, he thinks. He can see the shore from here. *We can make it.*

He looks up.

Clara's standing there, smiling.

He holds out his hand.

'Come on, quickly!' he shouts. 'Jump – *now*!'

The wind swallows his words. But she knows what to do.

She blows him a kiss and starts climbing over the side of the boat. The captain supports her.

And then a torch lights up her face.

'Quick!' he yells, his throat raw.

The wind whips around him. It lashes at the sea. A wave rocks the lifeboat up until it's nearly vertical. He sits down and tries to steady the boat with his arms.

Then another wave crashes into the boat. And another.

They don't stop coming.

He finds a handle on the side of the boat and looks up again. It's hard to see through the rain and the sea-soaked air.

He wipes the back of his palm over his face and forces his eyes open.

For a second, she's still there, her slim figure dark against the morning sky.

And then another wave comes.

As it seizes the boat, his feet lose contact with the deck, his body shoots up and he's thrown into the sea.

Before he's pulled under, he's able to hold his head above the water for a second – just long enough to take one last look at the fishing boat.

Just long enough to know that she's gone.

Constantin

A river cruise passes below them. Music. Dancing. Champagne flutes.

He feels light-headed and unsteady on his feet. His legs are growing weak and his knee aches from the long walk.

What does she think of him, now that she knows?

He sits down beside her on a bench.

'So, she drowned,' Isabel says, her voice shaky.

He realises that he and Sofia haven't said it out loud: how their little girl died. But they both know it.

'Yes.'

Does Sofia have the details? How long it took to find her? How they got her back home? Where they held the funeral?

There's so much still unsaid between them.

And here he is, with Isabel. He presses his hands over his ears.

Isabel pulls them away gently.

'I'm sorry,' she says.

He chokes. '*You're* sorry?' His eyes sting.

She nods. And then, very gently, she places her hand on his knee. 'I can't begin to imagine what you've been through – what you're still going through.'

He gulps hard. 'It was my fault, Isabel. All of it.'

She looks at him for a long time and then she says, 'I don't think it's as simple as that, Constantin.'

He looks down into his hands.

'You must wish you'd never met me,' he says.

She takes her hand from his knee, places her fingers under his chin, lifts his head and makes him look at her again. 'No, I don't wish that.' She strokes his cheek. 'Thank you for telling me what happened.'

Tears drop down his cheeks. It makes him feel foolish. That this is all he has to give her. And that even now, after everything that's happened, he can't be stronger.

For a while, neither of them talk. Then she asks, 'The elephant charm – it was Clara's, wasn't it?'

He nods. 'I bought it for her at an Indian market stand in Minsk before we moved to the forest. Clara knew I loved elephants – so she fell in love with them too. I read her stories about India, about places I wanted to take her, far away from the country where we lived.'

'And she gave it to you before you jumped?'

'Yes.' He shakes his head. 'I wish I'd never taken it. I wish . . . ' His voice breaks off.

Constantin takes a breath.

'I should never have let her come with me.' He turns to look at her. 'You must be angry with me – as a mother, I mean. That I took Clara away from Sofia. That I put her in such danger.'

Isabel bows her head.

A tear drops down her cheek. He draws her into his arms. He expects her to pull away, but she doesn't move.

Who knows what will happen after all this is over. Once Sofia has gone back to Belarus. Once River and Isabel and David and everyone else caught up in this go back to their old lives. Whether he'll get the immigration papers which will allow him to stay. Whether Isabel will ever want to see him again – whether she'll let him anywhere near River.

Perhaps this moment is their goodbye.

So he draws her in closer and places his lips on the top of her head.

'I'm sorry,' he says. 'For everything.'

She doesn't answer but, for a moment, he thinks he feels her body leaning into his.

River

River climbs out of Gabs's car – he lent it to Jules for the day.

River stretches, yawns and looks out across the car park of Whipsnade Zoo. There's hardly anyone here yet; they had to set off really early to get Sofia back in time for her flight this afternoon.

Last night, Mum told River about what happened to Sofia and Reg's little girl, Clara. That she never made it to England. That that was why Constantin's mind had stopped working properly. And why he looked so sad all the time.

River doesn't know all the details. For once, she's tried not to ask too many questions. But as soon as she found out that Sofia was going home again so soon, River knew that bringing her here, with Reg, was the right thing.

Wherever Clara was now, she'd want her parents to see the elephants.

And the weird thing was that all the grown-ups had agreed; even Mum didn't make a fuss about it being too short notice or too expensive.

One by one, everyone gets out of the car: Jules and Mum from the front, then Sofia and Reg from the back, where River had sat too. Everyone looks sleepy and kind of lost.

'Come on!' River jumps up and down. 'Let's go straight to the elephant enclosure.'

Jules locks the car and then they all follow River in a kind of daze.

The car journey from London was so quiet it gave River a headache. It's like no one wanted to start a conversation.

She knows everyone feels weird about everyone else right now. But that just makes coming here even more important.

It takes them a while to find the elephants.

River walks next to Jules, leading the way.

'I wish Dr Deardorff could have come with us,' River says. 'Maybe when he gets out of hospital, we could bring him too? He is going to be okay, isn't he?'

'He'd better be.'

River grins. 'You like him, don't you?'

Jules rolls her eyes again but she's blushing too.

'*Like*-like him?'

The whole of Jules's face goes pink.

'You do! You do!' River jumps up and down.

'Shush!' Jules says.

When they get to where the elephants are meant to be, the enclosure is empty and River panics that maybe they've been moved or that maybe the zoo keepers aren't going to let them out today for some reason.

'It's okay.' Jules leans in. 'They're probably having breakfast, or still sleeping.'

River bites her lip and nods.

'Is there somewhere I could get a coffee?' Sofia asks.

Everyone turns round to look at her, like they forgot she was there. She hasn't said a word since they left London.

'There's probably a café,' Jules says.

Mum steps forward. 'I'll come with you.'

Now everyone goes *really* quiet.

Reg stares down at his hands.

River looks back over to the elephant enclosure. A pigeon flies down behind the gate and pecks at some seeds on the concrete floor.

As Mum and Sofia walk away down the path, River's throat goes tight: she hopes Mum will be okay.

Reg takes River's hand. 'Thank you for bringing me here.'

Jules coughs. 'I'm going to get an ice cream,' she says and starts walking off.

Part of River wants to run after Jules and tell her to stay: she hasn't been alone with Reg since before he disappeared. And now that she knows about his wife and what happened to his daughter, she's not sure what to say to him any more.

When Jules has gone, River looks towards the path Mum and Sofia walked down a moment ago and wonders whether they'll be okay. She can't help thinking back to what Mum said about liking Reg. It's probably even weirder for her to have to talk to Sofia than for River to have to talk to Reg.

Reg settles on the bench in front of the empty enclosure.

River sits beside him.

'I think I'm going to have to go to school,' she says.

It's kind of a lame topic but at least it doesn't risk upsetting him.

River looks at the mouth of the cave which leads to the elephants' inside space. She hopes that Reg will get to see them before everyone has to go back to London.

He takes her hand and squeezes it gently. 'It'll be just fine, River.'

'How do you know?'

'Because they'll love you.'

River feels her eyes go wide. 'Love *me*? I don't think so.'

River thinks about how, whenever she was in the same room as a teacher, it was like she could feel their blood pressure rising just because she was there. And she knew the other kids resented that too, like it was her fault for making teachers stressed and snappy. No, no one was likely to love her, not at school.

'They will,' Reg says. 'When they realise how special you are –
and how good you are for them, they'll love you.'

'Good for them?'

'Difficult people are always good for teachers. For all of us.'

'*Difficult?*'

'Difficult is good.'

'Like you?'

Constantin smiles. 'Yes, like me.'

River takes a breath. 'Was Clara difficult?'

He nods. 'She didn't want to go to school either.'

'She didn't?'

River's certain she would have liked Clara. Which makes her
happy and really sad at the same time. It doesn't seem real, that
someone could just lose their child like that.

'No, she didn't. Especially when she found out she was going
to boarding school.'

'She went to boarding school?'

He nods. 'Things weren't very safe for me, back in Belarus.
And her grandfather wanted her to go to the same school as her
mother, Sofia, did. He paid for her school fees.'

'And you agreed?'

'I wanted to keep her safe.'

Reg goes quiet for a while.

'*Living* at school,' River says. 'That sounds awful.'

He smiles. 'It does, doesn't it? But you know, Clara grew to
love it.'

River feels her eyebrows shooting up. 'She did?'

He nods. 'It took her a while to adjust but, with time, she
found her friends and some teachers she liked, teachers who she
felt understood her.'

'Do those teachers exist?'

'Of course they do.' He gives her another smile. 'She was an artist, like me – like you. And artists are strange creatures. Sometimes we take a little longer to find people who understand us.'

For the first time, maybe ever, River thinks that maybe she could make a go of school. If Clara had to live at school and if she was a bit like River and if she ended up liking it, then maybe there's hope, after all.

'You're remembering more stuff, aren't you, Reg?' River asks.

'Yes, I am.'

River smiles but her heart feels heavy.

'I'm so sorry,' she says. 'About everything.'

Reg closes his eyes and River thinks that maybe she should stop talking for a bit.

She hears a shuffling sound coming from the enclosure and then she sees a tiny trunk poking out of the cave. She grabs Reg's arm.

'Look – *look*!'

His eyes fly open.

They watch a tiny elephant stumbling out into the sunshine, wobbly on her legs. The baby elephant's mother walks a few paces behind.

River's heart skips. 'They're here.'

Reg goes really quiet beside her and she knows he's thinking about Clara and how much she would have loved to see this. River doesn't understand much about what happens to people after they die but she wants to believe that Clara is here with them now: that she's seeing it with them.

'Thank you for bringing me here, River,' Reg says.

River leans her head on his shoulder and says: 'You're the one who brought me here, Reg.'

Isabel

Isabel walks over to the bench by the café where Sofia is sitting with her eyes closed, the sun warming her beautiful, pale face.

For a second, Isabel gets a picture of Constantin, sitting in the park in the rain: his knotty hair, his head bowed, his clothes drenched.

Today the sun is scorching: it's a proper summer's day. That rainy day back in July when she and River first saw Constantin feels like a lifetime away.

Isabel doesn't know what's going to happen after Sofia leaves. Where Constantin will go or whether he'll get the papers to stay – whether she and River will ever see him again. But she knows she has to do this.

So, she sits down beside Sofia.

Sofia looks up at Isabel.

'Thank you for finding him,' she says.

Isabel's heart sinks to her stomach. She's thanking *her*? She takes a breath.

'You don't need to thank me.'

'I do.'

Two small girls run past them, laughing, holding hands. They climb onto the swings in the playground next to the café.

'When we moved to our cabin in the forest, Constantin put up a swing for Clara,' Sofia says. 'She was too old for that kind of thing, but Constantin didn't care. And she loved it, of course.' Sofia pauses. 'She loved whatever he did.'

Isabel touches Sofia's arm. 'Are you very angry at him?'

Sofia looks down and tries to search for Isabel's eyes, but Isabel looks away. She still can't bring herself to look Sofia in the eye.

'Angry at Constantin?' Sofia asks.

'For what happened to Clara. That he didn't tell her to stay with you.'

'There are many things I'm angry with him about. But I can't blame him for that.'

'No?'

She shakes her head. 'Clara wanted to go.' She looks over to the girls swinging high now, their heads thrown back. 'I couldn't have stopped her – neither could Constantin. She was nearly an adult. And she would have followed him, even if we'd said no. She loved him more than anyone.'

Isabel's chest feels tight. 'She loved him more than anyone?' she echoes.

Sofia catches Isabel's eye. 'She loved him more than *me*, yes. It's not something we like to admit as parents: that our children prefer one of us over the other, but we are all human, after all. Our characters draw us to certain people. Clara loved me, I knew that. She liked me, even – we were friends, which I gather is rare for teenage girls and their mothers.' She pauses. 'But her spirit always leaned towards Constantin.'

Isabel had never considered this: that if River's father had been around, perhaps she might have loved him more. God knows Isabel and River have their struggles, but still, Isabel isn't sure how she would have coped with coming second.

'Did it not make you unhappy? That Clara—' The words stick in Isabel's throat. 'That she loved him so much?'

Sofia nods. 'For a long time, it did. I fought it. I tried to win Clara's affection.' She gives Isabel a sad smile. 'That sounds weak, doesn't it?'

'No . . . not at all.'

'Well, of course it didn't work. And when I saw that there was nothing I could do, I got angry with Constantin. Part of what Clara loved about him – his free spirit, his art, his constant questioning and his challenging of authority – was what was putting our family in danger. I wanted him to see that and to take responsibility for it. And I wanted Clara to see it too: that she couldn't just love him without understanding the consequences of who he was and what he was doing.'

Isabel looks over to the elephant enclosure, just visible from the bench where they're sitting. At River and Constantin watching the mother elephant nudging her baby forward with her trunk.

'But all my anger and my criticism did was push Clara further away from me – and so closer to him. I came to see that I was losing them both.' Sofia pauses. 'So, I let her go.' Her eyes fill with tears. 'It was my fault as much as Constantin's, maybe more so. I let her go with him because I knew that if she stayed, she'd end up resenting me – that I'd lose her anyway.'

Isabel thinks again of her parents. All this time, she believed that they wanted her to go, that they were so disappointed in her getting pregnant and then at her decision to keep River and drop out of nursing school, that they didn't want her around any more. But maybe it was more complicated than that. Maybe pushing her away was their way of giving her the freedom to go. Maybe losing her was a price they accepted they had to pay.

For two weeks now, she's looked at their number on her phone every single day, her fingers hovering over the call button, longing to speak to them. But it hasn't felt right, not with all this going on.

At last, Isabel looks at Sofia right in the eye.

'You could stay a bit longer if you wanted, I'm sure we could reschedule your flight.'

Sofia shakes her head. 'I need to go back to my father. And to be near Clara.' She pauses. 'She's buried in the family property, just outside Minsk.'

Isabel thinks about how Constantin might never see the place where his little girl is buried. Tears sting the back of her eyes.

'Did it take long – for them to find her?' Isabel asks.

She hopes for at least this small mercy.

'My father made sure they did. He went to Calais himself and brought her back to me.'

Isabel thinks of the man who made Constantin's life miserable, the same man who loved his daughter and granddaughter. And again, she thinks of her mum and dad. Every generation tries to do things better than its parents, and yet we seem doomed to fail our children. Maybe that is the hardest lesson of all.

For a while, the two women sit in silence. Isabel notices that Sofia is looking at River and Constantin. The baby elephant has moved a few paces away from her mother, but the mother's eyes don't leave her for a second.

'Was Constantin staying in Belarus never an option? Did he really have to leave?' Isabel asks.

'Staying was impossible.' Sofia sweeps her fingers across the slats of the bench, as though she's picturing the bench where they found Constantin.

Isabel can feel Constantin sitting here between them, his torso pressing into the wood.

'He was so very unhappy?' Isabel asks.

'He could not breathe in Belarus. When they took away his right to publish his drawings, he no longer felt alive. And his life was in danger. My father could protect us but Constantin had gone too far even for his help.'

Isabel takes a breath.

'Do you still love him?'

'Of course, but that's not enough.' She pauses. 'We're not right for each other. It took us a while to admit to that, but we know that we're better apart.'

Isabel's cheeks burn. She'd never contemplated that, if she'd found River's father, things might *not* have worked out. Wouldn't the very act of finding each other – and the fact that they'd had a child – mean that they were meant to be together?

Something in Isabel snaps loose. She feels free, suddenly. Maybe her love for him would have dimmed. Or maybe they would have fallen out of love altogether. Maybe it was possible to fall in love with someone completely, to have a child with them even, and to believe, with your whole heart, that they were the only person in the world for you – and then for that to change.

Maybe, in the end, everything gets distorted. Maybe nothing's ever meant to be for ever. And maybe that's why that boy in Italy left her while she was still sleeping, because he knew, on some level that she couldn't yet grasp, that it was better to walk away.

'I'm sure you understand this kind of love?' Sofia says.

Isabel lets out a long breath. 'No. I don't understand much about love at all. Romantic love, I mean.'

Isabel feels Sofia's hand on her arm. 'Constantin is very fond of you.'

Isabel's heart thumps in her ears. She knows about the kiss. More than that: she knows that Isabel had fallen in love with her husband.

'I'm sorry,' Isabel says.

'You do not need to be sorry. You saved his life, Isabel.'

'It wasn't me,' Isabel says. 'It was River, she's the one who understands him – better than any of us do. She helped him to find himself again.' Isabel pauses. 'She allowed him to breathe – like you said.'

Sofia's grip on Isabel's arm tightens. Isabel looks up into her big, clear eyes. 'You saved him, Isabel.' Sofia holds Isabel's gaze. 'He told me. We spoke last night, for hours.'

Isabel feels dizzy. They spoke about her?

'Will you take care of him for me?' Sofia asks.

Isabel can hear the words Sofia is saying but somehow, she can't make sense of them.

'I need to know, before I go, that you will make sure he is okay.'

'Of course we'll look after him. River wouldn't have it any other way. I'm sure David or Clem will be happy for him to stay with them, at least until he finds his feet. And Constantin will make a success of things: he's so talented.'

'No, that is not what I meant.' Sofia doesn't take her eyes off Isabel. 'I would like him to be with you. Then I can leave without fear.'

Fear? Isabel thinks. And then she understands. Sofia is worried that Constantin's mind will start to fall apart again. That as he comes to terms with Clara's death, he might go back to the place where they found him: sitting in the rain, on his own, the memories of what happened too painful to hold onto.

Isabel looks down at Sofia's hands, folded in her lap. A thin gold band on her wedding finger. She remembers what Constantin told her as they stood on Westminster Bridge: how he'd thrown his wedding ring into the sea because he didn't feel he deserved to be married any more.

And now Sofia is giving her permission? More than that: she's asking her to be with Constantin – the man she married? The man she had a child with? They've gone through so much together. How can she walk away from that?

'I don't know …' Isabel starts.

'What you said earlier – about not understanding love?'

Isabel nods.

'Love is not here to be understood.'

Isabel looks up.

Sofia smiles at her. Warmth fills Isabel's body.

'You love Constantin, a love that is good for him, a love that makes him the man he needs to be, that is what will heal him. That is all you need to understand.'

'I don't know what to say.'

'You don't need to say anything. You just need to promise me that you'll take care of him.'

Isabel doesn't know what that's meant to look like or how things will turn out between them, but Sofia's right: she loves him.

'I promise,' Isabel says.

SEPTEMBER

David

Jules thumps down David's overnight bag, along with a bag of groceries, and scans the flat. She'd brought him back from the hospital.

'God, this place is depressing.'

He'd forgotten, that in all those weeks they spent together, she never once came here, into his home.

She puts her hands on her hips and shakes her head. Her shirtsleeves are rolled up over her strong arms. The tattoo of a tiny bird sits on the inside of her left wrist. Just when he thinks he's seen them all, he notices another one.

'Bacherlorpad.com,' Jules goes on. 'And before you get any kinky ideas, I don't mean that in a *Fifty Shades of Grey* kind of way.' She shakes her head again. 'Where's all your stuff? And why's there no colour – like, anywhere?'

He pushes his glasses up his nose and sees the flat through her eyes.

He's embarrassed. Not in the way he was when Isabel first saw it – because it wasn't sophisticated enough. What he feels this time is different. He understands that – how did Constantin always put it when he talked to River about her pictures? It needs spirit. Yes, his flat needs spirit, only then will it be a home.

'I mean, you don't have to go painting River-like rainbows all over your walls, but seriously, Dave, this place is worse than the hospital.'

After selling the house he lived in with his mum, settling her into The Birches and buying this place, he'd run out of energy to do anything to it. And there didn't seem much point, living alone as he did.

'Sorry . . . I guess I didn't give it much thought before,' David says.

'Before what?'

He feels the tips of his ears go warm.

'We'll sort it out soon enough,' she says.

We will? he thinks.

She gives him a sharp nod.

'We got you back on track, didn't we? You've lost weight, you've stopped stuffing your face with those Jammie Dodgers, you've got some colour back in those cheeks of yours. And that was the hard bit. Getting this place sorted will be easy.' She looks at him and smiles. His insides melt. He *has* lost weight, he thinks. Got healthier. And he doesn't feel like eating Jammie Dodgers any more, not when she's around.

'But first things first. We need to get you settled.' She takes the bag of groceries to the kitchen.

While she's walking away from him, he notices the stick Constantin used as a cane still sitting in the entrance. That morning, the morning after David saw him kissing Isabel, the morning when he left without telling anyone – feels like a lifetime ago.

Jules comes back, picks up his bag, slips her arm under his elbow and guides him to his bedroom.

He stifles a yawn. And then remembers that she's probably been up much longer than he has. She was packing his bag at the hospital at 7 a.m.

'Aren't you tired?' he asks.

'I don't need much sleep.'

'You don't need much of anything.' He pauses. 'Do you?'

She stops walking for a moment, looks at him, blinks and then walks on.

When they get to his bedroom, David feels the warmth from his ears spread to his whole face: his room is even worse than the rest of the flat. The white bedsheets, grey with age. The wardrobe door hanging off its hinges. Books stacked on the floor because he'd never bothered to put up a bookcase. A bare light bulb hangs from the ceiling.

He sits down on the edge of the bed. 'It feels strange to be back here. So much has happened.'

'You really didn't know about Reg's daughter?' Jules asks.

He's been trying to explain it all to her: how he found out about Sofia through Clem. How he should have shared the information with Jules but that he was worried that, as her best friend, she'd feel burdened to tell Isabel.

'Clem didn't know about Clara either,' he says. 'Through all the interviews he did with Constantin and Sofia, they kept her a secret. It was part of them protecting her, I guess. She was sent away to a boarding school outside Minsk, all paid for by Sofia's father.'

'And then she came back to live with them in the forest – when they went into hiding?'

'Yes.'

David feels a lump in his throat. If only they'd known they were going to lose her, they'd have wanted her to be with them every second.

'Do you think they'll ever come to terms with it?' he asks Jules. 'With losing Clara, I mean?'

Jules shakes her head. 'No. No one can come to terms with losing a child. But with time, they'll learn that it's okay to live alongside the loss – that they don't have to push it away.'

He wonders whether this is how she lives with the loss of her mother. And in that moment, he feels the strength of her, sitting here beside him.

He doesn't want her to go, not ever.

Jules pats the bed. 'Well, it was time you came home, Dave. You were getting too cosy in hospital.'

'Cosy?'

She nods. 'All those nurses fussing over you.' She plumps the pillows and folds back his duvet. 'It wasn't good for you.'

'And you,' he says.

Her head snaps up. 'Me what?'

'You fussed.' He clears his throat. That's not the right word, Jules doesn't fuss. 'You were there, that's what I mean. More than anyone. You need a break.'

She waits a beat before she answers.

'I'm fine, Dave.'

Maybe this is just another part of who Jules is, like the piercings on her eyebrow and under her tongue, and her tattoos – like how she takes people under her wing and looks after them, as she's done with Isabel and River and all the kids she's ever looked after. And then him.

Only he doesn't want to be just another person she takes care of. Because if that's all he is to her, soon, when he gets better, she'll stop coming to see him. He'll go back to some kind of work and, later in the autumn, Jules will take on more children to nanny. Isabel will find a job somewhere else, far from the hospital. And they'll never meet again, not unless it's by accident.

The thought of being apart from her makes him feel sick.

She helps him out of his coat. He's wearing his pyjamas underneath. *No need to get dressed up just for a quick car ride between the hospital and the flat*, Jules had said. *And you'll need to have a rest when you get home. Staying in your PJs will save time.*

At times, he wondered whether, in her mind, he was just another child for her to look after.

She eases him into bed, settles him against the pillows and then unpacks his hospital bag.

He watches her moving around his room, her body reflecting the light from the window. She's right, there's no colour in his life, not apart from her.

She looks through the open door towards the kitchen. 'Hungry?'

He nods, though he can't remember the last time he had an appetite. His pyjama trousers are loose around his stomach. When he shaved this morning, he saw an angle to his chin.

Jules disappears through the door and he hears her pottering around in the kitchen: clattering pans, opening and closing cupboard doors, switching on the hob. Wherever she is, Jules seems to have some kind of internal navigation system that allows her to find her way. He can't imagine her ever being lost.

'I've bought some healthy stuff – and some stuff that you'll like.' Her voice bounces around his flat.

She's never scared of being loud, he thinks. He likes that about her. That she speaks up, makes herself heard in the world.

'You need a bit of both, right?' she goes on.

She keeps talking to him through the open door. She doesn't seem to expect him to answer so he just lies back and listens to the rise and fall of her voice.

A few minutes later, she puts a plate down on his bedside table. A bacon sandwich with some salad on the side.

'Make sure you eat the green stuff,' she says. 'Doctor's orders.' She gives him a wink.

Then she flicks her wrist and looks at her watch.

'It's late. I'd better go and get the kids.'

She slings her bag over her shoulder.

'I thought I could take you to see your mum – after work. I told her that you were getting out today.'

He sits up. 'You *told* her?'

'Went to see her a few times, while you were in the hospital. Thought she'd miss your daily visits.'

He just stares at her.

'She's cool,' Jules adds.

'She is?'

Jules nods.

'I'd like that,' he says. 'To go and see her. With you.'

'Good, good.'

And then she walks out of the room.

Slowly, he pushes himself up out of bed. The journey from the hospital has taken more out of him than he realised. Jules is right, he needs to rest.

Only he can't, not yet.

He pushes himself up to standing and follows her out to the hallway.

Jules is at the front door by the time she notices that he's followed her.

She spins round.

'What is it?'

He reaches a hand out towards her and then feels the foolishness of the gesture.

'I came to say thank you . . . and . . . ' He pushes his glasses up his nose.

'And?' She raises her pierced eyebrow.

His ears burn.

'And, I was wondering . . . '

'Spit it out, Dave. What do you need?'

He clears his throat. 'I need you.'

She blinks at him. And then she steps forward, takes David's face in her hands and kisses him.

After a while, she steps back.

His head is spinning. His whole body is spinning.

'Go and get some rest, Dave.'

And then she gives him a smile, and steps through the door.

River

River stands at the gates of her new school. Mum's gone in to have a chat with Mrs Endicott.

It's been raining all morning. There are puddles everywhere, but the sky's beginning to lighten.

She squints into the early morning sun and then she sees it: Gabs's old car, rattling down the road.

A second later, they're all here.

Jules is the first to get out. She gives River a wave and then goes to the boot to sort out the buggy for the triplets. Nula jumps out of the back seat, runs up to River and jumps into her arms.

'Can I come to school with you?' Nula asks.

River gives her chubby cheek a kiss. 'I wish you could.'

Nula nestles into River's neck.

She's going to miss seeing her so much.

River knows it's not the cool thing to do – to have everyone here, like she's starting pre-school or something. But she doesn't care what the other kids think; she likes that they're here, the people she loves, and that they'll be the ones she thinks of when she walks into her first day of school.

Reg gets out of the car next. He's living with Clem now. His papers haven't come through but River knows he's going to be allowed to stay. He's meant to be here.

He helps Dr Deardorff out of the car. Dr Deardorff has got really skinny since his heart attack, and he still gets these pains in his chest which make him wince, and he can't walk very far without running out of breath. But he's getting better. And he looks kind of happier than he did before he got sick.

Mum and River took the bus, so they could have some time, just the two of them.

She takes a breath. It's going to be okay. It's all going to be okay.

River adjusts Nula on her hip and walks up to Dr Deardorff.

'Thank you for coming, Dr Deardorff,' she says.

'I wouldn't have missed it for the world,' he says. 'And I needed to get away from all those paint fumes.' He looks over at Jules.

She's moved in with him and they're redecorating. And he's not planning on going back to work for a while; he says he likes hanging out with Jules and Nula and the triplets.

It's weird not having Jules living with them any more but she still comes round all the time and now Mum's got more space in her room, they're going to find a desk for her so that she can read her medical textbooks in peace.

'I can't wait to see the flat,' River says.

'Well, you're welcome to come over any time.'

Then he grabs a small, silver-foil-wrapped package from his pocket.

She picks at a corner.

'Jammie Dodgers!'

'They got me through the hard times.'

'Thank you!' She gives him a kiss.

Then she goes over to Jules and hands her Nula. She leans over into the buggy and gives each of the triplets a kiss on their rosy cheeks.

'Knock 'em dead.' Jules winks.

River gives her a hug.

Reg steps towards her. The physiotherapy has been helping; he doesn't walk with a cane any more.

He comes over to the flat nearly every day and he and Mum talk for ages. Sometimes, he'll sit at the kitchen table, drawing, while she reads her medical books. Sometimes, when Mum's in the right mood, she even joins in with the drawing. She's really good. Mum says they're taking it a day at a time, which River takes to mean that although Reg is still really sad about Clara and that he'll never forget what happened to her, he's going to be okay. And that they're part of him becoming okay.

Reg hands River a wooden box.

'What's this?' River asks.

'Take a look.'

She opens the box and finds a tin of watercolour paints, really posh ones.

'I thought you said pictures didn't need colour,' River says.

'My pictures don't. Yours are different.' He pauses. 'Your spirit is different. I think the watercolours will suit your style.'

'I have a style?'

He nods.

River notices a small card taped to the inside of the box. The drawing of an elephant, the same one as in the cartoon that got Reg into trouble. Only his ears are flapping and his eyes are wide open and his legs are free and his trunk is curled to the sky.

And sitting on the tip of his upturned trunk, looking at him right in the eye, is a pigeon.

'Thank you, Reg.' River leans in and gives him a kiss too.

The school bell goes.

Kids start running across the playground to the main doors.

'Time to go, River,' Mum says.

River puts the Jammie Dodgers and the box of watercolours into her backpack and walks over to Mum.

'If I hate it, will you homeschool me?'

Mum laughs. 'Me? Homeschool you? You'll be begging to come back to school in under a day.' She takes River's hand. 'And anyway, I've got my own studying to do.'

Dr Deardorff is helping Mum put together a grant application to go to medical school. She did her A-levels and everything, so she's got the qualifications to apply. Plus, she's got all this experience of the hospital – Dr Deardorff is going to write a reference for her telling them she's just as good as any of the nurses and doctors he's worked with. Jules has said that now that she's living with Dr Deardorff, she doesn't have to pay any rent so she'll give Mum the same money she always did to make sure she and River can stay at Gabs's. *You can pay me back when you're a famous neurologist*, Jules said.

'Promise me you'll give it a go,' Mum says. 'Even if it's hard?'

River gives Mum a kiss. 'I'll give it a go.'

'River?' Mum says.

River looks up at her.

'I've got a surprise for you, after school.'

'A surprise?'

River thinks about all the things that Mum could have planned. Maybe she's going to let Pablo live with them inside the flat, especially now that they have more space.

Mum nods. 'We're going to have some visitors. Two people who have been waiting a very long time to meet you.'

'Is it the people who were on the phone the other night?'

Two days ago, Mum answered a call and closed her eyes and went to her bedroom and when she came back her eyes were red and her skin was blotchy but she didn't look sad. When River asked her who was on the phone, she'd said that she'd find out soon. That she just needed to sort a few things out first.

'Yes,' Mum says. Then she takes River in her arms and holds

her tight and kisses the top of her hair and River closes her eyes and for the first time in ages she feels like maybe they're not so different after all. That maybe things are going to be okay between them.

Then she runs across the playground with the other kids.

When she gets to the main doors, River turns back one last time and looks at them all standing there, watching her. She holds her hand up and waves and, before she turns round again, she looks up at the sky. The clouds are still there, shifting in front of the sun. She feels a few drops falling on her bare arms.

A good day for a rainbow, she thinks.

And then she turns and goes inside.

Acknowledgements

This is the first novel that I've written on American soil; I wrote it as an immigrant to a new land and, like Constantin, I experienced great kindness from strangers – strangers who have now become dear friends.

Thank you Aryn Marsh, for giving me a place to write; for providing the shelter of your friendship as I settled into my new life; for supporting me as a mother and as a writer. And for your spirit. You inspire me every day.

Thank you Margaret Evans Porter, for being such a great writing-buddy, for reading my books with such enthusiasm, for growing the most beautiful roses and for showing me (and my little Tennessee Skye) such kindness this past year.

Thank you Virginia Prescott, for being a fan, for giving my stories a wider readership through NHPR – and for making me feel just as special as all those big name celebrities you interview!

And thank you to the hundreds of people, too many to name here, whom I've got to know as I wrote this story. Thank you for sharing your tables and plug sockets and stories with me; thank you for coming to my readings; for inviting me to talk about my books; for stocking my books on your shelves; for sharing my novels with your friends; for feeding me with juice and coffee and wonderful conversation; for keeping an eye on my bike; for looking after and loving my girls as I wrote; and for lifting my spirits just when I needed it. You know who you are: without you, my life as a writer wouldn't be possible.

Thank you to all those dear friends and readers in the UK who haven't forgotten me or my books, especially to Helen Dahlke, Jane Cooper and Linda Gibson.

Thank you, as ever, to Bryony Woods, my incredibly industrious and committed agent who, despite geographical distance, has not once wavered in her commitment to my writing.

Thank you to my outgoing editor at Sphere, Manpreet Grewal. For taking a chance on me with *What Milo Saw*, for helping me bring two more novels into the world and for laying foundations for this one. And thank you to Viola Hayden, my new editor, for taking up the baton, for dreaming up such a beautiful cover and for showing such enthusiasm for the future of my writing: I can't wait to work with you on my next novel.

Thank you to the rest of the team at Little, Brown: Kirsteen Astor, Emma Williams, Andy Hine, Kate Hibbert, Helena Doree, Thalia Proctor, Ceara Elliot and all the other talented individuals who help to bring my stories to the world.

Thank you to those of you who so generously shared your experiences of ADHD, to help me understand how this condition affects your relationship with yourself and the world.

Thank you to those who, through their writing, their life experience and their work with patients gave me an insight into the mysterious workings of memory, in particular Gae Polisner's beautiful YA novel, *The Memory of Things*; Su Meck's *I Forgot To Remember* and Naomi Jacobs's *Forgotten Girl*.

Thank you to Mama, for being so unwaveringly faithful and enthusiastic – and for pressing my books into the hands of everyone you know!

Thank you to my two little girls, Tennessee Skye and Somerset Wilder, for making me look at the world with fresh eyes every day. Motherhood is a central theme of my writing and lies at the heart of this novel: you've taught me everything I know about the rollercoaster of being a mother.

Thank you, finally, to my darling husband and soulmate, Hugh, for always, always believing in my stories and being such a fabulous sounding board for my ideas. I couldn't imagine sharing this journey with anyone but you.